CHRISTMAS HEIRS

LYNNE GRAHAM

MAISEY YATES

MILLS & BOON

First published in Great Britain 2024
by Mills & Boon, an imprint of HarperCollins*Publishers* Ltd,
1 London Bridge Street, London, SE1 9GF

www.harpercollins.co.uk

HarperCollins*Publishers*, Macken House, 39/40 Mayor Street Upper, Dublin 1, D01 C9W8, Ireland

Christmas Heirs © 2024 Harlequin Enterprises ULC

Greek's Shotgun Wedding © 2024 Lynne Graham

Pregnant Enemy, Christmas Bride © 2024 Maisey Yates

ISBN: 978-0-263-32030-5

11/24

This book contains FSC™ certified paper
and other controlled sources to ensure responsible forest management.

For more information visit www.harpercollins.co.uk/green.

Printed and Bound in the UK using 100% Renewable Electricity
at CPI Group (UK) Ltd, Croydon, CR0 4YY

GREEK'S
SHOTGUN
WEDDING

LYNNE GRAHAM

MILLS & BOON

Lynne Graham was born in Northern Ireland and has been a keen romance reader since her teens. She is very happily married, to an understanding husband who has learned to cook since she started to write! Her five children keep her on her toes. She has a very large dog, which knocks everything over, a very small terrier, which barks a lot, and two cats. When time allows, Lynne is a keen gardener.

Maisey Yates is the *New York Times* bestselling author of over one hundred romance novels. An avid knitter, with a dangerous yarn addiction and an aversion to housework, Maisey lives with her husband and three kids in rural Oregon. She believes the trek she makes to her coffee maker each morning is a true example of her pioneer spirit. Find out more about Maisey's books on her website: maiseyyates.com, or find her on Facebook, Instagram or TikTok by searching her name.

CHAPTER ONE

'I THOUGHT YOU were planning to be a no-show,' Jace's uncle Evander told his six-foot-four-inch-tall nephew.

Jace strode away from the helicopter with the silver logo flash that announced that the billionaire owner of Diamandis Industries had finally arrived for the funeral proceedings.

Apologising for his late arrival, Jace dealt the older man a regretful smile in which resentment, respect and fondness were all contained. Evander and his British husband, Marcus, had, after all, raised Jace when his own father refused to do so. Of course, both Jace and his uncle had been the *outsiders* in the Diamandis circle, Evander because he was gay and refused to pretend otherwise and Jace because his father, Argus, had refused to act as a parent and had abandoned his son at the tender age of six.

In actuality, Jace had lost both his parents on the same day. His mother had been an internationally acclaimed and famously glamorous opera singer, who had walked out on Argus for another man that day, leaving her son behind. When she and her lover crashed their car and died a few hours afterwards, Jace's father had burst into gales of hysterical laughter. And then he had looked only once at the little boy staring at him with his late wife's bright green eyes and her mop of curls before tucking Jace and his nanny into a limousine to be taken to his parents' estate, thereby repudiating his firstborn son.

It was a decision that Argus had never revisited over the twenty-two years that had followed…and now he was dead. Jace had indelibly remained a reminder of his father's lowest moment, a moment when not all the money in the world could compensate a man's hurt pride or save his shiny public image from malicious gossip about cuckolds. Even though he quickly remarried and had a second son, Argus had continued to reject Jace as his child. At one stage he had also attempted to cut Jace out of the family inheritance and give it instead to Jace's half-brother, Domenico, only to be prevented by their grandfather's lawyers.

Jace hadn't wanted to play the hypocrite and attend his reluctant father's funeral. Evander, however, had taken a very different stance. Evander had argued vehemently with Jace, pointing out that his nephew might be only twenty-eight years old and single but he was now the *de facto* head of the Diamandis family, and that it was a matter of good taste and common sense to accept his rightful place. Before Jace could think too much about it, he was engulfed in an embrace by his grandmother, Electra Diamandis. And if she could comfortably attend her son's funeral when the two of them had lived at daggers drawn, he believed that he had even less to complain about.

Jace was currently the cynosure of all eyes. 'Why are

they all staring at me?' he murmured as they emerged from the church.

'You're worth billions and they don't know you,' his uncle reminded him wryly. 'Bet they are now wincing for all the times they cut you dead.'

'None of them wanted to know me while I was growing up, apart from you and Marcus,' Jace agreed grimly. 'You took in the poisoned chalice and didn't care about keeping Argus sweet.'

'All your little nubile cousins have got wedding rings gleaming in their eyes,' Evander warned him, half under his breath.

Jace laughed with sudden intense amusement. 'I learned my lesson well with Seraphina.'

An unexpected smile curved his uncle's mouth. 'Yes, I did very much enjoy that visit from my brother Adonis when he demanded you marry my niece for stealing her virtue. You see, you can't go tantalising them all with the headlines you make and not expect to become a target for the gold-diggers in the family.'

'I'm all grown up now and rather more staid—'

'Absolute lies,' Marcus interrupted from his other side. 'Ain't nothing staid about your playboy lifestyle.'

'I'm only going to be young once,' Jace countered with raw assurance. Yet he remained grateful to the couple who had raised him with love, loyalty and care. A more conventional set of parentals might have given up on him when he went through an extended wild period as a teenager. Marcus and Evander, however, had stuck by him through thick and thin and he would never forget the debt he owed them for the security and stability they had given him.

'But you're heading towards thirty and you've never had a relationship with a woman,' Evander quipped. 'Maybe you need to think about that—'

'I don't do relationships.' Hell, no! Jace thought in horror. He did sex, not relationships. He kept his private life simple and straightforward. Since he had attained adulthood, no dates, no serious discussions with women and no boundaries had ever featured in his world. He did as he liked, when he liked and with whom he liked. And in truth, he honestly believed that he was happier embracing his freedom that way.

'You need to try it…at least once,' his uncle said.

Jace gritted his even white teeth. 'How much longer do I need to stay?' he breathed, feeling like a teenager again, but he hated it all *so much:* all the fawning attention from people who had ignored him all his life to meet Argus's expectations and curry his father's favour and *now?* The constant sidewise glances, the supposedly friendly grieving comments. As if he cared an atom for the father he had hardly known, who had hurt him beyond belief as a child when he'd chosen to punish him for his mother's sins!

'Speak to your brother before you leave. You don't need to do drinks and chat with the rest of them. You don't owe them anything,' his uncle told him.

'Why should *I* speak to Domenico?' Jace queried in a tone of literal disbelief.

'He had nothing to do with any of it and you're the *big* brother,' Evander reminded him drily. 'You've never even met him. Five minutes, Jace. He's the closest relative you have left alive. Make us proud…*please*—'

Jace breathed in slow and deep, rage hurtling through his big powerful frame at that piece of advice. But then he thought it through for the first time in many years and his temper receded because as always there was a lot of logic in Evander's words. Their father was dead now. Maybe there *was* room for him to look again at that particular relationship. It wasn't his brother's fault that Jace had been rejected, ignored and threatened with disinheritance. For all he knew, Argus had been a lousy parent to Domenico as well.

And affecting not to hear the remarks or see the languishing glances cast in his direction, Jace went off to meet his half-brother for the first time…

'What in the world…?' Gigi marvelled out loud as she stood at her front window and glimpsed the large animal dancing through the traffic with a dangling lead still attached to its collar.

Snowy, the ragged cockatoo in the corner cage in the sitting room, tried to mimic her voice—not very well. Humphrey the tortoise ambled in, munching a lettuce leaf. Hoppy, the terrier dozing on the sofa, didn't stir as much as a whisker. At the other end of the same seat, however, a big white and orange cat sat up, because Tilly was a knowing cat awake to her mistress's rising tension.

'Oh, for goodness' sake!' Gigi gasped because nobody appeared to be chasing the foolish dog and, on that acknowledgement, she was already racing out of her front door to stage a rescue bid.

Well, you are a veterinary surgeon, she excused herself and, without hesitation, she plunged into the busy street where the animal was capering about, seemingly quite clueless as to the danger it was in from the car wheels, the shouts out of windows for it to move and the squealing horns. Not a street dog, no, someone's pet and more like a baby than a child with some common sense. Others might have turned their backs on such a view but not Gigi, who valued animals more than people.

Gigi had spent eighteen months living on the Greek island of Rhodes. She worked there at an animal rescue centre but had primarily come to Rhodes in the hope of actually getting to know the Greek half of her family. Basically, it hadn't worked out like that and her hopes and dreams had slowly withered. That ambition had, seemingly, been naïve. But then Gigi was accustomed to disillusionment when it came to family members. If her own mother hadn't had any time for her, why had she expected her father and her half-brothers to feel any different? Even so, she *had* got to know her Greek grandmother, Helene, and although Helene had passed away three months earlier, Gigi had got on well with the older woman and had also learned to speak fluent Greek. Two pluses, she told herself, but more negatives than pluses had featured in her family experiences.

As she filtered through traffic suddenly come to a standstill after two cars collided trying to avoid the dog, she realised that the foolish animal had got its long fragile tail locked between the cars. As a spate of furious Greek male voices broke out over the accident, Gigi pointed out the dog's predicament but, evidently, nobody cared enough to help her free the dog. She pushed at the cars, trying to move them even an inch to free the animal and then both male drivers started to shout at her about daring to try and intervene on behalf of the dog. Meanwhile the dog started frantically licking her bare legs as if he knew she was striving to save him and a woman got out of one of the stalled vehicles to help her. But Gigi had managed to get that tiny bit of trapped tail released even if, in doing so, she had scraped her knee painfully and hurt her wrist. Thanking the woman for coming to assist her, she smiled even though blood was running down her calf, and hastened back to the house to treat the dog's injury.

'Oh, you're just gorgeous and a total pet,' she told the dog cheerfully and he bounced up on his hind legs like an acrobat, a couple of feet taller than she was because now she could see that he was an Irish wolfhound about three feet tall when on four legs. Huge but a fine specimen of an animal, pedigreed and wearing what looked like an expensive collar. She'd bet he was microchipped, which she would check out at the rescue shelter first thing in the morning, so that she could restore him to his probably very grateful owner. But first, he needed his tail treated before the wound turned into something more serious.

'And you probably won't like me so much by the time I'm finished,' she warned him as she fetched her vet bag. 'Oh, and you've scraped your poor leg too. Mo. Is that your name or your owner's name?' It was picked out in sparkly stones on the collar. 'That's a very girly collar, Mo, for a big boy like you.'

Mo was a pushover of a dog. He lay down for her, seeming to instantly recognise a sympathetic audience. He allowed her to clean his tail and even his leg, which required several stitches. He didn't even object when she fitted a surgical collar on him to ensure that he left his injuries alone and didn't lick at them and irritate them more.

'Oh, I wish you were a street dog I could keep,' she sighed as she fed and watered him and walked him until he eventually, tiring of his adventures, folded down at her feet and went to sleep like a total babe. 'What a wonderful temperament you have!'

Some time during the night Mo padded upstairs, and Gigi shifted in the early hours and saw a pair of adoring brown eyes beside her on her bed. 'Today we find your owner and take you home,' she told him regretfully.

Not noticeably impressed by that announcement, Mo went back to sleep, taking up more space on the bed than Gigi had for herself. 'You are a spoilt-rotten dog,' she told him ruefully.

He stuck to her like glue while she fed and walked him. She was about to head to her car to take him straight to work with her when she recalled that she had left her vet bag in her house. Although it wasn't *her* house, she reminded herself darkly, not with the big For Sale sign that had been fixed to it the week before. It was Helene's house and now her father's family were understandably keen to sell it, which was why she had decided to return to the UK with her pets as soon as she could make the arrangements. As she strolled back down the street, she noticed a crowd of men standing outside her door and banging the knocker as if some-one's life depended on it.

'What on earth's going on?' she demanded, trudg-ing through the clique of hovering men in dark suits.

'Mo!' a male voice cried with enthusiasm.

Mo reacted not at all. He licked Gigi's thigh ingrati-atingly and did not budge an inch.

'What the hell have you done to him?' the same voice demanded thunderously. 'He's been hurt...*injured*!'

Gigi stuck her key in the front door and moved in-side, Mo accompanying her. 'When I've checked out his microchip you can have him back...but not before. He hasn't even greeted you, which is weird when you're claiming to be his owner—'

'How *dare* you?' he demanded even louder.

'No, how dare you when I rescued this poor dog from traffic and treated him?' Gigi shot back at him without hesitation. 'That does not give you the right to come here and *shout* at me, you ignorant pig!'

To say that Jace was unaccustomed to such cavalier treatment from a woman would not have been an exag-geration. His jaw literally dropped as he gazed down at her, having already noticed that she had not deigned to look at *him* even once. And there she was, some impos-sibly tiny woman with a long, messy mop of brownish blonde hair, wearing shorts and a camisole like a...well, not like a streetwalker, he adjusted, for there was noth-ing come-hitherish about that outfit, nothing decorative or sexy. But she had stunning legs, he had noticed as she'd sauntered down the street with *his* dog. Mo was the one soft spot in Jace's hard heart. Hearing that Mo had broken free and run away while Jace was attending the funeral had sent him mad with worry.

'Treated him? How could *you* treat him?' Jace demanded, wishing that she would look up at him and behave more normally.

'I'm a veterinary surgeon, you dummy, and I'm not handing this beautiful dog back to you until you *prove* that he belongs to you. If you must, you can come inside and I'll explain what happened to him, but I should add that I have to be at work soon.'

'I thought he'd been kidnapped. There's a tracker on his collar—'

'He should be microchipped,' Gigi told him reprovingly as she stepped through her front door. 'That would be safer. I mean, what happens if the collar falls off or is removed? You couldn't find him then. Anyway, why would you stick a tracker on a dog, for goodness' sake?'

Jace breathed in deep and slow, as if he was bracing himself. What a weird woman—what a thoroughly weird woman! And then she finally paid him the compliment of looking up at him and he saw her for the first time…and she was gorgeous in that strangely natural way only a very few women could match. No make-up, nothing enhanced. Just pale porcelain skin, huge cornflower-blue eyes and a mouth, a sultry pink full mouth that could only exist for sin.

'Well. Come in if you're coming,' she told him impatiently. 'And I'm sorry but your friends will have to stay outside because it is a very small house and one stranger at a time is quite enough for me at this time of day.'

Dark colour edged Jace's cheekbones. A woman had never addressed him in that no-nonsense tone in his life. It felt exceedingly…wrong, he decided, wondering why she was reacting that way to him. Of course he had been rude, he reminded himself, attacking rather than pausing to first discover what had happened to his pet.

'Sit down,' Gigi urged. 'I'd offer you a coffee but I haven't got the time to entertain you right now—'

'Of course not,' Jace conceded, reeling back from her apparent indifference to him.

'Well, *sit*!' she shot at him. 'I can't abide someone so tall standing over me all the time and talking down to me like I'm a child!'

Gigi sat down on the sofa. Mo climbed up beside her and, beneath his owner's incredulous gaze, reclined across the entire top of her like the little lap dog he so obviously wasn't and could never be, not when he was the size of a pit pony.

'You're unusually small,' Jace pointed out almost apologetically.

'So?' Gigi replied shortly.

Gigi surveyed the big powerful male with the bad temper and no manners. He looked rich, sophisticated, everything she was not. He was also as impossibly handsome as a movie star. He didn't look quite real to her, seated as he was in Helene's former armchair in the very ordinary little sitting room.

Gigi told him in a few words about how she had seen Mo from her front window and how he had caused an accident and got his tail and his leg hurt. She explained her treatment much as if he were a potential adopter of an animal at the rescue shelter.

'Are you satisfied he wasn't being kidnapped now?' she enquired very drily.

'I apologise for that. I was upset, *worried* about him,' he stressed.

'Yes, you do leap to conclusions fast,' she conceded with a slight wrinkling of her delicious little nose. 'Perhaps I was a little hard on you. I'm not comfortable with volatile people.'

'What's your name?' Jace asked, relaxing a little from the sheer tension gripping him, a tension he couldn't even begin to understand beyond a barely acknowledged desire for her to like him.

'Gigi Campbell...and yours?'

Jace did not think he had had to introduce himself to a woman in living memory. It was unexpectedly refreshing. 'Jace Diamandis. You speak excellent Greek but going by your accent, you're *not* Greek—'

'No, I'm British...try and get your dog to come to you,' she urged, keen to get rid of him and get to work. 'I gather he's not microchipped? You should get that taken care of asap.'

'Tell me where you work and I'll take care of it,' Jace suggested in English.

'Yes, that would do,' Gigi conceded with innate practicality. 'Don't you realise that it's against the law *not* to have your dog microchipped? I work at a rescue shelter.'

Taken aback by that reproving response and casting a weathered eye at his dog, who had gone to sleep on his saviour's lap, Jace said, 'Let me take you to dinner this evening to thank you for rescuing him for me.'

'No need to put yourself to that trouble,' Gigi assured him cheerfully. 'I rescue animals all the time. It's my vocation.'

'I find that interesting. Taking you out for a meal would be a pleasure,' Jace asserted, wondering when she would crack and behave normally.

'Go on,' was all Gigi said in response. 'Try and get your dog to come to you…'

'Mo!' Jace grated.

Mo opened one eye, squinted at him and very carefully closed it again, playing dead.

'I think he's decided that he likes you better. He's not usually stubborn or disobedient,' Jace commented with a rare feeling of embarrassment, because he had owned the dog for two years and he was being royally ignored. 'I left him behind to attend a funeral yesterday and possibly he's sulking.'

'You'll have to carry him out then, because I *have* to get to work,' Gigi reminded him gently.

Jace sprang upright, opened her front door and two of the men left outside came in and carried a supine Mo out.

'Couldn't you have carried him yourself?' Gigi remarked in astonishment.

Faint colour flared along Jace's high cheekbones. She was the least tactful woman he had ever met, so why did he want her? And he did, he *knew* he did from the instant he had matched those legs to that beautiful heart-shaped face. Yet she wasn't even his type. He went for tall leggy blondes, not tiny, not impertinent, not anything other than conservative females. And this was a woman with a tortoise under her sofa, a bedraggled bird in a cage and a dog with one eye and three legs. Only the cat looked halfway normal in the assembly of animals. In fact, he didn't know what he was doing and it freaked him out more than a little. It was as if his brain went walkabout in front of her and he couldn't concentrate.

He would buy her flowers or something, forget about her because she didn't seem attracted to him in any way and that shocked him. In fact, it was the biggest shock Jace had withstood from a woman in many years.

There had been his best friend's wife, who had made a pass at him, all the employees over the years who had come on to him, every female student he had ever met. Jace had learned at a very early age that he was irresistible to her sex. He didn't kid himself that it was purely his looks and charm; he wasn't that innocent. No, it was literally the wealth and the lifestyle that made him so apparently irresistible to women.

'Thank you for looking after Mo,' he declared quietly. 'I truly appreciate your kindness.'

'Not a problem,' Gigi assured him, escorting him to the front door with enthusiasm.

'And if you should change your mind about dinner, here's my card.' Jace extended a business card to her. 'Maybe you have a boyfriend—'

Gigi raised both brows. 'Are you kidding? Men are more trouble than they're worth. I found that out years ago—'

'A girlfriend?' Jace persisted without even understanding why he was doing it, but he needed to know in that moment.

'Good heavens, no, I'm not gay, maybe just not that interested in…er…dating or whatever,' she completed in an oddly embarrassed rush of self-defence.

Jace nodded and he didn't get it, he *still* didn't get it. He wanted to change her mind, but he didn't know enough about her or what was happening inside his own head to understand why she was virtually indifferent to him or why he didn't wish to accept that fact. He went back into the street and she slammed the door behind him as if he had been an unwelcome intrusion.

'A strange woman,' his chief of security commented.

'You have no idea,' Jace responded as a limo complete with a still snoozing Mo drew up at the pavement.

So strange that he couldn't take his eyes off her! All curves in a very small package, eyes as blue as the Greek sky, hair as streaky as toffee in a pan that he recalled from his childhood and the most flawless face and complexion. Shaking his black curly head at such peculiar thoughts, Jace got into the limo.

'You're a traitor, a turncoat,' he told his dog without hesitation. 'I've loved you for two years and you wouldn't give me as much as a tail wag when I came to fetch you home!'

Gigi went into work with relief.

'Thought you were planning to sleep in today,' Ioanna, the shelter nurse, quipped without much surprise at Gigi's appearance. 'You're a workaholic…admit it!'

'I couldn't sleep late today. I had a dog I found last night and he needed walking—'

'Gigi…you could go to a blasted pop concert and come home with a dog!' the older woman teased. 'But it's no life for someone your age.'

'I'm quite happy with my life as it is,' Gigi lied.

But she wasn't going to reference her experience of men to anyone she worked with. Even on Rhodes within her own family, she had learned how unreliable men were these days. She had three half-brothers who were man whores with tourists and one whose marriage had broken up because he had cheated on his wife. And what about her father, who had insisted he was legally separated from his wife at the time that Gigi was conceived? Gigi wasn't convinced of that legal-separation claim after meeting her father's wife, Katerina, who had treated her very much as though she were some designing young female trying to muscle in on *her* family.

Her mother had been a committed career woman, a high-earning nuclear physicist, who had travelled a lot, often working abroad on government projects. She had placed Gigi in boarding school at an early age to remain free of the domestic burden of raising a child. She had informed Gigi's father, Achilleus Georgiou, that she had had a child after their fling in Athens while she was in Greece at a conference. But Gigi's father had never bothered to come and visit Gigi or write to her or even contribute to her care.

Achilleus owned three thriving businesses in the Old Town and he had four sons, all of whom worked for him. Had Gigi paused to consider such hard, revealing facts she would not have been foolish enough to come to Greece in search of a family after her mother's sudden death. Unfortunately, she had decided to seek out her roots in the hope of making a connection, but it hadn't happened. She had simply met up with a bunch of uninterested people who had their own lives and didn't need her in those lives.

'So, tell me about the dog,' Ioanna encouraged.

And Gigi did, from start to finish when Mo had been carried out like a parcel and she had been invited yet again to dinner.

'So, why didn't you say yes? Was he ugly? Too old?'

'No...er...no, he was extremely good-looking, probably only a few years older than me, and he even gave me a business card.' Gigi giggled in recollection of that unexpected moment of formality and dug it out of the back pocket of her shorts with a flourish.

Ioanna snatched at the card and her eyes widened and her mouth fell open. '*Jace Diamandis*...oh, my word, I don't believe this!' she gasped. 'Only one of the richest men in the world! And certainly the richest in Greece!'

Gigi pursed her full pink lips. 'He did look kind of fancy—'

'*Fancy?* Haven't you noticed that giant matt-black yacht anchored out in the bay?' Ioanna practically shrieked in excitement. 'It belongs to him and the funeral he mentioned was his father's. He was buried yesterday.'

Gigi winced at that announcement, feeling that she had signally failed to excuse Jace's loss of temper when it seemed he would naturally have been grieving. Poor guy, she thought helplessly, sympathetic for the first time towards her unwelcome visitor.

'And the worst thing of all is that you are not even impressed!' the nurse commented.

'Well, why would I be?' Gigi asked with a frown. 'What's his money got to do with me?'

'He asked you out and you said no! I can't believe that you said *no* to Jace Diamandis!'

'Well, he did seem a bit surprised that I was turning him down,' Gigi conceded reluctantly. 'But I got the impression that he was totally full of himself and that's a major turn-off for me. I wouldn't have had anything in common with him, so it would have been a waste of time meeting him again—'

'But you should have gone just for the *thrill*!' Ioanna carolled.

'I'm quite…shy with men. It wouldn't have worked and if he's that rich, it would have been just a plain peculiar experience. Look, who's first on today's surgical rota?' Gigi enquired, keen to get off the topic of Jace Diamandis and his filthy lucre and the unknown thrills he might be expected to offer.

On his legendary superyacht, *Sea King*, Jace was giving way to his curiosity and requesting an in-depth investigation into Gigi Campbell, who for some eccentric reason he couldn't get out of his head. He sent flowers too that evening when he assumed she would be at home.

Receiving a giant basket of glorious wildflowers absolutely bemused Gigi, who had never thought of herself as a flowery woman. She sat staring at them for almost an hour, and at the card, wondering what insanity had possessed Mo's owner. He was trying to say thank you, she supposed, failing to appreciate that she would have performed the same rescue bid on any animal running loose in busy traffic.

She wondered how Mo was getting on. She missed the dog. She had really, really liked Mo. Somehow, he had made her feel less lonely. She wondered if he performed the same service for Jace, but doubted that someone as handsome, powerful and wealthy could possibly feel in need of that kind of support.

On his yacht, Jace studied his disaffected dog, whimpering mournfully by the door as if he had been stolen against his will from Gigi, and he sighed heavily...

CHAPTER TWO

JACE THOUGHT UNUSUALLY hard about what he wore on the day he went to the rescue shelter. He ditched the designer business suits he invariably wore and picked jeans and a linen shirt, less formal, more approachable, he reasoned.

But *she* was all wrong for him, in any case, he reminded himself stubbornly. He had held a party the night before, a party attended by some very beautiful women, exquisitely dressed, flattering and polite women, and for the first time in his life, not one woman had appealed to his normally rampant libido. No, very weirdly, it was Gigi Campbell's image that he couldn't get out of his head. That truth was annoying the hell out of him. Was it the fact that she was a challenge? A challenge was something he had never met with in her sex. Could he possibly be *that* basic? He suppressed a cynical shudder at the suspicion.

At the rescue shelter, Gigi was attending to her usual duties without much concern. Ioanna might be champing at the bit for Jace Diamandis to come through the door for Mo's appointment to be microchipped but Gigi was not. In fact, with the vet nurse hanging about as if she were awaiting a visitation from a god amongst men, Gigi was more inclined to pity Jace for the excitement he seemed to engender in those who recognised his name. All the poor guy was doing was trying to get his dog microchipped. He had seemed shocked when she had mentioned that that, after all, was Greek law and it was a perfectly normal response for the man to attend to that oversight as soon as possible.

Even so, the prospect of his imminent appearance did fluster her a little and that bothered her. After all, she was a woman who had given up on men. One broken heart had been quite enough for her. Rory had cheated on her, blaming her for it because she had refused to give him her body, having known him only a few weeks. But in so doing, he had taught her a good lesson. She would never trust a member of the male sex again. They were all obsessed with sex and the number of women they could get into their beds. She was well aware though that there were women of the same ilk because she had known a couple like that at university, but the majority of her sex were a little less crude and more emotion-based than men.

'He's...*here*!' Ioanna squealed like a member of the Jace Diamandis fan club and Gigi said not a word, conscious that all the female shelter workers were equally enthralled and would be peering out of windows and hovering in doorways.

Gigi would not allow herself to look. For some peculiar reason, she *wanted* to look and that irritated her, particularly when his image was already stuck like glue inside her brain. The high sculpted cheekbones, the imperious ebony brows, the strong masculine nose, the wide sensual mouth. And the whole topped by the most gloriously cute glossy black curls, not to mention the unexpected eyes green as emeralds lighting up that lean dark face. Drop-dead gorgeous. Yes, Jace definitely had cornered the looks department with a meteoric score but, unfortunately, he knew that rather too well. As for his reputation? Well, that certainly didn't add to his image as a plus. She had seen enough online to decide that he was way out of *her* league.

'Good morning, Gigi,' Jace murmured perfectly politely while she busied herself rearranging the equipment she used, and she heard the faint strand of amusement edging his dark, deep voice.

'Good morning, Mr Diamandis…' she contrived to say flatly before she was unceremoniously engulfed by an ecstatic wolfhound who knocked her off her feet with enthusiasm.

'My apologies… I shouldn't have let him off the leash.' A lean strong hand closed over hers and virtually hauled her back upright from the floor, where she had fallen to her knees, while Mo tried to canter a circle round her in his excitement.

The warmth of his hand sent the most curious zing through her entire body and she glanced up at him, only to be consumed by the scorching flash effect of dancing emerald-green eyes. Her entire body heated up, her nipples prickling inside her bra, a sliding sensation tugging between her legs. Those feelings made her grit her teeth in annoyance and free her hand, which he was *still* holding, and drop back down to her knees again to give his dog her attention.

* * *

Jace wasn't accustomed to being blanked but he took it like a man, like a thrown gauntlet, because at the moment she had collided with his eyes, he had read her response as clearly as a shrieking alarm. The flush on her cheeks, her dilated pupils? Neither spoke of indifference. Gigi Campbell wanted him but at the same time she didn't *want* to want him, he recognised with satisfaction. He watched his dog fawn on her like a subservient slave. Indeed, he surveyed the delighted reunion with a curled lip of near disbelief because, in his experience, Mo was not that friendly an animal and rarely approached anyone else for attention. But Mo couldn't get enough of Gigi.

'Sorry about this,' Gigi said, unselfconsciously rising to her feet again with a final pat of Mo's head. 'But he's the most beautiful dog and *so* affectionate.'

'Is this…er…procedure likely to hurt him?' Jace enquired.

'For a split second…' Gigi wielded the tool and Mo stood like a statue for her, trying to lick at the knee that was all the skin he could reach below her lab coat. 'Stop that, Mo…'

The sunlight coming through the window lit up the blonde streaks in her light brown hair, settled lovingly on the porcelain-perfect skin of her profile, her slender neck, the thrust of her small firm breasts. Jace gritted his teeth because his body reacted like an adolescent's in her vicinity. That fast he was hard as a rock and it infuriated him, infuriated him in the only way it could a usually very controlled and reserved male. For the space of a timeless moment, he had been out of control, picturing her splayed across his bed like some kind of sexual sacrifice, picturing a *fantasy*. And Jace didn't have fantasies about women, had never had the need, had never wanted any woman that he hadn't had.

'There…that's done and, of course, you were a good boy,' Gigi told Mo, fondling his silky ears. 'Thank you for bringing him here so that I could see him again. I'm sure you could have sent him anywhere with an employee to have him microchipped.'

Yes, she knew who he was now, Jace savoured before it occurred to him that it had not changed her attitude one iota. She was rather more interested in his dog than she was in him.

'He may only have been with you one night but he formed an attachment to you,' Jace conceded.

'He slept with me. That's probably it. I didn't have the heart to put him back downstairs because he's *so* cuddly!' Gigi stooped to give another hug to Mo.

'You let him into your bed?' Jace elevated an ebony brow. 'I wouldn't dream of allowing that. No wonder he got so attached!'

'Sorry for teaching him a bad habit.' Gigi laughed, a low husky laugh, animation skimming her lovely face, her blue eyes sparkling, her soft mouth smiling to reveal a slice of pearly teeth. For an instant, she simply took his breath away and all he wanted to do was kiss her. The strength of that impulse spooked him into swinging away to put some distance between them. It was as if she had shot him up with pure adrenaline.

'Where do I pay?' he asked her, turning back around to face her.

'We charge the basic rate at Reception outside. I guess that won't be a problem for you,' Gigi framed awkwardly, striving hard not to stare at him. But he was so good-looking he kept on stealing her attention like a sneak thief. And never mind his beautiful face. He had an even more beautiful body. Tall, lean, fit, narrow waist, taut hips, powerful thighs and biceps, long, straight legs. Discomfiture relating to those reflections sent colour flying into her cheeks as she clashed with his amused green gaze. She stiffened at the intensity and the fire she saw in that scrutiny. He had watched her checking him out. Unnerved by that awareness, she dropped her head again.

'When did you find out who I was?' Jace asked carelessly.

'My nurse recognised your name. I think there's another patient waiting,' she prompted him very quietly, too aware of his volatile nature to be as blunt as she had been at their first meeting.

Thee mou, she was trying to get rid of him again, Jake registered in consternation. 'Why won't you have dinner with me when you're attracted to me?'

Utterly thrown by that confident assurance that she was attracted to him and by his unexpected candour, Gigi froze in her movement towards the door. 'Maybe I don't see what we would have in common...and I'm not the sort of woman who's likely to sleep with you on a first date, so we'd both be wasting our time—'

Jace threw his handsome head back in disconcertion, surprised that she would be that blunt. 'Doesn't it occur to you that I may not be that predictable?'

'Your reputation suggests that you're *very* predictable.'

'You think it's fair to judge me on the stories other people tell about me?' Jace lanced back at her a tinge harshly. 'I live in a goldfish bowl—'

'And you're very visible in it,' Gigi said in what she hoped was a soothing tone. 'But I *wasn't* judging you. Your life is none of my business—'

'Maybe I *want* you to make it your business,' Jace shot back at her without hesitation.

And Gigi almost laughed but dared not because he was acting defensively. But she was tempted to laugh at the concept of a guy with private jets, yachts and the like taking a genuine interest in a hard-working veterinary surgeon without an ounce of glamour. 'OK. I need to get back to work, Jace. There's a full waiting room out there.'

A stony aspect turned his carved jawline to granite. In silence he nodded, attached Mo's leash again and strode out. Jace had never been so conscious that he wanted to smash something with violence. His temper had rocketed up like lava in a volcano but he refused to show it around her when she had already labelled him' volatile'. And he wasn't volatile, not remotely volatile, he assured himself fiercely. He wasn't thinking that way because he wasn't accustomed to criticism, either. He had excellent relationships with his staff...*didn't he*?

She had blown him off *twice*. On one level he couldn't believe it, on another he was all the more determined to catch her. The investigation report hadn't come back yet. He wanted to know what the name Gigi was short for. He wanted to know what age she was. He wanted to know every damned thing there was to know about her!

But wasn't it a little unhinged to still be so interested in a woman after she had turned him down? An uneasy touch of ice trickled down Jace's rigid spine at that lowering apprehension. He would put her behind him, forget about her. Some strange notion had brought him back to her again and now he regretted it. Although it went against the grain to admit it, Gigi had been right: what did they have in common? And he would've only spent one night with her, in any case. It was insane to rate one woman any higher than the rest of the female sex, crazy to believe there could be some more special woman out there for him, especially when he was the last guy alive to want that *one* special woman.

Inside the shelter, Gigi's thoughts were travelling in the opposite direction. Possibly she had grown too rigid about protecting herself from predatory men, she was thinking abstractedly. And that very abstraction bothered her because no male had ever stuck around inside her head but Jace. Only wasn't she being a bit juvenile and hysterical saying no to a mere dinner invitation because he attracted her? So, she had got hurt before but sooner or later everyone got hurt in affairs of the heart. One person wanted one thing, the other something else. That was simply life and she had already warned him in advance that she wouldn't be inviting him into her bed.

Two days later, leash trailing again, Mo was sleeping on Gigi's doorstep when she arrived home. 'Oh, you bad dog,' she said very softly, stroking a silky ear while she considered the awkward prospect of having to phone Jace to tell him that his dog was with her again. She dug out his card.

'You've got him, haven't you?' Jace interrupted within seconds of her beginning to speak.

'Yes, sorry about that. He was waiting at my front door when I got home—'

'I wouldn't have believed that he could have retraced his steps from the harbour to your house last week. I'll collect him…or I'll have him collected—'

'Jace?' she broke in. 'I'll agree to dinner.'

A stark little silence fell.

'I'll send a car for you—'

'To go where?'

'You are so distrustful,' Jace complained.

'Merely mindful of my safety.'

'My yacht, *Sea King*—'

'I'd prefer a public place,' she said apologetically.

'Would you also enjoy the paparazzi surrounding us? That's what happens in public places when I'm visible,' Jace told her drily.

'OK, the yacht,' she conceded reluctantly, definitely not wishing to appear in newsprint in his company because she took her anonymous life for granted.

'Eight,' he specified.

'Eight-thirty,' she told him. 'I have to walk both dogs.'

And then the call ended without another word.

Well, did you expect him to turn verbal wheelies at

the end of the line when you finally agreed? Blinking, already wondering if she had made an unwise decision, Gigi set down her phone.

She went for a shower before taking a simple electric-blue maxi, sleeveless dress from her wardrobe. Her first summer in Rhodes she had assumed she would have more of a social life with her Greek family and she had extended her very practical wardrobe. But in actuality she had received few invitations. Everybody had been keen to meet her once out of curiosity, but their interest hadn't gone much deeper than that. Maybe if there had been a half-sister, *she* would have been more interested, only, knowing her luck, Gigi conceded ruefully, a potential half-sister would have been furious to discover that her father had a second daughter.

A limousine drew up at her door, paying no attention whatsoever to the 'no parking' lines. Gigi stepped out straight away, Mo walking by her side. She would've insisted on driving her own car to the harbour had it not occurred to her that trying to squeeze Mo into her tiny two-door car might make the big dog baulk. He stepped up onto the luxurious back seat beside her and flopped his head down on her lap for her to pat. 'Life's so much simpler for you,' she sighed.

Either the huge yacht had an enormous crew or it seemed as though an awful lot of them were curious about Jace's visitor because every direction Gigi looked in there seemed to be a face peering at her, and the captain, wearing his official uniform, greeted her as though she were arriving royalty when she stepped off the motor launch that had whisked her from the harbour.

That welcome, along with the opulence surrounding Gigi, just about deprived her of breath. She emerged from a lift into a vast reception area.

Clearly designed for his parties.

She was offered a drink by a stewardess who could have featured in a Miss World competition.

Does he perve on his staff?

Stop it, Gigi warned herself, you're being judgmental on nothing more than the headlines he attracts.

'Gigi. Sorry not to be here to greet you,' Jace intoned as he strode through an archway. 'I was taking a call.'

For a split second, she felt as though her heart stopped beating and the world suddenly swam into sharper focus on his lean dark face. Green eyes flaring like fireworks, startlingly intense and potent. It shook her up. She stole a fast glance at him and then walked over to the windows as if she were examining the fabulous view of the harbour and the winding road beyond it. She spun back, her heart now beating at an accelerated rate, and watched Mo trot over to greet Jace as normally as if the dog had just entered the room rather than run off on his owner again.

'I think, as far as he's concerned, *he* was retrieving *you*,' Jace quipped as though he had been thinking the exact same thing.

'Probably,' she agreed with a slightly nervous laugh.

'What do you like to eat?'

'I eat virtually everything, and I have no allergies.'

'Gigi…what's that short for? Or is it only a nickname?' he heard himself ask, startling himself with the level of his curiosity about her.

'It says Giselle on my birth certificate, so it must be my mother who shortened it because I've never been called anything else…or maybe it was one of the nannies who looked after me.'

'You were raised by nannies?'

'Yes, until I went to boarding school.' Gigi's eyes stung on the thought that she knew very little about her earliest years because Nadine Wilson had never been a sentimental parent, delighted to recall her daughter's babyhood. In the same way there were only a handful of photos of her between birth and starting school and some of them were on medical records.

'And after that?' Jace prompted, wondering why the hell he was still being so nosy.

'My mother sometimes worked abroad so for term breaks I often went to friends' houses or on study trips, which suited me the best. I was a nerd from day one at school,' she admitted calmly. 'There's lots of programmes out there for nerdy kids. Occasionally a short-term nanny would be hired but usually the housekeeper was capable of looking out for me.'

'There you are…we *do* have something in common,' Jace declared with satisfaction. 'Nannies and boarding schools. My parents were busy people too.'

A little uneasy below that shimmering emerald-green appraisal, Gigi parted her lips. 'You mentioned food…'

Recalled by the reminder that she had only just arrived and he had been interrogating her, faint colour enhanced Jace's high cheekbones. 'You can literally have anything you like because I have a team of chefs in the galley.'

'That's good. I find cooking a chore,' she confided lightly. 'It's a struggle to remind myself that I should eat a healthy meal when the easy options are often unhealthy. I'll have a Greek salad and…er stuffed veggies?'

'No appetiser?'

'Not for me. I'm not a big eater but feel free on your own behalf,' she urged, a little flushed as she sipped at her orange juice and sat down at the side of the polished dining table in the indicated seat across from his.

'I'm attempting to replicate the restaurant experience I denied you…and you won't allow me to do it,' Jace reproved.

'I guess that's because I'm really wondering what I'm doing here with you,' Gigi admitted frankly.

Jace gritted his teeth. 'Don't start that again.'

He snapped his fingers and the stewardess appeared to take their order. Apart from an aside to check that she wasn't vegetarian, he ordered food she hadn't requested and wine.

'I don't really drink,' she told him in a small voice.

Jace shot her a dazzling smile. 'No worries. I do.'

That smile made every cell in her body sit up and take notice. She simply stared back at him for a moment, mesmerised by that outpouring of charm but distrusting him all the more.

'What are you so scared of?' Jace asked her almost lazily, his bright green eyes suddenly as shrewd as cutting knives. 'Has some guy in the past assaulted you?'

'No!'

'That's how you come across,' Jace murmured. 'I

assure you that I have never laid a single finger on an unwilling woman.'

Gigi's flush had spread as far as her hairline. Indeed she felt as if she were being boiled alive with mortification inside her own skin. 'That's…er good to know,' she mumbled. 'No, I don't date or anything because I've rarely felt the need to do so. I did once a couple of years ago but he turned out to be a loser and that put me off—'

'*Once?* You're *that* easily put off?'

'You wouldn't understand—'

'Why wouldn't I understand?'

'You're an extrovert. I'm an introvert. I internalise stuff. Socially I'm a wallflower. I've always been that way.'

A lean brown hand came down to where her smaller hand was trembling and covered it with sudden warmth. 'It's all right to be who you are. There's nothing wrong with that. Stop apologising for it,' he urged, startling her with both those words and that physical gesture. 'Don't overthink this. It's only a meal—'

'On a freaking yacht!' she shot back at him with a choking giggle.

'On a freaking yacht,' conceded Jace, still smiling as he collided with those superb cornflower-blue eyes of hers. 'And you want to know why you're here? You're absolutely beautiful and I can't push you out of my head. It's like you've taken up residence there and I can't see anyone else and it's driving me crazy!'

As his dark deep drawl rose a little at the end of that final, disconcerting admission, Gigi's extreme tension gave and she suddenly smiled and relaxed. 'Same here.'

Jace dealt her a mock-stunned appraisal, his forceful gaze flaming over her. 'Are you seriously admitting that?'

Gigi nodded gravely. 'But what's the point—?'

'No...*no*,' Jace cut in with ruthless cool. 'Stop with the negatives. Slow that busy brain of yours. Enjoy the evening.'

Gigi knew that she suffered from a lot of negative self-talk but that underlying anxiety had always been with her. Her mother had been a very outgoing person and her daughter's different nature had offended her expectations. 'You talk sense,' she said, 'and that surprises me.'

Jace laughed out loud, amused by her ignorance. 'Gigi... I'm the CEO of a very large group of companies. Of course I've got sense.'

'Obviously I read the wrong stuff online when I looked you up.' Gigi frowned on her own behalf. 'I read the gossip. There's no real excuse for that.'

'In your position, I would probably have done the same. I came back onboard here and asked for a private investigator to check you out for me,' Jace admitted. 'And he still can't get back to me. He can't trace you, for some reason.'

Gigi was studying him wide-eyed and then she laughed with unmistakable amusement. 'I had to change my surname to my grandmother's to inherit her estate. That's my mother's mother. She never forgave my mother for falling pregnant outside marriage and she never asked to meet me, but she still put me in her will. That was a huge surprise. Growing up, my surname was Wilson because my mother was briefly married and divorced when she was quite young and she changed her name. Becoming a Campbell to match my grandmother meant that I could pay off my student loans, which was *huge* for me at the time.'

'I thought you'd be angry when I told you about the investigation I ordered on you—'

Below his arrested gaze, Gigi shrugged a slight shoulder. 'I guess that's your equivalent of the online snooping session that I did. I'm not annoyed but then I've got nothing I feel the need to hide.'

The first course arrived at the table. She ate with unusual appetite, savouring every tiny bite. Somehow, and she had completely no idea *how*, Jace had enabled her to relax in his presence for the first time. He made easy conversation. He was very polite. He was amazingly comfortable to be with. An enigma, she decided, seemingly quite unlike his glitzy playboy image. Or was she falling for an act? She suppressed that suspicion, scolding herself for that less than positive thought. Why would someone as rich and good-looking as Jace Diamandis go to so much trouble for someone like her if he *weren't* genuinely interested?

Jace whipped his hand from Gigi's only when he realised that he had retained his hold on those slender fingers. He was still recovering from the shock value of having told her that he couldn't get her out of his head. Never before had he been guilty of going in keen with a woman, because it handed out the wrong message and it wasn't fair...even if it was true? Every glimpse he got of her stuck to him like superglue.

Possibly that was the challenge she seemed to be for him. His intentions were wholly basic as usual, he reassured himself. A good time would be enjoyed by both of them; however, it wouldn't be heading beyond the bedroom door in any direction. No offence intended, no harm done, surely? So, why was he feeling like a bastard all of a sudden? Admittedly she was a sensitive woman and he didn't have a sensitive bone in his entire body. At least, he never had with anyone else. Why the hell was he even thinking along such complex lines?

'You seem preoccupied,' Gigi remarked, because he had been staring at her with brooding intensity.

'It's you…you preoccupy me.'

'That's a compliment, *isn't it*?'

'A foe worthy of my mettle,' Jace teased helplessly, because he could scarcely tell her the truth that being so drawn to her made him feel slightly on the edge of insane.

The main course arrived. He asked her about her animals and she worked through them one by one.

'How on earth could that little tortoise be too large for its owner?' Jace demanded.

'Because they got him when he was teeny-tiny and probably put him in an aquarium or something to keep him and he outgrew his space. I'm planning to let Humphrey go free when I find the right setting for him,' she explained. 'But he has to learn how to forage for himself before I can do that and he's pretty hopeless at the minute. He's very lazy—'

'Give him a break. Maybe the aquarium was very small,' Jace suggested seriously.

And Gigi laughed. 'You know, looking at your fancy suit, I would never have guessed it, but you genuinely do like animals.'

'Yes. Mo the defector who wants to exchange me for you isn't much of an advertisement in that line.'

'No, he loves you. I just think he's not used to female attention—'

'I'd like to think that, but there are several female crew members who like him and he's never gone missing to find them.'

Jace thrust back his chair with sudden restiveness. 'Let me give you a tour of the yacht and when we come back the last course will be waiting. Do you want coffee?'

'Tea's more my speed at this hour but I always sleep like a log anyway,' she conceded absently.

Not in my bed, you won't, Jace promised himself soothingly because he knew she was a very poor bet from his point of view.

She was clever but there was not the smallest attempt to hook him in her appearance or her behaviour and he wasn't stupid. The modest dress, the lack of cosmetics, the absence of flirtation. Right now, Gigi was merely tolerating him. He would probably have to fill out a thirty-page questionnaire before she would consider sliding between those sheets with him. She wasn't a woman likely to take a risk on him or one likely to succumb to temptation. She liked security, familiarity, safe bets and he offered none of those things. And yet it was strangely relaxing to be in her company, regardless of the reality that sex wasn't on the immediate agenda, possibly even because of that fact. Her lack of expectations and her sheer honesty were soothing.

'You're so different from me—'

'Stop building more walls between us,' Jace urged, exasperated at the manner in which she continually stepped further away from him, reinforcing her apparent conviction that they could never be together in any way. He swore to himself that he would teach her otherwise.

'Is that what I'm doing?'

Shimmering green eyes as bright as jewels in sunshine assailed her. 'You know you are.'

Gigi went pink and felt exposed as the unexciting woman she believed she was.

Jace wondered when he had last, if ever, been with a woman who blushed. Next time he met a woman who blushed he should walk the other way fast, he instructed himself. 'You haven't mentioned a father yet—'

'And you haven't mentioned a single word about your background,' she reminded him as he flung open the door on a plush cinema room and moved on to show her a gym.

'Most people already know all about me,' he declared. 'My mother died when I was six and when she was in the act of leaving my father for another man. She crashed her car with her lover. Both of them died. Thankfully she hadn't taken me with her.'

But his lean, strong features were taut as elastic pulled too tight and she grasped that it wasn't that simple for him. He might be grateful that he hadn't died in the same crash but he was still hurt that his mother had left him behind.

By instinct, in the same way she absently fondled Mo's ears as he walked with them, she closed a hand over Jace's fist. No, sophisticated he might be, but he wasn't good at hiding his emotions. But then few hot-blooded temperaments were, she reflected. 'That must've been tough.'

'No,' he disagreed. 'It got tough when my father decided that he couldn't stand the sight of me because I looked so like my mother and sent me and the nanny to live with my grandparents. And my grandfather was too ill to want to take on the burden of a young child.'

Her heart smote her for him. Gigi had always had a very soft heart and what had been done to Jace when he was a young child drove a compassionate knife through her chest. He had been rejected by his family and to some degree the same thing had happened to her. Her mother had raised her, feeding, clothing and educating her, but she had not loved her or looked for her when she wasn't there.

'What?' Jace chided. 'No words of wisdom now?'

'You don't like talking about it and I perfectly understand that and won't mention it again. However, don't get sarky,' Gigi warned him, removing her fingers from his.

'There *was* a happy ending,' Jace heard himself expand, missing that innocent physical contact with her and furious about the fact. 'My father's youngest brother and his husband offered me a home a few weeks later at a family meeting. Everyone was very grateful for that solution because my father was king in the family and nobody wanted me in the same household lest he stop visiting or favouring them.'

'And your father's brother?'

'He wasn't financially dependent on my father while the others were. He and Marcus are partners in a chain of very successful European art galleries. I was very lucky that they wanted me,' he breathed stiffly as she looked up at him, her wonderful eyes intent, her entire posture leaning in towards him in what he interpreted as an invitation.

Jace trailed a lean forefinger slowly up her arm, savouring the goose bumps that followed in the wake of his touch. He reached her delicate collarbone and traced it as well. Unlike him, she was slight in build, shockingly fragile to the feel.

'Jace…?' she whispered shakily.

And, like a male going for a gold medal, he tasted her soft, pouting lips gently and her head swam as if she had taken alcohol, a strange breathless weakness engulfing her as butterflies unfurled low in her tummy. He deepened the pressure and closed his arms round her without warning and just as quickly he was devouring her mouth as if he couldn't get enough of her.

And that was fine, she acknowledged dimly in the very midst of that hot, explosive kiss, because she couldn't get enough of him either. Her arms came up and closed on his broad shoulders as she stretched herself up to him, wishing she had worn heels. His tongue delved in her mouth and she shivered against him with sensation. It was like standing in a force ten gale. It was dynamite, everything she had ever hoped to feel and never found. There was no fumbling, no unease. It was as though her body had been waiting for Jace Diamandis all her life…

Both of them breathless, he pulled back from her and continued the tour, only this time around he kept a hold of her hand, reinstating that connection even when she had to step away.

CHAPTER THREE

GIGI LOOKED UP at Jace in the moonlight. His lean, hard-boned features were contemplative as the motor launch whizzed them back to the harbour. A phalanx of security staff ringed them because Jace did not like to be photographed against his will and had what struck her as an almost paranoiac need to ensure that his movements remained undocumented by the paparazzi.

Without warning, he folded both arms round her, pulling her close to the heat and solidity of his long lean length, and reaction went running through her like a crazy song rising in volume inside her. It touched every part of her. Her heart skipped a beat. Her nipples tightened almost painfully and there was a clenching low in her feminine core. Butterflies danced in her tummy. Concentration became a huge challenge.

'We're alone,' he insisted, against all the evidence to the contrary.

Gigi didn't want him to kiss her with so many men standing around, even though it was true that all of them were carefully looking in other directions. 'This is weird,' she hissed up at him, small hands braced and spread across his wide chest to forge some distance between them. 'You should've stayed on the yacht—'

'Didn't want to part with you yet,' he growled.

'You're seeing me in the morning,' she reminded him unevenly, her voice slipping and slurring as she collided with his intent gaze, the greenness blacked out by the low light but the expression no less forceful.

'You should've stayed on the yacht—'

'I have pets to look after,' she reminded him yet again, one hand sliding up off his chest onto a wide hard shoulder as she looked up him.

'I could've had that handled for you—'

'You're like a toddler sometimes!' she whispered in sudden frustration, leaning close to his ear. 'If you can't get your own way, you get angry—'

'I'm not getting angry,' Jace grated between evenly clenched white teeth and it was the biggest lie he had ever told, but he was damned if he was about to qualify for that demeaning 'volatile' label again. People who couldn't control their emotions, like his father, who had rejected him, like his mother, who had put her love life ahead of her son, often made mistakes they couldn't come back from. He had no plans to ever make those kinds of mistakes.

Her free hand mock-punched him on the chest. '*And* you're such a liar!' she countered in another tone entirely, a forgiving tone of understanding, because she had had to fight herself to walk away from him too.

And that had shaken Gigi deep, shaken her up, shaken her inside out because she had never felt anything like the connection she felt with Jace with any other man. He felt like something in her bones, something familiar and, oh, so precious and that was exhilarating but it was also terrifying. No matter what she felt, she didn't *know* him or, at least, she hadn't known him long enough. She didn't want to rush into anything with him. She needed to step back, take a breath and work out if it would be sensible to move forward. Her disillusionment on the family front had taught her to protect herself before she risked her heart.

'You're busy thinking of all the reasons why you shouldn't be with me,' Jace intoned knowingly in her ear as he bent his handsome dark head. 'Why do you think I tried to keep you onboard, even in another bed?'

Even the way he said that word 'bed' set her alight somewhere deep down in her body and she quivered, tapped out on words of wisdom, vaguely accepting that she was on her own with no guidance or easy solution to so powerful an attraction. It was intimidating that he knew what she was thinking almost before she thought it. 'Tomorrow,' she told him steadily, suddenly proud that she had retained that much resistance to a male she found virtually irresistible.

'Tomorrow,' Jace repeated in another tone entirely, his hungry mouth claiming hers with fierce hunger, his tongue delving deep, twining with hers, and her hands gripped his forearms to steady her stance because her knees were weak. And nobody had ever kissed her the way Jace kissed her, as if 'tomorrow' were a hundred years away.

He drew back from her and that was when she realised that the launch had already docked and that everyone onboard was looking to Jace to issue instructions. Her face burned as though hellfire had flamed beneath her skin and she lifted her head high as Jace handed her off the craft and she stepped down onto the dock, accompanied to the car that awaited her. Jace lived in another world, totally another world from hers and one with different rules and dangers. She refused to look back at him even though she knew he was still watching her and she breathed in deep and long to regain her calm. Unfortunately, when it came to her reaction to Jace, he had the same effect on her as an explosive device thrown into a tranquil pond.

Back home, sliding into bed for what little remained of the night, she was too tired to agonise and she slept almost as soon as her head hit the pillow.

First thing, she was too busy to think about anything other than the needs of her pets and getting to work for the short surgery she offered on Saturday mornings. She worked for a charity but she didn't get paid for Saturday mornings when she volunteered her services for those who could not afford to pay for treatment from more expensive places. Only when she was hurriedly packing a bag for the rest of her day did she allow her thoughts to stray to Jace.

About the last thing she was expecting at nine o'clock on a Saturday was a very loud rat-a-tat-tat on the front door knocker. And opening the door to find her Greek father and her four half-brothers waiting there was an even bigger shock. 'Has something happened?'

Achilleus Georgiou stepped through the door with a thunderous expression. 'Yes, something has happened,' he said very drily, extending a newspaper to her like exhibit A in a murder trial.

Frowning, Gigi peered and then her face lit up pink in mortification. In spite of all Jace's precautions, there they were in print on the launch kissing and there was another much clearer photo of her face as she stepped off the launch at the marina. Then and there, she scolded herself for assuming that Jace's concern about the paparazzi was paranoid. Evidently someone with a long-distance telephoto lens had spotted and caught them together.

'How did you meet him?' one of her four half-brothers demanded, all five men standing around her looking annoyed and accusing.

'I met him when I saved his dog from getting run over on the road outside,' Gigi advanced quietly. 'What's it to you?'

'What's it to any of us?' another half-brother piped up in apparent wonderment at her attitude. 'You're making an exhibition of yourself with a guy no decent woman would associate with!'

'Is that so?'

'Yes, I'm sorry to say it is,' her father stepped in to confirm. 'Diamandis has an appalling reputation with women but possibly you were not aware of that fact?'

Achilleus had the brass to look hopeful as he asked that question and Gigi squared her slight shoulders. 'No. I read about his reputation online—'

'Then why the hell—?'

'Are you crazy?'

'What man will want you after he's ditched you and moved on?'

'You're soiling the Georgiou family name!'

As that storm of male protest was unleashed on her, Gigi stood even taller. 'But I'm *not* a Georgiou. And I'm *not* a member of your family.'

'You are my daughter!' her father proclaimed.

'You are our sister!'

Gigi reckoned that it was most unfortunate that they had never once uttered such keen sentiments over the past eighteen months when she had hung around on the edge of their family group, unaccepted, never once sought out. No, she had arranged every meeting between them all, each and every one. And many of those encounters had taken place only because Helene had still been alive and, naturally, they had wished to visit *her*, their sick grandmother, with whom Gigi had lived.

'Ask your sons to leave,' she told her father. 'I will talk to you, nobody else.'

Her half-brothers shuffled out looking upset and angry at her apparent lack of understanding of their feelings.

'I can see that this is an intervention,' Gigi said quietly when she was finally alone with the older man. 'And doubtless well intended to protect me, but I'm a woman of twenty-three years of age and an independent adult. I do as I like and I don't wish to be in conflict with you but you have *never* been a father to me.'

'I'm sorry but I was worried about you. You're on your own. He's a womaniser and I don't want to see you getting hurt.' With this little unexpected admission, Achilleus backed off a step, his weathered but still attractive face a mask of guilt and disconcertion, and her kind heart smote her because he was not a man capable, it seemed, of sharing his feelings, of admitting what had actually happened between her mother and him. Her mother had refused to talk about that as well. He was an old-school man of a different generation, but he had had months to bring himself to that point of talking about what mattered most and he still hadn't done it, still hadn't grasped that nettle. Yet in spite of those facts, he had still somehow decided that he had the right to come to her and criticise her conduct as though he were a true father to her. That admission that he was genuinely worried about her getting hurt, however, took the edge off her irritation. I'm sorry,' She sighed. 'I'm all grown now. Nobody tells me what to do. I'm single and so is Jace. If he were a married man or engaged in criminal activities, I could understand your objections, but not in these circumstances. From what I hear, he is a perfectly respectable businessman—a very rich one, I will agree, but nonetheless there's nothing dodgy about him.'

'For your sake, I hope that is true,' Achilleus said anxiously. 'But he does have an unsavoury reputation with your sex, and you have never impressed me as the kind of ambitious woman who seeks a jet-set lifestyle.'

'I'm not but I like Jace,' Gigi responded. 'I'm not expecting a for ever and ever happy ending with him either, but I will continue to see him…for the present.'

Achilleus dipped his head a shade in grudging acceptance of her adult status and added very awkwardly, 'I wish it had been possible for things to be different between us—'

Gigi flinched. 'It could have been different but nobody made the effort,' she pointed out ruefully.

The older man turned his head away, his discomfiture palpable, and a few minutes later he was gone, refusing a cup of coffee while ignoring the opportunity to put their relationship on a firmer, closer basis. She thought it ironic that her entire Greek family had landed on her doorstep at an early hour when they decided that she had done something wrong but that the same family had been wholly uninterested in treating her like a daughter or a sister beforehand. It hurt, but not as much as their indifference had hurt eighteen months earlier when she was still all bright-eyed and bushy-tailed optimistic about developing those relationships. In spite of that, however, she felt better for having spoken up in her own defence and laid down boundaries. She had stood up for herself, said what she had to say without apology and that could only be a sensible move.

She went into work, relieved that there was no sign she had been identified by the paparazzi as Jace's companion. No, she was a mystery woman and, hopefully, she would remain one. That hope was crushed the instant Ioanna raced into the surgery to join her on a day that she did not usually work. 'So, tell all!' she vented straight off.

'You recognised me,' Gigi gathered with a frown.

'It's a very good photo. Everyone here recognised you,' Ioanna confirmed to her dismay. 'Someone somewhere will talk and you'll be identified…there's nothing surer.'

Gigi texted Jace that she would drive herself to the marina and she ignored his objections when she left the surgery, climbing into her tiny car with Hoppy and refusing to be menaced by invisible photographers out to make money out of her image. As a result she bore a closer resemblance to a bag lady than a woman Jace would date. Hair in a high ponytail, she wore sweatpants and an oversized hoodie in spite of the heat, determined to attract no attention. The launch was waiting for her and, cradling Hoppy in her arms, she climbed straight in, loving the breeze cooling her as the craft raced across the waves to the giant matt-black yacht anchored out in the bay.

She had expected to have a moment to remove her unflattering outfit before she joined Jace but she was stymied when he greeted her as she stepped off the launch.

'What on earth are you wearing?'

Gigi dragged her dismayed gaze from his lean, powerful physique. As usual he looked the height of casual sophistication, black curls tousled, long thighs encased in fitted chinos, muscular chest covered in a T-shirt, and every time he breathed she could see his incredible pec and ab muscles expand and release. Her mouth ran dry. Only realising then that he was still awaiting her reply, she muttered, 'It was a disguise. I'll take it off now that I've arrived—'

His flaring ebony brows creased. 'Why would you wear a disguise?'

'Because photos were published in one of today's newspapers showing my face and us *kissing*,' she revealed in unmistakable disgust.

Jace was taken aback by her attitude because all the young women he knew relished such appearances in print with him. He crouched down to pet Hoppy, who bounced over to him on his three legs and then wandered over to Mo to get reacquainted, not one whit nervous of the huge dog towering over him.

'I don't want that kind of public exposure,' Gigi added. 'I like my quiet anonymous life.'

Jace frowned. 'I'm sorry. I can only control the publicity when I'm in private places. In my company there's always a risk of photos being stolen.'

'It's not your fault. Let me get changed first,' she said.

Jace's bright green gaze arrowed down into hers. *Thee mou*, she was beautiful, unadorned as she was, sunlight glimmering off her streaky brown and blonde hair. She was a picture: the slender column of her neck rising from the jumbo-sized hoodie, the big blue eyes, the naturally cushiony pink lips. His groin tightened and he concentrated on having her shown into a cabin. She emerged within two minutes, disconcerting him once again with her speed. There she was clad in simple shorts and a T-shirt worn over some kind of swimwear, for he could see the straps at the neckline, and anticipation almost made his mouth water. He began wondering for the first time if it was sexier when a woman showed less skin. Certainly, it was not a female habit in his vicinity. His pool parties on the yacht almost always featured at least one naked exhibitionist and once one person stripped, others invariably followed.

'So, what are your plans for the rest of the day?'

'Lunch at a little taverna on a small, quiet island and bathing or sunbathing or whatever. Relaxed. I assumed you would prefer that.' Jace hesitated. 'Alternatively we could go shopping somewhere—'

Her delicate nose wrinkled. 'Why would I want to go shopping? This is time off. I want to relax.'

Why would I want to go shopping?

Jace was amused by that innocent question but not at all surprised by it as he led her out onto the upper deck and ordered drinks.

Having released her hair from her ponytail, Gigi stood at the deck rail as the yacht sliced through the waves, her hair blowing back from her face. Jace slotted a moisture-beaded glass into her hand. 'We'll be getting off in little more than ten minutes,' he told her. 'You must've got a shock when you saw that newspaper. With hindsight, it was foolish for me to accompany you back to the harbour.'

'I didn't see the paper until my father and my brothers brought it to me. They were all furious,' she revealed tightly.

'Your father and your brothers?' Jace repeated. 'Are you saying that you have a family on Rhodes?'

'Calling them family would be stretching the truth. I only met them eighteen months ago. Before that, my Greek father and my half-brothers were total strangers—'

'You're half Greek,' Jace mused in surprise. 'How come you didn't already know them?'

Gigi winced. 'I'm afraid I *still* don't know my parents' story. My mother was very private, and she got exasperated when I asked awkward questions, calling their brief relationship "old history"—'

'It was *your* history.'

'Yes, I thought so too,' she agreed, folding her arms. 'I hoped my father would fill in the blanks but it's quite obvious that he doesn't want to. I suppose that's because he was married at the time with four young boys of his own. My mother was in Athens attending a conference and that's when they met. She did tell him about me.'

'Is it really that important to you now?'

'After my mother died suddenly from an aneurysm,

I was looking for a family connection and Rhodes was the only place to look,' she confided with a shrug. 'So, I found a job on the island and then phoned my father—'

'And what was his reaction at that stage?' Jace pressed curiously.

'He seemed keen, he seemed pleased. Only he wasn't so enthusiastic once I was actually here.' Gigi sighed. 'He said I should move in with his mother, who had space…and I did, only to discover that what she really needed was a carer, so I became a convenient lodger there for the whole of my first year here. I loved Helene and got on very well with her though. Unfortunately, Helene didn't seem to know how her son and my mother got entangled or what the fallout was from it. My father obviously didn't confide in her at the time and she passed away about three months ago. I'm planning to return to the UK at some stage but I don't know when. I enjoy my work here and it's given me good experience but…'

Jace tensed at the news that she already had plans to leave Greece. 'Drink up…we're here.'

Gigi was pensive for a moment, acknowledging that she was not as keen to return to the UK as she had once been. Even working out the sheer expense of putting her pets into quarantine and the distress that that would cause them left her tummy churning. Furthermore, she had left no close friends behind, indeed had little to actually return for. At least, she recalled, until her mother's property in the UK finally sold and that last tie was cut. She drained her glass thirstily and stared up into the bright blue sky and then lower, to the rocky cliffs ringing a small unspoilt and empty beach. A haze of scrub and sturdy little trees growing out of the rock crevices clung to the steep gradient. 'Is it a big climb?'

'No, and you have appropriate footwear. There's a path.'

Clutching her bag and followed by the two dogs, Gigi climbed out of the launch onto the soft sand. Jace jumped down beside her, sunglasses anchored on his nose. She took notice of the four-man-strong security team that followed them. No, Jace was never alone except in beds and bathrooms, she reflected wryly. That had to be a drag for him but possibly he had grown up with similar protection and he had got so used it, he barely even noticed his silent backup any more.

He took her to the end of the path, a hand curved to her elbow as they began to follow the zigzagging path that slowly climbed upward. 'You've been here before,' she guessed.

'Many times, but this is the first time I've brought a guest. I come here when I'm in the mood for my own company. I hope you're comfortable with rustic surroundings. The food is amazing and the views are spectacular.'

He hauled her up the last few feet and steadied her as she studied the rock terrace built right on the edge of the cliff. 'Epic,' she pronounced, strolling up onto it to study the view of the glimmering sea in sunshine and the yacht far below them.

A little man came out and chattered up a storm about what was on the day's menu. Evidently, there *was* no written menu. Gigi sat down in the shade at a home-made table, which their host proceeded to clean and polish. A younger man delivered glasses and a jug of chilled water. The dogs lay down in the shade, Hoppy edging closer and closer to Mo, who treated him like a puppy.

Jace recommended the fish and she went with his choice. She sat back in her surprisingly comfortable chair.

Jace levelled narrowed shrewd green eyes on her tranquil face. 'Why did your family bring that newspaper to you?'

Gigi winced. 'Don't ask—'

'I've got to ask,' he parried. 'I'm assuming it relates to me in some way—'

'According to them, no decent woman would date you—'

'You're the very first woman I've…er *dated*.' Jace seemed pained by the word, his lean, devastatingly beautiful face almost sombre.

'How is that possible with your reputation for loving and leaving women?'

'That's not dating, that's sex. I *don't* love them. I've never been in love and they know going in that I'll be leaving them eventually,' Jace replied drily, watching her expressive eyes as closely as a hawk in search of prey. 'I don't play guessing games with women. Everything is open and upfront—'

Gigi's brain was whirling round as fast as a merry-go-round, troubled by his honesty. 'So, what on earth are you doing with me?' she asked, smiling at the older man as he brought bread and cheeses and a bottle of wine to the table.

'I haven't worked that out yet,' Jace admitted with a

compelling smile. 'When I have, I'll let you know. One glass?' He lifted the wine bottle.

'I'll have one.'

The bread was still warm from the oven and delicious with the salty cheese. The fish was fresh and tender and it melted in her mouth. It was a lazy meal and the conversation was good as well. Jace was astonished when she admitted that she was only twenty-three years old. He understood only after she admitted that she had always been on an accelerated programme of learning at school and had in fact graduated from university with her first science degree at the age of fifteen.

'So, nerd wasn't an exaggeration,' Jace quipped.

'No, not when it came to me. I was always with older students, which meant that my social life was a dead zone because I was out of step with my peers. It's only as I've got older that I've appreciated that it's not in my nature to be a social whizz kid.'

'You're sociable enough for me,' Jace murmured. 'I may have the reputation of a party animal, but I think that's the reverse side of the coin to working very long hours.'

They strolled back down the path to the beach, where a blanket had already been laid out with a drinks cooler. His life was smoothed and polished by great wealth and the wheels were greased by his many staff. Gigi shed her shorts and her T-shirt and then felt suddenly, unusually self-conscious. There was nothing daring about her halter neck denim-blue bikini, little cleavage and very little of her derriere on show. In fact, she owned more revealing underwear than what she wore to swim. But for all that, somehow Jace was contriving to look at her as though she were stark naked and in possession of one of those spectacular cover-girl figures that always captured male attention. Turning pink, she walked into the water and within minutes she was swimming, fast and strong and confident, the way she had been taught, but her mind was utterly focused on Jace.

That wasn't like her. As a rule, she was only serious about work. Her profession was her life and it gave her confidence. Her job was a vocation and she loved the animals she worked to help. She had had to be strong to succeed so young in her chosen field and, in many ways, it had validated the choices her mother had censured her for making.

Jace, however, was showing her that she had more layers of mental and physical response than she had ever believed. He kissed her and the world fell away and that sounded like an adolescent's dream, but it had truly happened that way. For the first time she had wanted a man. And Jace might be the wrong man in terms of a future, but, in reality, did she want a serious future either? She was twenty-three years old and hers had been a relatively sheltered life in terms of the opposite sex. She was just finding her feet in the world. She didn't want to be tied down, married or someone's partner. Her job was her world. She loved it. So, sex with the right guy was finally on the table and justifiable. Why deny herself what she wanted when a guy as uninterested in commitment as she was magically appeared in front of her? Yes, he *was* magic, she reflected dizzily.

She was an excellent swimmer into the bargain, Jace noted without surprise. Mo was sitting just above the tide line, Hoppy beside him whining, both dogs anxiously awaiting her return. Jace was thoroughly abstracted after that view of Gigi in her faded old bikini that concealed far more than it revealed. But her shape was...divine. Perky little breasts, tiny waist, a bottom as shapely as a sun-warmed peach. He had wanted to put his hands on her so badly he had dug them into the sand to prevent himself from making the wrong move. Since when had he behaved that way? Self-denial didn't come naturally to Jace Diamandis, any more than being serious about a woman.

He didn't do that emotional stuff. And that was what she wanted. She might not have said so but he could read between the lines. But emotions would blunt his killer edge in business, soften him, *weaken* him. He had learned one hard lesson from his chequered childhood: *don't fall in love*. Argus Diamandis had fallen madly in love with Alessia Rossi, Jace's mother, the famous Italian opera singer, and he'd been jealous, possessive and *obsessional* about her. He might have remarried but even Evander, who had thoroughly disliked his eldest brother, had conceded that Argus had never recovered from Alessia's desertion or her death. And the aftermath of an obsessional love of that nature going wrong was often the very reverse of love, as Jace had learned as a child when he had been rejected by his father. Love like that was like a dangerous thread of instability in a man's character and the very idea of it creeped Jace out.

His grandfather's bête noire had been Electra Pappas, an heiress, who had put him through hell with her tantrums and flirtations. Yet even knowing her inclinations, his grandfather had married her, only for the marriage to crash into divorce within months. Ten years later, the couple had remarried, and Electra was now Jace's highly respected, widowed grandmother, soon to make her eightieth birthday. So, his grandfather had been obsessional too when it came to that *one* woman. A chill filtered down Jace's taut spinal cord. He wasn't about to follow in his predecessors' footsteps. He should be holding Gigi at a distance, looking for casual, replaceable, *easy*, not toeing the line for some woman who couldn't even be bothered buying a new bikini for his benefit!

At that moment, Gigi walked out of the water, casually wringing the salt water from her long hair with her hands. And Jace took one look at her, that shapely body streaming with water, that pouting pink mouth smiling, and he vaulted upright instantaneously. A siren singing on some rocky outcrop could not have yanked a stronger response from a sex-starved sailor, he conceded grimly.

'My goodness...you look very serious,' Gigi remarked, dropping down to her slender knees on the blanket and reaching for a towel.

Towering over her in swim shorts, even though he wasn't smiling, Jace looked drop-dead, lethally and heart-stoppingly gorgeous and sexy.

Jace gazed down into those cornflower-blue eyes and crouched down to her level. His big hands carefully framed her cheekbones and he leant forward slowly to kiss her.

'We can be seen by your security—' she gasped.

'Don't care.'

And he kissed her and it was everything, a sweet vein of sensual delight that tunnelled straight down to her feminine core. Her thighs strained together, seeking to quiet the burn of response. He tugged her to him with strong greedy hands and as she overbalanced down onto his lap she could not have missed registering how aroused he was. *'Jace—'*

'I need to go into the water to cool down...or go back to the yacht.' It was the essential Jace, cool, straight, unapologetic. But there was nothing cool about the fire in the compelling emerald-green eyes trained on her for an answer.

'Yacht,' Gigi almost whispered, almost unnerved by her own daring.

Gigi glimpsed the flash of surprise he couldn't hide and a deep flush scored her cheeks. Jace dug out his phone, spoke not quite levelly into it and then walked out into the water anyway, grinning back at her with sudden scorching appreciation.

CHAPTER FOUR

JACE WRAPPED HER in towels like an Egyptian mummy and swept her off her feet to carry her on to the launch when it arrived to collect them all.

'I must look ridiculous covered up like this!' She hissed the complaint in his ear as the launch approached the yacht. 'Put me down...'

'I'm preserving your privacy.' Jace was fiercely determined that he alone would be lusting after that glorious face and body of hers. The crew and his protection team were mostly male and men would be men: they would look, wonder, fantasise. Only, he had deprived them of that opportunity because in the present and, naturally, for a limited time, the only man who would be picturing Gigi naked would be *him*.

'Put me down, for goodness' sake!'

'The towels would fall off,' Jace overruled, manoeuvring the two of them safely off the launch and heading straight for the lift to hit a button with his elbow.

'I don't like domineering men—'

'Of course not,' Jace murmured levelly. 'Given the chance, you'd be doing the domineering.'

'That's not true,' Gigi insisted, one arm round his neck to keep herself steady while her nostrils flared on the wonderful smell of his skin. Salt water, fresh air, cedarwood laced with something that was just intrinsically him.

Ought she to tell him that he would be her first lover? Why should she care if he thought that was a bit strange? After all, with Jace Diamandis in the starring role, there was nothing surer than the reality that this would be a one-night stand. That was how the cookie crumbled. She needed to keep that in mind from the outset. Jace might be a playboy but at least he was an honest one. He hadn't fed her a single line or pretended to be something he was not. Somewhere deep down inside her she was conscious of a sharp little pang of regret that she would not see him again because she liked him, honestly *liked* him and that was why she had decided to go to bed with him. That tempting and rare combination of liking and dynamite chemistry might never come her way again, she reasoned.

Jace set her down in a huge room and she wouldn't have known she was on a yacht if she hadn't seen, beyond sliding glass doors, the stretch of a furnished deck terrace looking out to sea. She turned uncertainly, letting one of the towels swirled around her fall to the floor. Her attention fell on a simply vast bed and her mouth ran dry.

'Would you like a drink?'

Gigi spun round. 'Some water, please.'

'You're very tense,' Jace breathed, ebony brows pleating. 'Maybe you need more time to consider this—'

'I didn't expect to have to talk about it,' Gigi protested, gulping down her water as though she would never see water again, feeling the hot colour climbing below her skin and knowing there was nothing she could do about it.

Amusement lightened the tension on Jace's lean dark face. 'You assumed I would throw you on the bed like some caveman and get down to it without a word exchanged? Even I am not that crass.'

'You're embarrassing me. I haven't done this before,' Gigi admitted half under her breath. 'I wasn't going to mention it but you made me nervous.'

His brow creased, intense green eyes narrowing. 'Haven't done it before? Sex? That's not possible—'

Gigi lifted her head high, cornflower-blue eyes unflinching. 'It's possible because here I am.'

Troubled more than he wished to admit by her admission, Jace dragged in a slightly ragged breath. 'I haven't been with a virgin before, but I'll be very careful,' he murmured huskily. 'But stop right now if you're not sure. I definitely don't want to be the guy you regret.'

And even as he told her that, he wanted to laugh at himself. Since when had he cared that much about a woman's finer feelings? Yet he definitely knew that he didn't wish to be Gig's bad memory. And even as he then began to wish that he would *not* be her first lover, he knew it would be a lie. It was absolutely an honour that he wanted for himself. In some strictly temporary way she felt special and he felt a strong need to make everything special for her.

While Jace agonised over whatever he was agonising about, Gigi flopped down on the side of the bed and kicked off her shoes. 'I need a shower. I'm covered in salt.'

Emerging from his fugue, exasperated by his inability to concentrate, wondering if he could lay that rare affliction at the door of overwhelming sexual hunger and relieved by that explanation, Jace strode across the room and thrust open a door.

The washing facilities were to die for, sheer glass and black marble that shimmered with metallic golden streaks. Stripping off her wet bikini, she stepped into the shower, wishing she had thought to ask for her bag, although, frankly, it hadn't occurred to her that she might decide to stay the night with Jace, so her bag didn't contain so much as a toothbrush. But the shelving contained everything that a woman might want, she discovered, wrinkling her nose at the obvious thought that Jace regularly had women in his shower. What business was that of hers?

'There are no fairy-tale princes out there,' her mother had told her sharply when she was fourteen, ripping down a pin-up poster of a boyband member from her daughter's wall and scrunching it before tossing it in the bin. 'Get used to that idea now and you'll be the happier for it. Take your pleasure from men if you wish but don't expect anything else from them. They're only good for that one thing.'

Suppressing that unpleasant recollection of her mother's cynical distrust of the entire male sex, Gigi dried her hair and freshened up, unsurprised to find a still wrapped toothbrush in a drawer full of them. And she thought the half-brothers closest to her age were man whores? She shut her eyes tight, reminded herself that if she was using Jace, he was using her and that there was nothing wrong with that physical exchange. Even her cold-natured mother would have agreed that point.

The same woman had insisted she went on the contraceptive pill at fourteen, saying that she didn't want any 'little mistakes'. Gigi had guessed right then that she had not been born the child of a planned pregnancy.

Even the effect of a cold-shower finish did nothing to lessen Jace's arousal. He was thoroughly fed up with his misbehaving body and the lack of adult control he was displaying. This was *not him* because he had never been desperate for a woman in his life.

A towel looped round her like a sarong, Gigi emerged from the bathroom, so nervous and awkward that her teeth were almost chattering together. The break between leaving the beach and arriving in Jace's bedroom had stretched too long for her relaxation to last.

Jace stretched back against the headboard, the sheet dropping to his waist, a vision of unashamed masculinity, revealing wide smooth brown shoulders and his muscular torso. He took in one glance of Gigi, blondish brown hair waving round her shoulders, blue eyes bluer than the sky, shapely curves safely covered in towelling, and he was off the bed faster than the speed of light without even thinking of moving. He scooped her up into his arms and then froze, struggling to think about what he was doing and why he was continually acting on some sort of subconscious inner voice that prompted him into weird behaviour around her.

Gigi let her head fall back against his arm, long silky hair brushing his thigh, blue eyes bright with laughter. 'I think I could get used to being carried around like a princess without your habit killing my domineering tendencies.'

'It takes one to know one,' Jace quipped.

And then just as she was thinking that she enjoyed his more sensitive side, which he had shown her when he earlier gave her the choice to step back from intimacy again, he kissed her. The whoosh of explosive hunger he could depth-charge through one kiss annihilated every logical thought. Her fingers crept up into his curly hair and held him to her, rejoicing in that shiny luxuriance and the smell of him that close. She felt as though every kiss she had had when she was younger had merely been a dress rehearsal for Jace and a complete waste of time. He dallied and he teased when he kissed, stroked her lips, nibbled a little, explored. It was so sensual, so sexy it should've been forbidden.

Slowly, gently, he began unwrapping the towel and sure fingers cupped the warm weight of a small breast, his thumb rubbing back and forth across the diamond-hard tip, sending little spears of desire hurtling through her. She quivered as he found the other, unexpected heat stabbing through her as the caress grew a little rougher and then he bent his head and took the throbbing peak into his mouth and sucked hard and pleasure engulfed her in a floodtide of response.

From that point on, it was a little like a dreamworld for Gigi because nothing happened as she had dimly expected it would. He shifted her down on to the bed and discarded the towel. He surveyed her as though she were a work of art and, later, she couldn't credit that she had lain there and simply let him look at her naked, but, in that moment, his rapt expression truly made her feel like the most beautiful woman in the world.

He came down to her, naked as she was but bronzed, muscular and beautiful, and suddenly she was as enthralled with him as he appeared to be with her. He kissed her again, skated a hand along one slender thigh while his mouth sought her breasts again and the surge of dampness she felt at the heart of her mortified her for a split second until she reminded herself that it was normal.

His fingers played between her thighs. He was very subtle, evidently gauging by her response what kind of touch she enjoyed. She appreciated how precise he was, the care he was giving to their encounter and she had no sooner thought that than she told him.

Jace lifted his tousled head to look down at her transfixed. 'Are you *rating* me?'

Gigi laughed. 'Well, you've got my vote—'

A smile chased the tension from his lean, dark face, lighting up his incandescent green eyes. 'You're very different from other women—'

'No, don't tell me that. I know I'm a bit off the wall. I don't need you to confirm it—'

'Even if I like it?' An ebony brow elevated.

'I shouldn't have interrupted you.' Gigi dealt him a teasingly pious glance and he laughed then.

As if they had all the time in the world, he worked his sensual path down her slender body and the little quivers of arousal began to build in strength. He settled his hands on the curve of her hips and lowered his head to the tender pink flesh between her thighs. She wasn't sure if she wanted something that intimate and then she reminded herself that essentially she was experimenting with Jace and exploring possibilities, so why not explore them *all*?

What she also wasn't expecting was how very fast his

expertise drove her totally out of control. Hunger was a drumbeat in her pelvis that made her writhe and gasp and moan. Intense sensation gripped her in a steely hold and before she knew where she was she was reaching an unfamiliar plateau of pleasure that lit her up like a thousand fireworks inside and out.

'Are you on birth control?'

Gigi winced. 'No. Used to be, not any more—'

'Why did you stop?' Jace asked curiously, not noticeably bothered by her negative response.

'My mother insisted I went on it at fourteen. I wasn't sexually active and I very much resented it. I stopped taking it about a year afterwards...it was my first rebellion against her expectations—'

'What was the next?' he could not resist asking.

'I suppose it has to be dropping out of medicine and choosing veterinary surgery instead. My mother wanted me to be a doctor but it wasn't for me. I'm better with animals than people,' she said quietly.

'I think you'd have been a winner with people as well if you'd had the right support to believe that,' Jace countered.

'My mother never forgave me for my change of heart. Once I reached eighteen, she stopped her financial support, which of course was her right...hence my student loans, but I've never regretted the decision.'

'I wouldn't have met you if you hadn't been a vet.' Jace tensed, not liking that idea but so irritated by that awareness that he immediately tugged Gigi back into his arms. 'We're losing focus here—'

'Don't you talk in bed?'

'Never,' Jace admitted, his sensual mouth compressing before he nipped at the edge of her shoulder and kissed a deeply sensual path across it to her throat, where he dallied at her pulse points, smiling again into that kiss as he saw the pulse at her delicate collarbone go crazy and her pupils dilate again.

Once they got out of bed, he would give her dinner and let her leave, he bargained with himself. No, that could make her feel *used* and no way was he doing that to her!

He let his fingers slide into her hair, relishing that softness, that absence of product that left the strands flexible. He gazed down into her blue eyes and felt triumphant that he had her with him and hadn't allowed the less presentable flaws in his driven nature scare her off. He was thinking too much. He didn't know what had got into him. Performance anxiety? He didn't want to hurt her. That was what was wrong with him, he reasoned with relief. Female friends had told him that their first sexual experiences had been basement-level bad, and naturally he wanted something better for Gigi. Only a selfish bastard wouldn't be concerned on that score. When did I *stop* being a selfish bastard? he wondered.

Gigi ran exploring hands down over his torso, fingers delighting in the indentations and the hard muscle that was such a contrast from her own softer curves. Jace almost shuddered beneath her touch and returned to kissing her with hungry fervour. She arched up to him in response and was empowered by his hungry groan. He shifted against her and she felt him hard and ready at her core. Without hesitation, she lifted her legs and curved them round him, urging him on. After all, she didn't think it would be that much fun for her and she knew it would probably hurt. Anticipation was not her friend at that moment.

Jace braced his hands on the mattress to stare down at her with exasperated green eyes that scorched her like flames. 'We do this slowly or not at all,' he breathed.

'There's two of us here and I have a voice too.'

'Gigi—'

'If you expect me to stay in this bed another thirty seconds—'

Put to the test, Jace flexed his hips and surged into her like an invasion force. As he tilted her thighs back to gain depth, a sharp pang of pain shot through her lower body and she gasped. 'Oh, well, that's done, then,' she pronounced with satisfaction. 'I expect that's the worst over with.'

Jace gritted his teeth together. 'You're making me feel like a science experiment—'

He sort of...*was*, as Gigi saw it. She cringed at that insensitive inner recognition and closed her eyes tight lest he could read her expression.

'So,' he breathed, mastering his temper. 'Stop talking. I don't need egging on to the finish line like a child in his first race!'

'I'm sorry,' she whispered. 'I don't have conversational filters.'

He pulled out of her, watching her try not to wince, and then pushed into her again with decisive speed. And on the strength of that single movement, Gigi forgot what she had been talking about, forgot what she had been worrying about and experienced that first seductive taste of sensual pleasure. He was an incredibly tight fit inside her, stretching her inner sheath with an efficiency that was uniquely enthralling. Her mind went blank as that glowing warmth filtered through her and all of a sudden she was in the moment again and wanting more. Excitement sparked as his pace increased, providing her with intense sensation that made her heart race.

'Good?' Jace checked, embarrassed by the fact that for the first time in his life he was concerned.

'Don't you *dare* stop!' Gigi launched up at him, her hips rising to his in a language older than time.

Jace bestowed a dazzling smile down at her and thought of all the many, many things he still had to do with her. He shifted position, picked an angle, watched the flush of response rise up over her face, picked up pace again.

An electrifying tingle ran down Gigi's spine. Her entire body was thrilling to the surfeit of pleasure she had never known before. He drove into her harder and faster and tiny jolts of lightning tightened like bands round her pelvis. She struggled to keep a lid on her excitement and that drowning desire but as it built and built like an alarm clock ready to go off, she realised that she couldn't control it, couldn't stop it if she tried. When another climax engulfed her, she quivered and cried out, moaned, hearing herself, despising herself and, out of control, she was sent gasping and flailing into an explosion of pleasure that utterly consumed her.

Jace threaded a line of tiny kisses down over her drowsy face. 'Admit it…you liked it—'

'Don't talk,' she urged, her body too heavy, her brain too drained at what she had learned about herself for her to stand examination of any kind.

She dozed off without even being aware of it. Jace surveyed her in fascination. That was another thing that had never happened to him before: a woman just going to sleep as if he weren't there. As if he had indeed merely been an *experiment*? He suppressed that toxic suspicion. He was grateful that she was so different from the other women he had known. No flattery, no calculation, no apparent greed, no false front, no lies, the complete opposite of his cousin, Seraphina, who was as artificial and treacherous as Gigi was not. Gigi's qualities were solid gold in the Diamandis family where no woman he had met within the family circle saw him as anything other than a rich trophy to be caught. Not that he wanted her long term, of course he didn't! He was committed to his freedom from all such ties.

And while reassured by that conviction, Jace got on his phone and ordered a dinner for them that evening and wondered where she would like to go when he took her out. A nightclub? It didn't strike him as a very good fit for her and she had nothing to wear. He went into the bathroom to clean up and only then noticed that the contraceptive he had used had torn. He groaned out loud in consternation. As Evander's name swam onto his phone screen, he walked out onto the terrace naked to talk without disturbing Gigi.

'I thought I'd have heard from you by now,' his uncle said tautly.

'Why?' Jace raked his fingers through his tousled curls, cursing them the way he always did but his pride was too great to get rid of them. It was the one reminder of his mother that he had and if his father had rejected him for his stupid hair and the colour of his eyes, he had felt stronger not altering his appearance in any way.

Evander swore in Greek, which was a rare enough event for Jace to tense and frown.

'It's your grandmother's eightieth birthday tomorrow!' Evander shot back at him a touch accusingly. 'There's a huge party for you to preside over on Faros with the whole family present. I told you about it weeks ago—'

'I know. I forgot.' Jace frowned, plunged into darkness at the prospect of a Diamandis family reunion at what was now, following his father's passing, *his* main home on the island of Faros. 'However, I made all the catering arrangements at the time. I've even bought the painting you suggested for her.'

'Good enough,' Evander grunted, soothed by those admissions. 'So, what time will you be arriving?'

'I'll text you.' Jace glanced through the glass doors at the barely noticeable presence in his bed.

Someone shaking her shoulder wakened Gigi. She stretched languorously before she opened her eyes and then it all came back to her.

'Where are my clothes?' she asked the stewardess.

The young woman pointed at the transparent garment carrier hanging on the outside of a swanky built-in closet. Gigi blinked and focused on the barely visible blue dress. 'That's not mine,' she said.

Jace strode in like a sudden gust of wind, instantly filling the space with raw energy and expectations. The stewardess looked relieved by his arrival and departed.

'Is it all right if I go for a shower?' Gigi asked uncomfortably, striving not to look at him, striving not to be sucked in by his compelling dark attraction. He was casually dressed in linen shirt and chinos, but they had perfect tailoring and bore all the hallmarks of expensive design and sophistication. His black curls were windswept, his bright green eyes luminous with sheer energy, his stance one of command.

His expressive brows rose. 'Why would you ask me that? Of course it's all right.'

'Where are my clothes?' she asked again.

'I've organised clothes for you to wear. However, if you want your own—' Jace drew out his mobile and issued instructions in that cool, polite way of his in Greek that always warned her that he was making specific orders.

'I'm going home,' she told him, even more uneasily. 'I don't need anyone to organise clothes for me. I'm sorry I fell asleep. You should've wakened me ages ago. I know I shouldn't still be here. I'm not that out of touch.'

'I don't know what you're talking about,' Jace said truthfully, dark brows drawing together.

'A one-night stand, you're supposed to get up and get out, not linger like yesterday's news—'

'This wasn't a one-night stand,' Jace objected with unexpected rawness.

'But you don't *do* anything else!' Gigi carolled in exasperation at his refusal to say it like it was while leaving her to gabble on in clumsy discomfiture.

'There's an exception to every rule.' Jace was studying her in growing disbelief that she could actually be attempting to ditch him. 'I had no indication that you were likely to wake up with such an idea. How could I have? I warned you that I didn't want to be the guy you regretted—'

'It's not that,' Gigi cut in, her face pink with mortification because she wasn't inconsistent. She did not regret what had happened between them but she did feel unnerved about the intensity of what they had seemed to share and deemed it the wisest course to immediately call time on seeing him again.

'That's good because you're trapped on *Sea King* for the rest of the night,' Jace revealed quietly. 'We're at sea…'

'At…*sea*?' Gigi gasped incredulously. 'How can we possibly be *at sea*?'

Jace laughed, which was the proverbial last straw in the dazed mood she was in. 'Are you worried about your pets? Don't be. The bird, the tortoise and the cat are all on board as well and I packed for you.'

'Are you seriously trying to tell me that you've kidnapped me and my pets from Rhodes?' Gigi shrieked at him, grabbing up the discarded towel still lying on the floor and anchoring it below her armpits to slide out of the bed.

CHAPTER FIVE

JACE STUDIED GIGI with incredulity. As she stalked into
the bathroom like an angry miniature Amazon warrior,
he was momentarily stunned by her attitude.

What was the matter with her? It was the weekend.
He already knew that she had no other plans. He had
taken care of the pet problem and the clothes problem.
Other women valued his attention to detail, his generosity and his talent for organisation. Why didn't she?

He knocked on the bathroom door. It opened a mere
crack. 'Yes?' Gigi enquired glacially.

'I thought you'd be pleased,' he admitted after a stark
instant of hesitation, because in Gigi's company occasionally he felt vaguely as though he were dealing with
an alien. Her reactions were never what he expected,
and her concerns were even more startling. He had de-
voted himself one hundred per cent to her entertainment. He had never done that for a woman before. Why
would she then assume that he saw her as being only a
one-night stand? Surely he had been obvious enough
that she could read the writing on the wall?

'How did you get into my house?' she demanded.

Jace gritted his even white teeth. 'The keys were
lying loose in your beach bag. I helped myself.'

Gigi rolled big blue eyes at him in disbelief. 'And you believed that doing that was all right? Sending strangers into my home?'

'I went with them. The cat was hard to catch. He wasn't for going anywhere. He hid under the sofa with the tortoise—'

'He is a *she* called Tilly,' she snapped. 'Are you saying that you personally went through my belongings?'

Jace compressed his lips. *What* belongings? he almost quipped. There had been a very large rucksack and a couple of drawers of casual clothes in a room as small and unadorned as a nun's cell. Even though that had been what he'd dimly expected from Gigi, he had still been taken aback by how little she owned and how very little she had personalised her surroundings.

'Yes. I didn't think you would like a crew member taking care of it.'

'Or…*you*!' Gigi stressed, slamming the door in his face, aghast at the idea that he might have rummaged through her underwear drawer or noticed that she hadn't made her bed up because the bedding was in the washing machine.

She showered. She fumed. She made up long ranting speeches inside her head. Where on earth did he think he was taking her? She marched back into the bedroom, scooped her obviously freshly laundered clothes off the foot of the bed and disappeared back into the bathroom to get dressed in her denim shorts again. There was no bra. She hadn't thought through that she would need one after she took her wet bikini off. What had he packed in her rucksack for her and where was it? The whole time, she thought anxiously about the way Jace made her feel. Feeling anything that powerful frightened her. Her mother hadn't shown her love and neither had her father. It only made sense to Gigi that she should always keep her emotions under control and never expect too much from people and situations. That was how she protected herself. Only with the animals she loved did she let her guard down.

Another knock sounded on the door. She wrenched it open. Jace handed her the dress in the garment bag.

Gigi simply set it aside because she had no intention of wearing it. 'You really don't take hints, do you?'

'Not when I don't want to hear them,' Jace conceded. 'I promise that I'll have you back at work on time on Monday morning. There won't be any problems—'

Gigi dealt him a fulminating scrutiny. 'You should turn the boat around and return me to Rhodes right now—'

'I can't do that. I'm taking you to my grandmother's birthday party tomorrow. It's her eightieth,' he informed her. 'If I turn back, I'll be late and, as I'm the host, that wouldn't be acceptable.'

Taken aback by that announcement, Gigi closed her hands into fists. 'Why the heck would you take *me* to a family party? You hardly know me!'

'I loathe Diamandis family gatherings but I believe it will be bearable if you are with me to lighten the atmosphere,' Jace declared with grim assurance.

'Why couldn't you just wake me up and *ask* me if I wanted to go?' Gigi demanded in annoyance.

'You had already told me that you were free this

weekend. I assumed you would spend it with me.' Emerald-green eyes fringed by lashes stark black and lush as lace rested hungrily on her. 'Particularly after this afternoon.'

A faint pink lit her cheekbones and a tugging sensation clenched between her thighs. Even the memory of being with him was shockingly physical. So, he fought dirty in a fight. How was that news? He was clever, manipulative and devious and, if she was honest with herself, he fascinated her because he was so different from her. But the fleeting vulnerability in his beautiful clear eyes when he admitted that he hated family get-togethers and that her presence would help touched something soft and tender inside her, something that made her shiver, something that made her feel weak. And she refused to be weak or sympathetic towards anything other than a voiceless animal, which depended on her for care. Jace was too risky. Dangerous energy and volatility ran through him like a life force.

She had been fifty per cent certain that what they had shared was a once-only encounter. She refused to have expectations of him. But Jace was changing the game, suggesting possibilities that were disconcerting.

'OK…you win. I'll make a large donation to the animal shelter where you work,' Jace announced without warning.

Gigi blinked in surprise and looked daggers at him. 'Is that how you buy yourself out of trouble?'

'You're not being reasonable—'

'You're not being reasonable. Why should I be?' she demanded.

'We can work it out over dinner,' Jace told her with an irreverent grin. 'I'm starving.'

'I want to see my pets first,' she told him briskly.

Tilly was strolling along a deck and wound herself round Gigi's ankles with a purr before moving on to investigate Jace's. Hoppy was nestling in a tiny corner of Mo's giant basket in the main saloon while Mo reclined in front of the basket as though he were guarding the smaller dog. Snowy was in the saloon as well.

'You don't choose your pets on the strength of their appearance,' Jace remarked.

'Snowy is moulting, so don't be rude. He'll look much better in a few weeks. Most of my pets are the no-hopers from the shelter. Hoppy's a street dog and he's a mixed breed. Add in his disabilities and there was nobody interested in adopting him. Snowy's owner just wanted rid of him because he's not a very good talker. Where's Humphrey?'

Humphrey was munching in a sizeable cage in a cargo compartment.

'What do you deem a large donation?' Gigi could not resist asking Jace as he guided her back to the upper deck.

He quoted a sum that left her bereft of breath. 'Think of all the good that money could do—'

A steward yanked out a dining chair for her and she sank down, unnerved as he shook out her napkin and placed it as well. She felt surrounded, inhibited by the presence of the crew. She lifted the wine glass that had already been filled. Jace hadn't needed the assistance of alcohol to get her into bed; she had done that all by herself, surrendering to that addictive chemistry, she reminded herself ruefully. She was trying not to think of what he had said. But cash would rebuild the outdated animal housing at the shelter. She could not deny that his money would do a lot of good and it infuriated her that he was making her think that way.

'I *am* thinking of the good,' she told him abruptly when they were finally left alone. 'But I don't like the fact that you're buying yourself out of trouble…or that you're trying to bribe me.'

'Squeaky-clean morals,' Jace groaned with a reproving appraisal. 'Doesn't it matter that it would improve the facilities for both you and the animals you tend?'

'Of course it matters. But I don't own or run the shelter and I don't know what the board of directors would do with such a big donation.'

'I could give it on the assurance that you must have a say in how it's spent because I know that you will put your patients first. I'm trying to say sorry, Gigi…but you don't make it easy.'

'Because if I make it easy it's like patting you on the back and encouraging you to do something like this again!' Gigi shot back at him, clean out of patience. 'And I will not be bought or bribed or blackmailed by your wealth! That's *wrong*, Jace. And you still haven't apologised.'

'I apologise.' Glittering green eyes held hers fast and her heart began to beat very, very fast, her mouth running dry because the power and intensity of his gaze burned her. 'But I *did* genuinely believe that you would freely agree to accompany me to the party. I also thought you'd be relieved that I'd considered the care of your pets and what you would wear.'

'Other women would be relieved, wouldn't they?'

'But I enjoy being with you because you're not the same as other women I've known,' he pointed out.

Gigi wrinkled her nose. 'But sometimes, like now, when I'm being awkward, you wish I *were* the same,' she guessed.

Jace laughed, a husky, sexy sound that brushed over her skin like the soft smooth brush of velvet. Goose bumps erupted on the skin of her arms, a warmth flowering at her feminine core.

'So, you'll come to the party.' Jace regrouped with that statement and disconcerted her afresh.

'Your presence will take the attention off me, at least a little,' he pronounced with satisfaction, draining his wine glass, a movement of his hand dismissing the steward who had moved forward from the far side of the room to refill it.

'I don't enjoy being the centre of attention. I'm a backroom girl.'

'No, to me you're something much more,' he contradicted. 'I want to show you off.'

Gigi tensed at the concept.

'I'm proud of you. Why wouldn't I be? You're an intelligent, independent and compassionate woman with a career you love.'

'Thank you. On the strength of your silver tongue, I agree to pretend to be plus one tomorrow,' Gigi conceded, smiling as she settled her cutlery down on the plate. 'I'll fake it until I make it—'

'Why should you have to pretend?' Jace demanded.

'Well, I'm not your girlfriend so of course I'll be pretending—'

Jace closed a lean brown hand squarely over hers. 'You *are* my lover. There is no need for you to fake anything.'

'I know next to nothing about you!'

'You know enough. My education? My birthday? My favourite colour?' Jace imparted those details. 'And what do those extraneous facts tell you about me? Precisely nothing.'

'Although if I were an astrologer, the birthday might be helpful,' she told him deadpan.

'Droll…'

The rest of the meal passed at speed. Gigi's anger had faded or Jace had charmed it away. He was great company, lighter in heart than her friends back in the UK. Of course, why wouldn't he be? Born rich, handsome and destined for success, he could have little in life to complain about, aside from a cruel, selfish father and, possibly, an equally egotistical mother, both of whom were now past history. Jace didn't need to worry about student loans or rent or saving up to buy a first home. In short, the world was pretty much his oyster.

'We'll have our coffee out on deck,' Jace decreed. 'We have something more serious to discuss.'

Frowning, Gigi glanced at him but there was nothing to be read in his lean, strong face. They sank down onto a wonderfully comfortable couch, a faint breeze lifting her hair and playing with the strands. She lifted her coffee and sipped, relaxing back into the upholstery. 'The something serious?' she prompted tautly.

'The condom ripped,' Jace spelt out grimly. 'I'd be less worried if you were on birth control.'

Shaken, Gigi set the cup and saucer down again with a slightly jarring crash. 'My word… I wasn't expecting *that*.'

'Neither was I. It hasn't happened to me before. I'm very careful.'

'I should have stayed on some form of contraception for my own protection. The trouble is, I wasn't counting on meeting you and I hadn't met anyone in so long that I decided that there wasn't any realistic need for it.' She sighed, contemplating the risk of an accidental pregnancy with a sinking heart. 'I've always wanted children but not this way, because I was an unplanned baby and I think my mother found me a huge responsibility and resented me for getting in the way of her work.'

'But from what I understand your mother was alone. *You* won't be. If there's a pregnancy, we'll handle the situation *together*,' Jace insisted, closing a lean hand over hers in emphasis. 'In spite of the way I may strike you, I'm not even a little irresponsible—'

'Only occasionally guilty of kidnapping sleeping women and unsuspecting animals from Rhodes!' Gigi chipped in with a rueful giggle. 'I'm not going to worry about what you've told me until there's something to actually worry about.'

But Gigi did feel embarrassingly guilty because she had urged him on when, had he gone slowly as he had clearly intended, the contraception might have worked fine. Unfortunately, she had been in a hurry to move past the potentially painful part to hopefully the more pleasurable conclusion.

'Come here,' Jace urged, stretching out to remove her coffee cup from her hold and settle it back on the table. 'I need to kiss you right now.'

He tugged her closer and then lifted her bodily over him, so that her legs fell either side of his. And as she came down on him, she could not miss out on the reality that he was hard and ready, his perfectly tailored trousers unable to conceal his arousal. She assumed that he didn't think that there was much chance of her falling pregnant because their discussion had failed to distract him.

'We're in a public area, Jace. I won't risk an audience,' Gigi warned him.

Jace groaned in her ear, the warmth of his breath fanning her jaw. 'You drive me insane!'

'It's your own fault. You've got a cast of thousands on this boat as crew and they are *everywhere*—'

'I only want to kiss you.'

'So you say, but I'm not sure you can be trusted,' Gigi confided, shifting back off him again and kneeling beside him instead.

Jace bent his proud dark head and dropped a brief kiss on her parted lips and then he sprang upright and scooped her up into his arms before she could even guess what he was intending.

'Let me down!'

'We have to go to where we won't have an audience,' Jace decreed, laughing as she punched his shoulder with an exasperated fist.

'Jace!' she protested as he finally slid her down onto her own feet in his bedroom.

'I'm succumbing to an overpowering need to get you horizontal.' As he spoke, Jace undid the button at her waist and ran down the zip on her shorts and then he lifted her up into his arms again, his big hands gripping her hips, and he crushed her mouth under his with such a surge of burning hunger that answering heat roared through her like a bonfire.

As he dropped her down on the bed, Gigi kicked off her shorts and canvas shoes and reached for him.

'I want you too,' she murmured intently, an electrifying thrill thrumming along every nerve ending as their eyes collided. 'I don't know what you've done to me.'

Halfway out of his shirt, Jace paused and braced both hands on either side of her flushed face. 'I wanted you the minute I laid eyes on you with my dog in the street—'

'I didn't look at you until we were indoors—'

'And what did you think?'

It was amazing the rush she could get from one hungry, demanding glance of those scorching green eyes of his.

'I thought you were too good-looking to be real and now I like you best when I've messed you up a little,' she quipped, ruffling his soft silky hair until it was thoroughly untidy.

And when he slowly tasted her parted lips again with sensual expertise, she gave herself up to the pleasure of it. She felt happier than she had ever felt. She felt wanted, appreciated, *special* for the first time in her life.

It was a crazy infatuation and she refused to agonise over it. It wouldn't last for ever. Such insane flights of fancy as put two such different people in a relationship never did last. But while it was current, she planned to make the most of it.

Tossing a handful of condoms on the nightstand, he curved a possessive hand to a small, pouting breast, his thumb rubbing across the prominent peak, watching her spine arch and lowering his mouth there to hungrily tease. Her hips rolled, that insane desire twisting inside her, no more easily ignored than a tornado. Her restive hands laced into his curls and then slid down to his wide shoulders, smoothing over his skin. He traced the heart of her where she was warm and wet and, oh, so willing to be touched. She rolled over onto her side and found his sensual lips for herself.

His tongue darted and dallied while his fingers played and toyed with her most delicate flesh, pushing her closer to the edge. The hunger she was struggling to control leapt higher and higher like a runaway flame. She felt almost frantic as he repositioned her writhing body and sank into her with potent strength. She climaxed instantly, unforgettably, and she was shocked. Fireworks shot up in multicoloured sparks behind her lowered eyelids while a whoosh of pure sensation seized her convulsing frame. She trembled and blinked rapidly in the aftermath, stunned by the power of the experience.

'Now let's see if you can do that again,' Jace murmured thickly, excited by the way she had lost control in his arms.

'Doubtful,' she mumbled shakily, barely able to think straight after that shattering flood of all-encompassing pleasure.

And the second time it was a slow, steady climb to those same heights, the very last word in sensual pleasure. She was drowning in the emerald-green depths of his eyes when he pushed her out of the comfort zone into a much faster rhythm and her body reacted as if it had been waiting all its life to experience that overwhelming excitement. Her heart thudded at an insane rate, her body jolting, wild elation grabbing her as she hit the heights again.

Afterwards, she was limp and on the path to sleepy exhaustion.

'So...' Jace murmured huskily as he leant over her and dropped a kiss on her damp brow, long fingers threading her hair back from her cheekbones in a slow, sure movement. His green eyes glittered as though someone had scattered stardust in them. 'You'll wear the dress I got you for the party...'

Gigi heaved a sigh. 'I suppose, since I really don't have anything else—'

'And wear the shoes—'

'I guess,' Gigi framed drowsily, snuggling into the pillow.

'And there's some jewellery—'

Gigi surrendered the pillow in dismay. 'I don't own any jewellery—'

'I have my mother's jewellery. I'd like you to wear a couple of the diamond pieces.'

Gigi made a face. Her mother had had no time for

such frivolous items as jewellery and had left her nothing in that line. When she was barely welcome in her own family, the idea of wearing *his* family jewellery made her feel horribly uncomfortable. 'No, thank you. I'm not showing off family jewellery when I don't belong to the family,' she told him tartly. 'That would make me look like a *very* ambitious companion as well as being one who lacks good taste.'

'It's mine to do with as I wish. It would only be on loan for the day—'

'Doesn't matter. I don't want to borrow anything,' Gigi said squarely.

'You can think about it—'

'I've already thought and the answer is no, Jace. *No!*' she slung back at him with furious stress, snatching up her shorts, climbing into them by the side of the bed and grabbing her T-shirt to pull it on as well.

'It was only a suggestion. There's no need to lose your temper,' Jace breathed tautly.

CHAPTER SIX

'ISN'T THERE?' Gigi spun back to look at Jace, still busy tugging her hair out from below the T-shirt, an arc of colour now enhancing her cheekbones. 'If you don't get the answer you want, you *persist*. You can't deal with a negative answer when you want agreement. It makes me wonder what you're doing with me,' she admitted frankly. 'I'm not a dress-up doll, Jace. I'm not a yes-girl either. I am who I am and proud of it. I'm not going to a party to pretend to be someone I'm not because you would prefer a glitzier version of me than you actually have!'

'That's not what I said. I am happy with you as you are—'

'No, you'd prefer an improved edition and sorry, but you're stuck with me!' she countered angrily.

'Where are you going?' Jace demanded as she reached for the door handle.

'To find another bed. One that's empty. Did you pack *any* of *my* things?' she asked flatly.

Jace indicated a door. 'In the dressing room.'

Gigi stalked into the dressing room and opened doors. Locating her rucksack, which had already been unpacked, she filled it again.

Wearing only a pair of black boxers, Jace lodged in the doorway. 'I don't want you to leave—'

Gigi gritted her teeth. 'You make me madder than anyone I've ever met!'

'Your temper is almost as bad as mine, just slower to rise,' Jace commented. 'Stay with me. I shouldn't have put on the pressure. I should've quit while I was ahead—'

Gigi groaned. 'It's too late at night for all this drama—'

'Drama was something I didn't do until I met you,' Jace admitted and a sudden sizzling smile lightened his expressive mouth while he carefully reminded himself that Gigi was only a temporary presence in his life. 'Lesson one, in a relationship listen to the other party. Lesson two, don't assume orgasms grant you a get-out-of-jail-free card. Lesson three, don't rile Gigi after midnight or she turns into a gremlin.'

An involuntary laugh escaped Gigi. She tapped a forefinger on his bare chest. 'No diamonds. We will get by fine without diamonds.'

Jace had already decided to get on his phone and find something that would be more acceptable to her than jewels, something that would make her smile, as she was smiling right now at him and it felt like liquid sunshine warming his skin. 'I'll have to make some calls early tomorrow—'

'It's already today and I haven't got a gift for your grandmother. I need a card, maybe some flowers—'

'I'll organise it.'

Gigi breathed in slow and deep and smiled again. What did he do to her? One minute she was raging and the next she was laughing. He had great charm when he wished to utilise it. Why did she feel as if she had known Jace for years? Where had the normal stranger barriers gone? She stuffed her rucksack back in the dressing room and undressed again to go for a shower.

The next morning, Gigi pulled on cool cotton trousers and a T-shirt. She wouldn't risk putting on the fancy blue dress until it was time to leave for the party. She was relieved that she hadn't worn it the night before.

Every tiny movement tugged on muscles somewhere inside her body and once or twice she winced and frowned, reminded more than she liked about the long, bold, brazen night that she had spent with Jace. Jace was like a wicked genie freed from a bottle. Every time he touched her, it was as though he bespelled her. A kiss, a fleeting caress and she was his again. She had never dreamt that she could want any man the way he made her want him and she didn't like that lack of control, that lack of true choice. It was as though her free will had been stolen from her. She had assumed that that intense sexual hunger would fade once satisfied but what did it mean when that didn't happen?

It was unsettling. Jace was supposed to be a fling, an experience, an affair and nothing more, wasn't he? She didn't want to get hurt, she didn't want things between them to turn messy, no, once the party was over, she wanted her life back the way it had been.

But how could she *truly* say that she wanted that? If she was honest, she had got lonely, living her independent life while stuck in her safe routine. Jace had splashed colour into her world, brought her alive and only now was she recognising just how much she had stubbornly denied herself.

'Breakfast is waiting,' Jace called through the sliding doors that opened onto the terrace.

Breathing in deep, Gigi braced herself. Jace had already been up and about before she roused and when she had stirred in that empty bed the first thing she had looked for was *him*. That had scared her, for a long time ago she had learned the hard way not to let anyone get that close to her. Sooner or later, favourite nannies, teachers or housekeepers always moved on somewhere else, often without even saying goodbye. In the same way, her mother had died without ever trying to repair their fractured relationship and Gigi had lost any prospect of forgiveness and acceptance as well. She couldn't afford to get attached to Jace. He was a free and easy playboy with a notorious reputation, and she was just one more in a long line of women.

It didn't matter that he had got up in the middle of the night to let Mo and Hoppy in when Mo whined outside the door. It didn't matter that he had hugged her most of the night like a precious teddy bear. She was neither a dog nor a toy and she wasn't here to stay either. No, she was only passing through his life.

Jace watched Gigi walking out to the table, small and slim and graceful. And yet that perfect skin of hers glowed, her blue eyes sparkled, and her luscious pink mouth smiled. She was beautiful even though she didn't know it and she was *his*. That thought thundered back through him again and his teeth gritted. She was his... *for now*. He wasn't a one-woman man. Soon enough he would tire of her and then it would be over. The dogs swirled round her legs like a moving carpet of fur, begging for her attention.

'That's the island of Faros on the horizon,' he told her, deliberately directing his thoughts away from her.

'Our destination?' Gigi queried, fighting to drag her gaze from his tall, dark frame, but that was a struggle when she didn't want to look anywhere else or when he had been out of her sight for a few hours and she literally felt starved of seeing him.

'Yes. It's a private island.' She studied him intently as he spoke. His dark suit fitted him with exquisite, tailored perfection blended with designer style. With his glossy black curls and potent emerald-green eyes, he was electrifyingly sexy. Broad of shoulder, narrow hips, tight waist and long, powerful legs. And below the suit, he was all lean, hard muscle.

'Your family own it?' All of a sudden, Gigi was finding it very hard to breathe.

'I do.' Jace shrugged, watching her frown down at the bewildering number of choices on the breakfast table before helping herself to a simple cup of tea. 'The island has the only house in the family that's large enough to entertain the whole Diamandis clan. It usually belongs to the head of the family but because my grandmother didn't get on with her son Argus—my father—my grandfather left the house jointly to my grandmother *and* me... Argus was hopping mad.'

'Why didn't your grandmother get on with her son? He was her eldest child and often the eldest is the favourite—'

'She couldn't forgive him for rejecting me and when he tried to disinherit me, it was the last straw. They had a massive fight and I think they both said things that the other couldn't forgive.' Jace shrugged a broad shoulder ruefully. 'Argus loathed the fact that he couldn't use the big house on Faros. He felt it lowered his standing in the family. Status, appearances, reputation? They meant more than anything else to my father. He built a mansion of his own at the other end of the island.'

'Was he a good dad before your mother left him?' Gigi asked curiously.

'I hardly knew him...*or* her, if I'm honest,' Jace admitted with rueful regret, even while he wondered why he was confiding that truth to her when that admission had never crossed his lips before. 'That was the nannies and boarding school phase of my life. Both my parents were very busy people. Evander and Marcus changed all that. Their care was much more personalised, much more hands-on and day to day. They took me to school. They attended prize days and Christmas concerts—'

Gigi was impressed by his sheer honesty and happy that he was sharing such personal facts with her. 'They're the uncles that raised you?'

Jace nodded confirmation, watching her select a yogurt, the plainest on offer.

Gigi dipped the spoon and licked it, savouring the creaminess, soft pink lips pouting for a split second. Jace felt the throbbing pulse at his groin start up again and he gritted his teeth. Gigi had been in his bed all night and he had taken full advantage of the fact. Why the hell was he still craving her like some wildly addictive drug? He glowered broodingly out to sea, his sensual mouth compressed over the lowering reality of her overwhelming appeal for him.

Gigi finished the yogurt and slid upright again. 'I need to hurry so that I can get dressed. You had better hope that that fancy frock fits.'

'It should do.' His ebony brows drew together as he swung back to face her, recalling a necessity he could not afford to overlook. 'I'll organise a blood test for you towards the end of next week and text you the arrangements. It will tell us whether you're pregnant days before an ordinary test would.'

Gigi glanced back over her shoulder in surprise. 'I didn't realise that you were that concerned about that.'

'Obviously it's a possibility that we shouldn't ignore. I'll be away on business next week,' he warned her.

'It'll give us a break...after we've spent the whole weekend together,' Gigi pointed out quietly, feeling that she needed that time away from him to plant her feet firmly back on solid ground again.

The dress fitted like a dream. It was blue, neither too short nor revealing and it suited her better than anything she had ever owned. She eased her feet into the high-heeled sandals with their opulent pearl trim. Her legs looked unusually long even to her own critical gaze. She sat down at the dresser and braided her hair to put it up.

'I need make-up,' she told him wryly.

'I didn't see any in your house, didn't think of that,' Jace admitted. 'But there's a beauty salon onboard.'

Gigi was reckoning that her few bits of make-up

were probably still in her bag under one of her coats in the hallway. She turned wide-eyed to stare. *'Really?'*

'And one of those beauty consultants.'

'Take me there,' she pressed without hesitation, knowing that a little primping was necessary for a high-society party.

He escorted her down to a lower deck and left her there with the chattering consultant. Thirty minutes later, she emerged again, convinced that she could hold her own in any gathering. Her enhancement was subtle and much better done than she could have contrived on her own. She looked natural and that was exactly what she had wanted.

Jace watched her step onto the launch and smiled. She looked amazingly beautiful in that dress, shapely legs on show but nothing else. She looked like a lady, elegant and collected. The neckline looked a little bare though, her slender neck unadorned. He still wished she had been willing to wear the diamonds.

The island was very green with trees and gorgeous in the sunshine. She glanced back at the launch leaving the small harbour again, white water eddying in its wake against the deep blue of the sea. A huge SUV whisked them through the bustling village, past the big Greek Orthodox church and uphill on a rough road. Within minutes they were turning up a paved lane bounded by palm trees.

'Does your grandmother live here?' Gigi asked.

'During the summer but once winter kicks in, she returns to the mainland.'

It was a very grandiose, palatial house stretching across the whole top of the hill. White walls, tall gleaming windows and elegant terraces overlooked the gardens and the bay below. 'Very impressive,' she muttered nervously.

The huge hallway was a rush of surging and busy people. 'Caterers,' Jace explained as an older man approached them, apologising in Greek for the disturbance.

Jace introduced her to Dmitri, who was in charge of the household, and asked how his grandmother was. He referred to her as 'Yaya', just as Gigi's family had labelled her late grandmother.

Dmitri grinned. 'Full of life today. Mrs Diamandis enjoyed her breakfast outdoors and even walked out to see her birds.'

'She likes birds?' Gigi queried in surprise.

'I've already told her about Snowy. She wants to see him. If he won a home in her fancy aviary complex, he would be fortunate indeed.'

His hand in hers, Jace strode ahead of Dmitri and led the way into an opulent sitting room that opened out into a shaded conservatory lush with tropical plants. 'Just in time for the festivities,' a lively voice announced.

And there in a basketwork armchair sat a little old lady with silvery hair and a delighted smile spreading across her soft, weathered face. 'Evander said you'd be late.'

'And yet, here I am in good time for lunch. This is Giselle Campbell... I call her Gigi. Gigi, this is Electra Diamandis.'

A hand was extended to Gigi as she was looked over from head to toe, but the smile remained, from which Gigi deduced that she at least looked acceptable. 'Happy birthday, Kyria Diamandis.'

She was offered a powdered cheek to kiss. 'Congratulations, Jace. You have finally brought a young woman home to meet me. Call me Yaya, Gigi, because you're obviously going to be family. Sit down and tell me all about yourself. My goodness, Evander and Marcus are in for a surprise!'

Lashes fluttering at that extraordinary welcome speech, Gigi wondered what was going on and she sank uncertainly down into the indicated seat.

'Jace always swore that the only woman he would ever bring home would be his intended bride.' Gigi's bare hand was lifted by her hostess. 'Taking your time about putting a ring on that finger, aren't you?' she shot at Jace with a warning look of concern.

Feverish colour lined Jace's high cheekbones as shock rocked him where he stood. He spread a troubled glance between the two women.

'Go and see your uncles,' Electra instructed. 'And by the way, I changed your catering arrangements for lunch. We're having a buffet instead of a sit-down meal. There's too many guests for the dining room.'

Looking a shade shell-shocked by the encounter, Jace studied Gigi's burning face and winced inwardly. He supposed he should have immediately contradicted his grandmother concerning Gigi's status in his life, but he had been too disconcerted by the reminder that he *had* once said that the only woman he would bring home would be his future wife. In addition, the old lady looked so happy with that interpretation that he had not the heart to disabuse her of the assumption. How many times had his grandmother bemoaned the fact that she was not yet a *great*-grandmother like her friends? Although it would be an even bigger shock for him if he turned out to be the *father* of that much desired great-grandchild, he acknowledged grimly.

'Jace told me you have a cockatoo who's looking for a home.'

'I didn't know that Jace had told you about Snowy—'

'Jace phones me every day,' Electra Diamandis revealed. 'There's not much he doesn't tell me.'

Gigi gripped her hands together nervously at that news and decided to keep the chat centred on Snowy as she advanced details on the bird.

'I have to apologise to you now in advance,' the old lady murmured very quietly. 'I didn't know until this week that Jace was bringing you and he hadn't invited many young people. I didn't want my party to be only the older folk and I invited a bevy of youthful beauties from the family to liven the men up.'

'Sounds exciting.' Gigi smiled and swept up the cold drink Dmitri brought her. She talked about her job and her pets while wondering why Jace's grandmother was so keen to see him married off. His reputation? Or did she just think it was time that Jace settled down? Why hadn't Jace put his grandmother right? Gigi felt as though she was being welcomed on a false premise and it embarrassed her. She was merely a girlfriend for the sake of appearances, not a future Diamandis bride.

Jace reappeared to collect her, allowing other family members to move in and sit down with Electra. He whisked her off.

'Why didn't you tell her that I'm not in line to become your wife?' she hissed at him.

'I didn't know what to say. I did say a long time ago that the only woman I would introduce to the family would be my bride, but I'd totally forgotten saying it,' he confided. 'It's just wishful thinking on Yaya's part and harmless conjecture.'

He took her straight to a pair of attractive older men talking in a quiet corner of the crowded hall. 'Evander... and Marcus. This is Gigi.'

'Evander Diamandis.' The tall man with the pepper and salt hair and beard gave her a firm handshake.

'Marcus.' Blond and British with wings of white over his ears and slighter in build than his partner, Marcus grinned at her. 'We've been waiting a very long time for Jace to bring home a girlfriend—'

'But we'll hold off on fetching my mother's engagement ring to give you,' Evander continued with wry amusement. 'I don't think you're quite ready for that as yet, but I'm afraid the rumours are flying round here already. Let my mother enjoy her eightieth, Jace, and dream her dreams undisturbed.'

'I intend to but thanks for not producing the ring on demand,' Jace murmured with a pained roll of his eyes.

'You can push off now and give us five minutes to get to know Gigi,' Marcus told him with amusement.

Jace had landed lucky with his second set of parents, she decided. Evander and Marcus were lively, entertaining company but Gigi was on edge, very much aware that she was being sized up.

'So, you're both still in the besotted phase,' Evander commented, startling her.

Taken aback by the observation, Gigi stammered, 'Er...no, I—'

'You can't stop looking for him and he can barely take his eyes off you for ten seconds,' Evander sliced in calmly. 'Not our business, I know, but it's good to see that he's opening himself up to more challenging possibilities.'

Jace reclaimed her as though he were snatching her from the jaws of death and she laughed with genuine amusement. 'They were very pleasant. Apparently, we're in the besotted phase.'

'Is that why I keep wanting to rip your clothes off?' His dazzling smile lifted the tension from his lean, dark face. 'Bless them, they do love to watch people. Let me show you around the house in case we get separated later.'

As they strolled around, she met more and more guests, including Jace's half-brother, Domenico, aka Nic, arm in arm with a very beautiful blonde. She found herself staring up at Nic, trying to see how much he looked like Jace, but the resemblance was only fleeting in his smile and other expressions.

The buffet would begin only when Electra Diamandis made her official appearance.

'You didn't tell me you had a brother,' she censured as he led her upstairs.

'I don't know him very well yet. My father remarried and he's the result. I first met him at our father's funeral. He's very successful in business and looks set to marry early. Perhaps he will make Yaya's dreams come true with a great-grandchild.'

'I hope we don't get faced with that issue,' she muttered unhappily.

'Never tackle trouble before it comes unless, of course, you can influence the outcome…and you *can't,*' Jace pointed out in challenge, pushing open a door on a wide airy room that seemed, by the number of doors visible, to yield entry to several other rooms. 'We are sleeping here tonight in the master suite. Your luggage will be brought here later.'

Trouble? Was that how Jace saw the risk of a pregnancy? Well, how else did she expect him to view it? Did she feel any different? At this stage of her life and career? For a split second, she had an image of a child who looked remarkably like a miniaturised version of Jace and, involuntarily, her heart lifted and warmed. If there *was* a child, she would raise her child with all the love and warmth her mother had denied her. She would make space in her busy life, she would make changes for her child's sake and put her child first. It didn't really matter how Jace felt about the prospect. She didn't need *him* to raise a child, she told herself fiercely, her natural independent streak taking charge of her.

'You've gone all serious now. I shouldn't have brought up *that* subject.' Jace sighed.

'*Are* we besotted with each other?' Gigi suddenly

asked in dismay. 'I don't want to feel like that. I don't want you to be that important to me—'

Jace grinned down at her, slow and assured. 'I feel the same, but it doesn't seem to be something we have much control over.'

And without warning, long fingers traced her delicate jawline and curled round the back of her neck and he kissed her with all the hunger that had built since early morning and, if anything, her response engulfed his. They made it down onto the bed, kicking off shoes, and she shouted when he wrenched at her dress. 'Don't you dare rip it! I have nothing else to wear!' she warned him.

Jace ran down her zip and unhooked the neckline at a very decorous pace. He lifted it off over her head.

'We shouldn't be doing this,' she sighed without much fight in her.

Jace released her bra with a skilled hand. 'I guess this is what besotted people do,' he breathed thickly.

The burning heat and hunger of his kiss overwhelmed her. She couldn't resist him when that ache clenched between her legs. It turned her into a total hussy, who flattened him to the bed and ripped off his tie.

Jace sat up, his dazzling smile never more evident as he casually, gracefully undressed, skimming off everything until he was reclining beside her unashamedly naked and bronzed. 'I'm all yours.'

And she thought then, *If only he were*, and just as quickly she caught up on that reflection and drove it out of her head again. She wasn't going to fall in love with him. She already felt more for Jace than she was comfortable with feeling. Whatever he felt for her was sexual, nothing deeper, nothing lasting. She would be a very foolish woman if she dared to think otherwise.

Passion glittered in Jace's spectacular eyes and she quivered with helpless anticipation, her body even more wound up than her brain. She almost passed out with pleasure when, having protected them both, he sank lethally deep and sure into her and then there was the long climb to satisfaction followed by a frantic rush to get dressed and presentable again. There was a flush on her cheeks and a ripeness to the pouting pink of her swollen mouth that set Jace on fire again before he even got back downstairs. If this was 'besotted' it was joyful fun and excitement, he reasoned, and he could happily live with it.

When they entered the big room where the buffet was being served and where the guests were spilling out onto the outdoor terraces, Gigi became aware of just how much she and Jace were under close scrutiny, particularly by the young and beautiful women sprinkled through the crush.

'I think Yaya's fondest hopes have spread,' Jace opined. 'It should keep everyone polite and distant.'

'Why wouldn't they be polite?'

'My female cousins always assumed that one of them would marry me, so you're treading on toes, which is good.'

'How…good?' Gigi asked thinly.

'Well, if you're assumed to be my future wife, few will wish to get on the wrong side of you.' Jace laughed.

'And they're probably too busy gossiping to spare the time.'

'I don't like anyone thinking that I'm your bride-to-be,' Gigi admitted tightly.

'I apologise,' Jace declared, a touch brusque in his delivery, his dazzling eyes narrowing. 'This is my fault because I was reluctant to contradict my grandmother and disappoint her.'

'Don't worry about it. When they never see me again, they'll know the truth.'

Jace's lean, darkly handsome features were now taut, his sensual mouth compressed at the prospect of never seeing her again. 'Obviously.'

There was a sharp little silence and it occurred to her that she had been tactless being so blunt, and her face flushed. Suddenly she was mortified at her lack of generosity. What did it matter if a pack of people she would never see again believed she was something she was not? And furthermore, when Jace inevitably moved on to other women, the rumours would be exposed as trivial nonsense.

They sat outside on a shaded terrace, soon joined by Jace's brother and the blonde beauty, who was apparently, in spite of appearances, *not* his girlfriend but actually his best friend. She noticed that Jace was very quiet, and her healthy appetite died long before she went indoors to the cloakroom.

As she crossed the hall again, a tall, curvaceous blonde greeted her. 'I'm Seraphina Diamandis,' she said, much as if she expected Gigi to already know who she was.

'Oh?' Gigi remarked awkwardly.

'Jace was mine first. I thought you should know,' she announced with a subdued melodrama that widened her eyes and made her sultry lips pout.

'It's not really something that I want to talk about,' Gigi said gently, keen to avoid any kind of confrontation.

'I'm Jace's cousin.'

It put new light on keeping it within the family, Gigi conceded.

'I'll be at every family gathering you attend,' Seraphina informed her ominously.

'I don't care who was with Jace first,' Gigi confided. 'I only aspire to be his last.'

After that uneasy meeting, Gigi caught her breath again while photos were taken of them all. A sea of camera phones flashed as Electra opened a handful of presents, one of which was Jace's, a superb modern painting. His grandmother insisted on showing Gigi her art collection with Evander and Marcus in tow. She had no idea where Jace had gone but she learned a lot that she didn't know about art in such knowledgeable company.

Snowy the cockatoo had arrived from the yacht and Electra accompanied Gigi out to see her aviary. The old lady had decided that she wanted Humphrey, the lazy, non-foraging tortoise, for her garden as well. Gigi had good reason to be grateful that she hadn't brought either Hoppy or Tilly out from the yacht, lest she find them being rehomed as well. She no longer needed to wonder where Jace had acquired his love of animals.

As Electra retired for the night, a DJ took over. Jace was drinking with a crowd of his male relatives and evidently not looking for her.

'Did you two have an argument?' Marcus asked while he put on a lively display of dad-dancing.

'A misunderstanding,' Gigi replied uncomfortably.

After a couple of hours socialising with Evander and Marcus, Gigi went over to Jace and told him that she was tired.

'I'll be up later,' he told her smoothly, catching her hand in his, lifting it towards his mouth and then letting it go again as if he didn't know quite why he had reached for it in the first place.

Gigi went up to bed, leaving Seraphina and her best friends doing some very suggestive dancing at the edge of the floor closest to Jace. So, she had put her feet in it with him, she told herself as she climbed into the comfy bed alone. She had acted insulted over being viewed as Jace's future wife and she had offended him. Why?

Her eyes stung. Perhaps her messy emotions were something to do with the fact that at that moment she had, crazily, wished it were truth and not mere rumour. And she was ashamed of that weak spot inside her that wanted a happy ending against all the odds. She swallowed hard and lay awake for a long time waiting for Jace to join her, but she was fast asleep when he finally did in the early hours of the morning.

CHAPTER SEVEN

GIGI WAS WAKENED early by her phone the next morning and she found herself alone in the bed, only a dented pillow beside hers letting her know that, at some stage, Jace had shared the room with her.

Sitting up, flustered and still half asleep, she came instantly wide awake when she recognised the voice of the CEO of the animal shelter, her boss, Thea. She learned that there was such a crowd of paparazzi camped out waiting for her arrival at work that Thea thought it would be best if Gigi took some time off on leave and they brought in a locum. Although the police had moved the crowd out onto the pavement, the staff and the usual visitors were being harassed for information about Gigi.

Gigi spluttered out a surge of embarrassed apologies only to fall silent when Thea congratulated her on her engagement. Her...*engagement*? Deeming it wisest not to tell the truth in such circumstances, Gigi thanked the older woman and came off the phone again. Getting dressed in her usual casual shorts and a top, she went downstairs in search of Jace.

Dmitri showed her into the grand dining room where Jace was chatting on the phone. He ended the call and turned to her, sheathed in fitted chinos and a casual jacket, a silk scarf at his throat, a warmer jacket tossed over a nearby chair. He looked effortlessly, sleekly European and as perfectly groomed as though he had walked off a modelling shoot. Her heart gave a stirring thud and stuttered inside her. She felt far too plain to be even seen in his sophisticated company.

'You must have risen very early,' she remarked, resisting the temptation to ask him what time he had come to bed. After all, he didn't owe her any explanations. Nor had his late night etched so much as a shadow on his lean, darkly handsome face.

Jace smiled as he sat down at the table. 'I'm always up at first light.'

'Someone's released photos of us at the party and announced that we're engaged to the media,' Gigi told him anxiously as she sank down into a seat beside him.

'One of the party guests with a phone,' Jace guessed grimly. 'We'll ride it out.'

'It's not so easy for me.' Gigi explained that she had been asked to take leave to minimise the harassment at the animal shelter.

'This is my fault. I'm sorry,' Jace said flatly, his exasperation making her feel mortifyingly raw. 'If I had stopped that rumour in its tracks, this wouldn't have happened. You can't even go home—'

Gigi frowned. 'Of course I can.'

'The paps will soon have your address as well. Stay onboard the yacht while I'm away,' Jace advised.

A lump formed in her throat and her eyes prickled and she looked away from him. 'I think we both need space right now and living on your yacht will only add substance to those rumours.'

Jace froze. For a split second, all he wanted to do was put a ring on her finger and tough the immediate future out, but that sudden surge of possessiveness and that desire for permanency appalled him, particularly when it pertained to a woman who had firmly rejected the concept of being his fiancée or his wife. Jace could never handle rejection easily because he came from a background full of similar rebuffs.

'That's a decision that only you can make,' he pointed out. 'But I don't agree with it.'

Colour flared in her cheeks again. 'How long will you be away?'

'About a week. You *could* come with me,' Jace murmured, startling himself with that impulsive invitation.

Gigi stiffened. 'Thank you, but no. But I'm sorry I offended you yesterday. I sort of felt trapped into a role I didn't feel comfortable in, and I took it out on you. I'm not very good at faking stuff…or lying.'

Long brown fingers closed over hers where her hands were knotted on her lap and her blue eyes flared up into compelling green framed with lush black lashes. 'I didn't think the situation through from your point of view—'

He leant closer, a lean hand reaching out to smooth up her slender neck and ease her closer. His wide sensual mouth drifted slowly across hers and her heart hammered like crazy. He kissed her slow and he kissed her deep: it was not a casual caress. She wanted to grab him, hold him close, say stuff that she knew she shouldn't say to him, and those impulses scared her. She needed to get back in control of herself fast.

'Guess who's kicking himself now for not coming to bed sooner last night,' Jace growled. 'Our last few hours together and I chose to waste the opportunity—'

'It doesn't matter.'

Jace groaned. 'Even if you decide not to stay on the yacht while I'm away, leave Hoppy and Tilly onboard because if the paps stage a vigil at your place, it'll upset them.'

'Hopefully, this will all settle down in a couple of days,' Gigi said brightly.

They didn't return to the yacht. She already had her stuff and they climbed into a helicopter to be returned to Rhodes. They parted at the airport because Jace was boarding his private jet there to fly to Japan. A limo stuffed with security guards ferried her home, cleared a path through the shouting, aggressive mob on her doorstep and saw her indoors, where she found her father waiting.

'I used my key and came straight inside because I'd prefer not to be identified,' Achilleus Georgiou announced with an apologetic wince. 'I've been waiting, hoping you would return. I went to the shelter first but your boss told me that you wouldn't be coming in to work for a while.'

On edge as she always was with her father, Gigi was already lifting the post he had set on the table to examine it. There was a letter from her solicitor and she tore it open, wondering if her mother's property had finally found a buyer.

'Is it true? Are you engaged to Jace Diamandis? It was a shock to see a picture of you at their family party,' the older man admitted.

'We're not engaged. That was just a stupid misunderstanding,' Gigi volunteered tightly. 'But we are still seeing each other.'

Even her ability to make that modest claim eased the raw tension that had begun to build inside her the night before when Jace had let her go to bed alone. And then he had kissed her again and the breach between them had been healed with sincerity. Her sense of relief was so extreme that it scared her even more. She was falling in love with Jace Diamandis. She didn't want to but it was already happening in a process that had begun very early on at that first dinner together on the yacht. That was when she had seen the male seething with emotion behind the smooth playboy façade.

'What's in the letter?' Achilleus asked, as keen as she was, it seemed, for a change of subject.

'When I came out here, I couldn't find a buyer for Mum's house because there was a problem with the tenant. Now that the tenant has moved out, there's an offer on the house and the buyer has discovered that there's still stuff stored in the attic. I never checked the attic,' she grumbled guiltily. 'Mum put her personal belongings in a storage locker before she rented the house out and I did sort through that. I'll have to go back to Oxford, accept the offer and empty the attic.'

'Is there no alternative?' her father prompted.

'No, I don't think so and, since I'm on leave, it's best

handled now. I didn't even know that Mum had ever used the attic!'

'I never thought I'd see my daughter at a swanky Diamandis party,' Achilleus confessed at the back door, from which he was hoping to make an unnoticed departure. 'You looked like a little queen, standing beside his grandmother... I was proud of you. Sorry I said what I did when I first knew you were seeing him. He's treating you with respect and I think the better of him for that.'

'Yes.' Gigi smiled up at him, for once at ease with the older man, even catching a glimmer of warmth in his dark eyes and heartened by it.

Gigi closed her front curtains, ignored the knocking on the front door and set about tidying and cleaning the house because she was restless. She phoned Thea to request a couple of weeks off and gained her agreement. She texted Jace to tell him she was travelling home to sort out some property hassles and asked if Hoppy and Tilly could stay on *Sea King* until her return. He phoned her to offer her the use of his private jet and she said no, thanks, and then he demanded to know where she would be staying and suggested that she use his property in London.

'I was going to book into a hotel.' A *cheap* hotel, she acknowledged, because even though her mother's property would be vacant, it had very little furniture and it wouldn't be worth buying bed linen and all the other things she would need to spend only a few nights there.

'Use my apartment,' Jace urged. 'I'd prefer that. I'd know that you were there and safe.'

Gigi parted her lips to argue again and then asked herself why she would argue. That he wanted to know she was safe and comfortable was reassuring. Not since childhood had anyone worried about Gigi's safety and comfort. 'OK.'

'And the jet?'

'Don't push it,' she told him drily.

Jace laughed. 'You'll be picked up off your flight and we'll have that blood test done while you're in London. Send me your flight details.'

Having booked her flight, Gigi relaxed a little. It would be a relief to finally settle her mother's estate. Once the house was sold, she would have the money to consider buying her own property on Rhodes. After all, her grandmother's house would eventually sell and she would have to find somewhere else to live. With her relatives on the island and closer friends than she had retained in the UK, that impressed her as a good plan. When had she stopped making such plans? When had she settled into a routine of only work and more work? Jace had sprung her out of that rut, but the price of their relationship would ultimately cost her dearly, she reflected unhappily. Nothing this good lasted for ever and she would be hurt.

Three days later she was collected by a limo at the airport in London and wafted back to a penthouse apartment. She was shown into a spacious, comfortable bedroom and served with an evening meal in the chic dining area off the large airy lounge with its views of the city. Breakfast awaited her when she rose early and a car arrived to ferry her to Oxford. The small, detached house that had belonged to her mother had few childhood associations for Gigi. She had vague memories of the rooms when they were still furnished but she had never climbed the folding metal stair that led up to the loft.

'Let us take a look first, Miss Campbell,' her driver and his companion urged, having already opened the hatch door for her to access the space.

Gigi let them climb up ahead of her and report back that there were only a few small pieces of old furniture and a couple of boxes. They brought the boxes down and she leafed through one, finding old files of her mother's and setting them aside to dump. The second box was more interesting, and she worked through it much more slowly because it contained family photos that she had never seen before as well as a photo of her actual parents posing together in sunlight, her mother smiling as she had so rarely smiled. There were old letters from people she had never heard of and right at the very bottom she found a dozen unopened letters that had been posted from Rhodes.

Her brow furrowed because she recognised her father's handwriting. Why were his letters to her mother unopened? The postal dates spanned the first six years of her life. Had an earlier letter from Achilleus angered her parent into rejecting all communication with him? Shaking her head over her mother's inflexibility, she tucked away the photos and the letters but she already knew that she wouldn't open her father's private letters. She would return them to him and perhaps that would prompt him to talk about the past and answer her questions, she reasoned.

When she rang Jace that evening, she told him about the letters. His attitude was very different from hers. He would have opened them.

'No, I'll be diplomatic and hand them back to him, see what he says,' Gigi argued. 'They're addressed to Mum and weren't meant for me to read.'

'It's your decision,' Jace sighed.

As soon as Gigi had organised the removal of the remaining furniture through a man who did house clearances, she visited the solicitor to sign the sale documents. It felt final and she was sad at the awareness that visiting her mother's former home had liberated no fond memories that she might have cherished. But then her mother had rarely given her daughter personal time. They had only ever shared occasional moments before her mother left on another business trip or Gigi returned to school. And her mother's main interest in her only child had always been limited to Gigi's academic achievements.

Late afternoon, Gigi went to the laboratory Jace had designated and agreed to a blood test taken from her arm. My goodness, she thought in sudden dismay, what if the result were to be positive? It would blow her entire future to pieces and set her on a totally different path. For the first time, she thought of how her mother had prioritised her career over family and she felt light-headed, acknowledging that, for a single parent, one's profession was all the more important when it came to financial security. Had she been a little harsh in her judgement of her mother? Even if she hadn't been loved, she had been well looked after. She breathed in deep. Her career was her security, she reminded herself. Helping animals validated her in a way family life had failed to do. No doubt she would deal with the upheaval if she was pregnant, she told herself firmly, refusing to let her fears and insecurities creep in. How would Jace react *if...*?

She refused to let herself sink into that craven state of anxiety. Wasn't it bad enough that she was twisting and turning in her bed every night remembering what it was like to be with him? She was reliving steamy moments and discovering that the sensual side he had awakened did not tidily go to sleep when he wasn't available. He was phoning her every day and it still wasn't enough. She was missing him more than she had believed it possible for her to miss anyone. Grow up, she told herself sternly. She was obsessing about Jace and it was unhealthy. And she would pay for it all in the future when he inevitably lost interest. Irritated by her state of mind, she contacted two university pals she had done internships with and suggested going for a drink the following evening to catch up.

'I can just call an Uber,' Gigi protested the next day when Jace's driver insisted that he needed to drop her off wherever she was going and Stavros, the beefy bodyguard, announced that he would be keeping her within view at all times. 'It really isn't necessary.'

'Mr Diamandis decides what's necessary,' Stavros responded. 'Perhaps you should mention it to him...but please don't quote me on that.'

Gigi gave up the argument and resolved to speak to Jace when she was dropped off at the bar. She had barely stepped onto the pavement when she was hailed by voices from an outside table. Glancing over, she saw Edison rolling his eyes at her and Marion staring at her with wide eyes.

She had forgotten that Edison was a chain smoker and always sat outside and she was grateful that she had a warm coat on because it was late October and, although it was dry, the breeze was icy.

'Gigi.' Edison stood up, his long, lanky frame towering over her. 'You've finally grown up. I can't believe it—'

'I think you're shooting for the moon here trying to chat her up when she arrives in a chauffeur-driven car!' Marion quipped and stood up, a small no-nonsense woman with wildly curly hair and warm brown eyes. 'But Ed's right. It's been four years. At my wedding, you still looked like a kid and now all of a sudden you're an adult like the rest of us.'

Accepting a brief hug, Gigi took a seat and ordered a drink while Stavros seated himself close to the entrance. 'So, you're a mum now,' she said to Marion. 'What's it like?'

'If you're going to talk kids, I'm out of here,' Edison threatened.

'What's it like?' Marion looked heavenward. 'Overwhelming and terrifying and wonderful and all at the same time and often on the same day.'

Talk about work and their various specialities took over. Edison worked almost exclusively with horses but

Marion was like Gigi, keener on dealing with smaller animals and pets. She was talking about the rescue centre when Marion answered her phone and almost instantly stood up and gathered up her bag. 'I'm going to have to cut and run. Damien has a fever and Steve is panicking,' she told them apologetically. 'Keep in touch, Gigi.'

'Looks like it's just the two of us.' Edison smirked at her and snaked an arm round her.

Gigi shook off his touch like a bristling cat. 'I should leave too,' she said wryly, reaching for her bag.

'Oh, come on, you're not that innocent these days… not when you're running around with an infamous Greek playboy,' he told her with amusement, catching a thick hank of her hair in his hand to prevent her from moving. 'I fancied you like mad when we were working together but you were way too young and naïve—'

'Unfortunately, I don't fancy you any more,' Gigi told him furiously. 'I have a boyfriend and I don't cheat—'

'You heard her…let go of her,' a masculine, achingly familiar voice interposed from behind her.

Gigi almost pulled her hair out of her scalp twisting to look behind her in disbelief. *'Jace?'*

Jace tugged her hair firmly free of Edison's hold and literally lifted her out of her seat, both arms wrapped round her as though she were a parcel. *'Any more?'* he questioned as Stavros pulled open the door of the limo and he settled her on the passenger seat.

Gigi was on a high. Jace was here with her in London and she didn't know whether she was on her head or her heels, only that suddenly life felt wonderful and full to the brim with exciting possibilities again. 'I had a monster crush on Edison when I worked with him three years ago but nothing ever happened between us. I'm sure he guessed but I wasn't the pushy, flirtatious type,' she revealed, her cheeks heating at the memory as Jace vaulted in beside her. 'Why didn't you tell me you'd be coming?'

'I wanted to surprise you...wasn't expecting to get a surprise myself and find some jerk coming on to you!' he admitted, arranging his long-limbed length in a re-laxed sprawl in the other corner of the back seat. 'Es-pecially one that yanks at your hair to imprison you when you clearly don't want to be touched. He's lucky I didn't thump him!'

Gigi collided with black-lashed witch-green eyes and simply succumbed to temptation. She scrambled across the seat separating them like a homing pigeon. 'I missed you so much!' she groaned, burying her face in the shoulder of his coat, drinking in the ocean-fresh scent of him as though it were an addictive drug.

Jace locked two powerful arms round her and held her close. 'I missed you too, more than I wanted to, more than I expected to...you've got under my skin.'

Gigi finally lifted her head and looked down at him. Her mouth fell open. 'You've cut your beautiful hair!' she wailed, slender fingers threading forlornly through the cropped black hair. 'I *loved* your curls.'

'I thought it was time for a change.'

'You should've discussed it first.'

'Are you serious?'

'I'll go out tomorrow and get my hair cut to two

inches long all over and see how you like it!' Gigi threatened.

Jace gazed up at her with a spellbinding smile tilting his wide, sensual mouth. 'I can see that being one half of even a temporary couple involves rules,' he murmured wickedly. 'It's time I started making some. No meeting up with other men when I'm not around—'

'Are you the jealous type?' Gigi asked with interest.

Her blue eyes were sparkling with considerable amusement and faint dark colour edged his sculpted cheekbones.

'I didn't used to be, but I don't like seeing another man put his hands on any part of you…most especially not without your permission.' Long, lean fingers threaded through her wind-tousled hair, spanned the base of her skull and drew her head down.

Her heart was racing so fast she was breathless with anticipation. He crushed her parted lips beneath his. He was hungry, urgent, demanding in flavour and it was exactly what she most wanted and needed to satisfy the hollow ache inside her. Unfortunately, it only whetted her appetite for more, her hands sliding below his coat and running down his shirt-clad sides, yanking at the fine cotton to reach skin. He flexed his hips up and she felt him hard and long and thick through the barrier of their clothes and lust almost ate her alive.

Jace sat up fast, his hands biting into her hips as he lifted and steadied her. 'Not here, not in the car.' He dropped a kiss on the crown of her head and she felt his lean, taut frame shudder against her. 'You could make me as reckless as a teenager, *koukla mou*,' he groaned, setting her beside him on the seat and belting her in.

'It's been a long week,' she mumbled, shamefaced that he had called a halt before she had.

He closed a hand over her smaller one. 'Did you go for that blood test?'

'Yes. I should get a call tomorrow,' she told him stiffly, finding it impossible not to tense when it came to discussing *that* controversial subject. 'I still think you're worrying about nothing.'

'We'll see.'

They made it as far as the private lift up to the penthouse and he grabbed her and kissed her with all the hungry urgency he had earlier restrained. Plastered to each other, they exchanged kiss for kiss, their tongues duelling, their bodies tangling so that he carried her out of the lift and down to the main bedroom. Gigi was quivering, every nerve-ending screaming with excitement, her heart hammering when he laid her down on the bed and stood over her, tipping off his coat, wrenching his tie off, toeing off his shoes, appraising her with fierce impatience.

'Yes, you definitely did miss me,' Gigi murmured with unconcealed satisfaction as he yanked her free of her jeans.

'I almost got ravished in the limo,' Jace traded smugly. 'You're unlikely to win a who-missed-who-most competition. I was shocked rigid by your enthusiasm, Miss Campbell. Only weeks ago, you were an innocent virgin.'

Gigi came up on her knees. 'Shut up,' she told him, reaching up to undo his belt and run his zip down because he wasn't stripping fast enough for her.

And then he was in her arms again as he had not been in days and everything in her world seemed to slot perfectly back into place again, as though he were the missing piece of her personal puzzle. The heat of him, the strength of his long, lean frame, the scent of him, the touch of him, all of it engulfed her like a tidal wave. His mouth on hers, his hand on her breast, the urgency of his answering arousal against her stomach drove her higher in the sky than a kite. Her heartbeat crashed inside her, thundered in her ears as Jace dug out protection and thrust deep inside her, joining them in the intimacy she craved. Nothing had ever been more exciting than that exact moment when she gazed up into his striking green eyes and realised that she truly loved him to a level she had never realised she could love anyone.

Jace stilled in the aftermath, both arms still solidly locked round her. He didn't want to let go of her yet. Nothing wrong with that, he assured himself, not considering how much he had missed her. He supposed it was an infatuation and he was overdue for the experience, but he reckoned that he would never ever admit to his uncle that a relationship could be so much more exciting than casual, uncommitted sex. Evander had lived long enough to already know that as a fact. But *naturally*, Jace, who was still *only* twenty-eight, would bounce back from this total immersion experience with *one* woman and want his freedom of choice back, he told himself without hesitation. He wasn't interested in a permanent relationship, not when his own history warned him of how dangerously unstable and messy such entanglements could become.

In the middle of the night, Gigi lurched out of bed and made snacks for them from what she found in the well-stocked fridge. 'When do you start back to work again?' she heard herself ask, dismayed by the anxiety that gripped her at the idea of him leaving her again.

'I'm working here for a couple of days, sleeping off the jet lag, spending time with you,' he framed lazily, lounging back against the kitchen island while he ate. He resembled a pin-up model, clad only in black boxers and his dazzling smile, all the lean, muscular, bronzed, hair-roughened beauty of him on full display.

And he still, at a mere glance, she acknowledged guiltily, stole the very breath from her lungs. There wasn't much she could do about that. She would see it through until the end and ensure that it finished without recriminations and with dignity. That was the only promise she made to herself.

'I miss the pets,' she confided.

'Of course you do, and you even had to part with two of them on Faros, but we'll be back in Rhodes in forty-eight hours,' he reminded her. 'And I've no doubt there are more Gigi rescues in your future—'

'I haven't much space. Once the money from Mum's house clears, I'm planning to buy somewhere with at least a small garden attached. My grandmother's house where I'm living will ultimately sell.'

'Stay with me on the yacht, instead,' Jace urged.

Gigi paled and tensed at that suggestion. 'Not a good idea for us to be blurring the lines that way—'

'What's that supposed to mean?' Jace demanded

starkly, his big shoulders straightening and lifting, all relaxation abandoned.

Gigi's mouth ran dry and she shrugged awkwardly. 'I don't want to be depending on you for the roof over my head when we break up.'

'Thank you,' Jace breathed with lashings of sarcasm. 'As a thought for the day on the same day that we *reunite*, that is kind of depressing.'

Gigi wrinkled her nose in semi-agreement. 'But realistic.'

Jace gritted his teeth on the truth that only hours earlier he had been thinking the same way, but the very concept of Gigi walking away, retaining her independence… Gigi with other men…still drove him crazy. He still hated rebuffs. Rejection always sucked him back to his birth parents' negative treatment of him.

He breathed in slow and deep and said nothing because he couldn't think of what he could say in the face of Gigi's immensely gloomy but intelligent practicality. He lived in the moment. Gigi lived on a much wider plane, foreseeing problems that didn't even occur to him. Did that mean that she was more mature than he was? a dark little voice whispered inside him and he immediately suppressed that suspicion. Much the same as he had done with the suspicion that, had she been a different kind of woman, she was clever enough to have run rings round him.

Hours later, Jace groaned. 'That's your phone, not mine. Switch it off,' he urged.

Gigi rolled naked out of bed in the daylight filtering through the curtains and dug through the pile of clothes spread across the floor to find her jeans and answer her phone.

'Miss Campbell?' the polite voice began. 'This is a confidential call. Could you give me your details before I give you the test result?'

It was the laboratory. As Gigi answered the questions to prove her identity, she paused. Jace had sat up in bed, shrewd eyes as green as polished emeralds pinned to her sudden pallor and the tension etched in her fine-boned features. A minute later she pushed the phone back into the pocket of her jeans.

'I'm pregnant,' she whispered shakily in total shock and denial, perspiration breaking out on her brow.

CHAPTER EIGHT

AND WHAT SHOOK Jace the most in that moment was the inexcusably weird shot of satisfaction that rocketed through him and the even less presentable thought, Try walking away now…

He was shocked by his own reaction and wondered what the hell was happening to his brain. A…*baby*? He didn't know any, so had little to say on the subject, but for the first time in his life in recent weeks, and ever since the risk of a pregnancy had arisen, Jace had started noticing babies for the first time. Babies…and pregnant women. That curiosity had freaked him out a little even while it had somewhat acquainted him with the possibility of becoming a parent.

'Pregnant!' Gigi gasped, stricken.

'It's not the end of the world,' Jace pointed out, feeling remarkably calm in the crisis. 'Come back to bed. It's too early to get up—'

'Come back to bed?' Gigi repeated, studying him as though he had sprouted horns and cloven feet in his apparent madness. 'Are you crazy? After getting news like that?'

Jace vaulted out of bed and clasped her hand to tug her upright and off the rug where she was still sitting like a woman felled by a lightning bolt. 'We were up half the night. You're exhausted. This is not the time to talk about this—'

'It's a nightmare…' Gigi looked up at him with tears swimming in her eyes.

'We're not having a drama over this,' Jace assured her with innate confidence, bending down to scoop her off her bare feet and tuck her with care back into her side of the huge bed. 'You'll feel better once you've slept for a while and will be more able to deal with it—'

'I'm not having a termination!' she shot at him accusingly.

Jace stretched out an arm and edged her close in a determined movement. 'I don't want that either—'

'But what are we going to *do*?' Gigi snapped at him in frustration, because his complete inhuman cool was not at all how she had expected him to deal with such an announcement. She had assumed that he would be shaken, horrified, angry…all likely responses from a young, single guy, who was in no way ready or eager for fatherhood with a woman he had only recently met.

Inside himself, Jace was in shock as well at the prospect of becoming a parent and the lifelong commitment that would demand from him. His birth parents had been lousy at the job, he acknowledged, little better than disinterested bystanders during his early childhood. He would have to do a hell of a lot better on that front than they had. But right now, he couldn't afford to reveal his panic to Gigi because it would only fuel hers. No, he needed to take a deep breath and step back and come up with a solution. That meant *not* getting emotional or dramatising the situation. He needed to concentrate on the practicalities.

'We'll get married—'

'What?' Gigi shot bolt upright in the bed, almost elbowing him in the face in her disbelief as he too sat up again, looking very much put upon.

Jace surveyed her aghast expression, mentally leafed through all possible arguments and came up with the one most practical, most likely to appeal to her as a future parent. 'All the Diamandis family holdings are in a trust. For my firstborn to inherit his or her share, the parents have to be *married*. I doubt that either of us are sufficiently anti-matrimony to disinherit our future child because we can't be bothered tying the knot.'

Thoroughly disconcerted by that very rational and unemotional explanation, Gigi slowly lay down again. Jace relaxed then and curved her back into him. 'Go back to sleep. You're catastrophising… I can *feel* it. We're adults and we have nobody but ourselves to consider in this. We'll handle it together—'

'Do you really mean that?' Gigi muttered worriedly.

'Do you truly not trust me enough to accept my word?'

Marriage? Marry Jace? Yes, she could do it for the sake of their child's potential prosperity, she reasoned in a daze, thinking that she had no choice on *that* basis. But what had Jace done with all the emotion she had initially sensed seething in him when she first made that announcement? Where had it gone? He hadn't said one word wrong. Was he always that tactful? Why did she have the suspicion that he had gone undercover with his emotions like some stupid secret agent on a mission?

Gigi went to sleep. Jace expelled his breath in a discreet sigh of relief. A baby. He didn't know anything about babies, but he had seen one or two in prams in

Japan that had struck him as being reasonably cute and interesting. None of his friends had a child. The Diamandis men, however, usually didn't marry until middle age and he would be breaking that cycle. He splayed a sneaky hand across Gigi's still flat stomach as she slumbered and he swore to that tiny life inside her that he would be a much better father than his birth parents had been to him.

Challenged, however, by the altered future now opening up ahead of him, Jace was restless. He slid quietly out of bed and went off to use his phone and share his news with his family. After all, it was his duty to control the narrative and ensuring that there were few surprises ahead would prevent him from dwelling on the emotional stuff.

Gigi wakened to having breakfast served to her in bed, Jace straightening to tower over her, fully dressed in a designer elegant suit. He looked stupendous even first thing in the morning and she knew that she did not, not without a brush through her hair, her teeth clean—and even some pyjamas would not have gone amiss. She dropped her evasive gaze to the beautifully prepared tray and wondered uncertainly when and just how they had become so intimate. She had fallen for him like a ton of bricks but that didn't mean she had to be dependent on him...for anything. Indeed, Gigi had based her entire life to date on not needing anyone for anything because she could usually take care of herself better than anyone else.

'I've organised a doctor's appointment for you this morning.' Jace fell silent as Gigi lifted stunned eyes to his. 'He's a top obstetrician. I assumed that move was only sensible…to have you checked out because we haven't had that done yet—'

'I don't think there's any royal "we" when I'm the one who's pregnant,' Gigi heard herself say tartly, even though all the while an inner voice was urging her not to be a five-letter word of a woman when he was only trying to take care of her. The way nobody had *ever* taken care of her, she reminded herself ruefully. Maybe that was why her hackles were raised, because that kind of treatment was new to her and it gave her an almost threatened feel, which her intelligence warned her was a ridiculous response.

'Seeing a doctor is normal,' she agreed in addition, cheeks flushing as she made that concession, disliking the irrational resentments assailing her. It wasn't *his* fault that they were in this predicament. If anything, it was *her* fault for not having taken the contraceptive precautions most young women in her age group did. Her fault for assuming that she would never meet a guy she wanted to have sex with. How realistic had that conviction been? For goodness' sake, he was standing right there now beside her and a dangerous, reckless and wanton part of her still wanted to drag him down on the bed and rip him back out of that business suit. He stole her self-control; he changed her into someone she felt uncomfortable with.

Sadly, she didn't seem to have the same effect on him. His shrewd and striking green eyes were impassive, his lean, dark, devastating face calm as a tranquil sea. *Businesslike?* She didn't know the side of Jace he was currently giving her and it…unnerved her more than a little. Not to know what he was thinking or feeling left her feeling shut out, distanced, and he hadn't given her one typical, normal extrovert Jace reaction since she had uttered that fatal word 'pregnant' first thing that morning.

Jace had never wanted so badly to peel back the layers in a person and see exactly what went on inside their head. Gigi was freaking out, *still* freaking out about the baby and he didn't know what to do about that. He was trying to be supportive, and she didn't like that either. His even white teeth gritted hard in frustration. An efficient can-do approach towards the practicalities would surely soothe her as any emotional reaction would not.

'Eat something,' he urged, since she had yet to touch a crumb of the food on her tray.

All her favourite items were on the tray. When had he noticed exactly what she liked to eat? My word, they hadn't been together *that* long! But there sat the hot chocolate and the yogurt and the fruit like a statement. And she hadn't a clue what he preferred for breakfast! Did that make her a very selfish, useless girlfriend? Exasperated by the constant clamour of anxiety and insecurity assailing her without warning, Gigi began to eat and Jace backed off a few feet.

Showered and fresh, Gigi pulled on her jeans and a somewhat shabby sweater and studied herself in a mirror, feeling unusually critical of her appearance. She had to buy some clothes, she conceded ruefully, never having been a fan of shopping. But she had next to nothing left to wear in a true winter climate.

'Why so serious?' Jace chided, striding over to her as he pulled open the door into the lift.

'Well, it's all serious stuff now, isn't it?' she framed bleakly.

A lean hand curved to her tense jawline and Jace lowered his head to claim a kiss. Not a light kiss, not a 'comforting the little woman in the lift' kiss, a downright passionate claiming kiss that shook her inside out and made her toes curl in her scuffed winter ankle boots. She blinked up at him in astonishment as he walked her out to the waiting car. It was the first thing he had done since they learned of her pregnancy that revealed emotion and she loved it.

In the back of the car, he offered her a drink and she said no, thank you. In a speedy sleight of hand that thoroughly disconcerted her, Jace produced a glittering ring and threaded it with great care onto her engagement finger. 'Er…what's this?' she mumbled.

'You know it's an engagement ring because we're getting married,' Jace pointed out flatly.

'Of course…for the look of things, for appearances,' she mumbled, a stiletto knife piercing her heart as she surveyed the truly gorgeous ring that was pretty much a fake as far as his intentions were concerned. It wasn't huge, which she would have hated, but a delicate, creative swirl of dazzlingly bright diamonds that would undoubtedly have cost the earth and some change. 'It's really beautiful, Jace,' she extended unevenly. 'Very elegant and not too much for my small hand. Thank you.'

A little mollified, Jace studied her taut profile until he noticed that her lower lip was wobbling as if she was on the brink of tears. 'What's wrong?'

What was wrong was that she could hardly tell him that she wished the ring and the supposed sentiments attached to it were real instead of fake to make them look like a genuine engaged couple. 'Nothing… I don't know what's the matter with me,' she said truthfully. 'I feel weepy and that's not normal for me.'

'It's probably stress. I don't want you stressing about *anything*,' Jace informed her in a forceful undertone. 'If there's any stressing to be done, let it be my problem, rather than yours. Evander and Marcus and my grandmother will take care of the wedding on Faros. All you have to do is choose your gown.'

Gigi swivelled in her seat in dismay. 'The wedding?' she gasped. 'You're *already* making arrangements for it?'

Jace dealt a sizzling appraisal. 'Why not? Since we're doing it, there's little point in waiting.'

With difficulty, Gigi held her tongue. She felt trapped, harassed, pushed into choices she had barely had time to consider. But was that reasonable? Hadn't she agreed to marry him? For the sake of their child's future inheritance? Which sounded horrendous, she acknowledged. Surely more should come into the decision than something so reliant on cold, hard cash?

'We probably won't like being married,' she warned him stiffly, while thinking that she would cope fine with the prospect of having him almost every day, *but* he had always been accustomed to more adventurous possibilities: fabulous underwear models, gorgeous screen stars, polished socialites. His past contained all of those options and how could she possibly compare?

'We'll manage,' Jace pronounced in a tone of finality.

Gigi went through the prior tests for her appointment at the surgery before Jace joined her in the consulting room and the obstetrician, a suave male in his forties or so, gave her an ultrasound to show them the tiny blip of their child inside her. The backs of her eyes stung with happy tears. Jace brushed her cheekbone to wipe away that bead of moisture when it trickled down without her noticing.

'I know, *asteri mou*,' he breathed soft and low. 'It's pretty special.'

He was calling her 'my star' and she almost wept all over him at the affectionate term. But that was *before* Mr Eames, the consultant, learned that she was a veterinary surgeon and revealed that his wife was one as well and that she had given up work for the duration of each of her pregnancies.

'Was that really necessary?' Jace asked in surprise.

'Toxic chemicals, dangerous procedures, the risk of infection or harm from an injured animal...what do *you* think?' the older man responded.

'Perhaps your wife works more with livestock than I do,' Gigi said stiffly even as her brain was spiralling with horror at the mere thought of not being able to work. Work had always been her holy grail, her anchor, what she based her whole life on. The threat of being without her job terrified her.

'Even so, there are a lot of risks for a pregnant woman in your field. Will you really take that chance with your baby?' the consultant prompted. 'Of course, if you're part of a big practice, your colleagues can handle the patients you can't...that would work.'

But Gigi didn't have that option. There was nobody else at the rescue shelter able to perform her job. Ioanna was qualified to do vaccinations and blood tests but that was about it. It would require another vet to do the surgeries and some other treatments. Her troubled eyes veiled and her slight frame stiffened.

'So, you quit for a few months,' Jace remarked without any expression at all as he tucked her back into the limousine.

Gigi's eyes widened but she said nothing because the prospect of losing her job was like a crack of doom sounding above her head that reverberated through her entire body. It was her security, her very foundation. She was going to lose everything that mattered to her, she reflected in a frantic, fearful surge of anxiety. Her whole life would fall apart without work.

'That's easy for you to say. It's not that simple,' she objected.

'Nothing about this situation is easy for either of us,' Jace countered drily.

And her heart sank to her boot soles because that was *finally* telling her, wasn't it? That all his careful plans were against his personal wishes? That he didn't want the baby or her and certainly didn't want to marry her? Gigi swallowed very hard and, in containing herself, she went rigid.

'What's wrong?' Jace asked in the lift on the way back up to the apartment.

'How can you ask me that?' she hissed at him, her messy emotions finally breaking through to the surface. 'My life is about to fall apart at the seams!' she shot at him in the foyer of the apartment.

'This is about your job, isn't it?' Jace murmured flatly, studying her the way a male might have studied a grenade about to blow.

'Full marks for perception!' Gigi gasped as she stalked down the bedroom corridor to their room to blow up in solo privacy.

Regrettably, Jace, it seemed, could not take a hint that just at that moment she was better left alone to deal with unwelcome medical advice. She felt as if the top of her head were about to blow off with anger and frustration. But Jace, cool as always, strolled in, closed the door and leant back against it. He looked almost insanely hot and sexy. Her breasts peaked under her sweater and something in her pelvis tightened right then, doubly infuriating her. It was bad enough having pulled the short straw with her pregnancy and marriage to a guy who didn't want *either* of them, but it felt like betraying herself to still want him so badly.

'Tell me what's wrong,' Jace murmured. 'I can fix most things—'

'You can't fix *this*!'

'Do you want this child?' Jace asked with lethal quietness, bright green eyes narrowed to an intimidating degree, and it was yet another side of Jace that she had not seen before. For a split second, he chilled her where she stood.

'No...no, it's not that,' she declared, devastated by that question, shocked he would ask because, of course, her baby was more important to her than her job. 'The baby's here and it's staying inside me until it's born. It's everything else...this wedding—'

'Which you agreed to,' he interposed drily.

'The impact the pregnancy will have on my working life. I mean, there would be risks I would have to avoid—'

'We'll get better advice, *qualified* advice,' Jace incised. 'And if it's still a potential problem I will cover the cost of another vet working with you—'

'For goodness' sake, you can't buy everything!' Gigi launched at him with scorn.

'I will pay for virtually anything that makes you happier,' Jace told her levelly, wondering why she didn't recognise how hard he was trying to shape the future into something that she could accept. 'That's not extravagance or foolishness when I'm your future husband, it's my duty.'

That word, 'duty', hit Gigi like a brick smashing through glass. 'Oh, take a hike, Jace. Leave me alone to get my head straight. I'm sorry. I'm in a bad mood. And it doesn't help *that*—' Her voice broke off. 'No, never mind.'

'Never mind about what? *What* doesn't help?' he pressed grimly, knowing that he dared not respond in a similar emotional way lest he lose control of the situation and made a mess of calming her down.

'That you're not giving me an honest, genuine answer to *anything*!' Gigi fired back at him, unable to silence that frightening conviction. 'I feel like all I'm being told is what you think *I* want to hear and that's not fair to either of us right now! I don't want to be manipulated like that. I can take bad news like any other woman!'

'I'm not manipulating you. I'm trying to keep you calm because I don't imagine it's good for you right now to get so upset,' Jace declared without hesitation, determined not to react. She was having his baby and he would do whatever it took to smooth that journey for her. Much good it would do them if he went off in an emotional scene and accelerated hers!

'Because I'm pregnant,' Gigi guessed, and she still wanted to slap him, slap him and drag him back into bed at the same time. But no, that wasn't where he was at in this moment. He was too busy suffering through a *scary* pregnant woman experience and handling her with velvet gloves like a dangerous science experiment. 'You're taking that far too seriously. As you said, it's not the end of the world,' she proffered, hoping to draw him out.

'You're the one still behaving as though it is the end of the world, so why are you questioning my behaviour?' Jace asked, logical down to the bone.

'That's not what I'm talking about!' Gigi flung back at him with spirit. 'I'm talking about the fact that you don't feel able to be honest with me any more and I can't stand that… It's like there's a wall between us now!'

Striding back to the door, Jace angled a scorching look like live green fire at her, his cut jaw line taut and hard. 'I don't know what I'm supposed to say. I don't do the touchy-feely stuff with women, if that's what you're expecting. Maybe it's because I'm a guy or maybe it's because… I'm emotionally repressed—'

'Or maybe it's because you're a coward and can't face the challenge of honesty,' Gigi interposed stiffly, aware that he was on the brink of losing his temper, wanting to push that, *not* wanting to push that in equal parts. Indeed, she was not even sure quite what she *did* want from him. All she really knew was that she felt torn apart and weak with insecurity and fear and that that, more than anything else, was what she wanted him to fix for her.

In the corridor, Jace stopped dead as though faced with a loaded gun and then he swung back to her, dazzling green eyes chilling as a polar freeze. 'Do you think you could strive to handle this situation with a little more maturity?'

It was Gigi's turn to ice over, knees stiffening beneath her to brace her and keep her taut back straight. 'Obviously you don't think so,' she parried.

'You say that you want honesty but, believe me...*you don't*,' Jace gritted, staring at her, wondering what had happened to the woman who had bewitched him without even trying to do so. Him? Was it his own fault? Was he supposed to lie down like a rug for her to walk over? Too bad, that brand of weakness wasn't in the Diamandis DNA. He could not recall ever being so angry with anyone and certainly not a woman, but at the same time he knew that he could not bear to utter a single word that she might take wrong. They could talk *after* the wedding, when all the fuss was over, when it was only the two of them and the baby news had settled in with her. So, he wasn't splashing his emotions round the place as she was...but that wasn't his job right now. She needed him to be sensible and controlled and consider the greater good.

'So you say.' With difficulty, refusing to show her vulnerability, Gigi simply shrugged a slight shoulder. Hadn't her own mother warned her times without number that men ducked out when the going got tough? Warned her that she had to be hard and independent and trust in no one other than herself? And from no age at all, Gigi had learned to live that way.

'Grow up, *glykia mou*,' Jace advised with icy restraint. 'Our baby comes first and we must learn to compromise for our child's benefit. That's the bottom line and agonising over it won't change it.'

And with that final uncompromising dressing-down, Jace strode off and Gigi backed into the bedroom again, sick at heart and even her tummy churning. Funny how the obstetrician had asked her if she had suffered any nausea and she had said no and now, all of a sudden, she felt sick as a dog. It wasn't funny, she acknowledged, lying down on the bed, wishing that Jace would come back and simply put his arms round her.

It was as though he had not the smallest idea of how much difference that one little gesture could make at a tense time. And was she likely to be the one to teach him? She, whose mother had never once hugged her, who herself had only ever shown affection to Jace? But possibly his omission was more honest than his words had been. She was hugging him because she was crazy in love with him. Why would he think to hug her in the midst of their current plight?

So, what kind of marriage was it likely to be? Gigi wiped her tears away. *Our* baby, he had said for the very first time. She supposed that label had finally answered all the questions he had refused to answer. He would marry her for their child's sake and not for any other reason.

When she rose after a sleepless night, it was to a text on her phone, informing her that Jace had flown to New York on business, apologising for the change of plan and for the necessity of her returning to Greece alone.

And now, she had contrived to drive him away, she thought wretchedly. Could she really blame him, though, for not wanting to spell out truths that, in all honesty, she did not want to hear?

CHAPTER NINE

ELECTRA DIAMANDIS TWITCHED the Elizabethan stand-up collar of Gigi's wedding dress straight and stepped back, beaming with satisfaction. 'You look beautiful, Gigi. You have classic taste.'

Gigi flushed. No, she didn't, she had simply fallen in love after trying on a welter of big bouffant dresses that swallowed her small stature alive. And the one she had chosen was a simple sheath with long sleeves, an upstanding beaded decorative collar and a narrow skirt that flattered her height and shape. The bodice was beaded with intricate rose designs. The costly fabric was pure silk with the weight to drop into elegant folds. And the colour was pure white because Electra had had very firm ideas about what even Jace's pregnant bride should wear and it hadn't been the ivory tint that Gigi had initially assumed would be expected of her.

Yes, the past two weeks had been a breathtaking whirl of surprises, shocks and constant activity, all shared with Jace's family while her future husband stayed safe from the bridal madness on the other side of the world. Evander and Electra had taken her to a designer salon to choose her gown. The wedding would take place on the island of Faros at the Diamandis home.

Humphrey the tortoise now rejoiced in a purpose-built cave and pond complex in the garden. He was living the life of one in a million tortoises and the perfect life for a very lazy one. Snowy was enjoying an equally fabulous existence in Electra's private quarters being hand-fed nuts and he was slowly beginning to speak. Retrieved from the yacht, her own pets were revelling in luxury as well. Currently, Tilly was sunbathing indolently out on the balcony beyond the bedroom. Mo and Hoppy were curled up together in a corner, having greeted Gigi's return with rapture and shared her bed ever since.

Her otherwise *empty* bed. She had not seen Jace since that last day in London and she was not quite sure that she believed that genuinely urgent business had demanded his long absence. She blamed herself, she totally blamed herself for exploding their developing relationship. She had wanted more than he was offering her, *so much more*, she conceded sadly, the sort of stuff a guy couldn't give if he wasn't in love. And Jace was not in love with her. She had come to terms with that, she reminded herself doggedly. They had very good reasons to marry for their child's benefit, not least the loving support of Jace's immediate family.

It had been a shock to arrive on Faros and discover that everybody already *knew* that she was carrying Jace's baby. He had told the lot of them, demonstrating a lack of discretion that had astounded Gigi. Electra, Evander and Marcus, however, could hardly contain their delight over the news, which she had to admit had been heartwarming in a manner to which she was unaccustomed for she had yet to share that same news with her own Greek relatives. Jace might hail from a dysfunctional background but the family who had stood by him at the age of six were still fully present for him... and very supportive of his bride-to-be. She was deeply grateful for that family warmth and unquestioning acceptance that had never come her way before.

She had chosen to invite her Greek family to her wedding. Leaving them out would only have hurt and offended her father. Achilleus, her stepmother, Katerina, and her half-brothers had travelled to Faros on *Sea King* to meet Jace's family. Understandably, they had been overwhelmed by the experience of the yacht, the house's grandeur and their welcoming hosts. Katerina had tactfully sidestepped the invite to help dress Gigi for her big day, recognising that she and her stepdaughter didn't yet stand on such close terms, and that thoughtfulness had convinced Gigi that she had made the right decision. Besides, the attitude of her father's wife had been so much warmer and friendlier than Gigi had dimly assumed it would be that she was now pretty certain that that relationship was set to improve.

As for the fuss over Gigi's career having to be put on hold for her pregnancy—that had turned out to be a silly storm in a teacup, a storm that Gigi now very much regretted setting off with Jace by being too precious and pessimistic. The day after she had freaked out in the wake of the obstetrician's advice, she had gone to see one of her former professors at university. And the truth was that, yes, she would have to take extra care, glove up, be cautious, but in a small animal practice there was no reason why she shouldn't work as late into her pregnancy as she chose to do. Given that safety procedures and risk assessments were respected, she would be fine.

'That's marvellous,' Jace had pronounced flatly when she had apologetically shared that welcome clarification with him on the phone. 'We'll use the yacht as a base so that you can remain close to Rhodes.'

And now into the bargain she had been invited to become one of the directors on the board of the charity that ran the animal shelter because of Jace's massive donation to their funds. In short, in the space of weeks, her life had evolved to an extent that she could never have foreseen while she was over in London. Indeed, life would have been perfect if she were not still cherishing such very strong feelings for Jace. After all, other people seemed to manage detached, unemotional relationships with partners. Why couldn't she be the same?

Why did she have to miss Jace every hour of every day? Why did she shiver just hearing his voice on the phone? Why did she lie in bed wishing he were with her with every fibre of her being? All that excess feeling in Jace's direction worried Gigi. Where had that inner intensity been hidden for the twenty-three years that had preceded Jace's appearance in her life? Now she was subject to emotions that felt too powerful to suppress or fully control. And in the future she would need to control her possessive, almost obsessive love for Jace. How loyal would he be behind closed doors to a wife he didn't love? He was twenty-eight, not fifty-eight, nowhere near any nominal age when sexual temptation might be deemed to be a little less potent.

* * *

Early on the morning of her wedding day, Gigi anchored a small hand to her father's arm as they stood at the foot of the aisle in the church.

His brother, Nic, by his side, Jace awaited her at the altar. He was tall, dark, startlingly handsome in profile. She could see that his hair had grown and started to curl again since their last meeting and a helpless smile put to flight her anxious expression because he looked so much more familiar: he looked like *her* Jace again. In almost the same moment, primed by the swelling notes of the organ music, Jace swung fully round and dazzling jewelled eyes locked to her as she moved towards him.

In the candlelit interior, Gigi took his breath away in that dress with diamonds sparkling in her hair and her ears. It had been the longest two weeks of Jace's life but suddenly it all seemed worth it. The dramas, the misunderstandings, the uncharacteristic restraint of having to bite his tongue. It had all been for the greater good to bring them to this moment when the future opened up and enclosed them both. Looking at Gigi, he decided it was definitely worth it. They might still have a load of issues to work through, but he knew he wanted her as his wife more than he wanted anything else in the world.

Gigi drowned in the burning intensity of Jace's appraisal. A full body shiver of awareness racked her slender body. That raw, seething intensity that was uniquely Jace got to her every time. For a timeless moment, all her worries disappeared, and it was just her and him, the packed church surrounding them forgotten.

'You look stunning,' Jace informed her before the priest began to speak.

A faint flush of warmth infiltrated Gigi's exposed skin. Her heart hammered, her pulses quickened and she snatched in a faint steadying breath. She felt her nipples prickle and push against the boned bodice of her dress, felt the tightening inner muscles clench in her pelvis. Embarrassment gripped her as she fought to concentrate on the ceremony. Some minutes later, she looked down in faint consternation at the wedding ring that Jace eased onto her finger because, for an instant, it didn't seem possible that they could be married. Only as Jace helped her to slide a heavier version of her ring over his knuckle did it dawn on her that in this, at least, it was real. For better or for worse and certainly on paper, they were now husband and wife.

As they climbed into the waiting vintage car, which was festooned in flowers, Jace curved an arm to her spine and whispered, 'It feels like a hundred years since I was with you in London.'

For a split second, Gigi was tempted to quip that she was sure that he had been glad to have an excuse to escape a woman ready to call him a coward for his reluctance to be honest about how he truly felt about her. But with hindsight, everything that had happened between them had since mysteriously taken on a different guise. Why trash what they *could* have in favour of what she couldn't have? If a guy didn't love her, forcing him to admit that and admit that he didn't really want to be married to her would only create tension and bad feeling. Why on earth would she do that to them both?

So, it sucked to be her, to love and not be loved in return, but she wasn't the first woman to be in that position and definitely wouldn't be the last. She was more intelligent than that, she told herself fiercely. Perhaps it would be wiser to put the past behind her and focus on the future, focus on what she did have, rather than what she didn't.

'I missed you,' she conceded ruefully. 'But your family have been amazing.'

'What about your own? Make sure I meet them all at the reception,' Jace urged her. 'Have you confronted your father with those letters yet?'

'No, not yet.' Gigi frowned. 'I want to talk to him about that when we're somewhere private and I haven't had that chance yet. I'm not planning to *confront* him either…he hasn't done anything wrong—'

'Except withhold the truth about his relationship with your mother,' Jace reminded her drily.

'Mum did that first. I'll find the right time to talk to him and return those letters,' Gigi declared with confidence. 'But it won't be today at our wedding.'

'And not for the next couple of weeks either,' Jace forecast as he handed her out of the car outside the Diamandis house. 'We're honeymooning in Oman. Evander and Marcus are loaning us their holiday retreat in Muscat but we'll only be using it as a base. We'll be travelling around.'

'I wasn't expecting a honeymoon. I haven't asked to

take any more time off,' Gigi muttered, her eyes wide with dismay.

'I organised it for you. Almost two weeks ago, I spoke to your boss and arranged for the shelter to retain your replacement until you return. You need a holiday, Gigi. As long as your work is covered, you're free as a bird.'

They moved indoors through the surge of bustling catering staff and walked out back to a shaded terrace where cold drinks were brought to them. Gigi started rising from her seat again to greet their arriving guests in the hall but Jace planted a staying hand on her knee. 'My family will handle them. We can enjoy five minutes alone,' he told her as he placed a jewellery box on her lap. 'Wedding gift.'

'You've already given me far more than you need to,' Gigi protested, colour lashing her cheeks as she thought of the entire wardrobe of clothes for all seasons that had crammed the dressing room upstairs. 'I mean, for goodness' sake, I'm wearing your grandmother's tiara, your mother's diamond earrings—'

'Those are family jewels. This is a personal gift from me to you,' Jace specified.

Gigi opened the box and lifted out a shimmering pendant. A diamond-studded wolfhound with golden eyes met her startled gaze.

'But for Mo, we wouldn't have met.' Striking green eyes levelly held her thoroughly disconcerted ones as he removed the item from her grasp and urged her to lower her head so that he could place it round her neck.

'Our first meeting wasn't exactly romantic,' Gigi protested even while she cherished the sheer shock value of Jace doing such a thing. He wasn't that type of guy, she could have sworn that he was not, yet…?

'But you warmed up to me,' Jace pointed out with a charismatic smile.

'An icicle would warm up to you,' Gigi mumbled, slender fingertips caressing the wolfhound pendant, but there was no hiding it: she was touched and impressed by a romantic gesture she had not expected from the once scarily honest male she had just married. 'It's absolutely gorgeous—'

'A perfect match for my absolutely gorgeous bride.' Jace sprang upright, offering her his arm. 'It's time for us to go public again. Shall we?'

The bridal celebrations and the crowds of guests swiftly engulfed them. As Jace finally guided her to the top table in the huge ballroom, one of his hands spanned her waist to ease her close. Bending his dark head, he ravished her parted lips slowly and thoroughly with his and whispered huskily, 'I can't wait until we're alone…only a few hours to get through now.'

As his lean, muscular body brushed against hers, her own blood ran hotly through her veins because she could feel him even now hard and ready through the fine layers of fabric separating them. Cheeks warm, she sat down, her knees no longer willing to hold her upright. Desire was spreading pulses of mortifying need through her entire body. She might get mad at him, he might often annoy her with what he said and what he did not say, but she never ever stopped wanting him back. Even though they still had a lot of undercurrents to steer safely across, she was determined not to think about them on their wedding day.

Polished, professional entertainment had been organised for the reception. Once they had eaten, Jace guided her round, ensuring that they spoke to all the guests and spending time with her father and half-brothers in particular. She could see that he found it a strain to exchange pleasantries with his own relatives, who had ignored him virtually until the very day of his father's death. She stepped in for him whenever she could, forcing herself to be a brighter, funnier and more outgoing person than she actually was, and it embarrassed her to appreciate just how much she wanted to protect him. Even when he was older, more sophisticated and a million times richer than she was? Yes, she acknowledged, even then. Where Jace was concerned there was a soft spot inside her that she couldn't harden.

Jace watched his cousins gather round Gigi on the dance floor, espied the spite glinting in Seraphina's hard eyes and narrowing them as she moved in Gigi's direction. He strode into the crush to steal his bride back to himself. He was damned if he would stand back and allow Gigi to suffer for one of his mistakes.

'Keep your distance from Seraphina,' he warned her soft and low as he steered her away from that group.

'I've already learned that lesson,' she admitted ruefully. 'She's a viper. What on earth did you do to her?'

'I'll tell you, only not here and now. But I will not tolerate her anywhere near us if she makes the mistake of targeting my wife with her nonsense.'

Gigi's eyes brightened at that possessive designation. 'I can look after myself, Jace.'

'But you shouldn't have to,' he responded in a tone of finality, his clean jaw line hardening with resolve. 'Particularly not when in any of the homes that we now share.'

'Gosh, you're being very inclusive all of a sudden,' Gigi murmured with a helpless giggle at the prospect of being included in the ownership of more than one home. 'How many properties do you own?'

'Six that I actually use, mostly inherited like the London apartment. My father hated hotels.'

Her fingers laced into the springy dark luxuriance of his hair, dallied there and spread to the base of his skull to draw him down to her.

'No,' Jace told her succinctly. 'If you touch me, I'll do something indecent in public, so play safe and *don't* touch me.'

Pink and roused more than she liked by the hard slide of his body against hers, Gigi broke his embrace to step back from him. As she crossed the floor to speak to Electra, where she sat with her closest friends in a quieter corner, Evander Diamandis came to a halt in front of her and kissed her on both cheeks with enthusiasm. Gripping both her hands, he smiled down at her. 'Thank you for making Jace happy—'

'No,' she demurred. 'Let me thank you, your mother and Marcus for making me so very welcome.'

She had barely exchanged more than a few words with Jace's grandmother before Jace was ushering her away again and urging her to change for their flight. 'We're leaving *now*?' she carolled in surprise.

'We're spending our wedding night in Oman.'

Jace practically lifted her out of the SUV at the end of the long, potholed track.

The ultra-modern villa was well lit. He walked her into a sleek entrance hall that opened into an even more elegant and contemporary living space. An ice bucket complete with champagne and two goblets awaited them. Jace strode through to the kitchen and dug into the fridge to produce orange juice for Gigi.

'You've been here before,' she guessed as she sipped the refreshing drink.

'Several times when I was a teenager and adventuring was still in my blood. While Evander and Marcus played golf, I went off exploring.' As she set her empty glass down, he swooped on her to scoop her up into his arms. 'Right now, all I want is to explore you—'

'Just when I was about to ask you about Seraphina—'

Jace groaned out loud as he carried her up a flight of shallow steps and into a cool spacious bedroom decorated in warm creams spiced with subtle hints of jazzy orange and turquoise. 'It's a sad little story of immaturity. I was eighteen and drunk. She was twenty-two. I spent the night with her. The following day her father visited Evander and Marcus. He accused me of taking advantage of her and demanded that I marry her—'

'What?' Gigi exclaimed in surprise. 'You were only a teenager and she was older than you were!'

'It was completely casual but I did make the mistake of crossing those boundaries. It was a set-up, of course. I was supposed to marry her to protect her reputation but, to be frank, she was no more an innocent than I was.'

'Oh, dear…she told me that you were hers *first*.'

'No, I was fifteen the first time I dallied with a lady.' Jace rolled his eyes in acknowledgement. 'And you're my one and only relationship.'

'And I got pregnant,' she sighed as she kicked off her shoes.

'No, *we* got pregnant,' Jace countered, dropping down beside her on his knees and pulling her into his arms. 'It does take two, you know…'

His warm mouth came down on hers with the kind of hunger that sizzled through her every nerve ending. Lean hands extracted her from her vest top and skimmed off her cropped linen trousers at speed, her lingerie vanishing at a similar pace. With an identical sense of freedom, she stripped off his shirt, stretching up to smooth reverent hands up over his muscular hair-roughened torso before he vaulted off the bed to peel off his chinos and his boxers.

He returned to her, a vision of bronzed masculine perfection and potent arousal, and kissed her breathless, clever fingers toying with the achingly sensitive peaks of her swollen breasts. 'Two weeks is too long for us to be apart—'

'It wasn't my choice,' she reminded him, slender fingers tracing the velvet smooth thrust of his erection.

'I thought it was best to let the dust settle—' But Jace gritted his teeth, knowing that he'd been craven when he had refused to admit that the baby announcement had knocked him for six, only he still did not feel up to the challenge of admitting that. Particularly not if Gigi might assume that he, who had once been rejected by his parents, was in some way now rejecting their child, because that was untrue.

'Never let the sun go down on a row,' she retorted in disagreement, silky, streaky strands of hair brushing his thighs as she bent her head to tease him with her mouth.

'I believed I was making the wisest move—'

'Well, when would you ever tell me or yourself that you'd been stupid?' Gigi jibed as his hips arched up to her and an almost soundless groan was dredged from him.

'Can't take that amount of torment, not right now,' Jace growled, suddenly hauling her up to him and rolling over to settle between her spread thighs. As she closed her legs round him in instant welcome, he tilted her back and surged against her tender cleft, discovering the warm wet heat of her and sending a current of electrifying anticipation through her quivering length.

'Exquisite…' He pushed inside her with a hushed groan of appreciation and angled his lean hips. Pleasure shimmied through her in heady waves as he stretched her inner walls with delicious force and friction. She flung her head back, her heart rate escalating as he began to move. The excitement began to climb, perspiration dampening her skin as she gripped him. A blinding wave of hunger powered her as he hammered into her at speed and the wild soaring excitement took over for endless moments. The intensity he induced sent her into an explosive, gasping climax that wrung her out.

'Sublime,' Jace pronounced, holding her close, his heart still racing against hers in the languorous aftermath. 'But for the record, I don't make stupid decisions—'

'Talk about it in the morning,' she whispered in cowardice, burying her hot face in the hollow of his shoulder and heaving an exhausted sigh.

'I was about to suggest a shower—'

'You get frisky in showers...wake me up at dawn,' she mumbled, feeling inexplicably secure and happy again.

In the morning, she wakened alone, however, which left her free to wash and dry her hair and slip into a blue and white sundress in honour of the scorching sunlight arrowing through the windows. Barefoot, she padded out to the outdoor terrace she had noted in the moonlight the night before and only then registered that it led out onto a clifftop platform suspended over the sea and the beach far below. There, Jace awaited her, a colourful breakfast already laid out in readiness for her.

'Wow,' she breathed in respect of that spectacular view of the Indian ocean, sunlight glimmering over turquoise seas that washed the edge of the long white beach.

'This is why the parents bought this place, plus Evander likes to golf and Marcus likes to sunbathe. I, however, simply want to spend time with you,' Jace murmured, closing a hand over hers as she dropped down beside him on the comfortable upholstered built-in seating.

'Where are the staff?'

'Maryam comes in at mealtimes only, unless we request otherwise—'

'And your security team?'

'In the housing at the foot of the lane. You should eat. We're leaving soon.'

Gigi poured her tea, sipped it, savouring the refreshment, grateful that the occasional bouts of nausea she suffered were still controllable as long as she ate little and often. 'Are we going to talk about stuff?' she asked stiffly, mentally bracing herself for that challenge.

'No. We're going to settle into being married first… and your objective is to learn how to relax and *rely* on me. You've lived through two frantic weeks of wedding excitement and naturally you're tired. Let me do the worrying for once,' he urged lazily, his thumb stroking the sensitive inside of her wrist.

Gigi breathed in deep. She did not rely on a man, never had, never would. She liked everything deep and hidden unearthed and out on the surface for her perusal. She wanted to know exactly how Jace felt about being married to her and a prospective father. But, being Jace, he had cut her off at the knees before she even gave her opinion. And what he wanted was crystal clear. There was to be no talking, no honest exchange of feelings and views or, indeed, any discussion about where their convenient marriage was even expected to go.

Her teeth gritted together. She cast him a glance that involuntarily lingered. In a white linen shirt, emerald eyes glittering, blue-black hair catching the sunlight, his lean dark classic features were breathtakingly handsome. Add in all the rest of him, the perfect physique, the little devil of teasing amusement that often danced in those eyes and the undeniable charisma he emanated, and he was a major challenge.

He was telling her to act like one half of a couple and she didn't know how to do that, didn't know how she was supposed to give him her trust when she already loved him. After all, give him trust as well and he would *own* her, hurt her with his indifference, his rich-boy polished wit and tantalising bedroom expertise.

'I'd just like to talk to you…in private,' Gigi told Achilleus Georgiou almost a month later.

'On the yacht?' Achilleus asked. 'Why not come to the restaurant and we'll sit in the courtyard and chat?'

'The yacht will be more private. Tomorrow? Around eleven? It's my day off.' Cramming her phone back into the pocket of her lab coat, Gigi made that decision for the older man and heaved a sigh. It was time to return her father's letters to him and hopefully that would finally open a line of communication between them and encourage her father to be honest.

It was the end of her second week back to work. Oman had been an amazing experience. They had travelled into the dramatic Jebel Akhdar mountains, dined on the edge of a magnificent canyon with the rugged mountains all around them, toured ancient tombs and forts and wandered through a deserted ghost village. Understanding her fascination and the reality that she had not travelled anything like as widely as he had done, Jace had promised to bring her back in the spring when the damask roses would be in bloom and the air would be full of their perfume. She had laughed and reminded him that she would be too close to having their child to fly anywhere.

There had also been lazy days on the beach with intimate dinners on the terrace. They had explored the walled old city of Muscat, sampled spices in the souqs and admired the sunlit ambience of the low white buildings with their ornamental Portuguese-influenced balconies. For the first time in her life that she could remember, she had totally relaxed, allowing Jace to take care of everything. And, given that freedom to manoeuvre and plan and organise, Jace had been in his element.

Their dinner had been served one evening by a campfire in the Wahiba Sands and it had been a magical experience. She had even tried to sleep under the stars before grumpily surrendering to her aches and pains and clambering back into the top-of-the-line air-conditioned RV Jace had hired for the occasion. He had laughed but she had still enjoyed the splendid tawny sunset that had rewarded their stay over breakfast. Jace had ruled out a camel ride or even a trip in an SUV through the dunes as too great a hazard for her in her pregnant state. His endless caution on her behalf had annoyed her once or twice because throughout their honeymoon he had treated her as though she were a fragile piece of china liable to break if allowed to overtax herself. Fortunately for her, he had not carried that approach into the bedroom with her. It was mortifying too that she had allowed Jace to ignore the issues between them but thinking about them only upset her.

A dreamy smile and a flush on her cheeks as she recalled that powerful passion of his, Gigi took her time tidying up her paperwork while Ioanna cast her knowing looks.

'What?' she finally paused to ask the nurse.

'You are just so in love with your husband…it's touching,' she opined with an apologetic smile. 'I don't know how you bring yourself to leave him every day.'

'Because he's working too,' Gigi pointed out wryly.

And had she got in the way of *his* work, he'd have driven her up the wall with his limitless energy. Round the clock, she had decided, Jace was best kept busy and occupied. If only she had that luxury, she reflected ruefully. No, she reminded herself dully, from now on, thanks to her pregnant state, she would only be working part-time hours. The arrangements were already in place.

Her new obstetrician in Rhodes town, a grounded, sensible woman, had warned her the week before that her blood pressure was dangerously high. She was to have less work and stress, more rest and daily walking and swimming exercise to try and bring the reading down to a safer level and lower the risks for her child and herself. All of a sudden, Gigi's pregnancy was dominating her life.

Only that morning, Jace had accompanied her to her most recent medical appointment, and she had had an ultrasound that had revealed the gender of their child. She was having a little girl. The joy of that discovery had been laced with anxiety for Gigi because now she knew that she could not have blind confidence in her own health. Jace had been delighted.

'She'll take some looking after,' he had remarked

thoughtfully. 'She'll be the first heiress in the Diamandis family for several generations.'

Jace had made not one single comment when she was advised that only part-time work was viable for her until her blood pressure reduced. And if that didn't work, even more far-reaching changes of lifestyle would be required from her. Her soft mouth compressed and downcurved.

The dogs greeted her the instant she stepped off the launch because they sat down there awaiting her return every afternoon. Jace stepped out of the lift as she was halfway up the first flight of stairs. 'Lift...' he stressed gently. 'You're supposed to be taking it easy and four flights of stairs isn't easy.'

With bad grace and feeling rather like a dog who had pulled rudely on her leash only to be yanked back into line, Gigi retreated back down the stairs and joined him in the lift. As always, he looked amazing, black curls tousled by the breeze, compelling green eyes lighting up his lean, bronzed face, raw energy still emanating from him even after hours of business calls and meetings. And Gigi? She felt utterly drained, her hair descending untidily round her cheeks from her once elegant updo, her face bare of make-up, mud on her jeans from an over-enthusiastic cocker spaniel.

'Time for a drink,' Jace announced, shepherding her into the main saloon, where she flopped down like a legless puppet into a comfortable armchair. 'You're exhausted.'

'Was that a criticism?' Gigi hated the sharp edge that had entered her voice.

'An observation.' Jace slotted a moisture-beaded

juice drink into her hand and settled a couple of glossy brochures down on the occasional table beside her.

'What are these?'

'Houses for sale on Rhodes. There's another one available but it's not officially on the market yet,' he volunteered. 'We need a home base other than the yacht.'

In silence, Gigi leafed through the small selection of very large, luxury homes on offer. 'We're perfectly comfortable here—'

'*Sea King* isn't a long-term solution. Not for us or the animals. And I assume you want to remain close to your father and brothers and the shelter, of course. We can continue to spend weekends on Faros but it wouldn't be feasible to live there. It's too far to commute—'

Gigi breathed in deep. 'Is it worth going to the hassle of buying and furnishing a house on a permanent basis?' she heard herself ask and, indeed, the question almost leapt off her tongue and it sounded a little tart. 'I mean…how long will our marriage last?'

The instant she said it, she regretted it and a chill ran down her spine. Jace stilled and studied her in apparent astonishment. 'I haven't got a crystal ball but—'

'I'm sure that you could give me an estimate.' Gigi was wondering what devil had got into her or if her outspoken tongue was simply a horrible eruption of the insecurities she struggled with on a daily basis. After all, Jace had refused to address her right to know how he felt about her and their child. She had been fretting about that since before their wedding. It was time he answered some of her questions.

Jace's lean, hard-boned features were pale and taut.

He expelled his breath in a stark hiss. 'I've always hoped that you would at least stay with me until after our child is born but—'

Gigi rose immediately upright, marvelling that she could stand when she felt as though he had plunged a knife into her chest. 'Perfect, we don't need to be looking at houses, then!'

'Even if we *were* to separate, Gigi, you and our child will need a proper home to live in on the island,' Jace asserted flatly.

Squashed flat by the lowering awareness that he had already calculated the practicalities of them separating, Gigi walked out of the room without looking at him again. Of course, of course, why hadn't she guessed what Jace intended all along? A marriage to legitimise their child and see it born and then soon after they would part, still being civil and friendly to co-parent. All of a sudden everything made so much more sense.

This had been his plan all along. This was why he had been willing to sacrifice his freedom, why he had been so impossibly delightful and soothing from the outset. Jace had always seen his escape on a not too far distant horizon. Anyone could contrive to make the best of a situation if it was only going to last for the duration of a single pregnancy. And, naturally, he hadn't wanted to make a point of saying that at the same time as he persuaded her to marry him. She suspected that he hadn't wanted his family to know that truth either.

Left alone, Jace downed two whiskies in record time. He had closed her out to keep his own emotions under control. He had withdrawn and she had noticed that he wasn't fully present or honest with her any more. Of course she had. How could he ever admit that he was terrified of losing her? Since the day she had married him, she had always had one foot out of the door.

And that was why he should not have mentioned the houses. Not when he knew that she was still agonising over having to accept working only part-time. Yet it was only for a few months. And how was he to straighten her out when she was supposed to be staying calm and resting as much as possible? He wasn't a miracle worker. Gigi seethed with emotion under her tranquil, collected surface but she didn't share her innermost worries with him…or trust him…or rely on him. So, what else wasn't new?

CHAPTER TEN

ACHILLEUS GEORGIOU SIPPED his coffee and studied his daughter with a frown. Her eyes were red-rimmed, her lovely face pale and strained, shadows suggesting a sleepless night. 'Tell me what's wrong,' he urged her, thoroughly disconcerting her with that personal question.

'There's nothing wrong,' Gigi hedged, even though she had barely slept the night before for fretting about losing Jace, losing her baby, losing Mo, losing *any* prospect of happiness. She had also fretted about her high blood pressure because now she had to doubt the healthy body she had once naively taken for granted. And then Jace, who had not come to bed with her because she had chosen to sleep with the dogs and the cat in the room next door, had greeted her at breakfast as though he had not a single care in the world. Furthermore, after learning that she was meeting with her father that morning, he had suggested that they lunch out later because she wasn't working. As if she were capable of enjoying a lunch out in the mood she was in!

'No, this is about something else,' she warned her father, lifting the bundle of letters from the bag she had stowed them in and extending them to the older man. 'I found them when I was cleaning out Mum's attic.'

Achilleus had stiffened and he went through the un-opened letters that spanned half a dozen years with frowning concentration. 'Did Nadine not even open them to read?' he muttered in dismay and astonishment.

'Apparently not...it's left me with questions I'd really like you to answer. What happened between you that she wouldn't even read your letters?'

'She said she would never forgive me if I left her and she kept her promise,' he acknowledged heavily. 'I need to start at the beginning. Katerina and I married as soon as we left school. We had the four boys, one after another, while I was building our first business. We hardly saw each other and ten years down the road she told me that she wanted a separation. I was devastated. At first, I didn't think she was serious. I moved in with my mother to give her some space to think but it didn't change anything. She went back to work and decided that she would be happier without me.'

Gigi had flushed with mortification because she had always doubted her mother's contention that her father had been separated from his wife when they met but now it seemed that that was true. Furthermore, it was disconcerting to learn that her father's marriage had broken down when they were both still young.

'Katerina and I lived apart for months and during that period I met Nadine. Your mother and I fell in love and planned to make a life with each other—'

'How long were you and my mother seeing each other for?' Gigi cut in. 'I always assumed you'd only spent a few days together.'

'No. After our first meeting, we met up several times in London and Athens before Nadine realised that she had conceived. We were together about six months before that happened. I planned to get a divorce and move to London to set up a business there...but I'm afraid that turned out to be very much a fantasy.' Achilleus winced in embarrassment at that memory. 'But I was thrilled when Nadine told me she had conceived because I've always loved children. And then, unfortunately for all of us, real life and misfortune stepped in and what I had with your mother fell apart.'

'What happened?'

His face shadowed. 'First, I did my sums. I didn't have enough money to provide for Katerina and the boys *and* start a new life in London. Your mother wanted to pay for everything but I refused to live off her and she couldn't accept that. We began to argue—'

'She could only see her own point of view—'

'And she couldn't compromise about anything. She wasn't prepared to even consider moving jobs even after she was offered lucrative work in Athens,' he confided heavily. 'And then everything else went wrong all at once. Katerina got breast cancer. She didn't tell me... my mother told me. I couldn't leave Katerina alone to deal with the boys while she was undergoing chemotherapy. There were problems with me trying to manage the business long distance as well. I came home because I *had* to. Understandably your mother was furious. She felt betrayed. We were a couple and I was leaving her to come back here to support my estranged wife—'

Gigi frowned. 'But your kids were still your responsibility.'

'But so were *you*—although at that stage you hadn't even been born. Nadine swore that if I returned to

Rhodes, I would never be allowed contact with you. And that's basically the whole story. Your mother ignored my letters and returned any child support money I sent. But I still can't believe that she didn't even read my stupid letters!'

'I'm sorry it ended like that. I'm sorry that you tried to have a relationship with me but she wouldn't allow it—'

'I could've visited, not often but enough that you would have known me as your father!' Achilleus argued plaintively.

Gigi leant forward and grasped his hand to squeeze it with sympathy because he had ditched his pride to tell her the whole story. 'It means so much to me that you *tried* to have a relationship with me,' she confessed. 'Why didn't you tell me all this when I first arrived on Rhodes?'

'It was so messy, and nothing can change the fact that I *did* let your mother down and she was entitled to be bitter and unforgiving,' he said heavily, guilt hanging over him like a dark cloud.

'You owed your first loyalty to the children you already had, and you had to support them as well. Mum didn't neglect me. She wasn't the most affectionate of mothers, but she did the job,' Gigi contended.

Tears shimmered in the older man's eyes and he looked hurriedly away before vaulting upright and taking an uncoordinated walk round the room. 'I would have loved you very much if she'd given me the opportunity.'

'I believe that.' And Gigi did. 'I gather that you and Katerina found your way back to each other.'

'Yes. Her illness made us both grow up fast and we grew together. It was hard for her to accept you when you arrived on the island. She assumed that you would hate her because I'd reconciled with her and that made her feel uncomfortable.'

Gigi forced a smile. 'She needn't worry. My mother's past isn't my present.'

But as her father was leaving, she did question her own final statement. In truth her mother's past and conditioning had always influenced her life. Nadine's bitterness and distrust of men had given Gigi toxic expectations of the opposite sex and had made her afraid of ever trusting a man or depending on one. Involuntarily, she had brought that baggage into her relationship with Jace, judging him before he even spoke, always making assumptions, never giving him the benefit of the doubt, invariably assuming the worst. She was in a troubled mood of reflection when she joined him for lunch.

'Where are we going?' she asked.

'It's a surprise.'

'Do you think I'm in the right mood for a surprise?' she muttered tightly.

'No, but you *need* one to lighten up…and we need to talk,' Jace decreed, steadying her to step into the launch with the dogs.

Her heart sank. What she had forced him into admitting the night before had made it impossible for them to continue breezing along as though they were any other newly married couple. Putting an end date on a marriage made a nonsense of that marriage being a normal one. She had brought her mother's bone-deep pessimism into her relationship with Jace and he fully recognised the fact. It shamed her to accept that she hadn't had the maturity to think for herself, hadn't once questioned her low expectations of him or compared his actual behaviour to her damaging convictions.

The limousine pulled off the coastal road into a leafy lane. Laced branches created a tunnel effect above them. 'Where on earth are we?' Gigi demanded.

'Wait and see,' Jace urged as the car pulled up outside a big sprawling cream house and he sprang out, letting the dogs run free as well.

'Have we met the owners?'

'They're not here. They've already moved to Corfu to be near their daughter.'

'So, what are we doing here?'

'We're having a picnic lunch,' Jace told her cheerfully. 'Indoors. It's not really warm enough to eat outside.'

Withdrawing a key from his pocket, he herded her to the front door.

'I've never had an indoor picnic,' she confided.

'You haven't lived,' Jace teased.

But she could see that he was nervous. Probably about the necessity of them talking and exchanging damaging bouts of honesty. Such as he fancied the socks off her, couldn't keep his hands off her but didn't want to be married to her for ever. Fair enough. No, it wasn't fair enough, another voice said inside her. It was blasted unfair, after he had tempted her into falling in love with him.

Jace led her into a cosy entrance hall and she shivered even though she was only cold on the inside, cold with fear about what confessions they were about to exchange. 'So, talk,' she urged him with helpless impatience, not wanting to wait for the axe to fall.

Jace held up a silencing hand. 'We eat first.'

He thrust open a door into a spacious room packed with comfy seating. A tiled Scandinavian stove emanated heat in one corner. The windows overlooked more trees that parted to frame a view of the sea. An elaborate picnic basket awaited them on the table and he opened it to set out plates and food and drinks.

Self-conscious as always, her mind in turmoil, Gigi ate several tiny snacks, prepared by their chef, and then embarked on a quiche. A sandwich in one hand, she paced the floor. 'That's a fabulous view,' she remarked.

'Do you want to tour the rest of the house?'

'We might as well,' she conceded as he drained his coffee cup and set it down to vault upright.

'Is this the house that isn't officially on the market yet?' she asked.

'Yes. It belongs to friends of Yaya's. If we like it, we can move in whenever we like and spend the winter here before we make a decision,' Jace told her.

Gigi strolled round, noting the spacious reception areas, seeing where updating would be required in utility areas. There was an indoor pool and a gym in the basement. She slowly climbed the stairs to find that there were plenty of bedrooms and a fabulous roof terrace, which overlooked the beach and the water.

'The house comes with several acres and it's very private—'

'It's a little big for one couple and a baby,' she remarked awkwardly.

Jace shrugged, striving to play it cool. 'But there might be more than one baby and then we'd be glad of the space,' he dared.

'I beg your pardon?' Gigi almost whispered. 'I thought you only wanted to stay with me until our daughter was born.'

'No, that is what I assumed you might decide when we first married but it was never *my* plan. I want to keep you until we're both old and grey, so room for more children in a house seems only sensible,' Jace countered steadily.

Gigi blinked rapidly, convinced she had imagined that statement.

'Of course, you're now about to come up with forty reasons why what I just said can't be true. But listen to *me* instead,' Jace suggested, hands closing over her arms to direct her to a seat in the corner of a big bedroom and gently push her down on it. He squatted down in front of her and gripped her hands in his. 'I'm sorry I checked out emotionally when we found out about the baby. I *was* in shock, but I wasn't willing to share that with you. I thought it would make you feel worse, so I attempted to focus on only the practical things, only that seems to have rebounded on me. I could feel that I was losing you…'

Suddenly she had the guy she loved back and he was finally talking to her again about what really mattered. She stroked the back of his hands with loving fingers.

Jace breathed in deep. 'I fell for you almost the same moment I met you, although it took me weeks to realise it. I don't know why I fell for you, so there's no point asking me why. Obviously, I was strongly attracted to

you, but I love your personality even more. Your loyalty, your intelligence, your fondness for animals, your
kindness, your warmth. I'm insanely in love with you
and I can't face my life without you in it. Before you,
it was empty, directionless, boring—'

'Jace…?' she whispered shakily, looking dizzily at
him. 'Are you really saying this stuff?'

'Are you finally listening?'

'Of course I'm listening.'

'Getting you to the church felt like trying to catch
a tiger by the tail and stick it in a cage. I wasn't at all
sure I could persuade you to stay with me, but I'd have
said anything to get that wedding ring on your finger.
I mentioned the inheritance issue because it was practical, and you are always *very* practical. I didn't want
to risk upsetting you by telling you that I felt more for
you than you did for me. I didn't want you telling me
that I was deluded or crazy to develop such strong feelings for you so quickly. So, I kept quiet because I was
afraid of frightening you off—'

'I'm not going anywhere…you couldn't frighten me
off,' Gigi told him dreamily. 'I'm mad about you as well
and that has been such a worry because I had no idea
at all you felt the same way. I just assumed you were
being charming and nice because I was pregnant—'

Gorgeous green eyes collided with hers. 'You love
me? Then why did you make me freak out last night
by asking me how long you can expect this marriage
to last? That was horrible!' he exclaimed with a look of
strong reproof. 'I want you with me for ever and ever
and you don't get time off for good behaviour or time

to think about how you feel about me…you're *stuck* with me! I need to be with you—'

'I think I would quite like being stuck with you for eternity,' Gigi admitted with a growing smile of happiness and the first sense of real relaxation she had experienced in months. It was a relaxation of tension, of constant worry and insecurity. The prospect of a real future with Jace filled her with pure, unalloyed joy.

Jace tugged her upright into the circle of his strong arms. 'Eternity mightn't be long enough, *glykia mou*. I'm fully committed and passionate about our marriage. And yet you fuss endlessly about all the small stuff. Like taking time off work when you'll only be restricted for a few months. I'll live anywhere in the world that you want…all I want is you and our daughter and I want you to be happy with me. You make me happy. It's simple enough.'

Gigi gazed up at him in growing wonder. 'I'm sorry I got so caught up in my work that I didn't realise what I was doing to you. Sadly, there wasn't anything but work in my life until you came along…and that was a major change for me. It made me vulnerable because I wasn't used to feeling what you make me feel. I've been worrying so much. I couldn't sleep last night—'

'Do you think I slept? You even took my dog with you,' Jace pointed out in reproof.

Gigi reddened and wrapped both arms round his neck. 'Only because he knows I'll let him into bed and you won't.'

'No dogs in our bed. That's an unbreakable rule,' Jace decreed.

Gigi pouted. 'I was going to tell you how much I loved you until you said that,' she teased.

'Not falling for it,' Jace warned, claiming a passionate kiss from her readily parted lips, edging her towards the bed.

'We can't…this isn't our house!' she exclaimed in dismay.

'We're about to become tenants. No reason we can't check out the bed. I mean, you do like this place, don't you?'

'Space for the dogs and us and our baby, what do you think? I like having the sea right on the doorstep,' she confided abstractedly, gazing up at him in slight amazement. 'You love me this much that you're happy to go the domestic route and lose your freedom?'

'Ecstatic. You're everything I didn't know I needed and my day looks a lot brighter with you in it,' he confided, spreading her across the bed, inching off her sweater by covert inches while kissing her, lean hands smoothing down over her slight frame possessively.

'Why did you tell your family I was pregnant before the wedding?' she queried.

'I was happy about it and I couldn't share that with you because you were freaking out. I was surprised by my own reaction. I realised that I was the guy who *wanted* to trap you with his child and it embarrassed me,' Jace admitted, gently tugging her out of her skirt. 'I don't think I could have hung onto you if I hadn't got you pregnant. I didn't think you were that struck with me. You were too suspicious of me. I wanted more from you from the start and I told myself all sorts of things before I realised that I loved you…and then it all seemed so simple.'

He made slow, careful love to her, gazing down at her with tender green eyes, and her heart felt as though it were swelling inside her chest. Happiness filled her to overflowing in the aftermath when he told her again how much he loved her.

'I fell for you the first night we had dinner…gosh, I was such a pushover!' she groaned in mortification.

'You were a total party pooper who went home and left me lying awake half the night fantasising about you,' he contradicted.

Gigi brightened and laughed. 'Serves you right. Oh, I have to tell you about my father…'

Jace listened, frowning several times. 'Your mother was hard on him. As I see it, he didn't have much choice.'

He talked about future plans for the house, one hand possessively splayed across the slight swell of her stomach.

Gigi snuggled close and listened. 'That unbreakable rule you mentioned about the dogs—'

'Not in the bed unless you want us to end up with a bed the size of Noah's Ark,' he quipped. 'You'll bring more dogs home in the future. You know you will. We'll make them comfy somewhere outside our bedroom… OK?'

'A Noah's Ark filled with dogs kind of sounds cosy to me,' she admitted drowsily.

'But we will have children as well,' he reminded her gently. 'And they might want to share our bed too. Go to sleep, Gigi…'

EPILOGUE

Five years later

AS SHE CAME downstairs, careful in her high heels, Gigi smoothed down her dress. It was red, silky and it clung to every curve. It was right up Jace's street while also being suitably festive.

It was Christmas Eve, but their children still had to wait a week for the seasonal bounty of gifts. In Greece, gifts were exchanged on the first of January, St Basil's Day. Lyra, their four-year-old, was already so pumped up on Christmas cheer that another week of waiting for Ayios Vassileios might send her shooting for the stars. In respect of Gigi's British heritage, one gift would be given to the children on Christmas Day.

Nikolaos, their two-year-old, was trying to scale the giant stuffed reindeer by the front door, his pyjamas at comical half-mast as he sidled past the table with the floral arrangement Electra had sent them.

'Nikolaos!' Gigi intervened before he could send the giant vase of flowers flying.

Lyra grabbed him, scolding him firmly.

'It's time for bed,' Gigi told her children.

Actually, getting them into bed was like trying to

herd cats up the stairs and into their respective rooms. Lyra chattered up a storm while grabbing the bedtime story she wanted and sliding below her duvet. She had inherited Jace's black curls and Gigi's blue eyes, his height and big personality laced with her mother's intelligence. Gigi's blood pressure had steadily dropped down to normal during her daughter's pregnancy and Lyra had been a textbook delivery.

Evander and Marcus swore that Nikolaos was Jace reborn. He hurtled headfirst into everything. He was a fearless, lively bundle of restless energy, the child most likely to be found clinging with one hand to a cliff edge while still laughing. But the reverse side of that extrovert nature was a current of fierce affection. As his mother sank down on the side of his bed, her son wrapped both arms round her and squeezed hard before wriggling down under his duvet. A paw appeared on the other side of his bed and, seconds later, a little black and white head nosed out. It was Houdini.

The little terrier had come into the household shortly after Hoppy had passed away, so at least they had still had a pet when Mo followed Hoppy at the age of nine, which wasn't a bad age for a wolfhound to reach. After Mo had come Roxy, a gangly, clumsy wolfhound puppy, who was so laid-back she was horizontal most of the time. Gigi tucked her sleeping son in and carefully scooped up Houdini to take him out to the landing. Tilly, strolling along towards them, pounced in front of the terrier and hissed, prompting Houdini to make a break for the stairs.

Humphrey and Snowy still lived on Faros and Humphrey even had a lady companion but Electra's fond hopes of the pitter patter of little tortoise feet had yet to be realised. Electra had had a minor stroke the previous winter and they visited her on the island most weekends. They had bought the house in which Jace had initially told Gigi that he loved her and, after that first deliriously happy winter there as a couple, they had updated where necessary and the house had slowly but surely turned into their much-loved home. Even with staff, it remained a somewhat messy, chaotic household that often took in rescue animals for a little while, particularly when the shelter was oversubscribed. Evander would look pained while he stayed over Christmas and he would earnestly suggest new and better ways of doing things. And they would listen politely and then go on much as before. Marcus, however, could sit in the middle of a hurricane without turning a hair.

Gigi still worked full-time at the shelter although she also took long breaks to enable them to have holidays. And they had ranged far and wide over the years, satisfying Gigi's desire to explore foreign climes, while also embracing all the time they could to enjoy simply being a couple. She saw her father most weeks and had since attended two of her brothers' weddings, the christenings of their children and their birthday parties. She was now fully accepted as a member of the Georgiou family circle and enjoyed a comfortable relationship with her stepmother, Katerina.

Loving Jace had brought Gigi more happiness than she had ever dreamt might be hers. She had her career, her children, but most of all, she had Jace and, although she would never admit it to him, her world revolved around him. He loved her and she felt that love every day, even when he wasn't able to be with her. He would phone or he would leave a note somewhere for her to find or send a gift.

Now as she picked her way down the stairs and heard the front door open, her blue eyes brightened. Jace came through the front door and she surged across the hall to greet him. 'Happy Birthday!' she carolled happily. 'The kids are in bed…and dinner is ready.'

Jace held her back from him to better enjoy what she was wearing. 'Like the dress…and the shoes,' he confided. 'Very sexy.'

Roxy sloped up to his side in her languid way and bumped his knee with her head before sprawling down at their feet in an untidy heap to go back to sleep.

'That's as much physical effort as she's made all day,' Gigi told him ruefully.

Houdini bounced out of a doorway and hurled himself at Jace, driven by frantic terrier energy. Gigi tugged Jace past the Christmas tree festooned in lights towards the dining room for their meal.

Before she could take a seat, Jace pulled her to him and said, 'I was expecting to walk into a party here. How the hell did you dissuade Evander and Marcus from throwing the usual party open house?'

Gigi winced. 'I didn't. You're still getting your big party tomorrow night on Faros…a whole family affair,' she told him guiltily. 'Tonight is just for us.'

'Terrific planning, *koukla mou*.' Jace ran a caressing hand across the pouting curve of her breasts and she quivered. 'Can we take a rain check on the food?'

'Er...'

'Of course we can,' Jace decided, bending down momentarily to sweep her up into his arms and head for the stairs. 'Am I allowed to ask what my present is?'

'Don't be impatient,' she told him with a secretive little smile as he settled her down on the big bed.

'You look so beautiful in that dress,' he said thickly, lean fingers tracing the pouting curve of her lips. 'You wore red just for me.'

'If you like to think so, Mr Diamandis.' But it was absolutely true. Red was a colour that she always thought wore her rather than the other way round. Red attracted attention and she never liked that much, unless it was Jace's attention.

He leant over her and crushed her parted lips beneath his, his tongue delving deep, and a little shiver of excitement gripped her. 'I love you,' he breathed huskily. 'I'm saying it now in case I forget to say it later.'

'You won't,' she told him confidently, lifting her arms to allow him to lift the dress over her head.

'And my present?' he teased.

'I'm pregnant, just like you requested three months ago,' she told him quietly. 'And that is the only present you're getting from me. Our third and final children will be born in the summer—'

'Child*ren*?' he queried.

Gigi looked smug. 'Always be careful what you ask for. We're having twins, two little boys to keep Nikolaos on his toes,' she told him.

With a huge grin, Jace wrapped both arms round her and hugged her tight. 'Who is the most wonderful woman in the world? Best birthday and Christmas present *ever*!'

'If I didn't love you so much, I wouldn't have agreed.' The bedroom door shook a little as a small foot kicked it and a wail sounded. 'Sounds like Nikolaos is looking for his father,' Gigi teased.

She lay back on the bed like a shameless woman in her red lace lingerie and slowly relaxed while Jace cuddled his son and talked him back into bed. He reappeared in the doorway and she smiled at him, totally relaxed. He was gorgeous and he still took her breath away and made her tingle in secret places when she looked at him. He loved children. He had learned to hug. He never failed to make her feel good about herself. As he returned to her, she heard the pitter patter of Houdini's little paws head for their son's room and the nice cosy bed he had in there. Yes, Jace still wouldn't have dogs in the bed but what he didn't know didn't hurt him.

Opening her arms to welcome Jace back, she was still smiling, a woman who had found love when nobody, least of all her, had expected to find it, with the male who had turned out to be the guy of her wildest dreams.

* * * * *

PREGNANT ENEMY, CHRISTMAS BRIDE

MAISEY YATES

MILLS & BOON

To mad sparks of creativity
that take us unexpected places.

This book was the greatest gift to me
right when I needed it.

CHAPTER ONE

I CLUTCHED THE strap of my shoulder bag as I waited for the elevator to reach its floor. I was far more nervous than I should be, given that I was prepared—if not overly prepared—for this.

The adrenaline in my veins was more energizing than any hit of caffeine, more electrifying than any shot of whiskey. It flooded me now, making it impossible for me to stand still. Thankfully the elevator was empty, so I had no audience as I bounced on the balls of my feet as I waited. And waited.

I would never dare show even a hint of nerves, excitement or any other emotion in a public space, where the media might take it and spin it out of control.

Florence Clare is a Head Case! We Knew it All Along!
Clare Heir Succumbs to Feelings!
Are Women Too Emotional To Be CEOs?

I would rather die.

Okay, not *die*. But I'd hate it.

The floor number illuminated on the panel. A sound chimed. I checked my reflection.

Not a hair out of place. I could never risk being anything like a human woman. I had to be CEO Barbie. Just pretty enough, just soft enough, just tough enough.

It wasn't fair, but nothing in life was. I was privileged and I knew it. So I wasn't going to waste time whining about the inequality I experienced when there were other women in much more dire straits than I. All I could do was try to change it by succeeding.

This was for a NASA contract. The press would be there.

And they were expecting a show.

I was ready to give them one.

I stepped out of the elevator and swept down the hall. I knew I looked flawless in my black suit, perfectly tailored, perfectly pressed. Not a wrinkle to be seen.

I'd better. I spent the whole drive from the hotel lying down flat in the back seat to keep everything from creasing. I'd practically rolled out of the car in the private garage my driver had pulled into.

For the last five years every move I'd made had been so high profile I couldn't even risk a sneeze at the wrong moment. Even that could be spun into a story about me. A badly timed photo could result in a headline about me crying or yelling at someone.

A photo taken at midsneeze painted a thousand lying words.

I knew this for certain.

Ever since my father had died and I'd taken over Edison Inc, I'd been under a microscope. But I'd trained for it my whole life.

And the truth was, I loved it.

All right, not every part of it. But enough of it.

I liked to imagine this was what it must be like to be a bullfighter. To be a boxer. An MMA fighter, even. To get high on adrenaline, anticipating the battle. To be en-thralled by the roar of the crowd.

To crave the fight. The impact of your fist hitting your opponent.

Oh, yes, I craved that most of all.

I moved closer to the doors of the conference room.

My heart surged. I smiled. Flawless, like I had to be. Invulnerable.

That was the image I had to portray. As a woman, possessing beauty was useful. But beauty was a mask that could be put on in the morning and taken off with makeup remover. Beauty was in the way clothing was tailored.

The real trick, the real necessity, was to never, ever show them a weakness.

As a woman who ran one of the single largest con-glomerates in the world, I had to be feminine, beauti-ful, and give the idea that I might be soft. I also had to essentially be a man in lipstick. I could never have real, female attributes. I couldn't have a pimple lest someone guess I was nearing my period, nor could I ever have an emotional outburst for the same reason. I had to be a woman in name and appearance only or my compe-tence would be called into question.

I never allowed that to happen.

Two men flanking the doors moved to open them as I drew near, and time stood still.

This was the pause before the battle began to rage.

I would meet my enemy in that room for the first of a series of presentations where we tried to get the lu-crative NASA contracts based on the rocket technology our individual companies had cultivated.

The media seemed to think I might be upset to have to go up against him again.

In truth, I relished it.

I never wanted to fight below my weight class.

I might hate *him* with very nearly the whole of my being. But he was also the only man who was strong enough to make it war.

In business, war was the only way it was fun.

My foot crossed the threshold of the room and time returned to normal. Cameras were raised, my photo was taken. I turned my head, and there he was.

Hades Achelleos.

The devil himself.

He was dressed all in black, just as I was, his dark hair swept back from his forehead. He had a fallen angel face, so beautiful he was almost unnerving to look at— or so many in the media had written in prose bordering on purple, I thought.

It was true, his cheekbones were sharp, his jaw square. He was tall and muscular. All of the things considered conventionally attractive in a man.

I had first met him when he was seventeen and I was fourteen. A massive charity event we'd been dragged to by our fathers. Our fathers, Theseus Achelleos and Martin Clare, had hated each other. As much as they had loved to fight one another.

The rivalry between their companies was the stuff of corporate legend.

Both starting out with hotel chains, expanding to travel—cruise ships, airlines, energy. What one did, the other would follow and try to improve on. Until they'd arrived where they were now. Unquestionably at the top of the industry with their children at the helm. Carrying on both their legacies and the vicious, cut-throat rivalry they had so cherished.

I'd been prejudiced against him before the first meeting. He had, all the years since, made certain that I hated him not simply because of his legacy, but because of *everything* about him.

Arrogant.

Insufferable.

The actual god of hell.

"Hello, Miss Clare." He stepped forward and reached out his hand.

I shook it. As I'd done a thousand times before. "Mr. Achelleos."

The room was filled with scientists, engineers, media and investors. It was set up for a panel-style talk, which would make it something like a debate.

Excitement ignited in my blood. Hades and I both made our way to the front of the room and took our seats. I looked at him. My stomach churned. Even his profile was arrogant.

He looked at me out of the corner of his eye, and the glint there, the certainty, it made me want to fight him even harder.

We were introduced to the crowd by a moderator— the introduction a formality. Everyone knew who we were.

And then it was time.

"Edison Inc is in the perfect position to pioneer the next wave of space exploration. Our commercial space travel has been successful, with our next prototype indicating that it will be possible to increase the accessibility of space flights."

"All well and good," Hades said, cutting me off. "But does space need to be accessible to the masses, or does it need to remain the bastion of scientists? It isn't as though British tourists can go lay on the sands of Mars."

He infuriated me.

"That is not the intent of space travel, and I think you know that. Surely, Mr. Achelleos, you are not so out of touch that you believe education is the province of the überwealthy?"

"I don't believe that's what I said, Miss Clare, rather I am simply suggesting that, like the Great Barrier Reef and the Arctic, there is merit in keeping masses of humans from crawling all over something unspoiled like ants at a picnic."

I hated him for that. As much as his acidic words ignited a fire in me. A fire I loved. A fire I needed.

I sometimes wondered if it would be possible to function as well as I did if it weren't for the sheer hatred of him. The electric excitement of having a nemesis.

"Are you bringing something to the table, Mr. Achelleos, or are you simply here to insult what I've brought?"

He shifted, directing his focus to the audience. "I am not putting resources into the commercialization of space. Rather what Mercury is focusing on is creating spacecraft with the very highest standard of scientific instruments on board."

As if I hadn't thought that NASA was going to need scientific instruments. Which I said, though not like an indignant teenager. Even if that was how I felt. How he made me feel. Like all my emotions were just beneath the surface of my skin. Reckless, unwieldy, like they never otherwise were.

We went back and forth, each shot like a blow in the ring. The slice of a knife.

"Arrogance. The assumption that access is equal to loss is the very height of privilege."

"Idealism that science can't afford."

Left hook. Right hook.

"Idealism is part of space exploration, Hades."

Uppercut.

"And practicality is what prevents catastrophe, Florence."

Finally our hour had concluded. The room exploded with applause and flashes, and my vision blurred for a moment as my heart beat a wild cadence that left me feeling dizzy.

Everything slowed. I looked at him. He looked back.

Those black eyes were always fathomless.

I could hear my own heartbeat. For a moment I thought I could hear his.

Then everything sped up again.

"Miss Clare!" came the shout of a reporter. "If you don't win the contract with NASA, will that halt the space arm of Edison?"

I turned my full focus to the reporter. "Absolutely not. We're committed to staying on the cutting edge of what's happening in the world of travel. The groundbreaking science we've employed in our rocket program has led to things like longer commercial airline flights, faster airplanes. It is research that has resonance in other parts of the industry."

"Mr. Achelleos! If you get the contract what will that

mean for the Super Ship set to be unveiled in four years' time?"

Hades slashed his hand to the side as if he was cutting through vines in the jungle. "The funding for the Super Ship is entirely separate. We are equipped and have the resources to make multiple breakthroughs at once."

"I see that the ocean is not as sacred to you as space, Mr. Achelleos?" I asked.

"I don't see a press badge, Miss Clare." His eyes dipped to my breasts, as if he were searching for credentials. I ignored the way his dark gaze made my skin burn and my breasts feel heavy.

"I would like to ask you a question," I said, turning from Hades and to the reporter who had just spoken to us both. "Why is it you asked me what I'd do if I lost, and what he would do if he won? Does his gender make this a foregone conclusion for you?"

The reporter sputtered. "No, not at all, only…"

"Perhaps it was the quality of my performance," Hades said.

"Or perhaps what you have in your trousers," I said, icy.

He stared at me for a breath. Then another.

You know what I meant. I thought that, as if he could hear me.

I wasn't thinking about his… I was only saying it was a sexist line of questioning and Hades should well know it.

Questions came fast and frequent after that and we could barely get a breath. By the time it was done I was stratospheric. It was unlike anything else. Riding into battle to face Hades.

Iron sharpened iron. And we were both as inflexible as the hardest steel.

We rose from the table and shook hands again. I walked ahead of him down the aisle and got into the elevator. The doors closed behind me.

The silence was like a blanket, settling over me. Smothering me.

My ears buzzed. It was so jarring to be in the quiet, the stillness, after such a frenetic hour.

We wouldn't know about the contract until we had another few presentations. The next one wouldn't be public. I already had everything prepared.

The elevator reached the bottom floor and the doors opened. I walked out of the building and straight to the black car that was waiting for me.

I opened up my phone and checked the details. "The Tomlin."

Penthouse One.

The virtual key was already on my phone so I would be able to go straight up without stopping at the front desk. Good.

Traffic was hellish, but that was DC.

I opened up my compact and refreshed my red lipstick. I eyed my overnight bag, considering changing en route, rather than getting out of the car in what would now be a rumpled suit. But now with the meeting behind me, some of my edges had been dulled. I didn't want to wrestle with getting the suit off, especially not with the elaborate undergarments I had underneath. No thanks.

While the car crawled through traffic, I replayed the whole thing in my mind.

The way he'd looked when I'd gotten a shot in. The relish when he'd lobbed one back.

I felt my adrenaline start to peak again as the car pulled up to the historic building in Georgetown. Red brick with stark white windows.

I took my purse and my overnight bag and got out of the car, assuring the bellhops that I did not need assistance as I went inside then into another elevator. It only took a moment to get to the top level of the building—there were only twelve of them—and I stepped out and onto the glossy marble floor, making my way to the room all the way at the end of the hall and unlocking it via my phone.

It was gorgeous. The chaise lounge by the window was plush and perfect. I moved into the bedroom and saw a giant four-poster bed. I walked inside and dragged my fingertips along the velvet. Then I touched the glossy wood on the bed frame.

I heard a sound in the next room and paused.

I turned and walked back into the living room, just as the door was closing.

And there he was. Dressed all in black.

My heart leaped into my throat.

"Hades."

It was time for the real battle to begin.

CHAPTER TWO

"Traffic was a nightmare," he said, beginning to loosen his tie.

"I know."

And my adrenaline hit its peak.

Because this was what we'd been walking toward all day. This was the real show. The one no one else would see. The one no one else would ever know about.

Through the haze that was beginning to descend I did think to ask about practicalities. "The room is registered under…?"

"Neither of our names."

"And you…?"

"Came in the back."

Hades Achelleos was a man of aristocratic and noble blood. But he walked through staff-only entrances, fire exits and side doors in alleyways for this.

For me.

It would be tempting to take that personally. But I knew from experience that with Hades nothing was personal. Especially when it felt like it might burn me alive.

He was fire personified. He couldn't help it if he scalded everything he touched.

Sometimes I told myself, if I could go back to the

moment when I'd first ruined everything, ruined us, I would. That I would make a different choice that night.

Lose my virginity to a waiter or some random dude I met on the beach.

But in my heart I knew I wouldn't.

Because doing battle with him in a boardroom was a high. But this was everything.

He crossed the room, his movements silken, like a big cat stalking his prey. Prey would run, though. And I wasn't running.

When he closed the distance between us, the move was lightning fast, his lips crashing down on mine the moment he brought me up against his hard body.

Victory.

I had him under my spell as much as he had me under his, and so while I sometimes felt helpless, a junkie addicted to his brand of pleasure, I knew he was no better. And that sustained me.

We were the only two people on earth equally matched to each other. In business and in the bedroom.

He propelled me back against the wall, his hands rough on my curves as he tore at my clothes. My perfectly tailored suit that I'd been so careful not to crease. He wrenched it from my body and left it on the floor like it was nothing.

And revealed what I had on underneath. What I'd had on the whole time. The look on his face was feral. I hadn't changed into a dress in the back of the car because it had felt too fussy, but what I hadn't counted on was this moment. I was glad then that I hadn't changed. Because this way he knew.

"You were wearing this the whole time?"

A corseted top with lace cups that were completely see-through and a lace thong to match. Garters and stockings. The sort of thing he'd said he found too elaborate to be practical when all he wanted was to be inside me.

I knew Hades well enough to know that if I did not oppose him, it wouldn't be as thrilling. Sometimes I gave him what he wanted. Me. Bare beneath my clothes so that there was no waiting. And sometimes….

If it wasn't rough, it wasn't fun.

So sometimes I liked to goad him.

Push him. Find his limits.

I nodded slowly.

He gripped my chin and forced my face to tilt upward, to meet his gaze. "You are wicked, do you know that?"

"That's what you like."

He was kissing me again, and it was such a rush. Such a relief. To be trapped between the unforgiving wall and the hardness of his chest. To be in his arms.

It had been a month since we'd last done this. And every day since had been like torture. I'd thought of what we would do, and how it would be. What the room would look like. When I'd walked in and spotted the chaise, I'd known what he intended to do with that. He would put me on my hands and knees and use the shape of the lounge to make it easier for him to take me from behind.

Then the four-poster bed…oh, yes, I'd known his intent for that too.

I would likely spend the night tied to it.

But first…first this. This runaway freight train of desire. It had to be dealt with. It had to be satisfied. Hot. Quick. Fast.

I felt his own desperation matching my own.

He moved his hands down my body then up again to cup my breasts, his large palms rough as he held me, squeezed me, while he left a blazing hot trail of kisses down my neck.

I moved my own hands then, ripping at his tie, at his crisp white shirt. Shedding his layers as I shed mine. As he left me in nothing but the thong and stockings. His body was so hard, so muscular.

Over the years it had changed.

I could remember him at twenty-one. Ten years ago. Lean and lithe, and the most beautiful thing I'd ever seen. Obsessed with him. It had been embarrassing.

Back then I'd had the dirtiest sexual fantasies of any virgin alive because my fantasies had starred Hades. And even a virgin couldn't make him innocuous.

He was broader now. Bigger. Harder. His chest had dark hair on it that extended down to his perfect, ridged abdomen.

My eyes met his and the breath left my lungs. How did he still take my breath away? Maybe more now than he had then. Maybe more now than ever before.

He pushed his hands between my legs, where I knew he would find me wet and needy. How could I be anything else? There was no need for foreplay. We'd just had hours of it.

Watching him answer every question with ease. Using his sharp intellect to cut everyone around him, including me. I gave as good as I got, I always did. With everyone and everything, but most of all with Hades. Most of all with him.

I brought my hand down to cup his arousal and he growled, leaning in and biting my neck as he stroked me between my thighs. The pleasure was white-hot, so intense. More, better than it had ever been. Or maybe I just couldn't remember anything but right now.

One blunt finger found the entrance to my body, and as he moved it inside of me, he kept his eyes on mine.

"This is what you wanted the whole time, isn't it?" he asked, his voice rough. "When you were sitting there answering their questions all you really thought of was having me inside you."

"It's true," I said, my voice a thready whisper. "But you were thinking of being in me."

That earned me another growl, and then his hand went to my hair, gripped my bun, his fingers speared deep in my blond locks, as he tilted my head back and kissed me roughly.

My hair, which had been in perfect order, now ruined.

By him.

Praise be.

I arched my breasts into his chest, rough with dark hair, the sensation glorious against my sensitive nipples. He stroked between my legs, pressing a second finger inside me. Taking me to the edge before drawing me back, over and over again. I couldn't withstand this. It had been too long.

Too long since we'd touched. Too long since I'd felt him inside me.

"Hades." I said his name as a plea.

"You will get what you want when I am ready to give it to you," he growled.

I wrapped my hand around his stiff shaft, squeezing him, knowing I could push him to the brink too. I let him take charge because I liked it. Because I enjoyed the feeling of all that strength being used to drive me wild. Because I relished his size, his firm grip.

But I knew full well that if I needed to, I could command his body too.

So I did. Moving my hand from base to tip in slow rhythmic movements until I felt his body begin to shake. He moved away from me for just a moment, returning with a condom that he deftly rolled on before returning to me.

He shoved my panties to the side, then gripping his length, sliding into me slowly. He filled me, made me moan with need before he withdrew and slammed back in hard.

It was rough. It was punishing. It was perfect.

The crescendo to the day.

The release we needed.

We both raced for it, our breathing fractured. We didn't bother to keep quiet.

In the boardroom I had to wear a mask. Here… I was free. Even as he held me fast in his strong arms, I was free.

He whispered things against my mouth. Explicit things that made me shiver. And I cried out with every thrust.

When the wave crashed over us both, he growled and I couldn't hold back a sharp cry, the cascading pleasure almost too much to bear.

After the storm we stayed like that. With me pinned to the wall. Him breathing hard against the crook of my neck. Finally we separated.

"Have you eaten?" he asked.

"No."

"I'll order something."

I nodded and looked around the room at our discarded clothes. This was the landscape of our lives.

Different hotel rooms. The same wreckage.

We never went to each other's homes. The chance for espionage was too great. We didn't…have a relationship. I didn't trust him. I wanted him.

I had wanted him from the very first time I'd met him, with all the limited understanding a girl my age could have for such a thing.

I'd been predisposed to hating him, thanks to his association with his father. Thanks to my own father's feelings on the matter. But I'd seen him and it was like the whole world had slowed down. I'd been fourteen and totally untouched, of course, and yet I'd wanted to know what it was like to kiss him. My fantasies had been fevered then, but romantic more than sexual even as fervent as they were.

By the time I'd been eighteen to his twenty-one, I'd known exactly what I wanted. It was an interesting thing. Our fathers had been rivals and yet they found themselves in the same circles, which meant I'd found myself with Hades. Often.

Back then I'd thought it was love, of course. Even though I'd never had a real conversation with him that hadn't devolved into us being cruel to one another.

That, I'd thought, might be the start of love.

I'd been certain the rush of feeling, the way my heart pounded, had meant something more than animal lust. A virgin's perspective, I realized now. And a protective one at that. Since I'd never wanted to be my mother—who bed-hopped with frequency, and worse, was always engaged in public, messy relationships that ended in court cases and lawsuits for alimony, palimony and child support.

I never wanted to be that.

It was one reason I kept a solid barrier between my desire for Hades and my real life.

Sex, not a relationship.

Sex, not screaming in the streets.

Sex, not headlines.

I didn't let it affect my life outside these rooms. That was how I was different from her. It was why I was successful. A CEO and not a woman who spent her days on a fainting couch in my Lake Como estate paid for by my myriad exes.

Not that I was proud of this. This messy, screwed-up connection we had.

There were reasons we kept it secret beyond my mother being my own personal cautionary tale. Our rivalry was storied in the media. Our companies' competitors. Our personal entanglement would be seen as a conflict of interest, as collusion. It would be…disastrous. Especially for me.

Evidenced by the line of questioning at today's event. What would I do if I lost? What would he do if he won?

I would be absorbed by him. If ever there was a public merger of our…persons, he would be the one who existed, not me. I would be his partner. His lover. My achievements would become his, somehow. I couldn't have it.

Even now that our fathers were dead—or perhaps even more now that our fathers were dead—it had to be secret.

And secret it had been, from the moment I'd slipped him a note with a dry mouth and a pounding heart at a massive charity event on my eighteenth birthday, asking him to meet me in one of the suites.

I'd begged my father for my own room, even though his room had plenty of space. He hadn't questioned me. I wondered sometimes if he'd had an idea that I'd wanted privacy for nefarious reasons, but hadn't minded as long as it hadn't become an issue for him.

That was my dad. He didn't want to know more about me than he had to, because then he might have to contend with something complicated.

That was fine in many ways. I was always grateful to have one parent whose sex life I didn't have to read about in tabloids. I knew too much about my mother. Very little about my father.

Neither of them knew me.

But whatever my father's reasoning, I'd gotten my own suite. And my plan had been set in motion.

Hades had come, his dark eyes glittering. He hadn't trusted me fully even then.

But I'd been thinking about that moment for years. Every time we'd fought, or even looked at each other across a crowded room.

You know what I want.

Do I?

Hasn't it been obvious all this time?

I'd been so afraid he would reject me. Send me away. Instead, he'd undone the top button on his shirt.

I know what I want.

He'd said it as if it was a question. Making sure we were on the same page. We were. Oh, we definitely were.

I want the same thing. And it's my birthday.

I'd heard that first times were awkward. That they were painful, messy affairs. Yes, it had hurt right at first when he'd thrust inside me, but there had been nothing awkward about it at all. It had been fire. And so had we.

He had been annoyed with me, though, that I hadn't told him I was a virgin.

I'd tried not to be hurt by it, but I was eighteen and the man who'd just turned my world on its axis was acting something other than completely thrilled with me.

Who else would it have been?

He'd paused then, and looked into my eyes.

Ten years on, Hades looked very different, but that intensity in his dark gaze was the same. He looked at me now as he had then, and maybe that was why he kept me bound to him. Ten years after that first time.

So many times in between I couldn't count them.

A blur of different hotel rooms, different pieces of torn clothing, different curses, promises and dirty words.

"They're bringing you a cheeseburger, *agape*."

My heart hit my breastbone when he returned to me. Those words were hardly poetry, and yet they were.

Agape. He called me that. I knew it didn't mean he loved me. I knew it was just a thing he said because it was Greek and exotic and it turned me on.

"Thank you," I said. I realized it was now the time for

me to offer to get my own room. "I don't have to stay.
I can leave after dinner."

This was a game we played.

He shrugged one shoulder, then went to put his pants
on. To deal with the room service, I supposed. "It makes
no sense for you to go."

Which meant he wanted more sex. Well, so did I.

I was careful, though, with the blurred lines that existed between myself and Hades. Careful to keep them
as unblurred as possible.

"The debate went well," he said. He moved to the
bar and picked up a bottle of scotch, pouring a measure for himself.

"Is that on the table to discuss?" I asked.

"We were both there." Meaning there were no potential secrets being traded between us.

"It wasn't a debate, really," I said. "It was meant to
be an informative session with the two leading minds
in the industry. That's us."

"Mmm." He lifted his glass and drank it all, then
poured himself more.

"Are you worried?"

"Me?" He arched a dark brow.

"You're drinking a lot."

He frowned and I knew I'd crossed one of our invisible boundaries. Something like that, acknowledging
that over the past ten years of being his dirtiest, secretest
secret I might have acquired some intimate knowledge
of him, was strictly verboten.

Then it hit me.

"Oh. Hades. It's…it's your father's birthday."

"It isn't. Because he's dead."

"I'm sorry."

"Sorry for what?"

"I don't know, for not acknowledging it sooner?"

He cleared his throat. "And when, Florence, would you have done that? At the event where it was required that we tear strips off each other's flesh? Or here, when I tore strips off your clothes?"

"We don't have an audience here. You can calm down." I moved over to him and stole the glass out of his hand and was gratified when his dark eyes moved over my partially clothed body, the lust there apparent.

"There is nothing to say. He died as he lived. A difficult bastard. You know that."

I did. Our fathers had been brilliant, complex men. I loved my father and I wanted to make him proud, but I had felt the weight of not being the son he wanted keenly. The need to never, ever make a mistake—particularly one that might be perceived as a gender-based mistake—drove me. Like a demon.

It was one reason Hades had always felt both so dangerous and so desirable.

It was a horrible thing to think, but I'd grown up rich, and if I'd ever wanted for anything, it was my father's attention. The truth was, I'd been denied little. But Hades had been off-limits. So I'd never wanted anyone more.

I'd never wanted anyone else at all.

It was his deepest secret, but mine too. If my father had ever known...

Our fathers' rivalry had not been friendly. Not even close. They'd hated each other. I wanted to hate Hades. Part of me did. For all the things he made me feel. But never quite all of me. He drove me insane. I wanted to punch him sometimes. But... I wanted him.

That first time it had been like we were inventing sex. We'd had a four-day event where we were turned loose. We'd had each other everywhere we could find privacy, in every position. I'd gone from novice to experienced very, very quickly, with his hands, his mouth, his body to guide me.

After I'd gone home I'd done my best to accept that it would never happen again. That by the time I saw him next he would have a new woman on his arm and in his bed. And it would be for the best, I knew it. I tried to find a boyfriend. I went on several dates, all ended without so much as a kiss. I couldn't bring myself to want anyone but him.

And when we'd next crossed paths six months later at a scientific symposium in Geneva, I'd expected him to barely acknowledge me. Instead he'd taken me into the nearest single person bathroom and locked the door. He'd had me on a highly polished marble countertop and I'd had no regrets whatsoever about it.

It had taken two years for me to accept that this was how we were.

We were each other's vacation. Each other's outlet. Each other's rebellion. Whenever we met, whatever was happening in his life didn't seem to matter. If he had other girlfriends I didn't ask, didn't want to know. When our paths crossed, that was all there was.

Then his father had died abroad on holiday. I'd been certain that he wouldn't want anything to do with me after that. Now the company was his. Now my father was his direct competition. At the same time, I'd been taking on more and more work for Edison and had been responsible for all the speaking engagements my father would have taken at one time.

We were both speaking at a think tank for the up-and-coming executives in different travel and leisure companies.

We'd been waiting in the same green room, waiting to be introduced, and he'd reached out and grabbed my bun, tilted my head back and held me steady while he kissed me deep and hard. I'd been dizzy when we'd gone out.

I'd gone back to his room that night. And he had been like a violent storm. He hadn't been like that before. He'd been more like that than not since.

I knew the subject of his father was a tricky one. And we didn't cover tricky subjects. The death of his father felt so…random. He'd been a vital man, even if my father had hated him, I could recognize that. The news had said he'd suffered a medical event and it had seemed a shock to me that such a larger-than-life man could have been taken by something so…common.

Part of me wanted to talk to Hades about it. Comfort him. But that wasn't us. This was dark for him. I could sense the changes in his moods. Hades' moods were like tides. They shifted everything around them. Rearranged the landscape of anyone who got in their path.

It was lucky then, that I'd fashioned my personal landscape into a rock garden a long time ago.

Maybe it was the function of never being quite right for my mother or my father. Maybe it was the necessary result of figuring out how to be what I needed to be to take over Edison, while also being able to smile at the woman who had given birth to me over mimosa brunches. I had a core of steel to make sure that, even as I flexed on the outside, I didn't lose my shape within.

"Perhaps you should dress," Hades said, breaking through my memories. "Unless you are planning on tipping the delivery person."

"I did not plan to be anywhere near you when the food arrived. I intended to hide under the bed."

The idea that I would be seen with him was ridiculous. And he knew it.

"Of course."

I gathered myself and my clothes and went into the bedroom, where I did not dress.

A few moments later, Hades appeared in the doorway, shirtless, wearing only those dark trousers, holding a tray of food. His dark hair was a mess now, thanks to my hands. His body a perfect testament to the masculine form. Sculpted muscular shoulders; a deep, broad chest; ridged abs.

I could look at him forever and never get tired of it. But looking at him only made me hungry. And not for food.

"You will be upset if you let your food grow cold," he said, pushing away from the doorframe and walking into the room to set the tray at the foot of the bed.

"Who said I was going to let my food get cold?"

"Your expression was asking me for more."

I shrugged, because I knew it would irritate him. "I was looking at the hamburger."

"Of course you were."

It was strange. How I knew this man, but didn't know him. How I liked him sometimes, but didn't. How in some ways he was my longest, closest relationship.

Perhaps that spoke to a measure of loneliness in my life. Or maybe I was lonely in part because of him.

I had a friend, Sarah, who worked at Edison, though there was…

I couldn't help but feel it was my fault that I wasn't as close to Sarah as I wanted to be. Because nobody knew about Hades. Nobody. I had never told another living soul.

I had made up mystery lovers. Because there were a couple of times that Sarah and I had been on the same business trip, and I'd disappeared overnight. So what could be said? I had fashioned a lie that made me sound maybe more adventurous than I was. I acted as if it was never the same man.

Of course it was. Distressingly, always the same man.

And with this man, there was only ever one way it could be.

I had imagined conversations with Sarah about it in my head before.

"And what is your plan?" Fake Sarah would ask. "To be with him like this forever? Until you both die alone and are buried with this secret?"

"I was thinking so," I would reply.

And in my imagination, my friend did not tell me that was ridiculous and sad.

There was of course, always the possibility that I would meet a man who made me feel half of what Hades did, but who made up for that by filling the other half with care, attention, soft feelings. Romantic feelings.

Not this hard and sharp need that made us both lose control at every opportunity.

I didn't need that. Not forever. It was just that I had never even met a man who made me feel half.

I could give this up. Someday. But surely half wasn't too much to ask.

I stretched across the bed and grabbed my plate.

"When will you next be in the city?" I asked the question casually, because he often worked in Europe, but the time he spent in New York was one of the few times we were able to meet up when we weren't at a special event. And maybe, sometimes, I found excuses to go and work in the London office of Edison so that it was convenient for us to meet up there.

A couple of times a year. But that was all.

"I will be there for the next month," he said.

The words hit me low. Hard. A month?

I imagined that. Going to his temporary residence more nights than not. Gorging myself on him. We never had that kind of time.

It would dovetail into the Christmas season and everything would be decked out. It would almost be…romantic. But we weren't romantic.

Undoubtedly he would be busy, but our toxic trait—one of the many, really—was that we always made time for sex. Even if it was just an hour of time, we would find a way.

I'd once met him on the tarmac when we'd been in the same city for an hour while his plane refueled and he'd taken me in the luxury bedroom on board. Then I'd deplaned trying to look like we'd been having a meeting.

Our level of determination and opportunism combined with that length of time was… Dizzying.

"I'll call you," he said.

"You will not," I said. "You'll text me an address."

He chuckled. "You never know if the media is listening in on phone calls."

"Not mine. They know that I'm terribly boring."

I took a French fry off my plate and reclined against the pillow, giving him a full view of my naked body.

"Terribly boring," he repeated. There was something strange in his expression. I couldn't read it. But then, when it came to feelings, I could never quite read him.

"Finish eating," he said. "I want my dessert."

That expression I could read.

Familiar and thrilling. My darkest secret.

One I was happy to keep forever.

CHAPTER THREE

HE HADN'T TEXTED. It was fine.

That night in DC had been…

I still felt wrecked by it. I couldn't quite explain it.

Maybe it was the intensity I felt over the event. Over that undecided contract. Or maybe it was him. The fact that it had been his father's birthday.

Either way, there had been something different in the way we came together each time that night. We had used the chaise and the bed in the exact ways I'd known we would, but there had been a layer to it all that was…it was just different. I couldn't pinpoint it. When I'd woken up in the morning, he was gone.

Not unprecedented, but it had felt strange and wrong after everything.

I didn't know why.

It wasn't different.

It was us.

Maybe I was romanticizing.

That thought brought me up short as I pushed away from my desk and moved to the corner of the office. It was all windows, looking down over the Upper East Side. Beautiful.

I loved the city. Though, I loved London equally. I

had dual citizenship, courtesy of my mother, who was an alarmingly excessive London socialite who had children with billionaires as if it had been her retirement plan. She worked. But not in a corporate sense. Her job was to be beautiful, engaging, *decorative*.

She did it well.

Consequently, I had an older half brother who was an Italian count, and one who owned Andalusians in Spain. They probably knew Hades. Those sorts of men, brooding and preposterous, typically flocked together.

Maybe they entertained socialites on their yachts.

That was the thing that wealthy men could do, which I could never be caught dead doing.

I bit the inside of my cheek. I did not like to think about Hades with other women. But we never spoke about that. I didn't own his body, whatever I might feel.

And for me... There had never been anyone else.

But I knew that I had benefited greatly from previously established skill the first time we were together. He had been no virgin. Anyway, he had been twenty-one years old. I had no reason to believe he had been anything like faithful to me in the years since.

Faithful?

Faithfulness implied the presence of a relationship. Which we definitely did not have.

I knew that. So the question of why I was preoccupied with Hades while at work was one I should probably sit down and answer. Maybe I should get my bullet journal and make some goals.

Do not think about sexy business rival while trying to get work done.

That seemed like a pretty basic skill that was really logical for anyone who wanted to succeed in business.

I looked at my phone, in spite of myself. There was still no text from Hades.

But there was one from Sarah.

Coming up. Crazy news.

I instantly Googled my name. Which was maybe a weird response to that, but of course when she said there was crazy news, I was instantly concerned that it was about me. Had somebody seen Hades and me at the same hotel in Washington DC? Of course, their go-to assumption would not be that we had been sleeping together. I didn't think.

I scrolled through endlessly regurgitated articles that popped up when I tried to filter the most recent entries first. None of it seemed to be real news. Just listicles about the best red lipstick worn by powerful women, and my best black suits.

Flattering. I had to admit. But not exactly crazy news.

The door to my office opened, and Sarah thrust her phone into my face.

"What am I looking at?" I asked.

"He's engaged."

"Who?"

"Hades."

The room tilted, but I could feel my face freeze. No reaction. My chest felt cold. She couldn't be right. I had slept with the man three days ago. He hadn't mentioned a fiancée. He was frequently in the news, but hadn't been photographed with anyone. It was impossible.

I couldn't say all of that.

So I just made a weird, inarticulate noise and took the phone from her hand.

Billionaire Hades Achelleos set to wed heiress Jessica Lane in lavish London ceremony.

"I… I don't understand."

"I wouldn't have expected it," Sarah said. "The man seems like he has ice chips in his veins."

"It's just… It can't be true. The timing is…" She could feel Sarah staring at her. "What I mean is, we are in the middle of competing for this NASA contract. Why would he plan a wedding during that? It seems silly. It seems like he's just handing me the win."

"That is true," said Sarah.

I was going to be sick. I was literally in danger of vomiting on the carpet. He was getting married.

He was getting married.

That bastard was getting married, and he hadn't even had the common courtesy to tell me?

He wasn't mine. He never had been. I knew that. I had known this whole time. Okay, maybe I hadn't known it at first. But I had tried to tell myself that. I had made an attempt to be sure that I kept my feelings disengaged from the whole thing. He wasn't a prop, he was a human being, so sometimes I might feel things, but that was to be expected. Because I wasn't a sociopath. But I was…

I sat down in my chair. Was I the other woman?

Was he in love with somebody else, or at least pretending to be, this woman who probably loved him, and he was cheating on her, with me?

That had never occurred to me. I had imagined him

perhaps entertaining vapid socialites on his yacht. I had not imagined that... Did he live with her?

"Are you okay?"

I looked up at Sarah. I honestly didn't know what to say. Except I had to find something. Something that wasn't the truth. "I'm just shocked."

I knew that I was acting like a weird robot. But it was that or cry, and confess that I had a terrible secret that it was especially important nobody knew.

The idea of what that would do to my reputation...

They would make me out to be some kind of barracuda. Someone who was sleeping with the competition in order to... I don't know...steal secrets from him? Engage in corporate espionage? Ruin his life? It would be unflattering.

I knew that, because I knew how the media wrote about women. I had seen them do it to my own mother, time and time again. Granted, it wasn't exactly a fabrication when they wrote those things about my mother. But I already knew that I would be tarred with the same brush. Easily. Quickly.

I trusted Sarah. But I could not bring myself to speak about what happened between Hades and myself out loud. Just the idea of it filled my mouth with a metallic tang.

"He is... He is the most vile man that I have ever met, and I hope that woman doesn't sign a prenup. I hope that when they divorce, and they will, she'll get everything. And I really hope they don't have children."

"Wow," said Sarah.

"You don't understand," I said, rage beginning to flood my chest. "He is... He is the single most vile human being that I have ever had the misfortune of knowing."

"You used *vile* twice."

"Well, it fits."

I pushed up from my chair and I began to pace the room. I couldn't sit still anymore. I was electrified with outrage. And thank God for it. It was saving me from the very real threat of shedding tears, which I refused to do.

"He would be a terrible father," I said.

The words fell out of my mouth like lead bullets.

"I actually thought you would find this funny," said Sarah. "The very idea of the man engaging in something quite as traditional as the institution of marriage."

"It isn't funny," I said. "Because she's a real woman. She's a real woman who has been… Tricked by him."

"You don't know that. She is a socialite. It's entirely possible that this is something of a marriage of convenience."

But what if it wasn't? What if she loved him. And he had spent last Thursday with me tied to a bed.

I told myself that was why I was upset. It certainly wasn't because he was stopping things with me without saying a single word.

Why would he? He didn't owe me anything.

That was my official stance.

"I have work to do," I said.

"Okay," said Sarah, frowning.

"See you later."

"You were just with him, weren't you?"

I looked up. Sarah was gazing at me now with no small amount of questions in her eyes.

"I wasn't with him," I said. "We just saw each other at the NASA event. Which you know already."

"Yes. You're right. I do. I'm going to call you later, Florence."

Sarah left me then, to my dark thoughts, which were teeming around inside of me like tussling eels. I tried to work for an hour. And then I did something... That I never did. I called my driver, and I gave him the address of Hades' office.

The entire drive there was a blur. I wasn't being discreet. But it was fine. I was allowed to go to his office. After all, we were business rivals. There were occasions when we might have to speak.

I walked into the office building, and the woman at the desk looked at me wide-eyed. "Ms. Clare," she said.

"Hi, yes," I said, trying to sound official. "I have a meeting with Mr. Achelleos."

"I don't have you written down."

"He'll see me," I said.

Because of who I was she let me in. Let me go up to the top floor. Elevators. I was always waiting in elevators, and that didn't really bother me normally. They were my safe private space to expel the energy that I couldn't risk letting out in public. But I didn't want to let any of it out in here. I wanted to unleash all of it on him.

The elevator doors opened and I got halfway down the hall toward his office before I realized I wasn't exactly sure what I was coming here to do.

It didn't matter, though, because once I set my mind to something, I was certain about it. I couldn't afford to be anything else.

I walked into the room without knocking. He was

standing at the window, facing away from me. "You should know better than to come here."

He didn't turn. Of course, the secretary had let him know that I was on my way up. But he hadn't locked the door. I did, because I didn't want anyone walking in on this discussion.

He turned toward me, and he had the nerve to look perfect. His dark hair swept back perfectly, his suit tailored perfectly. He looked well rested. He looked like a man who was on top of his game in every way. A man whose life was going exactly how he wanted it to.

I hated him then. More than I ever had.

"How dare you?"

"I'm sorry, what do I dare today?"

"Do not play dumb, Hades. It doesn't suit you. You're many things, but you're not dumb. You must know the news of your impending nuptials broke today."

He waved his hand. "Oh. That."

"That?" I was speechless. Which never happened to me.

"Yes. What of it?"

"You didn't tell me."

"How is it relevant to you? When have we ever updated one another on changes in our personal lives."

"You might have told me that Washington DC was the last time. I asked when I was going to see you."

Well. I should have actually planned a speech, because I hated everything that came out of my mouth just then. Because it sounded hurt more than angry. And hurt on my own behalf, and not poor Jessica Lane's, who was marrying a bastard that had been cheating on her.

Which was what I was supposed to be mad about. His making me the other woman against my will.

"I don't know why it has to be the last time," he said.

"What... Planet to do you live on?"

"As far as you and I go, my marriage changes nothing."

He really believed that. He really... He really thought that the wedding was nothing. Like getting a wife was like getting a pair of new shoes. That it had nothing to do with me because the encounters we had were so separate from his actual life. Because I was so separate from his actual life.

I knew that he didn't love me. I had never claimed to love him. Not since I was a virginal teenage girl. And even then, I had only ever claimed it in my diary.

Right now I was definitely acting like a woman scorned. It was one thing, though, to know we weren't in love. I never thought we were. It was another to realize what little regard he held me in. He didn't see me as a person. While I had at least seen him as my equal, as my nemesis, he had seen me as a plaything.

Of all things, that had never occurred to me.

"I hate you," I said. "I hate you and I never want to see you again."

"You came to my office, *agape*. If you did not wish to see me, that was perhaps a bad first move."

I found myself striding across the space, without even thinking. I walked up to him and I shoved at his shoulder.

He caught my wrist and pulled me forward. My stomach twisted.

I knew. I knew how this would end.

The way that it always did.

"After this, I don't want to see you. We will no longer

conduct meetings in the same space. We will contend with NASA in a different way."

"Fine by me," he said. After this. Because we both knew.

Perhaps that was why DC had been so intense. He had known. But I hadn't. I deserved this. I deserved the chance to make him feel what I felt. To pour all of my intensity out onto him.

I deserved this chance to know that this was the last time.

I wrenched the knot on his tie and flung it down to the ground. I tore his jacket off his shoulders, and then his shirt, violently. I made sure it lost buttons. I made sure that he couldn't simply put the shirt back on like I had never been here. I would not let him walk away from this unruffled. Because nothing had ever made me angrier than when I walked in to see him looking as beautiful and unstained as ever, as if he hadn't just unleashed news upon the world that rocked me to my steel core.

But he was no kinder to me. He ripped my blouse away from my body, and my bra, leaving me nothing but my pencil skirt, which he unzipped, so hard I thought he had torn the zipper down through the seam.

Maybe he had.

Right then, I didn't care. My eyes burned with tears, but I refused to shed them. I refused to show any emotion. Other than anger.

The color mounted in his cheeks, his need apparent. I slipped his belt out from the loops, and he took it from me, gripped my wrists and lifted them up over my head, and before I could react, he slipped the end of the belt through the buckle and tightened it fast around me, bind-ing my hands. I was too shocked to protest, and when he laid me down across the clear edge of his massive corner desk, he pushed my arms up above my head, his expression one of pure, violent need.

"I bet you can't do this with her," I said.

A betrayal. Of my jealousy.

I was jealous. I didn't care about her. I didn't care if I was the other woman. I cared that I had been wounded. I cared that I could no longer deny that he had been with other women. I cared that perhaps I was not singular to him in the way he was to me.

I cared.

I cared.

I cared.

And I hated him for it.

He didn't respond to me, not with anything other than a growl. But he tore the skirt away from my body, leaving me in my thigh-high stockings and black high heels.

He took the rest of his clothes off and came back to me, moving his hand to my throat as he kissed me, hard and deep. I wanted to touch him, but he held my hands down still.

He held me fast as he thrust deep inside of me, looked into my eyes as he claimed me, over and over again. I took my bound hands and lifted them up over his head, as his hold tightened on my neck, I held my arms around him, locked together as he took me.

I took him back.

Because I would be certain of one thing.

That he would not forget this. That he would not forget me.

That he would regret the day that he had chosen to take

half of what we shared in exchange for that bland, ordinary life. The one I had told myself I might take someday.

He had made the bargain before I did.

And it called to me. Wounded me.

I struggled against his hold, arched my neck upward and bit him, at the side of his throat. Hard enough that I left a dark mark behind.

His lip curled, and he looked feral then. As he went over the edge, and his own loss of control spurred mine.

We cried out, together. Uncaring if anyone heard.

We had wrecked this place. And each other.

For the last time.

For ten years this had been the landscape of my life.

The landscape of us.

It was over now. There was no more us.

He exhaled, hard, then pulled the belt back through the loop, freeing me, freeing himself. He stepped away from me and wordlessly went to collect his clothes.

I had a difficult time doing the same. My skirt was ruined, my shirt was too. I tucked the blouse in as tightly as I could, crossing the edges together. It would be good enough to get me to my car. Especially with my black jacket over the top of it.

It was a mundane thought.

But mundane thoughts were the only things that were going to get me out of this building without having a total mental breakdown.

I didn't say goodbye to him.

I didn't say anything.

I'd said all I needed to with my body.

And when I was finally in the back of the car, I put up the barrier between myself and my driver. And I wept.

CHAPTER FOUR

THE TROUBLE WAS my daily life didn't change after that last time. I went to work. I went home. I went out for drinks with Sarah. I called my mother and listened to her talk about the party she was putting together. She complained that my half brother Rocco wouldn't come with his new wife. She wanted him to add some class to the place.

I laughed.

My mum was often hilariously self-aware. It was no mystery why she'd managed to wrap so many men around her finger. While the press printed truths about her, they were half-truths. No one would believe she was funny, clever and very dry, because the press made her out to be nothing more than a vacuous socialite. She was a vacuous socialite. She was just also funny, clever and dry.

All of this, though, made it so hard for me to remember some days that my life had changed forever two weeks earlier.

I'd ended things with him.

We weren't between assignations. We were done.

I would forget sometimes. Then news about his wedding would be on my home page. Jessica Lane was apparently a very popular social media girlie. Which meant every choice she made, from venue to dress to stemware was much discussed.

I hated her.

It wasn't fair.

It was bad feminism.

I didn't care. But I didn't care in the privacy of my own head. Because the consequence of carrying on a secret affair for ten years was that the heartbreak was also secret. My own private hell. Just for me. Hooray.

Maybe what made me hate her most was that she got to be online in ruffles and pastels, with pink lipstick and softness. She got to be feminine and soft in a way I never felt I was allowed to be. When I was with Hades we weren't pastel. We were bold. Vivid. Sharp. Painful.

Maybe he'd needed soft.

I was so tired of myself.

I flew to Houston for another NASA meeting. Then I went to Cape Canaveral for the next. I didn't see him there. I'd made sure I wouldn't.

I went back to my hotel room after the meetings and stretched across the white bedspread with my arms out like I was making a miserable snow angel.

I went back and dived into work like it was my salvation.

He won the contract.

I watched his live stream about it in spite of myself, and then I took my phone and threw it so hard across the room that it cracked against the marble kitchen countertop.

I sat on the floor with my head in my hands, and for the first time I really contemplated the concept of failure.

Clare Heir Can't Hack It.

Florence Clare, Discarded by Hades Achelleos and NASA in the Same Month!

I could only give thanks the press couldn't actually write that headline. First of all, because no one knew about Hades and myself, and second of all because I'd discarded him.

It changes nothing...

How dare he?

I decided I needed a break. I called Sarah. "Do you want to work remotely for a few weeks?"

"Where?"

"Lake Como?"

Sarah laughed. "Are you kidding?"

"No. I'm not kidding. My mother has a house there."

"Well, yes, that would be amazing. You...you want to go stay with your mother?"

I did. Which was weird. I loved my mother, but I loved her with a bit of distance. The idea of being swept up into her sphere felt... It felt like a potential rescue.

Knowing Mom, there would be oiled-up men running around anyway. If I wanted to have a revenge lay, I could certainly find one. That made me feel ghastly.

"She's having a party. It will be fun. Also her house is so big it's more like staying in the same town than the same residence. We won't even see her every day."

I hadn't asked her yet, but as soon as Sarah agreed, I called.

"Mom, would you mind if a friend and I came to stay for a while?"

"Ooh, a friend, Flo?"

I grimaced. "No. Not like that. She is my actual friend."

It made me think of Hades. We'd never been friends.

I stared out my apartment windows, down at all the lights below. I couldn't remember why I loved the city.

I didn't tell my mother I'd lost the contract—she wouldn't have any idea I'd been competing for one. She saw the success of the company, that I had status, and that was really—not all she cared about—but it spoke of success to her so the details didn't matter.

The next day I overpacked everything floaty and feminine that I owned. I packed makeup I never wore and face creams I forgot to apply, and Sarah and I took the private corporate jet to Italy.

The flight attendant offered champagne but I didn't have the stomach for it. I didn't have the stomach for much of anything.

"It's all going to work out," Sarah said, gently as we descended.

"I don't see how."

I said that before I realized she meant for the company. After not getting the contract. Because she didn't know about Hades.

Both felt equally hopeless to me.

"What if it doesn't?" I asked. "I always thought it would if I just figured out how to be enough. But I haven't."

"It was one contract, Florence. It isn't the end of anything. You didn't need it to keep the company financially solvent."

"It feels like the end," I said.

I couldn't explain it. Not because I didn't have the words. Because I genuinely couldn't explain it.

I was temporarily distracted from my misery by the beauty of Lake Como. Apparently even in the depths of this…this despair that was entirely foreign to me, I could still pause to appreciate the beauty of Italy. I was glad of that. Maybe I wasn't going to need to see a therapist after all.

It shouldn't be like this. The end of whatever we had.

It was the contract on top of it. I knew that. Perhaps, it was even the bigger issue. It had to be. Because I was acting like my heart had been broken by someone I was in love with. I had been foolish in a whole lot of different ways when it came to Hades. But I wasn't that foolish.

My mother's house on the lake was gorgeous. The crowning achievement of one of her divorces.

She often said that, then laughed and said she supposed she would actually have to give that title to Rocco. He was her son, after all.

The house was a stunning yellow, with broad stone decks that extended out from the hill where it sat nestled over the lake.

When we arrived, my mother sent staff. She was on her way out to dinner and too busy to chat overmuch. She floated through like a butterfly, kissed my cheek and met Sarah enthusiastically. Then she was gone.

Her staff graciously allowed Sarah and I to take over a quadrant at one end of the house, and we were able to establish office space as well as our own bedrooms. I kept all of my focus on the company's internal network. I did not look at the broader internet. I refused to check any progress on Hades' upcoming wedding. I told myself that I definitely didn't know how many days away it was every time I woke up.

But I also did my best to ignore how increasingly tired and awful I felt every morning.

Because it felt like a weakness.

Not only had I failed, but I was allowing that failure to change me.

We were sitting out on the terrace one glorious morning, with a massive spread of food in front of us, jams and cream, croissants. Espresso, lattes and sipping chocolate. Cured meats, a selection of cheeses and olives. Because my mother did not care what time of day it was. It was always time for a charcuterie in her opinion.

One of the things I enjoyed about her.

"You seem heartbroken," she said, leaning back in her chair, wearing large sunglasses that covered half of her face.

Sarah had taken an instant liking to my mother, which was handy. Though I think my mother interpreted Sarah's desire to speak with her as frequently as possible as admiration, and I suspected Sarah was fascinated by her, like a specimen she was examining for research purposes.

Which was fair enough. My mother was eminently examinable.

"It's the contract," Sarah said. "Florence loves the company more than she loves anything."

"Flo needs to get more of a personal life," my mother said.

"Florence is sitting right here," I said. "Why did you name me Florence if you insist on shortening it."

"Your father named you," she said. "I wanted to name you Trixie."

Well. Then I never would've been CEO.

"It's the contract," I said.

My mother lowered her sunglasses. She was supernaturally smooth, her lips extending beyond the boundary of their natural line thanks to years of fillers. She was a beautiful woman, my mother, though natural beauty was not, and had never been, her priority. She made me feel dull. I could tell myself that I found her to be gaudy and over-the-top, but it didn't change the fact that next to her I felt like a pale, less vibrant photocopy.

"No," my mother said. "It is not the contract."

"It is," I insisted, standing up and grabbing a plate, determined to fill it. Determined to stop acting like I was heartbroken, because it was stupid.

Hades' wedding was tomorrow. That was just fine, and I wasn't thinking about it, because I wasn't looking at the news.

Just then, one of my mother's staff came out with a tray of pastries to add to the collection, along with a stack of newspapers.

I reached out and grabbed a piece of cheese off my plate and bit into it. Just as my mother grabbed hold of the newspaper and set it down on the table. And there it was. Front-page news on her favorite scandal sheet.

Achelleos Nuptials More Expensive Than Two Royal Weddings Combined!

Just then, the cheese that I was attempting to swallow decided it wasn't going down without a fight. My stomach lurched, and I ran from the balcony, stumbling into the nearest bathroom—thankfully they were all over the house—and found myself falling to my knees in front of the actual gold toilet. Where I did indeed lose the battle with the cheese.

I sat there for a moment, completely humiliated.

Hopefully no one had guessed what had made me react that way.

Maybe I could claim exhaustion. Overwork. A stomach bug.

Anything other than a headline about my supposed enemy's wedding.

I stood up and splashed water on my face before walking back out to the terrace, trying to look like I was fine. I was not fine.

Sarah looked worried. My mother had a small smile on her face.

"Oh, finally, Flo. I can see that you're my daughter."

"What?"

"You're like me after all!"

"In what way? Lactose intolerant?"

She laughed. "No. You've made a bad decision, haven't you?"

If only it was *one* bad decision. If only. It was so many bad decisions so many different times over the course of so many years. And I had convinced myself that by partitioning them off, separating them into a different part of my life, that I wouldn't be affected by them. Not seriously.

I had been in denial all this time.

Because the decisions that I had made in private could no longer be contained behind the door.

They were bursting through into the regular part of my life, and it was just so terrible.

"I'm just not very well."

"You're not pregnant?"

I froze.

"No," I said.

Sarah was staring at me now, and it wasn't concern on her face exclusively anymore. It was curiosity.

"I can't be pregnant," I said.

"Like you don't think you're pregnant? Or you *can't* be pregnant," Sarah asked. "Because those are two different things."

"It's…"

I was beginning to feel dizzy again. I closed my eyes.

"I *can't be*," I said.

Because there was nothing worse, nothing worse in the entire world that I could think of happening at this moment.

But I couldn't ignore the evidence that was flooding into my mind now. Very logical things that I had been ignoring for a good long while.

My period was late.

I was exhausted.

I was emotional.

I was nauseous in the morning.

I had just vomited up a piece of cheese like it was poison.

Most damning of all, I knew full well that we had not used protection in his office. I had wanted to think about it, I had wanted to acknowledge it. The entire encounter had been so painful that I hadn't wanted to play it over in my head. But I knew that he hadn't used a condom. I hadn't been aware of it so much right at the time. I wouldn't have remembered it then if a giant neon sign had flashed on reminding me to have safe sex. Later, when I'd started to try and gather myself again at home, it had become apparent to me.

But I pushed it to the side. Like I had pushed all of it to the side.

He and I were usually so careful. We couldn't afford to be anything else.

But we hadn't been careful that day. We had been dangerous.

"Oh, Florence," said Sarah, wincing. "You *are* pregnant, aren't you?"

"Is he rich?" This was of course my mother's first question.

That snapped me out of my momentary catatonia.

"That doesn't matter," I said. "*I'm* already rich."

"So was I," said my mother, waving her hand. "I wasn't estate in Lake Como rich, though. And now I am."

"Money is not my concern," I said.

I sat there for a long moment. And I tried to decide what I was going to do.

There was no use denying it, not to myself or anyone. As much as I wanted to.

It wasn't only my mum and Sarah I had to face. It wasn't only the board of the company and the public.

If I appeared suddenly, pregnant, *he* was going to know. Unless he could somehow be convinced that it was a rebound… Unless I could make him believe that I'd always had other lovers, and maybe I didn't even know who the baby belonged to. He wouldn't believe it. That was the problem. On some level, I was convinced that he had always known the degree to which he had me ensnared.

Also, he would be well aware at this point that he hadn't used a condom with me. The timing would be far too coincidental, he would make inquiries and demands about it. He was that sort of man.

But I couldn't wait until after he was married.

I really was trying to not care about his fiancée. After I had embraced my own selfishness, after I had decided to make love with him one last time, I thought it seemed a little bit hypocritical. But she should know. Before she married him, she needed to know that he was expecting a baby with another woman.

It was entirely possible Hades would want nothing to do with the child. Except...

I thought of the way he looked whenever the subject of his father came up. I thought of the way it affected him. And somehow, I knew the subject of children would be a thorny one, but also one he would not shy away from, because he was not a man to shy away from anything.

I couldn't hide it. Eventually, the media would find out, and they would take control of the story. We had a very short space of time where we could control the narrative. If he wanted to give up parental rights, to give up any claim on the baby, then I could simply say that it was artificial insemination and I had chosen to have a baby by myself.

That would be a great story. One that would make me sound like I was taking control of my life.

I did not let myself think about what a baby that belonged to both me and Hades would look like. I didn't let myself imagine a little boy with his dark eyes or little girl with glossy black hair.

No. I couldn't be sentimental about this. There was no sentiment. He was marrying somebody else. He didn't care about me. But everything would have to be entirely clear, entirely out in the open between us before it became public fodder.

That much I knew.

"I have to go. Right now."

"Why?" Sarah asked. "You could see a doctor, you could get a test…"

"We'll get one when we get back to New York. We don't have any time to waste."

"Why?" Sarah asked.

"Because we have to get there before the wedding."

CHAPTER FIVE

LEAVING LAKE COMO was interesting. Given I was losing my mind, and Sarah had forced the driver to stop in a minute market on our way to the airport to get a pregnancy test.

"You have to know," she said.

But I already did. It was like the veil had been lifted and I just couldn't deny the truth anymore. That's what I'd been doing. For weeks. Denying. Ignoring. I was so good at that, because in my position I'd had to be.

She had me take the test as soon as we reached altitude.

I knew she was mad at me. Because obviously I had been keeping a huge secret from her. But...

"Sarah..."

"Take the test, and then we'll talk. No. We'll make a strategy. I'm going to get out the Post-it notes."

"We don't need Post-it notes."

"We need Post-it notes and Washi tape, Florence. There is no other option."

I went into the bathroom as instructed. I didn't usually do what I was told. In fact, I was more or less allergic to it. But right now I didn't feel like I was in any position to argue. Right now, it kind of felt good for someone to just give me some instructions.

Of course, waiting for the test did not feel good. And watching that second pink line begin to materialize was...

I knew. At that point I absolutely knew, but still, seeing it like that...

I practically ran out of the bathroom. "It's positive. I knew it. We didn't actually need to stop for the test and..."

"He's probably going to want to know there was a test," she said.

I sighed. "You say that like you know him."

"I know his type. I don't know him, because I didn't actually think we were supposed to do any fraternizing with the enemy. Do you want to... Speak to that?"

"It happened after I found out about the engagement," I said.

She just kept staring at me, and I knew it was an insufficient explanation. I waited a moment. To just be very sure that she needed me to actually explain. That she needed me to tell her the whole story. Everything. Apparently she did.

"Because... It wasn't the first time."

"Oh, Florence," she said, pressing her finger to her forehead. "He was at every one of those conferences where you disappeared."

"How long have you suspected?" I asked.

"It occurred to me a couple of times that maybe... It's only that sometimes you get this look on your face when you see him. And it isn't entirely bloodthirsty. It is a little bloodthirsty, it just isn't only bloodthirsty."

"I never wanted anyone to know."

"I'm your friend."

"It's been going on for longer than I've known you," I said.

She threw her hands up in the air and sat there frozen, her expression one of near-comedic shock. Except nothing was funny.

"I seduced him on my eighteenth birthday," I said.

"*No*," she said.

"Yes. And ever since then… It just happens. It just happens. In cities all over the world, in different hotel rooms. In bathrooms, sometimes. Once a library at an English manor."

I had forgotten about that. Well. I had deliberately chosen not to think about that, because it had been one of the more lovely and romantic times. There had been an edge of danger to it. Because we had sneaked away from a party, and even though the doors were locked, he hadn't been fast, and I had been worried we would be missed.

He spread me out on the rug in front of the fireplace. He looked at me like I was special.

Or it had been a trick of the light. Because I had clearly never been special.

"So you have been having a secret relationship with your chief competition since before you were actually CEO of the company."

"It isn't a relationship," I said.

"When you saw that he was engaged, you looked like you were going to be sick."

"Because he slept with me when he was with her. I didn't know about that. I didn't know about her. I would never…"

That was a lie. Because I had.

"I can't forgive him for that," I said.

"No. Are you going to stop the wedding?"

"No. But I think that she needs to know. He also needs to know, but she really needs to know. Don't you think?"

"Yes," Sarah said slowly. "I think I would want to know."

"Well, that's what I think. Before she actually makes vows to him, she should know. Because this baby was conceived after their engagement." I stared out the window. "Their engagement was announced just a little over a month ago. You realize that means they were together for a very long time before that."

Sarah nodded. "Yes."

"I can't just let that stand."

"Are you motivated by justice? Or revenge?"

I shifted uncomfortably. "Does it matter?"

"Not really," she said.

Because she knew, I finally started talking about it. About the years of it. About how sometimes I convinced myself that having him after one of our big showdowns was my reward.

About how I tried to present myself as this very serious, very successful businesswoman, but I was as distracted by men as anybody. By one man.

"He's hot," said Sarah. "I just thought that you were…" She looked almost disappointed, and I hated that. "I thought you were as bulletproof as you pretended to be."

"Sadly," I said. "I'm not immune to all bullets."

We landed in New York, and the wedding was only ninety minutes away.

I texted him. In desperation. He didn't answer.

I went to his apartment. He wasn't there. I did not want to go to the church, but I was starting to see no other option.

"You want me to wait for you?" Sarah asked.

"I might need you to run interference."

Sarah nodded. "Whatever you need."

We got out of the car, and while we were dressed fairly nicely, we had just been on Lake Como on vacation, and I had brought pretty clothes, we weren't really dressed for a wedding that cost two times a royal wedding. I also wasn't dressed anything like I normally did. My hair was a mess, loose, and I was wearing pink. I also looked like I felt like garbage.

Only because I did feel like garbage.

So that was nice.

We ran up the steps to the big, stone church, only to be met by security.

"I'm Florence Clare," I said. "I'm obviously invited to the wedding."

He looked at me. "I don't have your name on any list."

"That is a mistake," I said. "Hades and I have a business relationship."

Sarah looked at me. I refused to look back.

"I don't have your name on the list," said the security guard. But he wasn't even looking.

"You just know that," I said.

"I know who you are, Ms. Clare," he said. "If you were invited to the wedding, I would have remembered seeing your name."

"It was an oversight." I opened up my phone and showed him that the last text I had sent was to Hades.

Showing him that I had Hades' personal number made me sweaty.

"I'll go inside and just check with his secretary," he said.

"You do that," I said.

He walked into the church, and Sarah caught the door. "Go," she said.

Without thinking, I skittered inside behind the security guard and dodged into a hallway out of his view. My heart was pounding. I felt like I was going to throw up again. I could not be skulking around the church where Hades was getting married and vomiting.

So I did my best to gather my courage, and I tried to figure out where he could be. I looked at the text again. Nothing from him. But suddenly one from Sarah came through.

It was a picture of the church's layout that she must have gotten from online.

She had circled two rooms that she clearly thought might be used for people getting ready.

I tried to orient myself.

Another text from her came in.

I'm going to tell the guard you weren't well and you left. I won't go far.

Thanks.

I made my way down the hall and tried to follow the map.

The building was old, and my steps echoed so loudly, in time with my heartbeat. I was sure that I was alerting everyone within a fifty-foot radius to my presence. I tried to move more softly, even as I kept my pace quick.

I peered into a window on the first door, and it was a room full of people preparing flowers. Definitely not Hades.

I made my way to the next room and saw that the window was blocked. The door opened suddenly, swinging out toward me, and I moved back.

"Are you one of the florists?" a beautiful, brown-skinned woman wearing a bright pink dress asked.

"Yes," I said.

"Okay. Do you have Jessica's okay?"

"Not quite yet. They're still putting the finishing touches on it. But will bring it down in a minute."

"Great," she said. Obviously the maid of honor. Thankfully, the wedding colors looked like they were pink, so I looked like I belonged here. And I wasn't especially recognizable with my hair down, and without my signature black.

The door closed again, and I stood there for a moment, wondering if I should just talk to Jessica first. No.

I did think she should know, but Hades was the father of the baby. He needed to know first.

I had no idea where to go next, though.

I looked back on the schematic and saw that there was an outdoor grotto in the middle of the church. I wove through the core door, looking for it.

I didn't know why, but for some reason I just thought that I might find him there. Just maybe.

There was a big wooden door with no window, but from the looks of the map, it was the door that led outside. I opened it up, and there he was. Standing with his back to me, the way he had been when I had come to confront him at his office.

And just like then, he straightened, as if he could feel me.

You silly girl, it's any person walking up behind him. It has nothing to do with you specifically.

He turned around, and our eyes clashed. For a brief moment, it felt like I was falling through the earth. It felt like the world had fallen away, and there was nothing. Not the earth, not the sky, not gravity. Only him. Only me.

"Florence," he said.

For some reason, hearing my name on his lips made tears spring to my eyes. It made me angry.

"I'm not here to stop your wedding," I said.

I refused to allow him to think, even for a moment, that I was so weak for him, that I would do something that silly.

"Of course not," he said.

"I'm just here…"

He crossed the space between us and grabbed the back of my head. His kiss was a shock. Cruel and hard. It was angry. And I found myself surrendering to him helplessly.

Even as my better self stood by and watched in horror as my weak self succumbed to his touch. I had no practice doing anything else when it came to Hades.

None at all.

He was my one and only.

He was the father of my baby.

That thought gave me the strength to pull away.

"I know what you came for," he said.

"I didn't come for that either," I said. "You don't know me, Hades. Even if you think that you do."

"I've been your lover for a decade, *agape*. Don't tell me that I don't know you. I know every sigh, every scream, I know the way that your blue eyes darken when you need me. I know just how dark your fantasies are. How the cold, calculated businesswoman likes for someone to tell her what to do as long as she's naked. How you wish for someone to tie you down and make your decisions for you. I don't just know what you want, Florence. I know what you beg for."

He made my knees weak. But while I had been weak with him for all of these years, I wouldn't be weak now. There was too much at stake. I was in shock, and I had had very little time to process any of this, so the part where I was having a baby still felt so… Distant. So theoretical. But right then, I realized that what I was doing was bigger than myself. Bigger than the two of us. Definitely bigger than the acid in my stomach, the anger and the lingering desire.

"I came because I have to tell you something. I'm pregnant, Hades. I'm having your baby."

He stood there. Immobilized. He said nothing. For one long minute, he said nothing. And then, he looked at me. With a black fire that chilled me to my soul.

"This changes everything."

CHAPTER SIX

I DIDN'T KNOW what to expect. He reached out and took me by the arm and began to propel me out of the grotto.

"You're certain?" he asked, just before we entered the church again.

"Of course I'm certain," I said. "I'm not the one that had a secret fiancée while we were... Yes, I'm certain."

"You are certain you're *pregnant*."

His eyes burned into mine. I could sense that he was at the end of his control. I'd experienced this in other ways, other places. When his desire for me had been beyond him. This was different.

"Yes. I took a test on the plane."

"And you're certain it's mine."

"It couldn't be anyone else's."

Ever. Because he was the only one. But I couldn't bring myself to say that, not now. Not while this was happening.

I was in shock, so I really didn't anticipate what he might do next. But he took me straight back to that room I had gone to only moments earlier and said that I was a florist. He knocked on the door, and it opened.

The maid of honor appeared again. "Hades," she said. "You can't see Jessica before the wedding."

"I will see my fiancée when I wish to. We have an important matter to discuss."

The maid of honor looked at me. "A flower matter?"

"Yes," he said.

He pushed his way into the room, bringing me with him, and looked around at all the bridesmaids. "Leave us," he said.

Jessica Lane was sitting there in front of the mirror, her dark hair styled into an artful updo.

I looked at her, and my stomach just about hit the floor. She was beautiful. In an iconic way. Soft and luxurious. Her dress was a cascade of silk, so beautiful and perfectly fitted to her. I was ruining her wedding day. Of course, I hadn't meant to. But that was the end result.

I felt so small then.

She saw me, and she frowned. "You're Florence Clare," she said.

"Yes," said Hades.

"What is this about?" Jessica asked.

"Things have changed," said Hades. "I'm sorry that this is happening right now. I will give you the allotted sum that we outlined in the prenuptial agreement."

"What?" she asked.

"We cannot get married."

Her jaw dropped. "Are you kidding me? We spent so much money."

"It was nothing to me," he said. "As is the money I offer you to go quietly."

"Hades," I said. "Are you for real right now? You were engaged to be married to her. You are practically jilting her at the altar. And you're offering her money? When you told me that your marriage wasn't going to change anything, I knew you were a coldhearted bastard, but I had no idea…"

I didn't know why I was defending her. Or why it made me so angry. Maybe because in part I looked at her and saw a woman I had something in common with. I had been foolish enough to get into bed with him.

As had she, apparently. It was apparent now that led nowhere good.

"And what do you have to do with this?" she asked.

"She's having my baby," said Hades.

"Oh," said Jessica.

"I see you understand why this changes things," he said.

Jessica blinked. "Not really. Can't you just… Come up with an arrangement?"

"The arrangement is that she will be my wife. My child will not be a bastard."

"Unless he takes after his father," I said. And then I realized what *he* had just said. "Wait a minute. You think I'm going to marry you?"

"I know that you're going to marry me, *agape*. There is no question."

"Wait a minute," said Jessica. "You two hate each other. It's literally all over the news. I mean, there's some fanfic but, that's all."

I blinked. "There's what?"

"You know, it's when people write…"

"*I know what it is,*" I said. "Why is there…? That. About us?"

"Because some people think that your apparent hatred of each other is just disguising your desire to sleep together. And… It seems like it's true."

I couldn't understand what was happening. Because

she should be crying. Throwing things. Maybe even threatening me. Instead, she was talking about the media.

"I'm really sorry," I said. "I didn't know about you. Not before… Not before the last time. There was one time when I did know, but I was really angry, and…"

"I'm not in love with him," she said. "He was looking for a dynastic bride, somebody who wanted to have his babies and take pictures in his gorgeous house. I have a media empire. It seemed like a good move. But I don't have any desire to get between you two. I mean, if we could have done a cool blended family thing for the internet, that would've been fine. But… I just need a way to come out of this looking good."

"You're a storyteller," he said. "Come up with something you have been doing ever since the engagement was announced. If you must make yourself into a victim, then do it, but don't paint Florence as a villain."

"No. People like to see women supporting other women these days. Also, you two are going to be a very big story." She tapped her chin. "Well. With all of my new money, I suppose I will embark on a year of wellness as I travel around the world. I'll do stirring posts about the importance of self-care. And how sometimes you have to get out of the way of true love."

"Love!" I sputtered. "I don't think he knows the meaning of the word."

Jessica laughed. "He doesn't. But then, neither do I. I'm a big can of self-love. But one reason that his proposition was so tempting was that it was going to leave me free to do whatever I wanted."

I felt like I was standing between two of the coldest people I had ever met. Jessica was likable, but I thought she had to be hollow inside. Because all she cared about was finding a way to spin the wedding. She didn't care that he was jilting her. In fact, it was almost like she thought being jilted was a bigger story, and therefore far more fun than wafting off to become a wife and mother.

"Perhaps you should escape the church dramatically in your gown. Maybe there is a photographer that can capture the image for you to put on your web page. You can claim that you had a feeling and had to follow your heart," he said.

"I like that. You really are very good with image."

I looked at him. And I was certain I was looking at a stranger. Yes. He was very good with image. But I wondered if there had ever been anything else there. Or if he had always been this...

This hollow man who saw people as playthings.

Perhaps I had deluded myself.

I had thrilled in his arrogance. I had let myself rage when he was stubborn. I had enjoyed the fight. Because in the end, I had believed there was something underneath that.

I had let myself believe that the man I let inside my body had more to him than that.

I had bought into a convenient lie, because I was no different than most women when it came to sex. I had told myself that we didn't have feelings for each other. But in the end, I'd had feelings.

Without another word, she slipped out of the room. I heard talking on the other side of the door. And I peered out for just one second, as she began to run down the stone corridor. And her maid of honor stood there, snapping photos on her phone.

I felt like I had just witnessed a play.

Because it was beginning to feel like a farce. That was for sure.

"Why didn't you tell me?" I asked. "That it was a marriage of convenience? Why were you even... Having one?"

"That's what you wish to talk about?"

I felt like I was sitting in the middle of the debris resulting from a detonated bomb. So picking which piece of detritus that we might talk about first seemed a little bit silly. It nearly didn't matter.

Because it was such a mess. How would we ever make sense of it?

He was supposed to be getting married in one hour.

"Is Sarah still here?"

"How did you know that Sarah was here?"

"I only assume that you would not come and do this without her. She is your best friend."

"She's here, but—"

"Excellent. I will have a selection of wedding gowns brought to you, what color bridesmaid dress would you prefer?"

"You are..." I sputtered. "*You are kidding me*. You think I'm going to marry you?"

"Yes," he said.

"I'm not marrying you. You were set to marry another woman not two minutes ago. I'm not going to be your backup just because I'm having a baby."

"I was marrying her to fulfill the terms of my father's will. I was to marry and produce children within a certain amount of time. I had five years. That has come to a close. You happen to already be pregnant with my child, and that is extremely convenient for me."

"Hades," I said. "You're forgetting something. We have kept this a secret for ten years because of the potential ramifications for our businesses. People are going to think that we… are price fixing and heading toward monopolizing areas of the marketplace. There might not just be financial consequences, there could be legal consequences."

"And we are going to have to work at figuring out how to manage that. We may have to dissolve different parts of the companies."

"Oh. Is this how you're going to get me to dissolve my space division."

"You don't have the NASA contract—you might as well."

Somehow, even in the middle of all of this, that enraged me. "And are you going to sell your cruise line to me?"

"Perhaps, Florence, but that is not my biggest concern at the moment."

My brain was spinning. His father had left a will saying he had to get married. He had to produce an heir. Technically, our child would be the heir to both companies. Unless we had more than one child.

I looked up at him. For one moment, it was like having an out-of-body experience. For one moment, I didn't understand why I shouldn't be wildly happy about this turn of events. Because he wasn't going to marry another woman. He was going to marry me.

He was on the phone.

He was ordering dresses.

"You didn't say what color," he said.

"Red," I said, and then clapped my hand over my mouth, because I was annoyed that I had answered the question at all. "My mother is in Italy," I said.

"Come now, Florence, don't you think that your mother will love the drama so much that she won't care that she couldn't be here? In fact, she'll probably like it better that she couldn't come, because it will allow her to tell the story and center herself as a victim of some kind."

I hated that he was right. And she wouldn't even really be mad at me because her new son-in-law would be a billionaire. And not only that, one that made for a sensational headline.

If nothing else, she would love it because my father would've hated it so much.

"I'm going to be sick," I said.

"Are you?"

For a moment, he looked genuinely concerned.

"I might be," I replied.

"We can stop for a moment, if you need."

"I haven't agreed to marry you."

"But you will," he said. "Because it makes the most sense."

"What happens to you if you don't marry?"

"The company reverts to the board."

"So you're telling me it would actually benefit me to not marry you."

"You're having my baby regardless. The production of an heir was the biggest issue. I am certain I could make the case to the lawyers that this counts. But is that honestly the legacy you want for the beginning of our child's life? Do you want to be your parents? Or worse, mine?"

We didn't talk about these things openly. I knew he

didn't have a functional home life, even without know-ing details. This was the first time it had occurred to me he might know the same about me.

I was still lost in the futility of everything. I had tried to hide myself from Hades, and apparently I wasn't as successful as I'd thought. I'd tried to hide us from the world, and now that was crumbling too.

My failures were mounting.

"But we kept it a secret," I said.

Mostly because the pain from the last ten years felt compounded in this moment. And futile. Because here we were. Ready to make this as public as we possibly could.

"If what Jessica says is true, we are poised to make a very popular move with the public. Many people will delight in being correct about the fact that we've been secretly carrying on for years."

I laughed. I couldn't help it. Maybe I was hysterical. It was entirely possible. "What was it all for? All of this. The years of sneaking around."

"Our fathers never knew. Your father never knew. I assume that's a big reason for the secrecy."

"If he knew that his grandchild was going to be…"

"We would both have lost our positions. There's no doubt about that."

Right then, all I wanted to do was let my guard down. All I wanted to do was to have another moment like the one we had in DC. When he'd come in and told me traf-fic had been terrible. When he kissed me. When he'd ordered me a cheeseburger because he knew exactly what I wanted.

That was what I craved. Another moment like that.

But I couldn't afford it.

I had to keep my wits about me.

"We have to get our legal team in here. Because there has to be a prenup."

"Wonderful. I'll put in another phone call. You keep all of your assets, I keep all of mine."

"Perfect," I said.

I knew him well enough to know if I defied him, he was going to start issuing threats. Still. I felt like it was time to give him the chance. To either be the man that I had wished he might be, or the man I knew him to be.

To tell me flat out he wouldn't be a monster. To say if I refused him he wouldn't try to destroy me professionally or personally.

I wanted to give him the chance to be…

Human.

"What if I walk away? What if I tell you you'll just have to deal with having your child on the weekends the way many men do."

The look on his face was enough to stop me cold. For the first time I realized that when he dealt with me he didn't unleash the full strength of his fury onto me. That he had never truly been the god of hell in my presence before.

The man I saw before me now, that man fit his name. Hades. That man would think nothing of dragging me down into the underworld along with him, where we could both burn together.

"I don't want to ruin you, Florence. But I will. We both know that a big reason you didn't want our affair coming out was the way you would be looked at as a woman sleeping with her competitor. If I let slip the wrong thing, imagine what it will do to your employees' confidence in you. To your investors' confidence. People might even be tempted to imagine I had the upper hand when it came to the NASA contracts because you took information from me and they realized it."

My stomach went cold. "I didn't."

"Later, I saw the proposal you put forward. Sections were alarmingly similar to mine."

"You know that I didn't take anything from you. We were very careful. I never wanted you to blame me for anything like that, and I know you wanted the same."

"It is not about what happened, it is about what is believable. And you know it."

"You would do that to me."

"I would. Where you got the idea that I am soft or movable, I don't know. But I learned one thing from my father of any value, and that is to never bend. I will have what is mine. The child is mine. You are mine."

"You," I said, "are not the man I hoped you were."

He didn't care about what I wanted. His priority would be what he saw as the right thing, whether I agreed or not. I was gutted to have it confirmed.

But I'd had to know. For sure. Because if I was going to do this, then I had to protect myself. If I was going to marry Hades, then I had to remember who he was, and who I was.

This was never going to be a union about feelings. Just like everything that had happened between us before this was not about feelings.

It was about control. It was about possession. Obsession. But it had never been about feelings.

"You will walk down that aisle toward me in forty-five minutes. Be ready."

CHAPTER SEVEN

SARAH AND AN entire team came into the room. Her eyes were wide, and she was looking around as if she was checking to see if someone was holding a gun on me.

"Are you actually insane?"

A red dress was thrust toward her. "Thanks," she said. "You're not marrying him."

"I am," I said. Because I knew that I had no other choice.

Or maybe you don't want a different choice. Maybe you're a sad deluded girl who thinks that this is a fairy tale.

No. I didn't. I knew who he was.

I knew…

"Is he blackmailing you?"

"Sort of. But I wouldn't expect anything different from him."

"You don't have to do this."

"Believe me. The wreckage if I don't isn't worth it."

If the various hairstylists and makeup artists were interested in exactly what was going on, they certainly didn't show it. A stylist looked at me critically and then took three different gowns off a rack that she apparently had determined would be best for me.

One of them was made from layers of floating, diaphanous material, the bodice draped over my curves with soft pleats. The skirt swished with each movement. It was the kind of thing that spoke of femininity. On a level that I normally would never allow myself to project.

I looked like a bride.

Next to Hades in a severe black suit, I would look nothing less than *soft*. It was the kind of thing that I would never risk in a meeting. But at a wedding?

Our wedding.

I looked at myself in the mirror. My eyes were large, my skin waxen.

Did I look like the spoils? Would he appear to be the victor?

I looked beautiful and I didn't know how to feel about it. Just like I had no idea how to feel about becoming a mother. About becoming a wife.

The wife of hell, basically.

But the only hell I'd ever willingly flung myself into, so it wasn't like I didn't know how I'd gotten here.

Play with hellfire and you might get damned.

"This is the one," the woman said.

"Perhaps something more tailored," I said.

A bid to try and find my balance. My comfort. In the middle of something that could not be less comfortable.

"No," she said. "This one suits you."

I knew that it did. And I knew that I loved it. It was only that something about it was terrifying. Like going into battle naked when what I needed was armor. Only I didn't have time to protest. Because then I was draped in a towel and given hairstyling and makeup. Bright blush to cover up the insipid color of my skin. Pink lipstick.

My hair was styled down. Loose, flowing curls.

For all the world to see, it would look like I had surrendered my power to Hades.

This was how he won. I hadn't seen that when I'd left Lake Como. All I'd thought about was that it was a race against time, and I had to win it. I'd made the classic mistake of not looking far enough ahead.

I had thought that I needed to get here so that I could give Jessica the chance to make a choice.

In the end, he had managed to twist it and make it so I had little time to make a choice of my own.

I could make him wait. And maybe I should have, but instead I was standing there in a wedding dress. I'd let him take control of this situation because I was still too shell-shocked by the last twelve hours to be anything but.

Or maybe I'd allowed it because the teenage girl who'd once thought she loved Hades still lived somewhere inside me.

Hadn't I learned better over these last ten years? Ten years of fraught sex. And he'd never grown closer to me. His moods were what made us. His intensity driving our encounters. He thought he set the rules, and I'd let him.

That was why he'd said nothing had to change, even after his engagement. Because he thought he got to decide. And what I wanted didn't matter.

Because I was nothing to him. Nothing but an outlet for his darkest, basest needs. Because there was no need to get me to sign an NDA, after all.

Who would I tell?

He knew, of any lover he could have possibly had, I

would be the one most motivated to keep all of his secrets in order to preserve my own self.

Before I knew it, the hour had passed and I was being
ushered out of the dressing room. A dressing room that
one hour ago had contained a bridal party and a whole
different bride. Would the sanctuary be empty? What
had he told the guests? Would I be marrying him in
front of Jessica's friends and family?

I stood outside the sanctuary wringing my hands,
and Sarah was directed inside. She looked at me, as if
waiting to be told the whole thing would be called off.
But I didn't call it off. So, in she went.

I felt another presence in the antechamber and turned.

My half brother Javier was standing there, looking
severe. We hadn't grown up together, but over the years
he, Rocco and I had found some sort of rapport. I was
shocked to see him here. "How did you…"

"I know Hades. He called because he knew I was in
the city."

My half brother was friends with my nemesis. I'd
had a feeling they might be. I wasn't shocked neither of
them had ever mentioned it.

Nemesis? You're marrying him.

True.

"Oh." He'd come to my wedding. Last minute. I was
so weirdly touched by it.

"Rocco sends his regrets that he couldn't make it.
He's in Italy, so of course there was no way for him to
fly in on time."

I laughed, though I didn't find any of this all that
amusing. "Well, it was my fault for replacing the bride
at the last minute."

"Do you need help?" he asked.

Did I? I wasn't sure. I was tempted to take it. Tempted to ask him to get us a helicopter and get us the heck out of Dodge.

I shook my head. "No, Javier. I don't. These are the consequences of my actions."

My brother treated me to one raised brow. "I hope that's in your wedding vows."

"What do you think marriage is?" I asked.

It was more a genuine question than I had meant it to be.

"If you ask our mother, a moneymaking venture." He stared ahead for a moment. "I'm not sure I can answer that. Or, not sure I should."

"Tell me."

"I don't believe in love, *hermanita*. At least not in the way of fairy tales. I believe in loyalty, and I believe in family. There is love in that. Otherwise I think it is a way we try and make lust into something palatable. A way for men to keep women with them so they can be certain their offspring are theirs."

"Romantic," I said, dryly, thinking about my and Hades' *offspring* then.

"Why are you marrying him?"

I looked up at the ceiling. "Offspring."

"Ah. Congratulations."

I gave him a disparaging look. "You don't mean that."

He looked back at me, the glint in his eye familiar to me. I'd seen it in the mirror enough times. Strange. I'd always associated that steel with my father, but Javier and I shared a mother.

It made me wonder how much steel I missed in our

mother because she camouflaged it so well with all the softness I'd always thought would make a woman seem weak.

"I do," he said. "A person needs heirs to carry on a legacy."

What was my legacy actually going to be? I'd never been less certain.

The doors to the sanctuary swung open, and my brother extended his arm. "Come, let me walk you down the aisle."

"Are you giving me away, Javier?"

"Only you can give yourself away. I'm simply there to provide backup if you decide you need to run."

The music changed and we began to walk forward.

Run.

The word echoed inside of me. As we made our way down the long aisle. And then I looked up, and I saw him. Standing there looking severe. Looking every inch the ruthless monster who had made threats to me in the form of a marriage proposal.

Looking every inch the avenging angel he so often was when he appeared in my hotel rooms, ready to claim me, take me.

Looking like the man I sparred with in boardrooms.

The man I surrendered to in bedrooms.

Hades was far too many things to me to ever be simple. And running would never solve the problem.

It hadn't yet.

Now he was going to be the father of my child. That was something I could barely wrap my head around. Because it required me fully taking on board the fact that I was going to be a mother.

I knew how to parent in the way my father had. I could imagine it. After all, I was also dedicated to my work. Dedicated to Edison. Dedicated to the future, to the family legacy.

But there was something missing from that. And I knew it. I also would never be my mother. Didn't want to be. Suddenly, I felt like I was falling through a void. Toward a man who knew as little about being a father as I knew about being a mother. What were we doing?

Would the child be raised by nannies? While he and I continued to battle against each other?

I couldn't see it. I couldn't even understand it.

But far too soon, we had arrived at the head of the aisle, and Hades reached his hand out to me.

I already knew there was no other option but to take it. I already knew that the devil's bargain had been made. Perhaps sealed with a kiss ten years ago, on my eighteenth birthday.

Perhaps then I had sealed my own fate.

Perhaps there had never been a different outcome.

Eventually, we were bound to be careless. In one way or another. Whether it was pregnancy, being discovered by the press or something else entirely, we had been destined for destruction. I had to figure out a way to make sure we didn't destroy the baby we had created.

I had to.

I was smart, and I could figure it out. I could figure out how to do this.

Maybe I would bring the baby with me to work.

I was going to be exposed as being a female. I was going to be a pregnant CEO. One who had fallen in the basest way. One who had slept with her business rival. And then married him.

There was no more hope left for me to wander through this landscape an untouchable robot.

There was a freedom in this disaster I had not anticipated.

I had made a mistake.

The biggest mistake, and it was being broadcast to the world even now.

His wedding had been upended. I was going to be portrayed as a home-wrecker, at least in part, whether Jessica was able to control the narrative or not.

Some people would enjoy the spectacle of us being together. Others would scoff.

And I had no control.

For the first time in my life, I felt the freedom in the surrender of that.

His dark eyes caught mine, and my stomach went hollow.

No. It wasn't for the first time.

Because I had found freedom in surrender and Hades' arms before. That had always been a part of who I was. But I had never understood how I could live my life that way.

I suddenly did.

I might not have all the logistics together, but I was not devastated.

I had lost control. And that meant no more trying so hard to hold it all together. No more desperate attempts at making sure the narrative was in my power. It wasn't. Nothing was.

I took Hades' hand, and he brought me to the head of the altar, facing him.

I looked out at the audience and tried to see who I recognized there.

It was full of Jessica's friends and family. Because everyone was glued to the spectacle.

And so I would give them one. Because the only acceptable way to spin this was...

I had to be the opposite of everything I had been up until now. I had to be soft. I had to be absolutely overcome by emotion. I was. It wasn't hard for me to play that part. I was angry, yes, frightened. But I was also...

Enthralled with him. As I had ever been.

The feelings that I had for Hades were complicated. I had wanted to call it *hate*, but it had never been able to be contained in such a short, simple word. Not honestly.

It was now, and had ever been, something bigger than the both of us. And so now, I did my best to let that show.

One thing that was never in short supply between us was passion. So I looked at him, with every ounce of passion that I had ever felt for him. And I felt a ripple move through the room.

Because our chemistry was undeniable. That much I knew.

What I hoped, was that this moment would seem undeniable to the people around us. As inevitable and essential as it suddenly did to me.

I could see a dark flame in his eyes. He felt it.

Good.

In some ways, I wanted to punish him. Here in front of everybody. He had been prepared to give himself to another woman. To make vows to another woman. On some level, I had been contending with my feelings of being the woman scorned for weeks now, and it felt good to remind him of what he had nearly lost.

The priest began to recite an extremely benign wedding script. It might have been for Jessica and Hades. It might have been for Hades and me. It didn't make a difference.

And I wouldn't allow it to be a problem.

Because I had found a small scrap of control within myself, and I would not surrender it. Not for anything. I would not allow him to see me crack.

So I made vows to him, promised myself to him, publicly, made vows that I had been keeping for the past ten years. Forsaking all others. Clinging only to him.

I had done all these things. Even as I had told him, told myself, that he was my nemesis.

He had nearly married another woman.

That stabbed me.

It wasn't fair, perhaps. Because I had never intended to take this public. Not ever. I had, somewhere in the back of my mind, imagined that I might marry someone else someday.

Still, he had devastated me.

But now I was here. I was the one having his baby.

I was the one marrying him.

It was time for us to kiss then.

I knew a moment of very real fear. What would it be like to kiss him in full view of all these people? What would it be like to kiss him and have to stop?

That had never happened. Because we kissed in private, behind locked doors. We kissed when we knew

that the kiss was tinder for a fire we would let rage all
night long.

We did not kiss as a destination.

And we certainly didn't do it with an audience.

He wrapped his arm around my waist then, his other
hand going to grip my chin. My breath left my body.
When he touched me like this, it was always the end
for me. The end of my control. The end of everything.

There was nothing but this. Nothing but those dark
eyes burning into mine. That dominant hold, the promise of what would come later.

We didn't have to manufacture a kiss for the crowd.
We had to find a way to keep from revealing ourselves
entirely.

The kiss was carnal. It was all we knew. I kissed him
back, because I was now, as ever, powerless to do anything but surrender to the driving need between us. In
truth, if we could control it we would have. If we could
have found control now, it would have made a mockery
of all that had occurred before. It would have indicated
we might have been able to stop this. But I already knew
we couldn't have.

It was, in that sense, a relief to be lost.

A relief to prove we had no other choice. Then and
now.

When we parted, he was breathing as hard as I was.
I knew it hadn't been a show. The wounded lover inside
of me wanted to claim that as a trophy. And I let her.

I was surprised when Hades addressed the crowd.

"My wife and I will not be staying for the reception,
but I invite all of you to do so. Enjoy the cake. Enjoy
the party. We have some things to discuss."

And with that, he gripped my hand and began to walk me down the aisle. I heard very fast footsteps behind us, and I turned to see Sarah close.

My brother was not far behind.

The four of us arrived in the antechamber of the sanctuary.

"You don't have to go with him," said Sarah.

Javier looked at her. "No," he said. "She doesn't."

"I'm going with him," I said. "Thank you. For being here with me."

Hades regarded both Sarah and Javier. "Your protective natures are admirable. But Florence made her choice when she came here today. She knows that."

I did. It was clear then, when he said that. I had always known what would happen. Somewhere, deep down. I had known he would marry Jessica. Not if I was carrying his baby.

I had known that he would feel a need to make his child legitimate. Because that was who Hades was. He was a businessman, in all things, and that meant acquisition was the purest of things in his mind.

He had acquired me.

He had acquired a baby.

In one fell swoop.

But that means that you've also acquired him.

It went both ways. It always had between us. I was not, nor had I ever been helpless. I had never been a damsel in distress. I had gone to him the first time. I was the one who had made it clear that I wanted to take the simmering attraction between us and turn it into something real.

I had more power here than even I had realized when I had first decided to go to the church.

Yes. I had much more power here than I had given myself credit for.

"I'm all right," I said.

"You're much more than all right," Hades said, propelling me out of the church and down the stairs, toward the limousine that had just pulled up to the curb. That was when I realized paparazzi were everywhere. Flashbulbs went off all around us. And he wrapped his arm around my waist, holding me up against him, pressing one hand to the top of the limousine, my body wedged against the open door. "You've won," he said.

And then he claimed my mouth. And I was lost.

CHAPTER EIGHT

WE DIDN'T SPEAK to each other in the car. I was entirely too frayed around the edges to form an intelligent sentence, so I didn't bother.

Instead, I stared out the window, up at the towering buildings.

"No questions, *agape*?"

You've won.

What had I won? I had just been forced down the aisle and now I was following him wherever it was he had decided to take me.

"What did you mean I won?"

He looked at me, and for a moment I saw a crack. "You didn't want me to marry her," he said.

Rage spiked in my blood. "No, Hades. I don't care what you do or who you marry. What I care about is that you didn't tell me. What I care about is that you thought I was the type of woman who wouldn't care that you'd married someone else. What I care about is that I treated you like an equal, a rival. You treated me like a whore."

He growled, the feral sound shocking me. "I did not treat you that way. You assume I could stop this, Florence. And that is what you don't understand. You have won because in the end my well-ordered plans are for nothing. Because of you."

His words left my stomach churning, rage rolling through me. Unease.

I wasn't surprised when we ended up at the airport.

I just needed a moment. To simply move. To react. Not fight against him, not try to plan the next move. But to breathe.

It wasn't until we were on the plane—a plane we had made love on before—that I decided it was time to figure out what the plan was.

"Where are we going?"

"We have at least six hours until we land in Switzerland."

"Hoping the famously neutral country will help in our communication?"

"No. I have a chalet there. Perfectly out-of-the-way and impossible to access if one does not have a helicopter. Well stocked. It will see us through this initial storm, and the holidays. Isn't that romantic. Off on a secluded Christmas honeymoon."

It made my stomach churn. Because I had been thinking about how lovely it was that he and I would have a month together in New York, just a while ago. It hadn't gone that way.

And now we would be shut in a house together. Albeit, a house that I assumed was large enough we could also never run into each other if we wanted. It didn't fill me with the same sort of uncomplicated thrill that it had two months ago.

Though it did still thrill me. Even if it was a dark, twisted sort of feeling.

"We have six hours," he repeated. "Plenty of time to cover whatever ground you need."

"I haven't slept." And I didn't think that I could sleep even if I wanted to. Not after all of that. I was utterly and completely undone by the events of the day, but it had left me supercharged.

"Sleep if you wish," he said.

I wouldn't let him tell me what to do on top of everything else, even though I was so tired I was in danger of losing consciousness in my seat. "I don't. What is the plan? Do you honestly expect us to be married forever?"

"I don't see why not. This makes sense. We can make it work. Why be competitors? What would be the end result of our continuing on the way we have been anyway? We would destroy one another eventually, I assume. I don't actually want to destroy you, Florence."

I looked at him, my stomach sour. "Then what is it you want?"

He lifted a dark brow. "I want to navigate this without our empires crumbling. It would be best if you were a help and not a hindrance."

"Hades, I am carrying your baby. I never had to tell you. I chose to come and speak to you. I chose to handle this with as much integrity as I could. I chose to keep the pregnancy. I chose to walk down that aisle toward you. I had ample opportunity to escape. Do you not think my brother was standing by with the means to spirit me out of the city if I wanted him to? I chose to marry you. You might ask yourself why."

"Because I threatened you."

"Because it is useful to me. You underestimate me. At every turn. I have the control here. I could have denied you access to this child, and you know it. The whole world was ignorant to the fact that we were together. I could have let you marry her. I could have let you have your children with her."

"But you couldn't," he said, his eyes dark, burning into mine. "Or you would have. You wouldn't let her have me."

"You bastard. You let me find out about your engagement in the press. You were as cruel as you could have been, and that was a choice. You…" I stood up. "Let's talk about it then, Hades. Let's talk about the ways in which you are *the actual devil.*"

"You and I had a sexual relationship," he said. His gaze was dispassionate then. A stranger's. "I never promised you fidelity of any kind. Likewise, I never promised Jessica fidelity. When I told you my engagement changed nothing, I was being honest with you."

"But you didn't explain it to me."

"Given the nature of our relationship I didn't think it mattered."

That made me even angrier. "You treated it like a business matter. You were the CEO of the sex so it didn't matter what I thought because I'm just beneath you. Because you never saw me as a human being, did you?"

He looked past me. "As you said yourself. I'm the very god of hell. And think about that, Florence. That is what my father chose to name me. Whether that speaks to his view on me, or what he hoped I would become, is nearly irrelevant. I was never shaped in the mold of a good man. And I never pretended to be. You… You came to me. Far too innocent, and far too young. I should've turned you away."

"But you didn't. Not once. Not once over the last decade," I said.

"Guilty." His dark eyes gleamed. "And you kept coming back."

That was the truth. The ugly, awful truth of it. There was no innocent party here. We'd used each other. He'd never gotten to know me, but I'd never gotten to know him either. I'd put the company, my reputation above any potential relationship with him.

I had thought I might be as cold as he was at one time.

I didn't feel cold now.

I felt raw. Bruised.

"This is our consequence, I suppose," I said, quietly.

He reached over and poured himself a glass of whiskey, settled deep into the couch and stared across the expanse of space between us. "Quite the consequence. You might as well vent your rage at me. Get it over with."

He said it so casually. So dry. So...controlled. As if none of this touched him. As if he could be here with me or with Jessica and it would make no difference to him. As if my feelings were an inconvenience he would allow just for the moment.

"Is that what you think this is? That I'm... Angry and need to vent?" It wasn't untrue. But there was so much more to it. Of course, I hadn't even begun to work out what all my feelings were, so I felt like I was treading on dangerous ground.

"It seems as if that's the case."

"What did you feel?" I was so angry at him. He was such an impenetrable wall. I knew him in business. And I knew him in bed. And in the time in between he had gotten so much more of me. Because I had shown my

hand, hadn't I? I had shown my hurt over his engagement. I had gone to him and given him that loss of
control. Even if I had scraped some power back by reminding him that I'd chosen to tell him about the baby,
I was the one who'd given more of my…heart. And what
had he given me?

Nothing.

An orgasm.

A child.

Our consequence.

And yet I was no closer to having any idea of what
he felt for anyone or anything. Perhaps he really did feel
nothing. I'd known a moment of true relief followed by
true panic listening to him and Jessica worked out the
story for the dissolution of their engagement. Because
both of them had been so utterly dispassionate. So cold.
As if they were made of stone.

Meanwhile I was not made of anything of the kind.
I knew that now.

I was entirely made of the sorts of feelings I didn't
want at all.

"When?"

"When I denied you. When I told you that I wouldn't
be with you anymore after you were married. Did you
feel anything?"

He leaned back, a shadow concealing part of his face.
He was starkly beautiful. High cheekbones, a square
jaw, that mouth that had done so many wicked things to
me. I could barely catch my breath when I looked at him.

"I knew you would never be able to manage it." He
took a sip of his whiskey, all arrogance. "If you had been

able to control yourself with me, *agape*, you would have done so years ago."

"You're wrong." At least I was confident that I was telling the truth. "I wouldn't have shared you. Do you have any idea how angry I was, knowing that you had slept with me while you were planning to marry somebody else?"

"It angered you that I was having sex with another woman during our time together?"

"Of course it did. But I never thought that I had an exclusive claim to your body, Hades. I did not think that you would get engaged without at least speaking to me."

He frowned. "So it is the perceived emotional betrayal that bothers you? Even though you and I have never had anything like a relationship?"

"Yes."

It all bothered me. In truth.

"Put your mind at ease, Florence. I did not love her. Neither was I sleeping with her."

I let that truth settle over me. I had figured at that point that he didn't love her, but the idea that he hadn't slept with the woman—who had been exceedingly beautiful—had not occurred to me.

"Why didn't you tell me that?"

Yet again, it was like the mask slipped. Giving me a view of something more feral. An intensity normally reserved for sex.

"Because. Because it would've been better if you would've stayed away. Don't you think? It would have been better if I could have married her and kept you away from me." It was an intensity that I was only used to when we were engaged in work battles and bedroom games. It was not something I was used to in conversation with him. But then, we didn't do conversation. We didn't talk. We didn't share pieces of ourselves. Only our bodies.

"If you think that, then why did you marry me at all? Why did you… In your office that day, why have me then. If you were getting married to get rid of me, then why? Because if you hadn't, and if you would have remembered the condom, we wouldn't be in this situation."

He was across the space, and over to me before I could draw my next breath. His large hand resting against the base of my throat. "Because if I could, I would have. As it is for you, it is for me. You know that."

The words were like a balm to all those wounds in my spirit. It was easy to believe that it wasn't as enthralling for him as it was for me. Easy to believe he had other lovers, that this was just one flavor of sex he enjoyed.

But his face now told me otherwise.

I really was his shame.

If he wasn't a slave to it, the same as I was, he would never touch me.

But he had touched me. Over and over again for years.

I had power here. I needed to remember that.

"I do," I said. "So why sit there and hurl those things at me like accusations, when you know you are no better."

His lips curved, his body relaxed and he moved back to the couch across from me. My heart was pounding hard. Not with fear.

With desire.

Because it was always like this. It didn't matter if it

should be. It didn't matter if it was wrong, toxic, obsessive.

It was always this.

If we could have stopped, we would have stopped.

"I act with control at all times, Florence." He took another sip of his scotch. "I understand that you may not know that. Because the one exception to that in all of my life has been you. I knew that I shouldn't touch you. That first time you came to me, I knew. Do you have any idea… If my father had found out, let's just say the punishment likely would not have been worth the reward I found in your arms. And yet. I made the same mistake with you. Over and over again. I let myself have you, even knowing that I should not. When I saw the terms of my father's will, I saw a means of escaping it. When the time ran out, I knew that I had to choose a wife, and when I found Jessica, I knew that I had found someone with goals that were the same as my own. She did not want love. She needed to marry to help inject something new into her image. I needed to fulfill the terms of the will. Both of us needed to fulfill external obligations."

I watched him, the way that he moved, the way that he spoke. I was fascinated by him. Because this was not the kind of thing we ever engaged in. This was more conversation than we ever had.

I felt desperate then. To close this gap between us. And yet, I knew that it would be foolish. Dangerous. Already…

I had said that he felt the same way I did, but I feared it wasn't true.

Already, I feared that my feelings ran far deeper than his.

I refused, utterly refused, to name them.

Anyway, if I thought that I felt something... Anything like love for him, I was simply delusional. A woman looking to explain away her behavior as something other than pure unadulterated lust. We didn't know each other. And what I did know about him did not make him the sort of man I ought to have feelings for.

Sex wasn't love.

I knew that.

Respect in business was not love.

But right then, my mind clicked back to the first thing he had said.

"What do you mean your father would've punished you?"

"I mean exactly that. My father ran his company with an iron fist. And he ran his home the same way. My mother was not like your mother, Florence. She did not run away seeking adventure. She sought safety. Peace. But had she taken my father's heir with her, my father would've never stopped looking for her. She had to find safety, and to do that she had to leave me. Without his preferred target for his rages, my father had to adjust his focus on to me."

I didn't know what to say to that. Because of all the things that I had thought about his father, and the relationship Hades might've had with him, I hadn't ever considered that he was physically abusive.

There were no rumors about it in the media. Nothing.

He was such a strong man, and proud. Hard. Things that made him impenetrable at times, but the idea of him being…harmed by his own father. Broken. I hated that. Whatever anger I felt for him was replaced by shock. By the unending sadness that I felt thinking about how he'd been hurt…and I hadn't known.

His father's death had been a shock. He'd been healthy, and while her own father hadn't liked him at all, he'd been strangely upset about the death of his rival. Or perhaps it was death in general. He'd died two years later of a heart attack. I supposed there was a lesson there about overworking yourself.

I didn't know how to learn it.

"Hades…"

"It is nothing. Do not waste your tears for me, a child who grew up with access to the greatest education, the best means of travel in the world. There are many in life who have struggles, and I would not consider myself one of them."

"Your father physically abused you, and you don't consider that a struggle," I asked, feeling incredulous.

"No. If I did, perhaps I would speak of it with a therapist. As it stands, I'm fine."

I looked at the strong, remote man sitting across from me, and I had to ask myself how he thought he was fine. How I had ever thought he was fine.

What I knew about him for certain was that he was a wall. Until the wall came down, and then he was passion personified. And then he was fire.

Are you any different?

Maybe not. Maybe I compartmentalized things just the same as he did.

Maybe I had to keep myself protected too. But it didn't come from a place of having been… Abused.

"I'm sorry," I said. "I wish I would have known. All that time we knew each other… You were twenty-one the first time we were together."

"If my father had access to me, then he would hit me. And I allowed it, because… He told me that if I ever displeased him, he would find my mother. And he would kill her. I had no reason to disbelieve him."

"Why are you only now telling me this?"

"Because we have only now just decided to have a conversation. You are marrying me, and you need to know the manner of man you've married. My father wasn't a safe man. I never had any desire for a passionate marriage. Things… They will not be the same between us now."

I tried to process that. Tried to understand what he was saying. "You think that we are suddenly going to not have passion between us?"

"We have to figure out how to arrange our lives so that we can work together. Things have changed. Where once we could fight one another, act as opponents, we cannot now. We are having a child."

"I understand that."

"I don't know how to be a good father," he said.

It felt like a warning. Combined with what he'd just shared with me about his father but… I was angry with Hades. Hurt. But I wasn't hurt enough to allow myself to believe he was the sort of monster his father had been.

Yes, he'd hurt me.

He would never hurt me physically.

I had been with him for ten years. Even if it wasn't a relationship. He had been my lover.

He was difficult. He wasn't evil.

"I don't know how to be a good mother. And I realized as I walked toward you down that aisle that we are both ill-suited to this, but it is what's happened. We will make it work."

"We must make it work," he said. "Sometimes I think my father simply wanted me to have a child because what he really wanted was for me to pass down the pain he meted out on to me. He said that once. That when I had children I would understand. What a trial they are. How difficult it is to try and shape one in the way that you need them shaped. He said one day I would understand."

"Your father was weak," I said. I had many opinions about his father, mostly given to me by my own father, but none of them had been about his actions as a man. They had simply been about the way he ran his business. My father had known. But I knew now. "A weak man has to rule with tyranny. That isn't you. It never has been. You might not have always been my favorite person, Hades, but I have always respected you. I have always respected the brilliance that you brought into our competitiveness. I have always preferred going up against you than anyone that I could beat easily. And you have enjoyed the fight as well. The truth is, you've never tried to crush me. Not even once. Because that doesn't bring you joy. You like a fight. But you're not a bully. They are two different things."

"I will never touch our child in anger," he said. "You have my vow."

I believed him. Because hadn't he experienced enough uncertainty? A mother who had left him for her own safety. A father who had used his fists on him.

I felt despairing.

For him. The child he'd been. The man that he was.

The man I had known all this time, who perhaps could've at least been my friend, whose pain I might have known, and yet I didn't, because I had been so focused on him as an object of desire.

And then later as my competition.

"We will merge the companies. There is no other option. We simply will not be able to conduct them as two separate entities. Nobody would believe it was possible, first of all."

"I don't like that," I said.

"Think about it," he said. "The heir to your throne is now the heir to mine. And so what difference does it make if we keep them separate for the next thirty years? Eventually, the company will belong to our child. And so, we might as well make them into one."

I couldn't deny that he had a point. I also felt like he was doing his level best to try and push the conversation away from personal things.

"What about fidelity?" I asked.

"That has nothing to do with our companies."

"It is the holiday season and we have gone away for a honeymoon. I say we wait to speak about the logistics of the companies."

"Not something I would have expected to hear from you."

"Well, I didn't expect to be married and having a child either. I find the topic more concerning than I did only twenty-four hours ago."

"The truth is, we have to come to a consensus on what

we're going to do with the company and release a joint statement by tomorrow."

"Why?"

"Because it matters," he said. "Because we cannot afford to have any speculation or accusation that we do not have total control over what's happening. Do you not understand that? I have taken a contract with the government, and nothing can appear untoward."

There was a level of intensity to him that I had experienced in business meetings, but there was something different as well. I wondered if it had to do with what he just told me about his father.

There had been punishments. When he had made mistakes, he had been hurt.

That was what he was acting like now. As if a mistake was going to come with a heavy price.

"Then we can merge," I said.

I felt myself give. But it did not feel weak. I didn't feel like I was letting him win. I felt like I was finding a path to peace in my own life. Like I was taking this moment and turning it into something better. I'd had the epiphany standing there at the altar that there was something powerful in this loss of control. I experienced it again just now.

I had always imagined that my spine was a core of steel. Because when it came to dealing with my parents, I felt like I had to bend too often. But this was not a reshaping of myself. It was a strength. He was being rigid, and he couldn't find his way around it.

But I could.

"I will—"

"We must maintain equal power in the company," I said.

He looked at me. "My company is worth more."

"I don't care."

"That simply isn't how these things work."

On this, I would not bend. "I've worked far too hard to surrender everything to you now."

"Perhaps you should've thought of that before you surrendered to me the way you did in my office."

"Which of us surrendered truly, Hades? Can you answer that question?"

His lip curled. "We will have equal positions," he said.

"Good. Come now, you would not wish to elevate yourself above me using blackmail. I don't even believe you would ruin me if you had the chance. Because again, you're not a bully. You don't want uncontested power. You want a fight, because it makes you better, and you know it. We have always made each other better. Iron sharpening iron."

He chuckled. "Perhaps. Though in my experience when a person with a hard head goes up against another it is usually bone bruising flesh."

I let the silence lapse between us, and I tried to imagine the treatment he had received from his father. Let it reshape the things I'd assumed about him all that time ago.

I had thought that he had been his father's pride.

I would never have assumed that Hades was being physically harmed by his father.

Not ever.

"You can tell me," I said.

"Do you really want to hear this? I will say the worst of it is always what ends up in the mind. With the body... you can learn to shut yourself down. But when you are locked away for days at a time. When your father buys you things only to destroy them..." His throat worked. "That was the only reason he ever gave me anything. To make me care for it, so that it could be used against me." His smile then was like a dagger. "He loved Christmas. He would make an elaborate setup and throw a huge party for his clients. He would wrap presents and put them beneath the tree. Sometimes none would be for me. Other times there would be. One year he burned them all, wrapped, in the yard." He frowned. "The worst, I think, was never getting to know what they were."

"That's horrible. Despicable. You don't have to have had a good father to know that's wrong and you would never do it."

He shook his head. "No. I never would."

Silence between us was dangerous, because the minute we stopped speaking, there was only tension to fill the space between us.

"The matter of our marriage," I said.

"Yes?"

"I don't want to share you."

He looked at me, as though he pitied me. "You will regret that, later. When you are tired of our fighting. When you are weary of having to deal with my moods."

I didn't understand why he couldn't simply tell me what he wanted rather than speaking in riddles. But then I supposed this highlighted the true problem. I had known him for all of these years and never really known him.

"What is it you wanted from a wife?"

"I told you. Children, and no demand on me. I did not wish to get married to make my life more complicated. I wanted to get married to solve a problem. That's all."

I felt like my chest had been punctured. "And I've never been much of a solution, have I?"

"No," he bit out. "If you think this is a convenience to me, you would be incorrect."

I still felt…sorry for him. But that gave him no excuse for trying to hurt me. Simply because he was trying to force distance back between us.

"I'm tired," I said. "I'm going to bed." I stood up. "I already know where the bedroom is."

And then I left him there, and some part of myself.

Things were already too complicated without splintering my feelings for him even more.

I was angry at him. For being…

Human.

I preferred him to be the devil.

Because at least then I could fight against him with no pity whatsoever.

CHAPTER NINE

I WOKE AS we touched down in Switzerland. I felt disoriented for a moment. And then the nausea reminded me. I was pregnant. And I had married Hades.

I had little time to marinate on that before the bedroom door opened. I had changed into a luxurious sweat suit I'd found hanging in the closet before going to sleep—I chose not to ponder whether it was for Jessica or for me.

"Are you well?" he asked.

"Not especially," I said.

But it didn't matter, because we were landing. I changed into a dress I found in the closet and soon we were transferred from the airplane to a helicopter. And I couldn't help myself, I clung to his arm as the unwieldy vehicle took off in the wind.

He put his hand over mine, a gesture so comforting it made my eyes well up with tears, and it made me want to punch myself. Because I shouldn't go getting emotional over him. Not when he didn't actually care about me. Physical connection was something we had. But we'd never had anything more.

It took twenty minutes in the helicopter for us to arrive at the top of a snowy peak, surrounded by white-capped pine trees, and an awe-inspiring vista of the Alps. It was definitely a place to go to disappear.

We got out of the helicopter, and the chill from the wind shocked me. He shielded me with his body as we walked toward the house. He put his fingerprints up against a pad on the door, and it unlocked, allowing us entry.

The interior was stunning. All light pine and glass that looked out over the craggy Alps. We were cocooned in silence, wrapped in the blanket of all that snow.

For the first time in my life, I was alone with him and it wasn't only for a matter of hours. For the first time, we weren't a secret. The whole world knew about us.

But here it didn't feel like the world existed.

Bizarrely, I found myself thankful he'd taken us here. Bizarre because I didn't think I really owed him thanks for much of anything right now.

He pushed a button on the wall and the glass-encased fireplace roared to life. I could see through it, straight to the outside, where the flames danced on the snow. There was a time when I would have relished this. A chance to spend days exploring his body? A chance to try and exhaust some of the need that constantly burned between us?

But it was different now. This wasn't temporary.

We were looking at something much more permanent.

I had never dreamed of forever with Hades. Though in some ways I'd dreaded it. The idea that I would never be able to want any other man. That I would end up alone because my body had found his, so my heart would never find anyone.

This was the inglorious inevitable.

Here we were, expecting a child. Married. And yet we were the same two people who met in secret rooms and communicated using only our bodies. We had no practice at this.

We were competitors. We had never shared our personal space.

Though, looking around this room, I could not say whether or not there was anything especially personal about it.

"How long have you had this house?"

"Five years or so," he said, discarding his suit jacket, mesmerizing me as he undid the cuffs on his white shirt and began to roll the sleeves up over his forearms.

In the past, that would have been an invitation to only one thing. I could imagine what might have happened only a few months ago with ease. Everything about his body had always excited me.

I really did like his forearms.

I tried to focus on the information he had just given me, not the skin he had just revealed. He'd owned this house for five years, and there was nothing personal anywhere. No marker that it was anything different than one of the many hotel suites they had stayed in together.

"Dinner should be ready for us."

"Is it dinnertime?"

It felt like morning to me. But I realized that I had been awake for twenty-four hours, changed time zones during that time, slept for about six hours, then changed time zones again.

Time, at this point, truly was relative.

"It is dinner hour, but you may call it whatever you wish."

For a moment I thought it was significant we were sharing a meal. And then I realized we had done so many times. But we had never sat down to a table together. It had never been officially having dinner, going on a date or anything like that. We had eaten together in bed. Countless times.

In many ways, we shared a lot more intimacy than I had given us credit for.

He knew what my favorite thing to get from room service was.

He didn't know what I would order at a restaurant, though.

And that highlighted just how turned inside out our intimacies were.

He walked ahead of me, and I followed, since I didn't know where anything in the house was. He led me into the dining room, where there was a massive, long table with candles flickering in candelabras. Food was spread from one end to the other, as if he had been expecting a dinner party, and not just me.

"Not exactly a cheeseburger," I said, looking at the potatoes, steak and glorious roasted vegetables, along with the basket of rolls and platter of cheese and meat set out on the table.

"If you would rather have a cheeseburger, then I can call the staff back."

"This will do," I said, doing my best to keep my tone dry.

I was learning about a third version of Hades, I realized.

Whatever this was. I didn't think it was the real him.

But then the real him wasn't the man that I saw in different business meetings either. Not entirely.

The closest thing, I really did think, was the man who took me to bed, but even that man had secrets.

More than I had even begun to guess at.

"What is this exactly?"

"Dinner," he said, his voice hard. He sat down at the head of the table, as if he expected me to take a seat at his right hand. To be spiteful, I sat at his left, with one chair space between us.

"I can see that it's dinner," I said. "But I'm not entirely certain what farce this is. We know each other far too well to engage in this kind of behavior. You can't pretend to be civilized with me, Hades. I know who you are. I know what you like. You pretend. Every day you pretend. And when you first get the chance, you come to my room, to my bed, and you tie me to it. You're not civilized. Any more than I am."

"Do you want to live that way? Because I don't. I lived with a father who didn't bother to engage in civility in his daily life. Better, I think, to have an outlet for it in the bedroom, than to leave it all over the dining table, don't you think?"

I could understand what he was saying. He was equating the passion between us to the abuse his father had meted out, and that wasn't fair. What we did was intense, but it wasn't abusive. We both wanted it. We both enjoyed it. No one was a victim of anything. He knew that, I knew he did. If he thought for even one second that what he did might cause me harm, he simply would never... He would never.

"Eat," he said.

I would have loved to shout back at him that I wasn't hungry. Sadly, I was. The nausea had begun to shift into peckishness, and I found that I really did want something to eat.

"You were going to marry Jessica Clare, and... Never sleep with her?"

"Of course I intended to sleep with her. I intended to sleep with her and produce children."

"But you wouldn't have slept with her until then."

"I didn't especially want her," he said. "However, I am a goal-oriented man and, given a reason, I could have roused myself to do so."

I looked down at my food, my lip curling. "I see."

"Did you never have plans to marry?"

I frowned. "No. I did. At least, I hoped to someday. I hoped to find someone that was nothing like you. A man who would give me a gentle, easy life. Who would support my ambitions. Who would... Be nothing like either my mother or my father. Someone I can have a partnership with."

His black eyes were fathomless. His lips flat. "How cozy."

"Does it sound cozy?" I looked around the stark space. "If this is your version of *cozy*, Hades, we have a long way to go."

"Sweet summer child. My version of *cozy* is the underworld. Or hadn't you figured that out yet? This is me attempting to be human." He smiled, but it wasn't nice. "I had thought that you might like it better."

I couldn't tell if he was being dry, if he was exaggerating to prove a point, or if he was actually being sadly, extremely honest.

But that was the problem. I knew compartmentalized, masked versions of him.

And he knew the same of me.

"I'm still not sure what the performance is. We got married with an hour of planning. I found out I was pregnant... It hasn't even been a day. I am exhausted. I can't even begin to picture... To picture what the future looks like. A child, Hades. You and me."

I didn't think I imagined that his skin went slightly waxen then. "We will hire professionals," he said. "People to care for the child who are experts in development, and in psychology."

"You think that's what the child needs?"

"I know what a child does not need. I know what my father did to me was..." He looked off into the distance. "He made me into an exceptional businessman. He made me into a weapon. I have one weakness. That has proven to be you. Over and over again. Oddly, it is the weakness I find more concerning than any of the emotionless strengths. Because at least when it comes to other areas of my life I can act dispassionately. With you it's never dispassionate."

I didn't know whether to be flattered by that or not. And because this wasn't a few stolen hours. Because this was our life. Our relationship. Our future. I decided to just go ahead and say it. "Is that a compliment? You keep talking about me like I'm a venereal disease that you can't get rid of. There aren't antibiotics strong enough to rid you of Florence Clare."

"You speak of me as if I'm the same."

I knew that was true. I wasn't any more flattering to

him than he was to me. I only knew how to talk about the thing between us in a way that could protect me.

If I spoke of it like it was a sickness, something that was being done to me, something that I didn't want, then somehow I wasn't at fault for it. And perhaps couldn't be hurt by it. But when he had said that he was getting married, it had been proven to me that I could be quite hurt by it. I was far too vulnerable with him.

But if he was ever going to change…

No one had ever made him feel safe. No one had ever shown him what a family should look like. I wasn't sure I had a lock on that, but maybe I could…show him.

"This is something I never wanted to do to you," he said. "Do you want honesty? I am the son of a black hole. A man who absorbed and destroyed everything that came into his sphere. I never wanted to put you in a position where my hand would be in your business, but here we are. It is how we must go. I never wanted to put you in a position where your life would be directly connected with mine."

"You should have thought of that before you took my virginity, Hades. Because our lives have been bound together ever since, and you know that."

"Sex, Florence. And for a while that's what it was. And it was fine. We took risks. That day, a risk that… Had its reward, I suppose. Now we must figure out what to do with it. But you act as if you want something else from me than this." He swept his hand along the distance of the table. "From a nice dinner, from a warm dwelling. How? And why? Because this is not temporary. Nor is it a few stolen hours. We must think about what we can maintain. What can be sustained."

Was he worried? About us drowning in desire for each other now that we had an endless amount of time?

I looked at him, and I honestly couldn't say.

He was a man who made little sense to me.

My feelings for him made little sense to me.

He was like a puzzle that I could never quite put together. I had been a foolish girl but I was eighteen. I had looked at him and seen myself. The child of a powerful man, who didn't have his mother around. Who had been dragged to all of these events. Who wanted to do well. Who had a sense of exceptionalism. I had looked at him and I thought I had found the other side to myself.

Or maybe it was something I had convinced myself of so that I could justify wanting to sleep with him.

But we weren't the same. I had been telling myself we were all this time. But while this experience was showing me where I was vulnerable, where I was soft, he was doubling down on artifice.

And wanting me to thank him for it.

I wondered then how we would handle it if what had happened was a one-night stand. If we didn't actually assume that we knew each other. If it wasn't the product of ten years' worth of risky behavior that had finally caught us out.

But if we had been true strangers, rather than this… strange thing that we were. Strangers who had watched each other brush their teeth.

Strangers who knew each other's room service order by heart.

Something had to give.

He couldn't.

Maybe it would have to be me.

"When I was little," I said, "I thought my mother was the most beautiful woman in the world. I used to love to watch her get ready to go out. Once, I told my father that. He laughed at me. He asked me if I had ever read a newspaper. He asked why I didn't know that when my mother went out it was to humiliate him. He said that she was a whore, and that everything beautiful she put on her face and everything lovely she wrapped her body in were lures to catch men like they were unsuspecting large-mouthed bass." I flinched inside, even thinking of it. It had been such an unnecessary thing to say to a child. I had loved both my father and mother so much. I loved my father all the way up to the end, even knowing that he was flawed. Even knowing that in that moment his hurt had allowed him to be so unkind.

I swallowed hard. "All I knew then was that I could never be like my mother. Not really. I had wanted to be. What little girl wouldn't? She is quite simply one of the most stunning women in the world. And maybe now she has changed. Some of it was too much plastic surgery, but isn't that the mark of pain for a woman who has spent her life being defined by a certain sort of beauty? All I know is in that moment I was taught to fear beauty. I was taught there was something cynical, dangerous, beneath that sort of femininity."

I leaned back in my chair. "Then I looked up the articles on my mother. Like he suggested. I was eight, maybe. Reading about how my mother was suspected of having multiple affairs. Do you know, until that moment I hadn't realized that the older boys who came around sometimes were my half brothers? You probably know Javier and Rocco better than I do. My father actually wasn't cruel. Not habitually. He made mistakes. He certainly said the wrong things out of anger. Even without the intent of being cruel, he took my view of the world and twisted it. He made me afraid of being a woman. Because when I saw the things that they wrote about her, I knew I never wanted that to be me. It will be now, don't you think?"

I shook my head and laughed. "Here I am, her daughter. Felled by the absolutely wrong man. By my inability to resist desire. Temptation. Caught in a snare of my own beauty."

He stared at me, his eyes blank. "And why are you telling me this?"

"Because you don't know it. Because for all these years, for all of this... History between us. We don't know each other. We can't sit down and strategize what kind of marriage we are going to have like we are having a business meeting. We have to actually make allowances for the people that we are. Maybe we even need to get to know each other."

"Do you even know yourself, Florence?"

The words were like a slap, directly across my face. "Excuse me?"

"You strike me as one of the most disingenuous people on the planet. You wear a mask all the time. The only place that I have ever found you to be remotely authentic is when you're naked. On your knees. Tied to a bed. Then I see glimpses of who you might be. You go into business meetings like you are dressed for war."

I flinched, because it was nothing less than the truth. Except... I did know myself. I did. I understood why I turned away from the things that I wanted. Why I forced myself to be a specific kind of strong, because I had decided that being soft was too weak.

I understood that I had decided to pattern my life more after my father because...

Because I would be more successful. Because I didn't want to be an object of ridicule. Yes, my mother had monetary success. She was famous. But not for the things that I wanted to be famous for.

So the only other way that I could even begin to think to find success wasn't behaving like my father. I knew that I did that.

And when I went home, I... Worked more. I went out for drinks with my friend, and I didn't tell her that I had an obsession with my business rival, because...

Because the real things about myself embarrassed me.

Because the truth of me was something that not even I wanted to know.

And that he saw that, while he remained an enigma to me, made me so angry I wanted to pick up my plate and throw it in his face.

"What makes you so confident that I am myself with you?" I asked.

"Because you have no reason to perform. You never wanted anything from me but my body, and that means you are an exceptionally honest lover. You only take what you want. And nothing more. And everything you give is something that you want to give. It is not an insult."

"No. Just the idea that I don't know my own mind."

"Am I wrong?" he asked.

"What about you? Who are you, really? You're not any better than I am. You were looking to style a marriage to keep your business. You have no heart. No soul."

"Ah, but the difference between you and I is I don't believe that I do."

"No, the difference between you and I is that I do. You will recall my reaction to your engagement."

His face went blank. "Yes. I do recall that. If nothing else, Florence, I do enjoy your passion."

Something about that sent me over the edge. An edge I couldn't see the bottom of. I found myself standing up, moving over to where he sat at the head of the table. He turned toward me, looking up, his eyes glittering.

I was trying to find something new between us. But this was…familiar. This was us.

Our connection.

Maybe I could find something new in it.

I reached behind my back and unzipped my dress. Letting it fall to my waist, down to the floor.

I had succeeded in shocking him. I could see it on his face then.

He had not expected that.

I took off my bra, pushed my panties down and stepped out of my shoes.

Then I maneuvered myself so that I was straddling his lap, completely naked, while he sat there fully clothed.

I gripped his face in my hands, and I kissed him. Not the performance that we had engaged in at the church, for the paparazzi. But a kiss for him, a kiss for me. A kiss to prove to him that I was not cold-blooded. Not in any capacity.

"Why?" he asked, gripping hold of my hands, taking them captive.

"I don't know how to talk to you," I said, because that was honest. Because it revealed something, when normally I never would have. But this had to be us and new all at the same time. I would find a way. "But I have more than enough practice wanting you. Whether I'm angry with you, whether I think I hate you, or not. And I'm tired. I am so tired of living in all these moments that I don't know how to handle. I want you. Because at least I understand that. I've had years to come to terms with it. There is no logic in it. There is nothing right about it. But it simply is. And I need something that makes sense."

He growled, wrapped his arm around my waist and stood, moving his other hand to my thigh, bracing me as he carried me away from the dining table and down the vast hall toward the bedroom. The lights came on automatically as we entered the room, and he deposited me in the center of the bed.

I watched him hungrily as he began to undo the buttons on that white shirt.

As he began to expose his gorgeous chest, a feast for my eyes that I would never tire of.

He moved his hand to his belt, undoing it with one hand, then he untucked the shirt and shrugged it from his shoulders, depositing it on the floor. He slid his belt from the loops, but did not bind me with it this time. Instead, it went down with the shirt, followed by everything else. Until his gloriously familiar body was pressed against mine. Naked and perfect and everything that I had ever desired.

He looked down into my eyes, and he kissed me. It was familiar, and yet…

It was our wedding night.

It was our wedding night.

I could not push that thought away once I had it.

This wasn't the same. It wasn't a few stolen moments in a hotel room. An hour between meetings.

This was our wedding night.

Hades was no longer my dirty secret. And I was no longer his.

He was my husband. I was his wife.

And it was like he could read those thoughts moving through my mind, because something changed. In the way he held me, in the way he kissed me. It was still desperate.

But there was… Something else in it that I couldn't put a name to.

Like the tone of the desperation had changed. As if the melody of the song had shifted.

His tongue slid against mine, claiming me deep. And I clung to his shoulders, broad and magnificent. I moved my hands down his back, gloried in those familiar muscles.

This wasn't the last time.

That thought stabbed me. Made tears prick my eyes. It wasn't the last time.

Every other time it had felt like it might be. Had felt like it had the potential to be.

In the time when we had conceived the baby…

I had been so sure that it was a goodbye I wasn't ready to have.

I'd given one that had felt necessary. One that had felt like the right thing. Except it had torn me to pieces.

But this wasn't the last time.

This was the first night of something else. Something different, if we could find a way to make it work.

Yes, I had done the familiar thing by kissing him. Perhaps taking him to bed had, in the moment, felt like the easy thing.

This wasn't easy, though.

It never had been.

It had always been a fight for something. For something that didn't have a name.

For a satisfaction that might never see its end.

Just like I had realized there was strength in softness as I made my way up to the head of the altar at the church, I realized there was more to this than I had ever let myself believe.

The sex was a conversation. In a way that I had not ever let myself understand.

His hands spoke volumes as they moved over my skin.

Whether it was rough or soft.

His mouth, commanding, soft, cruel, caring, could speak without words.

He kissed his way down my body, forced my legs apart and licked me directly at my center.

His tongue over my slick flesh was hot, perfect. And I arched my hips up against him, grabbed his head and held him there as he feasted on me like he would never get enough.

He wasn't sorry that he had married me.

That was another strange and clarifying thought.

This was not a man who wanted another woman.

He would've slept with her. That wounded me.

But he... He hadn't wanted her. It would never have been this.

Not ever.

Maybe he really didn't have this with anyone else.

Because this was singular. This was him, and it was me. And maybe he had been right about that too.

That this was the most myself I ever was. In his arms. Because it was the only place I could actually be soft. The only place I wasn't afraid of what I wanted. The only place I wasn't scared of my own pleasure.

I had been wounded, thinking about how I was the one person he never had to worry would sell stories about him. But it occurred to me that I had often felt safest with him for that very reason.

He could not betray me without betraying himself.

And so we had real trust. Real safety between us and I had never truly appreciated why. Or how deep it ran.

He pushed two fingers inside of me and I reached my peak, crying out his name until he moved up my body and kissed me again, swallowing my pleasure whole.

Then he thrust inside of me in one, smooth movement. I lost my breath.

I held his face in my hands, and he pressed his forehead to mine as he began to move.

As he claimed me. Possessed me.

"Hades," I whispered against his mouth.

He growled, his movements becoming a frenzy. I felt desire begin to build in me again, higher and higher, harder and faster.

We were a storm. Fire. Destruction. Everything bad that I had ever labeled us.

But we were something else too.

Even if I couldn't find a name for it.

His pleasure unraveled him, as he shook and found his peak, gripping my hips as he poured himself into me. And I found my own oblivion, biting his neck to keep from saying his name again. Because I could only strip myself bare so many times.

Afterward, as the oblivion cleared, I realized that we had nowhere to run to.

Because he was my husband. I was his wife.

And I was in love with him.

CHAPTER TEN

AFTER THAT I couldn't sleep. He did. And deeply. Which struck me as the most infuriatingly male thing that had ever occurred.

I loved him, though.

And I found myself sitting up by the window, gazing thoughtlessly out into the darkness at what I knew was the vast expanse of wilderness below.

Hades was like that wilderness. I had been looking at the trees and not beyond. Into the darkness. At the vastness contained there.

This revelation made me rethink everything. From that very first moment. Because if I evaluated the things that I had done through a lens of feeling, rather than simple lust, I saw him differently.

If I took the things that he had just told me, and I mixed them with the realization that had just come from my own heart, then I saw things differently.

That first time. When I had invited him to the hotel room. What had he been thinking? Had he been worried about the consequences if his father were to find out that we met? Did he think that I had been about to ask him corporate secrets? Or had he known from the beginning that we were going to...

I had never asked him. We needed to talk. That was one of the very simple truths that I stumbled upon over the course of the night.

We had to stop defaulting to sex, because that was easy for us.

I had convinced myself that we had no intimacy. That wasn't true. But we had gaps in our intimacy.

Like knowing each other's room service order, but not what we like to have at a regular dinner.

I knew a strange, vacation version of him, as he did of me.

And we needed to build a home together. That was the way that we were going to find the parts of each other we hadn't seen before. That was the only way that I was going to get to know the man behind the mask.

He was so determined to make rules. I didn't agree with that. I didn't agree with the concept. I wanted something that felt more real.

But he was the way that he was. Which meant we weren't going to fall into that. Not accidentally. I was going to have to do something.

I had started this.

I was going to have to keep pushing to change it.

I finally slept, for a couple of fitful hours, though I didn't sleep beside him. I opted to curl up on the chaise by the window. Mostly because I didn't trust myself. Mostly because I knew if given half the chance, I would make love to him again. Because I wanted to. Because I loved him.

The sex last night had been different. Maybe because I knew I loved him.

Maybe because we were married.

I considered that as I brooded over a cup of coffee far too early.

He came out for a moment, shirtless, stunning.

"Thank you for the coffee," he said. As he poured some from the coffee maker.

"It was a byproduct of my own need for caffeine."

I smiled. He looked surprised by my expression.

"What?" I asked.

"I thought you were mad at me."

I shook my head. "No. I'm not. I was thinking, though. About our first time together."

He cleared his throat and leaned against the counter. The muscles in his torso shifted, and I found myself powerless to look away.

"One of my favorite memories," he said.

This felt like the sort of bubble we often found ourselves in after long nights in hotels. Where we were too tired, too satisfied to keep our guard up. When he would smile like it didn't hurt him to do it. And I would tell him a story about my friends. When he'd tell me about his time at university—the one moment when he hadn't always been serious—and he'd done fantastically dangerous stunts like leaping from yachts with his friends. And for a moment, we would be like this. Just us. No businesses, no shields. I wondered what it would take to get us here all the time.

Because this was what I was in love with. These moments. The spaces.

Liar. You love him when he's intense too.

Well. That was true. I couldn't actually separate all the different versions of him that I knew. I couldn't say that I loved one and not the other. He was complicated.

And I was beginning to realize I loved him even in his complication. Perhaps because of it.

"Is it?"

"Yes. I thought all my dreams had come true."

Those words felt fragile. Like if I moved too quickly, spoke too quickly, they would evaporate. And there would be no evidence that they had ever been there.

"I was curious what you thought initially. When I sent you the note. When I asked you to meet me."

"I… Of course, being a man, I thought perhaps you wanted me. But then I thought perhaps it was also wishful thinking."

I looked at him, avidly. Hungrily. I wanted to know what he was thinking now. What he'd been thinking then. Sometimes I felt like I wanted to slip beneath his skin and inhabit him entirely. So that I could finally know him.

Would I ever know him?

"Wishful thinking, what do you mean by that?" I asked.

He lifted a brow. "You're not naive, Florence. Come on now."

"Maybe I'm not naive, not in general. But there are things about you that I have never been able to figure out, Hades. So maybe I just need you to tell me."

He looked mystified. A crease forming on his forehead. I wanted to smooth it, but I also wanted to analyze his every muscle movement to try and glean more information. So I didn't smooth any of it away.

"You must know that I wanted you for…" He shook his head. "An inappropriately long time. I met you, and there had never been anybody like you. You infuriated me. You are so opinionated. My father hated your father, and that made you…"

"Forbidden," I whispered.

He nodded slowly. "Yes."

"I thought that. That perhaps I wanted you so badly because you were the one thing I really couldn't have."

He leaned just a bit closer. "And what was your conclusion?"

I shrugged. "But it doesn't matter why. Because it's real either way and there's nothing I can do about it."

"Fatalistic." He moved away slightly, some of our tension broken.

"I think both of us are entirely fatalistic in the approach to our affair, don't you?"

"Perhaps. But yes. I think you were sixteen the first time I noticed that you were beautiful. But I set you at a distance for obvious reasons. I was too old for you."

"And my birthday magically fixed that?"

He paused for a moment, as if considering. Thinking.

"No. It didn't. When you were eighteen you were still too young for me. But you made plain what had been secret before, and once you told me you wanted me I wasn't going to turn you away."

"So you hoped that I was going to try to seduce you?"

"Yes," he bit out. "Because I never would have seduced you. I would never have touched you, for so many reasons. It was the wrong thing to do, even with you being insistent it was what you wanted. It was the wrong thing to do. I knew it. But the attraction that burned between us was uncommon. Then and always."

"Yes. It was."

I couldn't help but smile. He wanted me. It had felt

inevitable to him, as it did to me. Or we had been lying to ourselves because we want it so badly. Whatever the answer was, whether it was fate, or a lack of desire to resist, it didn't matter to me. Because it boiled down to the fact that I wasn't alone.

That it hadn't only been me burning.

"Afterward, what did you think?"

He laughed. Hard and bitter. "When we left the resort, I was determined that I would never touch you again. After that weekend, when I made you mine in every way possible. I was… I should not have treated you that way."

"What way? Like a woman who wanted some incredibly hot sex and got it?"

"I should not have treated you like a woman with experience."

"I certainly walked away from that weekend a woman with experience," I said, smiling softly.

"You were a virgin. And I gave no quarter for that."

"You certainly ruined me. In the sense that I could never have wanted anything more mundane afterward." I was quiet for a moment. "Why did you come for me again? The second time? If you were determined not to…"

"I will never be able to say. Why you test my control when it is something I have always otherwise found so easy to keep hold of. Why… It was like you fundamentally changed something in me. Before you, I had never set a foot out of line. Before you, I had never defied my father because of the sword he had dangling over my head. The safety of my mother. I was angry. I was… Well, you saw. Everything that you saw in me as a young man, that was my simmering rage at my father.

But I never let it out. Not around him. I never let anything off leash. And then there was you. You touched me, and you kissed me. And I was powerless to do anything but take what you had on offer. To show you exactly what our bodies could do together. And then in Switzerland…"

I realized then that we were in Switzerland. What a funny thing. Our second time together had been in Geneva. At that glorious hotel with all the high-gloss marble. He had me in the bathroom.

I looked up at him, and I knew that we were in the middle of a shared memory. His eyes burned.

And in that fire I saw so much.

This was so much of him, a look behind a normally locked door. I didn't want him to close it, I felt panicky at the thought. I was hungry for him. More of him. All of him I could have.

"Geneva," I said.

He pushed away from the counter and walked out of the kitchen. I followed him. He was standing there with his back to me, facing the vast wilderness below. "Geneva is just there," he said, pointing to lights that I could only just barely see beyond the fabric of the mountains. "When I looked down there, I always think of that. Of us. In Geneva. Of the moment that you walked in, wearing some lovely, floral dress. Nothing like what you are now. It was very soft. And you looked impossibly beautiful. I had been drowning in my need for you for those months. I wished… So much, that I could find a woman and ease the ache inside of me, but I could not force myself to want anybody else. I went out. I had drinks. I couldn't force myself to lose control when you weren't there. And then the minute you were there... It was like the fabric that made up the core of my being torn apart. Six months without sex, Florence. And I grabbed hold of your hand and took you into a bathroom and... I behaved like an animal."

I was trying to process all of this. The revelation that he hadn't been with anybody in those months between our first time and our second.

"I love that," I said. "I thought it was the most glorious... Romantic..."

"Taking you on the bathroom counter was hardly romantic."

"It was to me. Because I had done nothing but think about you. I made myself ill with it, Hades. I had tried to tell myself that you would have forgotten me thirty times over by the time we ever saw one another again, and that we were never going to touch, let alone kiss, let alone make love. And then I saw you and the fire was just as hot as it ever was. We never have been able to put it out. I can't even express what a relief it was when you kissed me. When you locked me in that room. When you stripped me naked. When your skin was on mine. I had never wanted anything quite so badly as I wanted that. Hades, I wanted it. More than you'll ever know."

He looked away from me, and I studied his profile. There were so many things I did not understand about this man. But I knew that we were in a house in Switzerland with a view of Geneva, and he thought of me when he looked out that window. I knew that I loved him.

That he was my husband, that we were having a baby.

That this was forever, and would not be the scattered, passionate encounters that had fueled us for so long.

Things had changed, and we could not behave the same.

"I have to work," he said. "We need to get press releases ready. I have paperwork to review from my lawyer."

"I'll need to look at it too," I said.

"Florence, let me. Let me start this. You rest. You're pregnant," he said.

Hearing him acknowledge it, in a way that wasn't just him railing about me having his baby, but about my actual condition and his concern for it, made me feel something warm.

"All right," I said. Because at some point I was going to have to let my guard down. At some point I was going to have to trust him. I cared so much about the company. And yet, it wasn't the sole source of my identity. That had never been clearer. I was having a baby. I had married Hades. Making it the sole source of my identity was half my problem. It had made it so that I couldn't fully see myself. Hades had been right. I didn't know my own heart.

I loved him.

I loved fighting with him in the business arena because I loved having his attention. Because I loved having him look at me. Because I liked showing him that I was good at my job.

Because I wanted him to think so too.

I wanted him to respect me.

My father was gone. The only other person in the whole world whose opinion mattered even half so much was Hades.

I wasn't going to examine that too closely, but I was determined to make changes.

To fill in our gaps. I made some phone calls, and arranged for Christmas decorations to be brought to the chalet. Along with an extremely elaborate dinner.

I was going to make this a home. Because we needed to become a family. We were something. We had been from the beginning. I understood now that for me it was love.

I couldn't say what it was for him. Powerful, certainly. He made it sound like an illness, and in fairness, I had often felt like that's what it was.

But maybe that was how love unnamed felt. Love without boundaries and security. Unspoken. Uncertain.

Now suddenly that I found a place for it, something to call it, now that I was his wife, it felt less like a sickness and much more like peace.

I had no real idea how our marriage was going to unfold or what kind of husband he was going to be. But I knew that for the six months between our first and second encounter he hadn't been with another woman.

He had said that I wouldn't want him to be faithful to me because I wouldn't want to be the focus of all of his desire, and yet… It seemed that even when I wasn't with him, ten years ago, I had been the sole focus of his desire.

That he couldn't manufacture it for somebody else. And he hadn't slept with Jessica.

It was a question I didn't really want to ask, because it felt unrealistic to assume…

But perhaps I was not the only one who couldn't find it in them to take another lover. Perhaps I wasn't the

only one who would rather be celibate than with somebody I wanted less.

By the time Hades was done with his meeting, I had
the entire house bedecked. It glittered with decorations
of champagne and gold. It went with the minimalistic
Norwegian design all around, but added glitter. Sparkle.

Maybe this would begin to show him what I wanted.
What I felt.

He looked around, completely stunned.

"What is this?"

"Christmas," I said. "Because we are going to be a
family."

He looked at me, and the expression on his face was
like shock. "And why would Christmas matter?"

He'd said that Christmas had been used as a weapon
against him.

"Because we get to choose who we'll be," I said.
"I spent Christmas split between houses. It wasn't a
weapon in the way your dad used it, but it often felt
fraught to me. I don't want our child to have that experience. Our family will be different."

"Family?"

"Yes. We're having a baby. And… I understand why
that scares you. I understand why you think we need
nannies and psychologists, and I'm not opposed to any
of those things if you think that it would help. But I think
that we can find family between the two of us. Because
there is so much between us, Hades, and I truly believe
that we can spin it into something lovely. We are not our
families. We are making a new one."

This felt like a gambit. The kind of risk I normally
took in the boardroom, not in my personal life. But

nothing mattered more than this. If I couldn't make this work, if I couldn't find my way with him, what future was there?

This wasn't a contract. No merger or business deal.

It was only our whole lives.

"Florence…"

"I made dinner. I mean, I called and had dinner delivered."

I took his hand and led him into the dining room. It was not set with a massive spread that would allow us to have distance between each other. Just one corner of the table, with bread and meats and cheeses. The chairs pushed up together. "Talk to me," I said.

"I have been talking all day," he said. "Making sure that we do this legally is complicated."

"Tell me about it. All of it. Because we are no longer hiding our business dealings from one another."

So he did. And I felt myself falling in love with him all over again, because what was sexier than listening to this man talk about business? Businesses we both cared about, things that we both loved.

"I really would love to be involved in the super ship," I said.

"You really like the cruise ships?"

"I love them," I said. "The ocean just feels so free to me. I love the idea of being able to feel at home while you travel. And I just loved the adventure of it."

"You are secretly quite intrepid."

I looked down. "I suppose I am. I always tried to shut the wilder parts of myself down, because they reminded my father of my mother. And… You know how he felt about her."

"It was unfair of him to say all those things to you."

"I agree," I said. "But I think it made me a better CEO. Except... I don't know. In the end I got pregnant with your baby, so maybe it didn't. Maybe it had to find other ways to leak out. In my love of the ocean and my love of jumping on you whenever I had a spare moment."

Humor gleamed in his eyes, and I felt proud of that. "You're brilliant, you know," I said.

A crease appeared between his brows, and something that looked like a smile stretched his lips. It was the oddest expression. "Thank you?"

"I'm serious. You know, I have often thought that I enjoyed fighting with you so much because nobody else really feels a challenge. I really appreciate the fact that sometimes you're better than me. Not always. But sometimes. It's nice to know that I can lose."

"I suppose I like that about you too," he said slowly. "I don't like to lose."

"But have you ever lost anyone else?"

"No," he said.

I wanted to ask him if he had ever... Since us... But those words stuck in my throat, because I felt vulnerable about the whole thing. About what my answer would be.

But then... What was the point of holding back? I was sitting there surrounded by Christmas decorations I had procured, having dinner with the father of my baby. A man who knew my body better than I did. And I was embarrassed to tell him that he was my only lover?

Or maybe I was just afraid of finding out that it had never been as special to him as it was to me.

"There's never been anyone else," I said. Because I

decided to lead with my own vulnerability. As much as I hated it.

Because that wasn't something either my mother or father ever would've done. They were so committed to their roles. To the characters that they played. My mother to her daft socialite persona, which kept everybody from getting too close to her. My father to his steely businessman facade. Neither could admit that they were wrong. Neither could open a vein, not even if they chose to. So my mother was forever creating arterial spray that would do Hollywood proud. It was a facade. A ruse. I wasn't going to continue on that pattern.

We had to break our patterns.

For all the reasons that I had just said to him, we could be a family in a different way.

I was going to have to lead by example.

"What?" He looked fierce suddenly.

"You know that I've never touched another man. Never kissed one. I wanted you, from the first moment that I ever saw you, and I told myself… When I planned on maybe marrying someone else, I had hoped that perhaps I could find somebody that I felt half of what I felt for you. A man who made me burn only half as bright, I thought that seemed reasonable. But I couldn't even find that. I dreamed of you in between."

He looked past me, at the wall.

"There've been no other women, Florence. Not since we were together the first time. I might not have been a virgin the first time we came together, but I have not touched anyone since."

It was so huge an admission I almost couldn't take it on board. It made me want to weep. So I sidestepped.

I wasn't proud, but it was easier to focus on something that had wounded me than on whatever this deep emotion in me was.

"You were going to," I said, accusing.

"I felt I had no other choice. I wanted… I lied to you. On the plane. I told you that I thought you would simply not be able to resist me. I did think that you would. I thought you would be so angry with me, so disgusted that I was married, that you would never touch me again. I thought that it would set us both free, Florence, and that was what I wanted."

I felt like I'd been stabbed. He had wanted me to go away. He had wanted to end this.

"Then why didn't you just end it?"

"If I was strong enough to end it…"

I knew the answer. I already did. Because it was the answer that we both always came back to. If we could stop, we could stop. If we could be finished, we would be finished.

If we could save ourselves from this, we would.

So he had hoped that he had put up a wall so tall that I wouldn't want to scale it.

"You are one of the most moral and upright people I know," he said. "There is nothing shadowy about you. I knew you would never touch a married man."

"And then I had the bad luck of getting pregnant." Tears filled my eyes. "Hades, I wish that I could tell you your plan would've worked. I have never been quite so—" I avoided the word *heartbroken*. "When I found out about the engagement I was sick. Because I imagined you sleeping with her just after you left me. I imagined you touching her just before you came to me. But it was jealousy. It wasn't moral outrage in the way that I wished it could be. I tried to fashion it into moral outrage. I tried to tell myself I was hurt for her. Because she didn't know what you were.

"But I was hurt for me. And when I went into your office to yell at you, I didn't even consider resisting you. I am afraid that it would've continued that way."

Something in his expression was tortured then. But in a breath it was gone, and it had been so singular that I couldn't quite remember it as it was. Couldn't sit there and pull it apart and try to put names to each and every flicker of emotion that had crossed his face then. I felt robbed. Robbed of the moment when I could have tried to understand him. Just a little more. Just a little better.

"The pregnancy made the decision for us. This is not something…" He shook his head. "I did not want to trap you in this."

"The merger?"

He looked at me. "Yes. The merger. But now… Now here we are."

"You will be faithful to me," I said.

Because now it was clear that he would be, because he always had been.

"If you ever wish it to be different, just say so. If you ever regret any of this…"

How can I regret it? I had never wanted another man the way that I wanted him.

I loved him. And I wanted to spend this time we had away showing him.

"Hades, do you know what we've never done?"

"What is that?"

"We've never been on a date."

CHAPTER ELEVEN

IT TOOK SEVERAL days for Hades to be able to come up for air after dealing with all the legality of the merger.

We signed off on the paperwork extremely late on the fourth day, and that was when he told me he had a surprise for me.

"I will take you out tomorrow," he said.

"It's not even Christmas yet," I said.

"I know," he said. "But I was thinking about what you said. We have not been on a date."

The last few days had been strange for us. We had sex, but we had managed to talk quite a bit in between. And do work. I was right; we needed to fill in those gaps. And we were. Much more competently than I had expected us to.

We had breakfast together. Lunch. Dinner.

We moved in the rhythm of each other's life. Rather than existing in stolen fragments of time.

It was that shot of intensity, but with everything in between.

I liked him. And that was an interesting thing. I had realized I loved him first. But it still felt very sharp.

A bit uneasy.

But I liked everything about him. Well, not all of his

mercurial moods, not while they were happening, but I didn't think that he would be him without them.

Because without them, he wouldn't be intense. And I did love the intensity. Especially when it was all focused on me.

I liked the way he talked about business. I like the way it felt to sit next to him. I like him as much as I ever thought that I had hated him, and that was saying something.

But I had only ever been protecting myself. That much was clear.

I had only been able to make space for myself to love the company, because I thought that I had to succeed at that or everything else would fall apart. Or I wouldn't matter. Or I would be my mother. I couldn't see a middle ground. But that, in and of itself, was flawed thinking.

It didn't let me be a whole person. And I really badly needed to figure out how to be a whole person.

I could love my job—I did love it. But I could also love myself.

I didn't need to be subsumed.

Because I had lived with people who had become parodies of themselves, and that kept you from being what you needed to be for the children depending on you. I knew that well.

It also didn't help a marriage. And my marriage to Hades meant a lot to me. So much.

I opened up the closet when it was time for us to get ready for dinner and gasped at what I saw.

There was a gold dress inside that glittered like all the Christmas decorations I had bought for the house.

It was so deliberate, it had to be intentional.

"Hades," I breathed.

"I want badly to see you in that," he said. He moved over to me, kissed my neck and wrapped his arm around me, his chest hot against my back. "More, though, I want to take it off of you."

"That can be arranged," I whispered. "Maybe we can make it like old times. Find a coat closet."

He growled. "I'm done with coat closets. You're mine. And I'm going to show the world that you're mine. Then I'll take you home to our bed, where I will stretch you out and feast on you like I have all the time in the world. Because I do."

Nothing could have been sexier. But then, that was how he was. Nothing could be sexier than him.

We had to take a helicopter down the mountain, and I clung to him again as we did so, but this time I didn't resent it, or him.

"Geneva," I whispered, as the glittering city came into view.

"Good memories," he said.

"Yes," I whispered.

A car was there to pick us up after the helicopter landed on the edge of town, and whisked us to a glorious restaurant in an old palace. If people were staring at us, I didn't care. Because for the first time, I was out in public with him.

For the first time…

Yes. There had been headlines and all kinds of things about our wedding, about our kissing. There had been a storm. But I had ignored it because I was with him. And when I was with him nothing else really mattered.

Now we were out together, making something new.

Something we had never experienced before.

It was amazing how much had changed in the past two months, but then, also how nothing had changed.

It was like the hard knot of my feelings that had lived in this deep place inside of me had been given room to grow and expand. So that I could finally see what they were trying to become all along.

It was always supposed to be love. For me, that was always what it was supposed to be.

I still couldn't quite figure it out with him, though, and I didn't want to disrupt what we were building.

I had to be patient. Though, patience had never been my particular strong suit.

I was, after all, the same person who had seduced Hades on my eighteenth birthday, because I hadn't been able to wait another second.

But now I would have to wait. We had all the trust in the world in each other's bodies. But the rest of it… We didn't have practice with it. Not yet.

I was trying to figure out how to learn this. How to learn him.

How to get over the walls inside of him.

Or maybe it wasn't walls so much as a series of locked doors and different rooms. Sometimes he let me into one room, but it closed off another. I could never access all of him all at once.

He had shared some things, but it always felt like it was being dragged from him. And there was more. I could feel it. He could be so remote, so hard. And yet he was so passionate too. I wanted to feel the passion. All of it. Always.

I wanted everything.

I let him order for us.

"I like it," I said.

"What?"

"Letting you make decisions for me sometimes. I'm exhausted. From deciding everything all the time." I looked at him. "What can I do for you?"

He raised his brows. "You already do it."

He meant sex. And that was not particularly flattering or romantic, but I can understand how he meant it. Because for him, that was maybe when he was his most honest.

"I am always happy to accommodate," I said.

But I determined that I was going to figure out a way to make moments in his life better. Not just naked moments.

I became aware after our plates were put in front of us that we were drawing a bit of attention.

I looked up at him and moved my eyes to the left, knowing his gaze would follow. And it did. There were two girls giggling and raising their phones, clearly taking video or photos of us.

"You know," I said softly. "At one time, that would have been my worst nightmare."

"Yes," he said. "I know."

"You know why, though. It was never because I was ashamed of you."

"My ego is fairly healthy," he said. "I don't know that I was ever concerned that you were ashamed of me."

There was something, though. A slight hollow note in his voice. Something that let me know he felt something. Even if he wasn't going to fully articulate it.

I put my hand over his. His eyes dropped to that space

on the table. And I felt his entire body relax. Not something I had ever felt it do.

Even after he had an orgasm he was breathing hard, all of his muscles strung tight. He didn't even fully relax and sleep, but in that moment, I felt give. Beneath my fingertips. I saw it in the slope of his shoulders.

I was shocked by it. Maybe that was what he needed. For someone to touch him. For someone to care for him. He did a lot of caring for me, I realized. Yes, it was often in physical ways. But it was all very thoughtful. He never allowed me to be cold or hungry. He made sure to see to my comfort at all times. And that was something that seemed to go well beyond sex. Deeper into something else.

"I couldn't figure out how to have everything," I said. "I realized something when I was walking down the aisle toward you. I had lost. All of my intent was burned to the ground. I had nothing. I was going to be exposed to the world. And then I realized that I was free because of that. That I didn't have to hide anymore. Try anymore." I want that for you.

I left it wordless. Because I knew he wasn't quite ready to be confronted with that in a way he couldn't sidestep or deny. I didn't know how I knew it. Perhaps it was knowing *him*.

He hadn't hidden me for fear of his father being disappointed. He hadn't hidden me because of what it might say about his gender. Or the position he occupied in his company and his ability to do his job.

He had initially hidden our relationship because he was afraid his father would beat him.

And I had to wonder how much of what he did was

purely the response of a boy who had been hit when he should have been cared for.

It was almost impossible to say.

"I'm glad of it," I said. "Because I was going to exhaust myself. There was just nowhere else for me to go."

"Except I would've married someone else."

I could pivot here. I could put my own shields back up. But then we would just be caught in the same circle we'd been trapped in already. I had to be the one to keep moving. To keep breaking through barrier after barrier. It felt like a risk. To expose myself like this. But I could feel myself getting stronger the more vulnerable I became.

Like I was becoming more myself as I tried to connect with him.

"Nothing about that would've been a relief," I said. I chewed on the inside of my cheek. "I went to my mother, because if she knows one thing, it's how to deal with heartbreak. That was what I felt, you know. I wasn't just angry at you. I was… I was devastated."

"I didn't want to hurt you," he said. He looked down at his plate. "Whatever you think about me, I want you to know that."

He looked up again, and I saw that same sort of lost darkness there. "I believe you," I said.

And I didn't have anything else to say on the subject. Except that I believed him. For some reason, I thought that might be important. I knew that it was to me.

We talked about business until dessert. And then we talked about chocolate cake, because we both liked it. And considered it the pinnacle of dessert.

"That is one thing I have always resented," he said.

"What is that?"

"The snobbery my fellow Europeans have for the sweetness and decadence of American food. I for one am a fan."

"But you like dark chocolate," I said. "Which is not historically the sweetest."

"I like it at every point on the spectrum," he said.

He smiled. And I felt something like joy resonate inside of me.

Afterward we left the restaurant and he put his coat over my shoulders. We held hands and walked down the streets, bathed in the streetlights. Even this was something we'd never done before. This simple act of walking and holding hands.

This ordinary togetherness that most couples tried out before they ever kissed. Certainly before they had ten years of torrid sex.

But not us. There had never been lightness for us. There had never been simplicity.

We had been trying to gorge ourselves. Trying our best to have every bite at a feast we were certain we had a limited time to experience.

And now forever stretched before us. Which meant we had the luxury of time.

I laughed.

"What?"

"You're a billionaire," I said.

"So are you," he pointed out.

"Yes," I said. "And it would be silly to say that our lives weren't absolutely replete with luxury. But one thing we've never had the luxury of is time. So here we are."

"Yes," he said, his voice rough.

"We can walk down the street for the next four hours if we want to."

"Well," he said. "It's possible there might be traffic that makes that difficult."

"You know what I mean. We don't have to worry about anyone finding out. No more going through back doors or staff entrances. No more fake names. No more hiding. We were so busy figuring out what all of this meant for the company, and then thinking about... Well, about the baby, that I didn't really think about what it meant for us. I want to know you." I turned to him, standing on the street, holding his hands as I had done at the altar on our wedding day. "Everything about you."

His expression looked pained. "You say that as someone who does not know me. And the problem is once you do, you'll never be able to go back to the bliss of your ignorance."

"Doesn't it ever get tiring," I said. "Playing the part of King of the damned."

"Does it ever get tiring, playing the part of persistent, bulletproof CEO?"

"Yes," I said. "That's why it was a relief for you to pick my dinner. That's why it has always been a relief, to find myself in your arms, to have you be in charge of making me feel good. Because I am tired. Because I needed a place to break down. To cry out. Because I needed to be able to be naked. To be able to be honest. And with you, I found that. Yes, it gets tiring. That's why I'm asking you if it's ever the same for you."

"If it was ever an act, I have forgotten. Simply become who I am."

"But you love chocolate," I said. "And you kiss me like a dream."

"Some girls dream of the devil," he said, a regretful note in his voice. He put his fingertips beneath my chin, tilting my face up. "And some would say those dreams are untrustworthy."

"But they're the only dreams I have."

I realized then that I would give up the company for him. I would give up anything he asked me to. He was more important than anything else, and the actions that I'd exhibited over the past ten years actually did suggest that. I had been willing to risk everything to be with him. I hadn't been brave enough to actually set everything on fire, but I had not protected my position entirely.

I had been much more interested in protecting my connection with him.

That had been the most important thing. That had been the thing I really cared about.

It hurt me, knowing the same probably wasn't true of him. And I knew a moment of deep shame. Was it inescapable, this softness inside of me? Was it a fault of my sex? That I had this latent desire to be his housewife somewhere inside of me.

No. That wasn't the revelation I was having. It was only that if I had to lay out my priorities, right now, the top one would be this. Him. Our family. The life that we were building.

I no longer needed to impress my father. I no longer needed the press to write glowing things about me. I no longer needed to live as an act of defiance to my mother's frailty.

I just wanted to live.

I just wanted to love him.

Of all the things that I had succeeded at, being loved had never been one of them.

It was what I wanted now. Really. Truly. More than anything.

But I didn't say that yet either. Because I wasn't quite sure how.

Because I didn't quite know what to do.

Or maybe I just wasn't quite ready to risk it.

I had risked the company, marrying him. He had agreed to a merger that kept me in an equal position, but he might not have. I had risked my reputation by marrying him. I didn't care.

But I was not ready to risk him.

This was terrifying. It was like standing on the edge of a cliff, staring down into a void I couldn't see the end of. Because what if?

What if he never loved me?

I couldn't think that. But I had to take a moment. A breath. I had to proceed slowly.

Especially when I was not quite certain of my own feelings anyway. Well. I was certain of them. But I wasn't sure of what to ask for. I wasn't sure of how exactly to go about telling him.

I just needed some time. Some more time to turn it all over.

We went back to walking.

"Do you have any good memories of your childhood?" I asked.

"Yes," he said. "My mother. She taught me how to ride horses. We used to go out early in the morning.

Especially on summer days. We lived in Greece then. It was magnificent. We would ride through the olive groves and out to the sea. I didn't know then that we were wealthy, or that I was going to inherit a major company. All I knew was that my mother loved me. And the world was beautiful. That is the happiest that I have ever been."

I ached. I wanted him to be happy with me.

But at the same time, I was glad there had been some happiness for him. That he had known love in some capacity.

"Where is your mother now?"

He looked away from me. "Greece," he said.

"You never visit her?"

"I do," he said. "Our shared experience made a relationship difficult. My father made a relationship difficult. Also, I suspect her guilt made things hard."

"That isn't fair," I said. "She made the choice that she felt she had to make, and I can't be overly judgmental about it. I don't know how terrifying your father was."

"He was a dangerous man."

"I believe you," I said. "But now, in the fullness of time, at the end of all things, I don't understand why she would allow that choice to drive a wedge between you."

"Things are complicated. Much more so than I would like them to be. But…"

"You could talk to her. Tell her that you don't want those years to stand between you. If your mother is your happiest memory, then…"

"What?" He paused midstride, and turned to look at me. "Are you an expert now in repairing fractured family bonds, Florence?"

I shook my head. "No. Though I did have to figure out how to maintain a relationship with both of my parents when they hated each other. When I wanted desperately to please them both, and no amount of loving my father would ever make my mother happy, while he was endlessly disapproving of my continued relationship with her. I don't know about dangerous family dynamics. I admit that. But I do know about difficult ones. I had to forgive my father for the things he said to me because he was angry at my mother. I had to forgive my mother for being… For being something I couldn't understand. The truth is, for a long time I was bitter at my mother for not changing. But my father never changed. It was only I found it easier to fit into the mold that he set out for me. If I had wanted to trip around Europe bagging rich men, my mother would have been a fantastic role model." I laughed. "She's strong, is the thing. I never saw it as strength when I was younger. I didn't see how much work she did carving out a place for herself to live."

He surprised me by laughing. "Many people might have taken that route, Florence. It does seem a bit easier than this endless road of perfectionism you've been walking."

"But surely you understand that sometimes perfectionism is its own reward."

"And its own hangman's noose."

"Absolutely," I said. "But nothing is simple, is it?"

"No indeed," he said.

"You should call your mother. Tell her she's going to be a grandmother."

"She's already a grandmother," he said.

For a moment, I struggled to understand that. "What?"

He chuckled. "Not me. One of her stepsons. Also, she had other children. They are all fifteen years younger than me at least. She had another family. I'm glad for her. She found happiness. Less complicated happiness. I am a complicated joy for her. She loves me. I know that. But sometimes love does not look like being able to be there with someone every day." His dark eyes burned then. "Sometimes love looks like giving someone space. Sometimes love hurts as much as it heals. Sometimes love is itself a sharpened blade."

"I feel like I read somewhere—I don't know, some little book—that love was patient and kind."

"I wish it were so simple. I do. But my experience of it has not been simple. My mother and I are both tied to violent memories. We are that for each other. She has a husband who is good to her. She has children with him."

"And you feel like a bruise."

"Exactly that. An old wound that is pressed whenever she sees me."

"It isn't your fault."

"Fault has nothing to do with it." He leaned in and put his hand on my face. It was a surprisingly gentle gesture contrasted with the ferocity of his voice. "It does not matter who is responsible for pain, not when it lingers, not when the effects, the damage, carry on. You can be twisted through no fault of your own, and yet it does not change the result. Blood can poison you. And you are poisoned whether you consented to it or not. And love is not enough to change that."

Somehow, just then, I did not feel like we were talking about his mother. But I couldn't get a firm enough hold on what he might be talking about. It stirred inside of me, a strange beacon of hope that also felt hopeless. Because he was telling me he couldn't love. Regardless of what changed in his life.

He was telling me what he couldn't give me.

But at the same time, I felt like he was telling me he wished it could be different.

And one thing I couldn't reconcile was the idea of hopelessness in this man. This man who was so determined, so successful. This man who rivaled me for success. How could he want something and not obtain it? How could he desire something to be different and not make the change.

It wasn't him. It never had been, not for as long as I'd known him.

So even while a part of my soul flailed in hopelessness, another part felt like it had just had the sun shone upon it for the first time in ages.

He had bought a house with a view of Geneva.

I wanted that to mean something.

"What is your best memory?" he asked, as if the change in subject would shift the mood completely. Like he could control it with new words and a flick of his wrist. With a step onward.

I wanted to share with him, and that was why I let him change the subject.

"I'm lucky. There was a lot of happiness in my childhood. I remember going to work with my father and sitting on his desk. I loved the frenetic pace of the Edison offices. I loved the thrill of discovery. Of innovation. When we would get to go out on the cruise ships, take their maiden voyages, I was always so excited. I loved staying in a new hotel. Flying on the newest airplane. It was an exhilarating way to experience the world. Magical, in a way. My passion for this industry doesn't just come from inheriting a company. It doesn't simply come from the amount of money there is to be made. I really do believe in the beauty of it. I'm captivated by this world. By the universe."

"Do you think that you'll make a flight to space?"

"Yes," I said without hesitation. "Because I want to see it. Everything that I do is about the drive to discover. I really do believe that as humans we will never fully understand each other, understand how to make our world better if we don't see it. If we don't see one another."

"An interesting perspective to gain from the creation of luxury travel methods."

"It isn't all exclusive. We have the most affordable cruise options for the amenities of any other line. We have more flight options and more hotel package options at budget levels than any other large travel conglomerate. We also invest a large amount of money in different charities. Primarily education. Because I really do believe that learning and exploring are the keys to a person discovering all that they can be."

"All because you sat on your father's desk when you were a child?"

I blinked rapidly. "And because my mother took me to different places around Europe. Because I have citizenship both in the US and the UK. Because I was someone who lived in different worlds."

"And you feel like you know yourself?"

"No," I said. "I feel like I know aspects of myself. I

definitely learned what my professional dreams were. I formed a lot of my core values from those experiences. I ignored what I wanted personally. I will admit that. I didn't think that I could have it."

I looked at him for a long time. I didn't feel that my expression was terribly ambiguous.

"Why is that?"

"I felt like what I wanted was wrong. I didn't feel like I could trust what I wanted. Because… The most damaging thing that my father told me was the thing he said about my mother. He made me feel like the things in me that might be feminine—that might relate to desire or romance or sex—were flawed. Like I couldn't trust them. Obviously, finding myself attracted to you confirmed that."

"Obviously," he said, but there was a faint smile on his lips.

"I couldn't see a way around it. I couldn't figure out how to take all the passion that I felt for Edison, for wanting to be the CEO, for wanting to please my father, and also…"

"Live?"

I breathed out hard. "Yes. I guess I was more committed to figuring out how to create experiences for other people than I was committed to finding happiness in my own life. I convinced myself that professional ambition and personal goals were the same thing. But the end result of that was that I pretty much only had one thing to claim as a personal life."

"Surely you don't mean sex with me?"

"I do. You have been my closest friend for a long time."

That stopped him again. He turned to me. "That is possibly the most desperately sad thing you've ever said."

Except it wasn't sardonic. He sounded as if he had been hit in the head.

"Why? If you think about it, it makes sense. Who else could have ever understood even part of what my life was like growing up." My stomach crumpled. "Though, I didn't know what you were going through. And I am sorry for that."

"I didn't want you to know. Because you were my escape."

It was my turn to stop and look at him. "I thought I was your loss of control."

"Don't you understand," he said, his voice rough. "That was an escape. It was the only place that I could…"

Be human. Be a man.

It was my turn to touch his face. I did it slowly, deliberately. My breath caught. I was on the edge of that cliff.

Could I jump?

His gaze pulled me into him. And I had no choice. "You have me all the time," I said. "I promise you that."

He looked like he wanted to say something, but couldn't find the words. I had never seen Hades speechless. I was used to sparring with him. I wasn't used to sincerity. I wasn't used to connection.

Nothing about this was familiar. This was one of those intimacy gaps. And we were finding a way to fill it.

As best we could. I had to believe that he wanted it too, on some level. Or he would have simply strode off into the night without answering any of my questions. Without speaking to me at all.

But he didn't. He stood there instead. He looked at me, like he wanted to say something, but couldn't quite find the words.

"I arranged for us to stay in town tonight."

I was surprised by that.

"Really?"

"Yes."

I felt… I wasn't sure. Because this was us, back in a hotel. Not in the place where I was trying to make a home for us. It made sense. Rather than taking a helicopter back up to the top of the mountain, he was giving us a place closer to go. He knew that I didn't especially like the helicopter.

And yet, something about it felt like a step backward. Whether that made sense or not.

I didn't say that, of course. Instead I took his hand and let him lead me on. We hadn't been walking toward nothing. I thought we were. Just walking to walk. But no, he had been taking us to a hotel.

"You're annoyed with me," he said.

"Annoyed?"

"Yes. I can tell."

"There's a lot that I could say about how this transcends your typical ability to read other people's emotions."

"See?" He paused walking. "Annoyed. You were being very nice to me."

"I thought… I don't know. I thought we were taking a walk. It ended up being something more calculated."

He frowned. "Is that what you think? That this was

calculated? Nothing that I have done with you for the past ten years has ever been calculated. I wish to God that it were. That would be easier. If I could claim to you that I had control over this the entire time, then… If I had control of it the entire time—"

"I know. You would never touch me."

"As you have said many times."

Gripping my hand, he brought me down the sidewalk with him until we came to the front of the well-lit, lovely historic building with Swiss flags waving over the front.

"Lovely," I said.

He always had great taste in hotels.

"You're still annoyed with me," he said.

"I'm not."

"Do you not want me now?"

There was a strange light in his eyes. I frowned. "What makes you ask me that?"

"It would not be completely shocking. Perhaps it was the danger, the element of the forbidden that enticed you."

Was Hades honestly feeling insecure? Thinking that I didn't want him?

I stopped him, right there in front of the hotel doors. "I want you now and forever. More than I have ever wanted anyone or anything. Hades, I have never even kissed another man. Because I can't begin to disentangle desire from you. I could never want you less."

"But you wish that you could."

"In the past, yes. I've wished that. Haven't you wished the same?"

"No. Never. As I said, if I could have resisted you, I would have. But I have never wished it was different."

Then he turned and walked through the revolving doors of the hotel, and I had to scurry after him.

"I have the key already."

Of course he did. We moved far too quickly through the beautiful lobby, and it took me a moment to realize that I'd been here before.

This was our hotel. The one we had been together in that second time.

"You…"

This wasn't an anonymous thing. It wasn't to disentangle us from our history. From the reality of our feelings.

He was… It was borderline sentimental. I felt foolish. And I felt small. For having been petty only a moment ago.

As soon as the elevator doors closed behind us I leaned in, and I kissed him. As unhurried as the walk here had been. An expression of the shift that had taken place. Of who we were now.

Of who we had been then.

I could remember how impatient we were. I felt it now.

But it didn't cut so deep.

Before I knew it, we were at the top floor. I was dizzy.

I looked up at him. At that familiar face. My lover. My husband. The only man that I had ever wanted. The only one I had ever loved.

I traced his lips with my fingertips. Because I felt like I could. Because I felt like we could have some softness, instead of that endless, driving storm.

It was still there. That storm. But it wasn't all there was.

He led me to the room and unlocked the door. Took

my hands and brought me into the center of the living room. He cradled my face in his hands and he kissed me.

Kissed me like he had nothing else to do. Ever.

Kissed me like it was the destination.

I had thought we didn't kiss to simply kiss only recently. And yet that's what this was. The luxury of a kiss.

I had never thought of them as being particularly luxurious. They were an aperitif, impatiently swallowed while waiting for the main event.

Not now.

I focused on the feel of him. Running my fingers through his dark hair. Touching his face. His cheekbones, down to the stubble that covered his jaw. Down his neck, to that muscled wall of his chest, his thundering heart.

It was amazing how this man could be familiar and a stranger all at once.

I supposed, in the way that he was mine, and not mine.

I couldn't say why that thought hit me with quite so much force.

Hades had always been a man apart. Not just for me. From everyone. But I didn't want that. Not anymore.

I unbuttoned his shirt slowly, moving my hands over his chest. Reveling in the feel of that coarse hair over firm muscle.

"We have all the time in the world," I whispered.

The sound he made was more like a growl than a groan, his eyes electric on mine.

He reached around behind me, trying to get at the zipper on my dress, and I moved away. "Patience," I said.

"I'm not patient," he said.

"Because you've never had to be." I wanted him naked. I wanted to see him. I wanted to have him. All of him. With the luxury of time. With all the love in my heart.

I pushed his shirt from his shoulders. I admired every tanned, toned inch of him.

I moved my hands to his belt.

His body was so familiar to me. So beloved.

And yet the thrill could never be gone.

The thrill in knowing that he was mine was endless.

The thrill in knowing that since I had touched him no other woman had put her hands on him was more than I could have ever imagined. Mine.

"Mine." It was my turn to growl. My turn to grab hold of him. I gripped him tight, squeezing his arousal. I held on to his shoulder with my other hand, dug my nails into his skin there. He looked at me, his eyes hooded. I could feel that I was in danger. That he was only allowing this for a limited time. That he was lying in wait.

Hades.

Perhaps I had finally assimilated the underworld. Perhaps I had finally accepted that as long as he was in it, hell would be my home. Or just maybe…

Hope sparked in my chest.

What if we could be new? What if forever could make us into something different?

And the same all at once.

What if we could be us?

Whole and together and in love.

I loved him. I kissed his neck, openmouthed. He grunted and wrapped his arm around my waist, his large hand going to cup my rear. Then he claimed my mouth, hot and hard. The control was no longer mine. It was all right. I didn't want it.

I surrendered. To whatever it was. To the depths of hell or the heights of heaven. I surrendered.

Because I knew myself. I was more than making my father proud. I was more than distinguishing myself from my mother. I was more than a good CEO. I was Florence. As I had been all along. And I was the woman that had captured his attention all those years ago, never to lose it.

So perhaps I was enough all along.

He stripped my dress from my body, my underwear. Took me down to the floor and lifted me up over him.

"Take me," he said.

I tilted my hips and accepted him into my body. I let my head fall back, but only for a moment, because I couldn't resist looking down into those deep, black eyes. As he filled me. As he made me wild with need.

As the storm began to rage inside of me. Because there would always be a storm.

Always. Because we would always be that. Even as we shifted and changed.

He drove me higher, faster than I had ever gone before. And when my orgasm crashed over me, he pulled my face down and kissed me, reversing our positions. So that he was over me, and I was pinned to the floor.

He kissed me. My neck, my breasts. He thrust into me, over and over again like he was making vows. This time with his body.

I saw something feral in his eyes. Wild. And if he had not been Hades Achelleos, I might have said it was fear. But he was never afraid.

Least of all of me.

When his release came for him, he resisted it. Put his hand between my thighs and stroked me, calling another climax from deep within me before he gave himself to his own.

And the storm raged on and on.

And as I came back to myself, back to my body, the truth loaded up between us. One that I couldn't deny. One that I couldn't hold back.

"Hades. I love you."

CHAPTER TWELVE

HE SAID NOTHING. Instead, he moved away from me and withdrew. I listened as his footsteps took him away from me. This was different. Different than any other time he had ever walked away from me. And he had done it countless times before. When the evening had to end, and we had to go back to being rivals. When the necessary separation came, taking us back to our real lives.

But this was supposed to be our real life now. He wasn't supposed to leave me.

He might not have left the hotel, but the way that he had pulled away was profound. I pressed my hand against my chest. Felt my beating heart. Didn't feel pieces of it fracture and launch themselves through the front of my breastbone, as it felt like they might. As I feared they must be.

Because it hurt so bad.

So very badly.

I took a breath, and then I stood. Naked. I found that I wasn't ashamed. Or afraid.

I was too strong for that.

We were too strong for that. Ten years, and nothing had broken us. Not really.

We had ample opportunity to find other people. To

want other people, and we hadn't. We had promised our bodies to one another all those years ago, without even being conscious of it. We had promised our souls to each other. And I was willing to fight for it now. I would be damned if I let this be the end. I would be damned if I let those footsteps down the hall be the last word on my love for him.

I kept my own footsteps soft as I walked toward him. As I reached the sanctuary that he had ensconced himself in.

"Hades…"

"It is the one thing," he said, his voice dark. "The one thing I did not want between us. And I never imagined… I did not think there was a danger of it."

"Love?"

"I already told you. Sometimes things are simply too broken. People are simply too broken."

"I don't know what you're talking about. How could… How could we ever be too broken? We are just the right kind of broken for each other. Or have you not been paying attention all this time. We are maybe the only people who could ever understand each other. Really."

"You don't know."

"Are you going to tell me that you're afraid you're like your father? Because I've known you for far too long to believe that."

"You didn't know my father was abusive. And yet you think you have great insight into me?" he asked, his voice fierce.

He was a wall still. No matter how I'd tried to break it open for him. I felt like I was tearing strips off myself. Leaving myself raw.

But I kept going.

I kept doing it.

"You are my lover. That's what you are. You're not a dirty secret. You were not some clandestine affair. You have been my lover for ten years. I have let you hold me. I have let you kiss me. Taste me. Touch me. You are the father of my baby. I know you. I have seen you win battles and lose them. Only to me. I have seen the way that you handle setbacks. I have seen who you are when things don't go your way. You are not an abusive man."

I could feel him resisting my words. Resisting me.

"But I am as easily corrupted by love as he ever was."

"I don't understand what that means." I pushed. And pushed.

"Don't you?" he asked.

"No. Because you don't tell me anything. Because you are… An impenetrable wall, Hades, and you have been from the beginning. You didn't tell me that I was the only woman that you were with."

My own voice fractured. I could feel myself breaking. I wouldn't let this break me.

His face was hard. Stoic. "You didn't tell me that I was the only man."

"But I was the virgin. When we came together. I was the one that… You never gave me a hint of vulnerability. Not to the degree that I gave it to you."

"I'm sorry—did I never soften enough for you? You didn't act as if that was distasteful to you, given that you flung yourself at my hardness every chance you got."

"Hades… Don't. Don't be hateful now because this is too much for you. Just tell me why."

"It is not too much for me. It is sadly ground that I

have gone over already. Over and over again, Florence. Why do you think you weren't the woman that I asked to marry me?"

"The business."

"Little idiot. Do you think I care even one bit about this empire? In light of... You're a fool," he said. "I would let it all burn. Why do you think I made an attempt to set out rules for how we should let this marriage be?"

"Because you're a control freak."

"And why do you think that is?"

"*Stop it*!" I shouted. "Stop making me work for every damn thing. Give something to me. I deserve it. I am the one who has given everything. I came to you. I had to tell you that I was having your baby. I had to stop your wedding. I was the one... I was the one who had to find out you were marrying somebody else. Give me something without making me debase myself, damn you."

"My father found my mother."

I was shocked. Immobilized. The look on his face was raw, tormented. Tortured.

"He found her house in Greece. Her husband, her children. Because of me. I went to visit her, and he had a tracking device on my phone. He had been lying to me all those years, saying he hadn't known where she was. He was using that to keep me in line. He found her and followed her there. When I saw him in the villa, his eyes were like a wild man. He was beyond himself. He rushed her, holding a knife. I grabbed hold of them, and I disarmed him."

I watched his face as it contorted, as all the defenses fell away, and I saw, not a monster, but a man so filled with grief, self-loathing and fear that I almost couldn't bear it.

"You saved her life," I said.

"Yes. And then I hit him. I didn't need to. Then I hit him again. I also didn't need to do that. He went down, hitting his head on the edge of the stone steps of the villa. It triggered a seizure. He died. It was easy to change the story around just a little bit. Easy to say that he had hit his head and it caused the seizure. There was no bruising. He died too quickly."

"The media said your father died on holiday," I said, aware that it was a foolish thing to say because the media didn't know more than Hades himself.

"We made a story. One that would protect me. Protect the legacy of the company. What was any of it for if we destroyed the thing I was…created for. It was my chance to have control."

My heart felt bruised. Bloody. "Hades…"

"So you see. I am as dangerous as my father ever was."

"You did it for your mother. You did it for love. I don't care if you killed your father. I don't care if you shot him in cold blood. He threatened you. He held your mother's safety over your head for years and allowed it to become a method to manipulate you by. His death is something that no one is sorry for. He was useless. He was evil."

"It is not danger in the way you're thinking. Look at how love betrayed my mother. My version of it. It made me careless. Selfish. It led my father to her."

I shook my head. "Hades, your love isn't selfish…"

"It is. It has been. It has been all about keeping what I want near me when I want it. And never about giving."

"Hades," I said. "I love you. And I know you. I'm not afraid of you. I have loved you. From the beginning. Don't you understand that? If there was one thing

I didn't know about myself it was that. And it was because I was terrified. I was terrified of what loving you would mean. Of what I would be willing to give up. Because the answer is simply everything. I don't care about the company either. Not if I had to choose between it and you. So I never wanted to put myself in that position. I forced myself to deny those feelings. To keep them locked away."

"I wish that was why I kept myself controlled. I will never hurt you. I will never..."

"No. You won't."

"You should be disgusted with me," he said. "You should be horrified. By the manner of man I am. By my capacity for violence."

He just looked broken. Stripped apart by the admission. He had held all of this in for so long.

But I'd seen him look this way before. In that moment I'd first seen him after his father's death and he'd devoured me.

This was the truth of him.

"But I'm not. So, where does that leave us? Because I don't see a violent man when I look at you. I see a man who was abused by his father. A man who was very nearly destroyed, but wasn't. A man who fought for his mother when he needed to. Don't you understand? Your father fought to make you afraid. But he didn't succeed. Instead, you were stronger than he was. You were as brave as he feared you were. He had to keep you in line because he knew that he couldn't crush you."

"He was poison," he said. "If he would have ever known what I felt for you, he would have..."

I saw it then. Real, deep fear. Deep and dark. And I

had to wonder what he was really afraid of. He was a man who had started out as a boy. A boy who had been scared that the thing he loved most would be taken from him. Because his father had used that, manipulated that. His mother had left him to protect herself. Left him with a monster. And even if I could be sympathetic to what she had lost, I felt for him.

He was lost in a maze of feelings. A maze of fear. Where he didn't even know who the enemy was anymore. He had decided it must be him.

But I knew that wasn't true.

"Hades," I said softly. "Tell me. Tell me everything."

"It isn't that simple."

"I know it isn't. Because we never could be. We have always been more. Bigger. We have always been…"

"No. We haven't. We were lust, pure and simple. And it is all we can ever be."

I felt like he had stabbed me. What he didn't understand was that for me, his *words* were violence. What he didn't understand was that for me, this was death. I had tried so hard not to love him. And now… He was going to stop us. From having everything. From having all that we could be.

And if this was true, if I had cut myself open, and he had arrived back at the very place we'd started, then there was no winning.

I had no more left to give.

I had jumped off the cliff.

Bared my entire soul.

"What are you so afraid of?" I asked, exhaustion, anger, overtaking me.

"We cannot live together," he said. "We will raise

the child, but we will not live together. We will not be as man and wife."

"You don't get to decide that," I said.

"Yes, I do."

"Or what? You'll ruin me? That is where you're like your father, Hades." It was a cruel thing to say, but I didn't care. Because he had to realize. "It's this… This ridiculous need to control everything, that's where it comes into play. You would never hurt me, not physically, but this is a threat. Because you don't know how else to make me do what you want. Because you don't know how else to control me."

He looked stricken.

"You have to… Let go. I am my own person, and I will feel for you what I feel. You can't force me to feel any different. You cannot make me into what you think I should be."

"Florence…"

This was the end. It had to be.

Because if there was one thing I'd learned from my mother, it was that you couldn't let a man take it all.

You had to save some spark for yourself.

For your child.

"I'm leaving you. If you don't want to be married to me, then you won't be married. Technically you will fulfill the terms of your father's will. He won't have won. But I don't have to stay married to somebody who doesn't love me. Because I have done enough contorting to last me a lifetime. I will not tone myself down for you. I won't hide myself, not now that I have just found who I really am. I love you. Desperately. But if I can't have you in the way that I need you, then this really is the end."

Forever. We were supposed to have forever. I hated him as much as I loved him then. Because he had made me hope. And now he was taking it from me. Because of fear. Because he couldn't see past the things he had done, because he...

No. I didn't believe him. Not for a moment. I didn't believe that he truly regretted the death of his father enough that it was what kept him from love now.

"You're just scared. All these years you've been able to keep me with you without having to risk yourself. And that was the thing you really didn't want. You know you're not a monster. You play the part of one well. It suits you. It makes you feel comfortable. You want people afraid of you. You *wish* that you were like your father, Hades, because that would allow you to hold everybody at a distance. You want the evidence of your violence to scare me so you can care for no one but yourself. But it isn't you. Your father acted out of hate. You did it out of love. And you've allowed yourself to change the definition of love so that you can deny it. I won't let you. I won't give you any place to hide."

"Florence."

I stared him down, my fury a living thing between us.

He released his hold on me. I walked out of the bedroom and collected my clothes. I could get my own damned private jet and fly out of here. And so I did, with my heart absolutely breaking. So I did, hating myself, even as I made the call.

I didn't want to leave him. But I knew that I had to.

I cried the whole way back to New York. And I questioned myself. I had taken what I could get of him for so many years, I questioned my own sanity, drawing a line under this the way that I had. Now that we were having a baby. Maybe I should've been more flexible. Maybe I should have given more.

But I wanted to be loved. Most of all, I wanted him to open himself up to me. To be able to love me. I couldn't be with him as long as he was a wall. In quite that way.

I needed him to be honest with me.

I needed to know him.

For ten years, he had been a locked box. And I needed the key. I needed it.

I called Sarah as soon as I was back at my apartment. She came right away.

"What happened?"

"I love him. And he won't love me back."

"He's a jerk," she said.

"He's afraid," I said.

"I'm sorry," she said. "I really am. I know that you care about him. I know…"

"I have loved him from the first moment I saw him," I said. "I think deep down I always hoped he felt the same."

"It's not your fault that he didn't."

But it felt like it. It was worse than the NASA contract. Worse than anything. Because I'd had everything in the palm of my hand. And now it was all gone.

My hope, that beautiful future I had wanted so desperately.

I put my hand on my stomach. I was having a baby.

So much of my impending motherhood had been swallowed up by my feelings for Hades.

By the shift in our relationship.

I wouldn't crumble. My parents had lost themselves in

their hatred of each other. They had hurt me, even when they hadn't meant to. I wouldn't do that to my child. I refused. I would be stronger than that. For their sake.

"I might not be able to have everything," I said softly. "But I will have better. Because I'm strong enough."

I'd never managed this before. For myself.

I'd gone back to him every time. An addict who needed my fix.

But not now. Because these weeks of vulnerability had made me new. Here I was, a butterfly fresh from the cocoon, with wet bedraggled wings.

But I had changed.

I needed him to do the same.

I could imagine the headlines now.

Clare Heir Single Mother After Marital Implosion.

Every Other Weekend for Achelleos and Clare: Though now it's Custody! Not Wild Hookups!

It made me want to vomit. But I knew that I could survive it.

Because I didn't care what anybody said. I only cared that for my part, my child would never have to defend themself this way and that to please me or their father. They would be enough for me. I wouldn't need them to hate Hades just to make me feel better. I wouldn't feel compelled to be derisive of him to try and shake my child's opinion.

I was heartbroken.

But I was determined to give my child a life that was anything but shattered.

I had a core of steel. And I would be using it indefinitely.

CHAPTER THIRTEEN

I WAS STANDING in my office, looking out at the view below. It was Christmas Eve. I was trying to remember why I loved the city.

And then I imagined walking my baby through Central Park. I imagined holding them up so that they could see a statue. So that they could put their chubby baby hands on the leaves as they changed for fall. I imagined Christmas. Like the one Hades and I didn't get to spend together. Opening presents for them. Making a home.

My chest ached and I couldn't breathe for a moment.

I could see it. What we could have had.

If he would have only...

I steeled myself. I wouldn't let myself go down that path. I couldn't.

I had not lost everything. I hadn't.

There was a future there. And it wasn't the one that I had hoped for. But it was still bright with hope. To have a home and a family that had some semblance to what I had wanted.

Because I was the mother, and I got to shape so much of what my child would experience. And I had decided that it would be good. Beautiful.

The city was blanketed in snow now, the glow of the

holiday salt in my wound. Or it had been, until I thought of the baby.

Because there was always next year. Next year I would have this baby.

I heard a sound, the door to my office opening, and I turned, expecting to see Sarah. But it was Hades.

I stood there, completely in shock. "What are you… Doing here?"

"I have come to cut myself open," he said, his voice hard.

"What do you mean?"

"You were right, Florence. I am afraid. And I have… I have done my best to hide my innermost self from you, from myself, from the world, because I never wanted you to know me. The truth is, I feel shame about what happened to my father, but I also know that if that hadn't happened he would've tormented my mother till the end. Until he was able to kill her or someone that he loved. He was twisted with rage. In some ways, I have made my peace with what happened. But I used it. As another reason."

"What reason?"

"Another reason to stay away from you. I…" He paused for a long moment. And I let him. And when he looked up at me again, I saw it. All of it. The truth of him. In all its brilliance. "I have loved you from the first moment I saw you."

"Oh." It was all I could say. A breath, a sound, of pure emotion.

"I did not think you loved me," he said, his voice rough. "I told myself you didn't. You couldn't. It cut me, every time I touched you, but it made me feel safe too.

If you didn't love me I couldn't hurt you. If you didn't love me, we could keep it in hotels and bathrooms and coat closets. If you didn't love me it wouldn't hurt you when I decided to marry another woman."

"But I did," I whispered.

"I know now. It blindsided me. It…it made me feel so much regret. And so much…fear. Fear that has lived in me since the first time we touched. Because the things he could do to me if he knew there was a woman that I cared for. The daughter of his enemy? It would've been so much more than him beating me, Florence. My fear over what he would've done to you…"

This was him. All of him. I felt bowled over by it. I felt…singed. Burned by the endless glory of him. Of his truth. Of all that he felt. And all that he was finally, finally letting me see.

I truly didn't know what to say. And then, I decided not to speak at all. I decided to give him the floor. I decided to listen. Because for all these years, I had known him, but it had never occurred to me that he had loved me from the very beginning.

"When you asked me to meet you in your room, I hoped. I knew that I had no right to you. I knew I should stay away, but I wasn't strong enough. Florence," he said, my name a whisper. "When you gave yourself to me, I knew that I could never touch another woman. Not ever again. I thought of nothing but you. After that weekend, until I saw you again in Geneva, I thought of nothing. And when I held you in my arms again after six months, it was like breathing for the first time."

My heart felt bloody and bruised, thundering rapidly in my chest. An endless gallop, as if it was trying to race toward this truth faster than he could speak it.

"Everything was nothing, until those moments I was with you. When my father died, and I told myself... I told myself that I would never put those hands on you. Those hands that had been so violent. I hated myself for it. I told myself it was when I would stop tormenting you. Me. Both of us. But I couldn't stay away."

"I remember when you kissed me. Before we went on stage."

"I could think of nothing else but you. I wanted to push you away, but you were also what I needed. At the exclusion of all else."

I tried to reshape everything. With the knowledge that he had loved me. And it was like I had discovered a whole new thread in the tapestry of what we were. Gold that ran right on through. When I looked at his intensity and saw more than lust, my heart lifted. When I realized that he and I had been coming together because we loved each other...

"I was afraid," he said. "The whole time. That someone would take you from me. That I would lose you. I thought of every reason that I should stay away. It isn't the violence I exhibited toward my father that scarred me that day. It was seeing my mistake nearly cost my mother her life. It was facing losing the only other person on this earth, other than you, that I love. It was a window into pain I did not want to imagine."

He let out a hard breath. "And finally, I decided to marry another woman. With the clock ticking down on my father's will, I thought I would simply cut ties. Set us both free. But when you came to me, pregnant with my baby, it was the perfect excuse to let myself have you. And I didn't have the restraint to say no. I thought that I could control it. And you're right. That is where the danger lies. I thought that I could manipulate you. Turn our passion into something that it was never able to be. Something softer. Something that didn't burn quite so bright. Something that didn't threaten me. Something that I didn't fear the loss of."

"Your father…he used Christmas. He used your love to make you afraid. Of course…of course you feared it. He used it like a weapon."

"Yes," he said, his voice rough. "But I love you. I love you, and it is killing me. It has been, slowly, for all these years. I love you, and I worry that it will be the death of me."

It all dawned on me, like the slowly rising sun casting light over all the shadows.

"You said to me, that sometimes love was too broken. You meant your love for *me*."

He'd been trying to tell me then. But it was all bottled up. Behind a protective wall. Because his father had taught him that loving something was dangerous.

"Yes," he said. "I did. But I realize that my love for you is perhaps the only thing in my whole body that is not corrupted. It is perhaps the one good thing in me. Or maybe I just need it to be, because I don't want to live a life without you in it. Because I cannot want anything but you. I don't want to live in a world where I don't have that."

"Hades," I said. "I will never leave you." I tried to smile. "If I could have…"

He laughed, rough and hard. "You would have."

"I wished away the feelings, because they terrified me."

"I never wished mine away," he said. "Because they were the only thing that kept me sane. The only thing that kept me going. My life was a wasteland, Florence. And you were the one oasis. You were the one thing that mattered. The one thing that I wanted. The only good feeling inside of me. The idea that we could just be together. That we can have a family... I spent so many years believing that wasn't possible. I spent so many years pushing that aside. When my father died, the violence didn't stop. It echoed. Lingered. I felt like a failure in some ways because I felt like I had given in to the creature he made me. He demanded that I marry because he knew there was a real risk I wouldn't want to carry on the bloodline. Because he knew how much I despised him. I hated the ways in which he won. But now... Florence, watching you be so brave, so vulnerable, I have challenged many of my beliefs. He thought that he had control over me, leaving those terms in the will. He thought perhaps that he won the day that I hit him and ended his life with the same violence that he had lived with. But he didn't. Because I'm different. Because something had already changed inside of me. *You.* The way that I love you. He never had the capacity for that. I told myself that he loved my mother at one time..."

I was close to bursting. I hurt for him. I rejoiced for us. He loved me. My journey had shown him how to walk out of the darkness. Just as I'd hoped.

"He didn't," I said. "That was never love."

He shook his head. "No. I love my mother, though. And she left me. And in the end of all things, that is what terrified me most. Giving love again only to have it taken away."

"I won't leave you," I said. "You were my destiny. From the first moment I ever laid eyes on you. You were meant to be mine. I know it. I believe it, down to my soul. From that first moment. Do you have any idea how much time I spent convincing myself that it couldn't be love? We were lying to ourselves."

"Not me," he said. "I always knew."

"Well, I did. I was simply a coward protecting myself."

"I was the same. However different a shape it took. I love you, Florence Clare. Every chance that I ever took to spar with you, to kiss you, to be with you, was just about you. About having the chance to have your attention. To have your eyes on me."

"I love you so much," I said.

I knew then that this was the truth of it. That we had always been meant to be. That our times together had never been an interruption of a path that we were supposed to be walking. It was the real path. We had simply taken a long time to figure out the truth of it. This was where we were meant to be.

"I will spend every day of the next ten years at least, telling you exactly how much I love you. Twice."

I smiled. "Why twice?"

"Because I'm ten years behind."

I wasn't worried about that. Because I knew that we were on the right path now. Because I knew that we had finally found where we were meant to be.

I had always believed that he was my match.

I simply hadn't realized how true that was.

"I love you," I said. "As much as I ever thought I hated you."

"And I love you. As much as I've always known I have. Without fear. And nothing holding me back."

"I can see the headlines now," I said.

"And what do they say?"

"Clare Heir Lives Happily Ever After."

EPILOGUE

Hades

I KNEW THE moment I saw her for the first time that my life was ruined. A good thing, that in the years since, I've learned that I can be wrong.

Because the moment I met Florence Clare—now Florence Achelleos—was the moment my life was saved.

The first time she kissed me I knew it could only be a weekend. But after that, I couldn't let her go. I thought of her when I should have been thinking of business strategies. I planned meetings around the cities I wanted to have her in.

For all the world it looked like the company was my reason for breathing.

But it was her.

It was always her.

I told myself it was all we could have. Stolen kisses, stolen moments.

Now we have everything.

Ten years of sneaking around. Ten years of hiding. Now we've had ten years of marriage. Four children. One very successful merger. But we leave the running of things to other people now. Our family is what obsesses us.

Our mothers make doting grandmothers, and our children are lucky to spend time in Lake Como and in Greece. But our favorite times are when we're together, in the house we bought by the sea, so Florence can always look out at the horizon and plan her next adventure.

I look out at the horizon now. My wife went down to the harbor earlier to look at one of the new ships, and I've been waiting impatiently for her to arrive home. I am always impatient for her.

"Traffic was a nightmare."

I turn and see her standing in the doorway. Like I conjured an angel, just by thinking of her.

Florence.

"But you came back to me," I say, as she crosses the room and stretches up on her toes. Kissing me like it's the first time and the last time all at once.

Even though we both know it isn't.

We both know it's forever.

"Always," she says. "I never could resist you."

We used to tell each other if we could have resisted, we would have.

Not now. Now we would never stay away. Not by choice, not for any reason.

Florence Clare is my forever.

And I am hers.

* * * * *

MILLS & BOON®

Coming next month

GREEK'S ENEMY BRIDE
Caitlin Crews

The priest cleared his throat.

Jolie took one last look at Apostolis, soaking in this last moment of blessed widowhood before he became her husband.

He looked back, that gleaming gold thing in his gaze, but his expression unusually serious.

For a moment, it was as if she could read his mind.

For a long, electric moment, it was almost as if they were united in this bizarre enterprise after all, and her heart leaped inside her chest—

'Stepmother?' he said, with a soft ferocity. 'If you would be so kind?'

No, she told herself harshly. *There is no unity here. There is only and ever war. You will do well to remember that.*

And then, with remarkable swiftness and no interruption, Jolie relinquished her role as Apostolis's hated stepmother, and became his much-loathed wife instead.

Continue reading

GREEK'S ENEMY BRIDE
Caitlin Crews

Available next month
millsandboon.co.uk

COMING SOON!

We really hope you enjoyed reading this book.
If you're looking for more romance
be sure to head to the shops when
new books are available on

Thursday 19th December

MILLS & BOON

afterglow BOOKS

Afterglow Books is a trend-led, trope-filled list of books with diverse, authentic and relatable characters, a wide array of voices and representations, plus real world trials and tribulations. Featuring all the tropes you could possibly want (think small-town settings, fake relationships, grumpy vs sunshine, enemies to lovers) and all with a generous dose of spice in every story.

♪ @millsandboonuk
⊙ @millsandboonuk
afterglowbooks.co.uk
#AfterglowBooks

For all the latest book news, exclusive content and giveaways scan the QR code below to sign up to the Afterglow newsletter:

SCAN ME

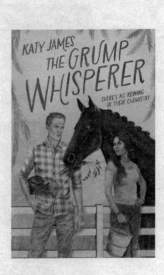
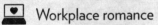

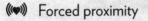